HEART OF SNOW

ONCE UPON
A FOREST

HEART
OF SNOW

RACHEL GROW LAW

to Courtney Willis
Thank you for your insights, your late-night Marco Polos to calm my freakouts, and your constant encouragement and praise. You are an amazing friend and the best cheerleader and critique partner a girl could ask for!

Cover image: *Woman with Historical Cloak in a Forest Under Snow at Sunset* © Nature by Louise / Trevillion Images. *Hand Holding Apple* created using generative AI tools.

Cover design by Christina Marcano © 2024 by Covenant Communications, Inc.

Published by Covenant Communications, Inc.
American Fork, Utah

Copyright © 2024 by Rachel Grow Law
All rights reserved. No part of this book may be reproduced in any format or in any medium without the written permission of the publisher, Covenant Communications, Inc., PO Box 416, American Fork, UT 84003. The views expressed within this work are the sole responsibility of the author and do not necessarily reflect the position of Covenant Communications, Inc., or any other entity.

This is a work of fiction. The characters, names, incidents, places, and dialogue are either products of the author's imagination, and are not to be construed as real, or are used fictitiously.

Library of Congress Cataloging-in-Publication Data

Name: Rachel Grow Law
Title: Heart of Snow / Rachel Grow Law
Description: American Fork, UT : Covenant Communications, Inc. [2024]
Identifiers: Library of Congress Control Number 2024938428 | 978-1-52442-773-3
LC record available at https://lccn.loc.gov/2024938428

Printed in the United States of America
First Printing: January 2025

31 30 29 28 27 26 25   10 9 8 7 6 5 4 3 2 1

ACKNOWLEDGMENTS

In over fifteen years of creating this novel, there are so many people who have been instrumental in making this long-held dream a reality.

Primarily, I want to thank my husband, whose love for me overcame his distaste for romance novels. He helps me brainstorm, solve plot problems and character motivations, and gives me all the romantic inspiration a romance writer could wish for.

Thank you to my children for your interest and enthusiasm when I over-explain my plot ideas. Your acting skills will get you far in life.

To my parents, for raising me with unending love and unearned confidence. You brought me up to trust in Heavenly Father and believe in myself. That education has been the foundation for a lifetime of joy and an ever-growing relationship with the One who has made my writing possible.

To the *many* beta readers who offered feedback and insight. Particular thanks to my sister-in-law MaryAnn, who read this book in its many forms and encouraged me with each iteration.

To the team at Covenant for taking on an aspiring writer and turning me into an author. Thank you for your hard work in making this book the best it can be.

And lastly, to the wonderful authors who have become my dearest friends and network of support. You are not an afterthought. You are my entire motivation. Thank you.

Part One: *April 1547*
Wildungen, Waldeck Countship, German Territory of the Holy Roman Empire

CHAPTER 1

Margaretha

I DID NOT LOOK AT the pyre in the center of the crowd.

I watched boys in hooknose witch masks chase screaming girls toward their mothers' skirts. I watched celebrating villagers dance, kicking up the dust of the open field as they pounded their feet to grating tunes from slide trumpets and shawms. I even watched drunken men staggering and spilling ale from their cups. All so I might avoid seeing the woman of twigs and straw propped atop an ominous pile of logs, waiting to burn. The villagers paid her no heed, carrying on with their throbbing noise and chaos, forgetting what I could never forget.

I remembered when the woman who burned was real.

"You're shivering, Countess." My lady-in-waiting, Belinda, rubbed my arm. "Let us warm you with some ale."

"It isn't the cold; it's the place." Despite the nearly ten-year absence, dark memories hovered around me like fog clinging to the forest's trunks.

Belinda's eyes turned sympathetic. "Do you wish to leave? Perhaps we can sneak away without your father noticing."

My heart swelled at the idea of escaping the mock burning, and I nodded excitedly. "Yes, let's do. Only, first I must deliver these electuaries." After reaching into my pocket, I pulled out the small vials.

"Margaretha, you brought your medicaments to a festival? Do you never rest?"

"Ailments don't cease simply because it's Walpurgisnacht." I rolled onto my toes to search for the blacksmith. "I've only two left to dispense."

"Very well. Let us be quick." She slid her arm through mine, letting me lead her along as I weaved through the crowd. Heads turned as we passed, young men staring after me, old men's eyes going wide. I batted away my rising embarrassment from their attentions, until my sights landed on a nobleman, his brown eyes following me with interest as his foot relentlessly tapped the dirt.

I nodded a quick acknowledgement, though it was not quick enough. Belinda had already followed my line of sight to the man, a broad grin coming over her face. "Is that Baron von Dalwigk? Well, this will be diverting. Let us have a chat with him."

"Belinda, no." I tugged on her arm to steer us away from another of her attempts to have me speak with a man, but Belinda was stronger, dragging me toward him. Before he'd even pushed himself up to greet us, my hands trembled, and it seemed my tongue was swelling in my throat. As Belinda and I dropped our bows, I locked my gaze safely on his boots. His tapping toe indicated he welcomed this conversation as much as I, but he returned our bows, greeting me first to show deference for my higher rank.

"*Guten abend*, Herr von Dalwigk," Belinda said. "You're looking quite a man now. Are you yet five and twenty?"

"Eight and twenty, Baroness, and I see you are as lovely as ever." He took her hand to kiss it, and peeking at the pair, I suddenly saw Belinda as he might, with the advantage of five years' maturity over my nineteen and beauty enough in her own right. Her darker features were not as fashionable as my fair ones, but she had a cleverness about her eyes, and her mouth was bent in a soft, knowing smile.

Dalwigk turned to me next, and I dropped my sights back to his mud-splattered, fidgeting boot. "But could this really be the young countess? Lady Margaretha, I would not have thought it possible you would grow to be such a beauty."

His compliment was part insult, but at the insistence of Belinda's elbow in my side, I stammered out my thanks.

"What calls you from Burg Lichtenfels, sir?" Belinda asked. "Would you not rather be feasting with your own people?"

"Not when there's such company to be had here." Dalwigk caught hold of my hand and lifted it to his lips, but before I realized what I'd done, I wrenched my hand away. Cheeks warming from my blunder, I risked a glance at the frown that dropped the corners of his mouth. Annoyance colored his words as he added, "I own a second motive for my presence. I bring news for the count."

News?

His fingers joined the rhythm of his foot, drumming a beat on his leg that made my head heavy. This was not good news. My thoughts flew to my brother, and I cast Belinda a nervous look.

"About the war?" she asked, perfectly anticipating my anxiety. "Not unpleasant news, I hope."

"Ah, here is the count now." Dalwigk ignored Belinda's question, stepping past us to greet my father with a bow.

Father's mouth was already set in a frown as he acknowledged the man, then nodded to our private tent. He said nothing until the four of us were safely inside.

"My man tells me you've come to report."

Dalwigk's nervousness did nothing for the weight on my brain. "It's not good, I'm afraid. Mühlberg was a loss. Your troops were defeated, every man either captured or killed."

Father's face drained of blood, and he sank into his chair. "Every man?"

Dalwigk nodded, his face solemn.

My throat seized until I could only whisper a strangled, "Samuel."

"The kaiser is sending his Spanish troops to every rebelling German territory," Dalwigk continued. "Unless you keep fighting, it will only be a matter of weeks before your county is overrun and you're forced to renounce Luther and return to the Catholic faith."

Father gave him a dark glare. "Keep fighting? Every man in my army was at Mühlberg. Whom would I fight with? And it's no different for the other nobles in the league." He ran a shaking hand over his beard, letting out a low curse. "All that work, yet in one battle the Reformation is dead."

The Reformation. For nearly thirty years our lands had been aflame with reform. Ever since Martin Luther bravely nailed his criticisms of the Catholic Church to the Wittenberg chapel door, each beat of his hammer echoed throughout the German lands in the drums of war. If Luther and all our territories denied the Catholic faith, then Luther and all our territories would deny the kaiser his God-given right to rule. And with the core of the kaiser's empire free from his control, how much longer till Burgundy, the Netherlands, Spain, Sicily, Naples, and the rest of his lands wrestled for independence? No, the kaiser would put down such rebellion here, enforcing with sword and ball his divine right to govern and fighting whatever hordes of men dared rise against him. Men like my brother.

"But what of Samuel?" I asked, finally meeting Dalwigk's eyes. "What fate befell my brother?"

Father leaned forward, just as eager for Dalwigk's answer, but the grim set of Dalwigk's mouth was not encouraging. "I admit I do not know. But take heart." He offered us an unconvincing smile. "Count Samuel is a fighter."

That was precisely what worried me.

I wrestled back the threatening emotion, rubbing a hand over my nose until I caught Father watching me. He shifted his sorrowful eyes to my lady-in-waiting, his voice weary as he addressed her. "Mistress Hatzfeld, why don't you see Lady Margaretha back to the festival."

She nodded, giving him a sweet smile and pulling me toward the tent door. "But—"

"Look," Belinda whispered, holding back the tent flap. "The sky grows dark. Let us deliver the vials and be gone."

Behind the orange and pink clouds loomed a darker purple hue, and I knew Belinda was right. We hadn't much time.

I let her lead me away through the field's matted grass, plunging back into the thick of the crowd to resume our search for the blacksmith, but I passed faces without seeing. When would I learn what had become of Samuel? No doubt it took time to identify the bodies of war's mutilated dead. But no, I shouldn't think that way. Samuel could well be alive.

"Your brother is all right, Margaretha. He has to be." Belinda's fierce tone matched her grip on my arm. She was every bit as worried as I, though she would never admit it. "And anyway," her posture relaxed, an air of indifference slipping over her like a comfortable chemise, "we have our own troubles to fret about. Your sorry showing with Dalwigk . . . You must be more sociable if you hope to succeed in Brussels."

She was intentionally diverting the conversation, but I allowed it. "Will you persist in dragging me to speak with every nobleman in the empire?" I shot her a glare.

"Until you can learn to look a man in the eye and say two words together, yes." Her smile was infuriating. "Oh, don't furrow your brows at me. It's my duty to prepare you for the courts of Brussels."

"Why all this talk of Brussels?" I pulled to a stop. "Has Father asked you to speak to me?"

She suddenly seemed very interested in searching for the blacksmith.

"Belinda?"

Meeting my eye, she heaved a great sigh. "As it happens, another invitation from the queen arrived today. It's quite a distinction, you know, being asked as her lady-of-honor."

I shook my head and resumed the slow push through the crowd. "You know full well I'm not going to Brussels."

Belinda huffed. "Why would you refuse the queen's invitation now? As the kaiser's sister, she could sway him to—"

"The war is lost." I rounded on her. "Any plans to promote our reformist cause have been slaughtered. I do more good here with my healing medicines."

Belinda pressed her lips in a tight line, her usual countenance when she had much to say but not the composure to say it with. She kept silent, following behind me until I found the blacksmith. Upon seeing me, he whipped off his cap and gave a bow so hasty he nearly knocked his head with mine.

"I thank ye, m'lady," he said, taking the vial I offered. "Weren't never a better brewer than you. Or a prettier one."

His wife slapped his arm.

I pretended not to notice. "Can you point me in the direction of the harness maker's wife?"

"There," he said, "beyond the pyre."

At the mention of the pyre, I glanced at the forest and dark purple sky beyond. There was little time left before the burning would begin. Torchlights flickered about us, sending shadows dancing over the villagers' faces as I squirmed between them, hurrying to reach the harness maker's wife.

"Frau Baumann?" I asked, breathlessly dipping into my pocket for the last vial. "For your son."

"Oh, *dankeschön*, my lady. But I worry his wound's not healing like it should. Would you mind takin' a look at him?"

I nodded, crouching beside the boy to unwind the bandage from his head. There had been some bleeding, but nothing troubling. Head wounds always bled more than other injuries.

Belinda knelt in the grass next to me, holding him steady as she quietly asked, "Margaretha, what if your brother was captured? Would that not be reason enough for you to go to Brussels?"

"Belinda." I sighed.

"You could be the means of saving him. With your exquisite beauty, I'd wager you could win the love of any man in Brussels. Just be sure he's a man sympathetic to our cause, and with power too. If he has the queen's and kaiser's respect, once you marry, your brother is as good as free."

"Marry?" I gave her a piercing look, then twisted the bandage around the boy's head. "The man could be an ogre. I won't marry for mere advantage."

"But if it meant saving Samuel's life? Is there any sacrifice too great?"

My bandage winding slowed. If there was a chance my brother was still alive, I'd do anything to keep him safe.

"My people!" Father's booming voice made me jump, and I turned to find him standing atop a bench, gripping a flaming torch in his right hand.

The witch burning.

I had to escape. Hurriedly tucking the bandage into itself and handing the boy to his mother, I squeezed my way through and around the people listening to Father's speech.

"Tonight is Walpurgisnacht, when the veil thins between the living and dead and the devil's followers are in full power. As it's a night for witches to meet their master, Satan, on the high mount Brocken and cavort in all manner of evil, should we not speed their journey to the inferno and burn them all to hell?"

The crowd roared their approval. I ducked beneath a few raised arms, noticing a thinning in the throng. We were nearly free.

"It has been tradition for my son, Count Samuel"—Father coughed, as if trying to conceal emotion—"to set the witch ablaze. In his absence, I give the honor to another. Lady Margaretha."

I stopped cold, the blood draining from my face. My feet were stone, rooting me to the spot.

There was no escaping now.

Belinda nudged me from behind. "You must go to him."

Casting a final, longing look at the road to home, I slowly pivoted to face my father. He inclined the torch, offering it to me, and I stumbled forward, my motions awkward and wooden.

"My lord." I bowed when I reached the bench, then lifted my face to whisper, "I don't wish this. Give the honor to another."

"Send the witch to the devil!" an old man called out, and the people cheered.

Father's glistening eyes were soft, oblivious to the pain he caused as he pushed the torch closer. "For Samuel," he whispered.

I drew in a steadying breath and took it from him, squeezing the stave in my trembling hands while I turned to face the witch. Her stained white rags stood stark against the backdrop of an inky sky. Though I'd kept my eyes from her all night, finally seeing her now, I couldn't look away. I felt drawn to her. Moving one foot forward, then another, my steps came easier as I walked in a trance through the parting throng. At my left, a woman whispered to her child, "Watch for the black smoke. That's when the witch flees the fire and flies to hell." A sudden gust threw the torch's smoke back in my eyes, and I blinked against the burn and tears, focusing ahead on the blurred figure before me.

Reaching the crisscrossed logs of the pyre, another gust snatched up the witch's tattered gown, slapping it against the wooden cross onto which she'd been tied. Unbidden, the image of a mud-stained chemise thrashed by churning smoke flashed through my mind, then was gone. My breath came quick at the memory.

"Light her!" a woman called out. Others joined her, echoing the cry.

I swallowed and pushed the torch through the chinks, holding the fire against the kindling until it smoked and smoldered and burst alive. Yellow flames licked the logs, biding their time, teasing their wooden prey before they slowly, unrelentingly consumed it. I remembered flames equally hungry and merciless crawling over a different pyre to taste the naked feet of the woman tied above.

Because of me.

The bonfire grew to an unbearable heat, forcing me to retreat, but my gaze stayed riveted on the straw witch. As the flames curled around her face, her eyes remained blank. Expressionless. Devoid of pain or agony or reproach. Completely unlike the real woman who'd burned. The plumes of blazing air had churned around her—the town healer—lifting her ebony hair and blurring her features until the only thing visible was her anguish.

Guilt scorched as much as the swelling fire before me, and I stepped farther back, pushing myself to the outskirts of the crowd to shield my face from the intensity of the heat. Yet it was nothing close to what the healer had endured, not even a start to comprehending the pain she'd suffered. How could I ever understand?

At the edge of my vision, my torch flickered. I pulled it closer, watching the fire writhe, mesmerized by the shifting shades of yellow and orange. I lifted my hand and stroked it over the flame as though smoothing the hair of a child. Heat singed across my palm, the sensation quick and painless, the warmth transfixing me further. I found myself raising my hand to try again.

Strong fingers wrapped around my wrist, waking me from my trance as a man behind me spoke.

"You'll find noble flesh burns the same as common."

His touch startled me, and I wrenched my wrist from his grip, the action flinging my hand into the flame. Burning pain shot through my palm, rippling out to my fingers. Unable to hold back a shriek, I nearly dropped the torch, but the man caught the stave, slipping it from my grasp. I used the torchlight to study my burning hand. "What could you be thinking, attacking me without warning?" A large blister was already forming in the center of my palm.

"You looked ready to do yourself an injury, and I—"

"You think me mad?" My fingers weren't red yet, but I knew they would be soon. "There was no danger of injury until you came along." I lifted my glaring eyes, but my scowl faltered as I took in the face of the traveler. His cheeks were smudged with dirt, and the blood-encrusted gash above his brow was conspicuous despite his attempts to conceal it beneath his cap. Yet it was his eyes that arrested my attention. Storm gray and so familiar, as if I ought to remember them.

And then I saw his livery, striped black and yellow. Father's colors.

Worry for my brother returned in force. "Have you come from Mühlberg? Do you know of Count Samuel?"

His answer was drowned by the sudden cheers of villagers, and I rounded, following their collective gaze to a column of black smoke rising from the fiery heap that was once the witch. My earlier preoccupation now dissolved in my anxiety for my brother, I turned back to the stranger just as he faltered, stumbling forward. Catching him by the arm, I could feel his body trembling and the heat of his skin burning through his sleeve. "Are you ill?"

He winced as he pulled himself upright. "Where is Count von Waldeck?"

"You're hurt."

"It's nothing," he growled but wrapped a protective arm about his waist. "I must speak with the count."

"You must speak with a physician. At least let me look at it." The burning in my hand revived my anger toward the man, but I tamped it down. He was sick. I would never neglect my duty to any ailing person, no matter how infuriating they were.

Ignoring his protests, I pulled back his arm, revealing a dark-brown stain on his doublet. Old blood was a good sign, but the heat of his flesh told me he was not out of danger. With my good hand, I unbuttoned the doublet, lifting his shirt to find a hastily made bandage covering a gash, long and thin, like a slice from a sword. Redness and swelling hinted at infection.

"There, you've seen it. Now take me to the count." His limp hands fumbled as he tucked his shirt into his hose.

"I have an angelica powder to help with your fever."

"The only help I need is finding the count."

"Perhaps some yarrow root," I continued. "Though I'm not certain we have sufficient stores in the castle—"

"Countess, please." His earnest entreaty made me pause. "It's about your brother. Count Samuel was captured."

CHAPTER 2

Friedrich

THE COUNTESS HAD CHANGED. I secretly studied her as she helped me sit against a tree trunk and was shocked by the difference in her looks. Her childhood roundness was gone, her once-awkward nose and ears now in perfect harmony with her face. Even her freckles had melted away, leaving snowy, flawless skin. But more surprising was what hadn't changed. The deep sadness that had darkened her blue eyes as a child still remained.

She caught me watching her, and I dropped my gaze, angry with myself for noticing her at all.

"Wait here. I'll be back with help." She blew on her hand as she disappeared into the crowd, and my gut shifted uncomfortably. I was to blame for her injury. If I hadn't taken it upon myself to try to help . . . and why had I? She was nobility, after all. The whole class had a pretty tidy way of getting themselves out of trouble.

A violent shiver raced through me, and my eyelids drooped. Exhaustion threatening, I wrapped my arms around myself for warmth and leaned my head against the trunk. Food had been scarce since Mühlberg. Being seen at an inn or caught traveling the main roads was too much of a risk, and what little I'd eaten was either foraged or begged for. But not even the smells of ham and ale wafting from the feast tempted me. Right now, I wanted nothing more than a bed.

The scuff of shoes nearby jolted me awake. I instinctively pushed myself farther back into the shadows of the forest before realizing the steps were faltering and uneven. Not the smart clip of a soldier.

I risked a glance around the trunk at the man staggering toward me, his swaying steps all too familiar. Even if he'd been sober, he wouldn't have recognized me, but I crouched lower behind the trunk, trying to rein in my shivering as the town bowyer passed by.

It could have been a few moments or a few hours before the countess returned; my sense of time had warped into uselessness, and my head was growing hazy. I almost didn't notice the countess's soft step.

Her voice whispered from the other side of the tree. "Do you think you can get up?"

I leaned around the trunk to find a gangly boy standing beside the countess as she twisted a dripping rag around her hand. "I brought a servant if you—"

"I can stand." I made an effort to rise, but the shivered crouching had taken its toll, and I sank back to the ground.

The countess winced. "Help him, Ulrich."

I gave the servant a quick appraisal. He was likely somewhere near fifteen years of age and had the tall, bony build of a boy who'd just sprouted. I didn't trust that he could carry me, but he seemed determined, dropping to the ground beside me and wrapping his arm around my waist. When his hand bumped against my gash, I had to squeeze back a cry, only letting it escape my lungs once I'd stifled it down to a groan. He had enough sympathy to wait until I'd recovered before draping my arm over his shoulder and hoisting me up to meet the countess's worried gaze.

"Our coach is practically resting atop the ale tables. How will we get him there undetected?"

"Why hide him, my lady?" the boy asked.

"If reports prove correct, in a few days our town will be overrun with the kaiser's soldiers. We don't need anyone remembering a man in Father's livery limping through the feast." She pulled off my cap, tucking it under her arm and ruffling my hair. My eyes went wide at her forwardness, but she was already busy surveying the festival. "Just keep to the outskirts of the crowd, Ulrich. Pull him toward houses or barns whenever you can."

Ulrich nodded and half-carried me as we shuffled along behind the countess. "Didn't you say the war is over?" he whispered.

"As good as." The countess fiddled with her bandage. "But until a treaty is signed, the war continues."

Which meant I was still a soldier in that fight, subject to either capture or death whenever the Spaniards arrived. The countess seemed to understand this, for she moved with quick, sure steps through whatever shadows she could find. Poor Ulrich was struggling to both keep pace and support me, though I did my best to carry my own weight. Each time we ducked behind a darkened home, he'd lean me against the wall to rest his trembling arms. Still, for as young as he seemed, he had surprising strength.

We were fewer than two rods from the coach when a woman grabbed the countess's arm and pulled her to a halt.

"Mistress, where have you been? You vanished after the burning."

"Belinda, we must go. Now."

The woman's eyes took in my livery, and she fell into stride beside me, shielding me from view until we arrived at the coach where the count stood, balanced on the step and drumming his fingers against the roof. Though his temples were now streaked with gray, he still wore the familiar fur-lined overgown with rubies along the neck chain. They sparkled in the light of the bonfire as he snapped at Ulrich to hurry up.

Poor Ulrich was wheezing when he deposited me into the coach. I fell into the seat with a groan, resting my head against the window frame and sucking in the stale air until the ache from my gash dampened.

The coach creaked as the count settled in his seat across from me. "Friedrich Rowohlt. I thought you were dead."

Even after a year, the count's voice still left my nerves twitching in irritation. "Sorry to disappoint, Your Lordship." Digging into my doublet pocket, I pulled out Count Samuel's signet ring and dropped it in the count's gloved hand.

He looked up at me, anxiety tightening his eyes, until the coach tilted again and the countess set foot inside. Her father moved to block her way.

"You and Mistress Hatzfeld must stay," he said. "Else who will oversee the feast?"

She kept her foot in the coach, lifting her chin with a determined gaze. "He's wounded and febrile. I must see to his care."

I expected Count von Waldeck to hold his ground, but he sank back to his seat with a nod. His daughter climbed in, followed by her lady, and the three of them crowded together on the opposite seat, their eyes fixed on me.

"Rowohlt, tell me what happened to my son."

The coach lurched forward, and I took a deep breath but regretted it the moment pain shot through my gash. At my grimace, the countess squeezed out from between her two companions and nearly fell into the empty space beside me, quietly rolling back my shirtsleeve to press her fingers against my wrist. Her touch was ice, making me shiver even more.

I clenched my teeth against the chattering. "Count Samuel was taken captive."

"Captured? When? How?" Mistress Hatzfeld's questions pulled my attention from the countess and back to the bloody field by the river Elbe. The kaiser's army bursting through the fog, the deafening crack of bullets mingling with the scent of smoke and soured eggs. The screams of men dying.

"He was injured. Shot in the leg." I'd done my best to stay by and defend him, but the kaiser's men were closing in. "When they started collecting prisoners, the count pushed me away and told me to escape and find Your Lordship to bring word of his capture."

"And where are they keeping him?" Count von Waldeck asked.

"With the kaiser. He took the Elector of Saxony captive too. I suspect they're being held together."

Hatzfeld whipped her head toward the count. "Didn't Dalwigk say the elector has been—"

"Condemned to die," the count finished for her.

With such speed I might have imagined it, Hatzfeld rested a gentle hand on the count's wrist. Was this behavior typical?

I glanced at the countess to see if she'd noticed, but she was rubbing a hand across her nose, blinking so quickly she had to be fighting tears.

"Father, we can't let that be Samuel's fate too. What can we do to save him? Is there some way to break him free? How will we see that he gets the care he needs for his wound?" Her voice grew more frantic with each question. "Could you not send me to him?"

"I'm afraid there is little to be done as of yet." The count clenched his jaw, looking out the window. "The prisoners will be in the company of the kaiser wherever he travels, and with the war on the brink of ending, there's no one place he'll settle long enough for us to seek him out."

"But what of Samuel's injury?" the countess continued. "If he's not properly cared for—"

Her father lifted a hand to stop her. "The kaiser will treat his noble captives with the respect demanded by their rank. Samuel's needs will be looked after. So long as he is allowed to live." He ground out the last words. "I will send Dalwigk to search and see if we can't learn more of Samuel's welfare and whereabouts, but in the meantime, Margaretha,"—he leaned forward, his attention fixed on her—"you should seriously consider accepting the queen's invitation."

The countess fell into silence.

I couldn't understand the importance of the queen's invite and was too tired to think about it. The nobles continued their discussion, talking past me, as they apparently no longer needed my input. When the coach tilted back, climbing the steep hill to Wildungen's old fortress-castle, I sagged into the velvet cushions. Before we'd even arrived at the gates, the steady bounce of the coach tempted me toward the oblivion of sleep. I gave up fighting and welcomed it.

CHAPTER 3

Margaretha

I FLIPPED THROUGH THE JOURNALS, catching Belinda watching me from her pallet on the floor. "Have you had another nightmare?"

She scoffed. "I never have nightmares."

I left her lie unchallenged and ran my finger down the page of the journal.

"What are you doing?" She leaned up on her elbow.

"Research."

Belinda's pallet creaked as she threw back her coverlet and climbed up to my bed. "Make room." She gave me almost no time to move before squeezing her way under the blankets, pressing her cold feet to my leg.

"Gah, your toes are icicles!" I kicked her foot away.

She nodded to the books in my hand. "What do you read?"

"Elizabeth's journals from Brussels."

"You've decided to go, then?"

"I don't know what choice I have. I can't sit by and leave Samuel to his fate." I tossed the pile of journals to the foot of the bed. "Why does Queen Mary persist in inviting me anyway?"

Belinda shrugged. "It is the way of things, having noblewomen of lower rank working for their betters. It's why I serve you."

"Yes, but she could have maids from any territory in her brother's vast empire. The daughter of a poor German count hardly seems worth her notice."

"Your sister served her well as a lady-of-honor. It's not unreasonable the queen would hope the same of you."

"Much good Elizabeth's service did her," I muttered. Elizabeth had always been our parents' favorite, earning the bulk of their attention and lofty expectations. She'd been trained to marry well, and marry well she did, though her first child had still been in her belly the day she'd died.

I leaned against the wooden headboard, the smell of it musty and ancient, just as it had been when I was a child. All those years I'd spent away—off in Waldeck, then in the Netherlands with Uncle—and yet the room remained unchanged, as if I'd never left. The blood-red drapes brooding over the bed; the small, smoking fireplace; the cracked looking glass in the empty corner. Each part of the room revived memories I'd long struggled to bury.

But the searing burn of my hand trumped them all, refusing to be ignored. I tugged at the bandage, unwinding the wrappings until my burn was exposed.

Belinda pulled herself up beside me, sucking a breath through clenched teeth as she looked at my hand. "What befell you?"

My anger with the soldier had already dissolved, acknowledging my own fault in the event. It would never have happened had I not been so entranced, so bent on understanding what pain I'd inflicted . . . so full of guilt. "Utter foolishness," I answered, angling my hand to study the blister in the dim firelight. The salve I'd applied offered scant relief from the unrelenting burn. At the bonfire, I'd been absorbed in my own guilt and suffering, but it all seemed selfish and narrow compared to the threat Samuel faced. I had to save him.

Reaching down the bed to retrieve Elizabeth's journals, I sifted through pages till I found the one I sought. "I may have a better idea of how to help Samuel. Elizabeth writes here of Queen Mary's love of hunting, saying the queen's so fond of it that she fancies herself ill if she's kept from it for more than a few days. And over here"—I flipped to another page—"Elizabeth describes the queen as a great horsewoman, with a seat as good as any man's. I'm a fair horsewoman myself, and I think, given a few months' instruction, I could learn to hunt too."

"And what would that do for Samuel?" Belinda swiveled herself on the bed, pulling the blankets down with her as she sat by my feet.

"What if"—I tugged the blankets back to my chest, forcing her on top of the coverlet—"instead of marrying a man who could plead for Samuel, I concentrate on winning the queen's favor? Surely she could speak to her brother and beg for—"

"I doubt a few months' study of hunting would give you enough mastery to impress such an avid huntress as the queen. Even if it did, she's only queen regent in Brussels because the kaiser granted her the position. It's unlikely she'll risk the regency or her brother's ire by asking for the freedom of a religious rebel."

I blew on my hand. "Then let's have *you* be the one to win a man over. Your chances of success would be much higher than mine."

Belinda's eyes lit up, and I knew she was letting herself imagine it: the luxury, the opulence, the attention of powerful suitors poised to raise her up in the world's estimation. She was an amazing friend and guide—something closer to an older sister or even a mother—but I'd never cared much for her social aspirations. Perhaps they were a product of being raised even poorer than I. I shouldn't judge her for it.

The sparkle left Belinda's gaze, and she shook her head. "You perpetually undervalue your beauty. Besides, the queen's invitation is for you."

I grasped at another objection. "Well, what good would it do me, winning a man with the kaiser's favor, if the kaiser isn't even in Brussels?"

"Not yet, but he will be, come autumn. Your father said the kaiser is bringing his son up from Spain to let the people meet their future sovereign. Oh!" Belinda gasped, grabbing my knee. "You could woo the kaiser's son! Surely a prince would have the power to free Samuel."

"Belinda, you go too far. He would never support a Protestant. Besides, I haven't the skill to win myself a German baron, let alone a Spanish prince."

Her smile faltered, and she released my knee. "True."

"I say we focus on gaining favor with the queen and see if our hunt master will teach me to shoot."

Belinda scoffed. "Old Bernhold can't hit a target with his tremors. You'd be better off asking the half-dead soldier in yonder room to teach you. I suspect he's nearly as young as you." A slow smile lifted her cheeks. "And he cuts a handsome figure besides, don't you think?"

I did think so, but I was not ready to admit as much. I still had that nagging sense I should know him from somewhere.

"Maybe he could teach you a thing or two *more* than hunting," Belinda said.

Throwing her a quick glare, I rebandaged my hand.

"You know, that's actually a useful idea." She pulled herself up to kneel. "It could be just the thing, in fact. You only want for some practice, some time around men to give you the confidence you need at court. This soldier could be the one to provide it."

"He's ill, Belinda. He's hardly in a state to countenance my feeble advances."

"'Tis only a fever. You said yourself his wound wasn't deep, that he'd recover in a matter of weeks."

I chewed the inside of my cheek. "And then what? I've no idea how to flirt. I haven't even an excuse to spend time in his company."

"As I said, have him teach you to hunt. And you needn't fret about flirting. Do your best, and whenever you err, I'll correct and tutor you. Then once you've procured his confession of love, we'll move on to another man and then another, until you're ready to conquer the courts."

"Confession of love?" I huffed my disbelief. "How could I even . . . Despite preference, despite compatibility and taste, you expect me to make this man—no, a string of men—fall in love with me?"

Her brow rose. "That's precisely what you'll be doing in Brussels."

That was true. I wouldn't have the luxury of hoping a man would take me as I am. I'd have to choose the most powerful noble and mold myself into the kind of woman he desired. I shivered and pulled my knees up to my chest, hugging them. This all felt wrong.

"Is he not handsome enough for you?" Belinda misinterpreted my silence.

I laughed. "Old Bernhold's looks would suit me better. A handsome man only makes me more nervous." Already I was twisting my chemise into knots around my ankles. "But I don't know that it's right, toying with a man's affections for the sake of . . . education."

"Oh goodness, we needn't trouble ourselves over a common soldier. He will bear his disappointments and find a woman on his level. No doubt sooner than he should," she muttered. "But don't think of him; think of Samuel. What's a month's worth of this soldier's injured pride when compared to the possibility of saving your brother's life?"

I shook my head, still feeling uncertain.

"Have you considered, Margaretha, what else Samuel's freedom would signify for you? For me?"

"What do you mean?"

She rested a hand on my wrist, drawing my eye to the bandage covering my burn. "Freedom from this haunting guilt. Saving a life to atone for the life we took." She raised her eyes, giving me a penetrating stare. "Redemption."

"Redemption?" As I whispered the word, a strange pressure built in my chest—a dull push, repeating slow and quiet, like a distant thudding of a drum. It felt as though my heart was stirring, fluttering to life after years of numbed silence. Could saving Samuel's life truly make amends? Could I really be absolved of the healer's death?

All the years spent studying healing, bandaging cuts and brewing electuaries for the infirm, had never felt enough. But perhaps this . . . this could be enough to rescue our eternal souls from hell.

I straightened my back and met Belinda's gaze. "I'll do it."

CHAPTER 4

Friedrich

THE BED, SOFTER AND WARMER than any bed I'd ever slept in, was my first reminder that I was in Count von Waldeck's castle. I relaxed each muscle into the mattress before opening my eyes to see a walnut canopy above me. Black wood posts twisted down to the coverlet, and I let my fingers run over the fabric, smooth as velvet, before sitting up with a groan. Looking down at myself, I saw my tattered livery had been replaced with a simple shirt. All my personal belongings were gone.

The letter.

Panic-stricken, I patted down the blankets and mattress to find it. I dug through the pillows but came up empty. Flipping back the coverlet, I gingerly stepped out of bed, crouching on the ground to look under the frame as a timid knock sounded at the door. I had little time to hoist myself back onto the mattress before the door clicked open and a beautiful face peeked around the corner.

The countess raised her brows in surprise. "You're awake." Pink colored her cheeks, and she lowered her eyes to the ground, stepping inside the room with her lady-in-waiting close behind.

"How long have I been here?" I asked.

The countess wouldn't meet my eye as she walked to the bedside and put her hand to my forehead. "Three days. Your head is cooler now. Do you feel any chill?"

What I felt was the softness of her skin on my face. I never knew hands could be so soft, but it ought not surprise me. Nobles never did do much work.

"No chill," I answered.

"Belinda, the electuary." The countess waved her companion forward.

Mistress Hatzfeld brought a silver tray for the countess, who picked out a corked flask full of an alarming brown liquid. She gripped the flask with her fingertips, careful not to let it bump her bandaged palm. That uncomfortable tug in my gut was back, and I squirmed. Apologies had never come easy for me, but I couldn't ignore my wrongdoing.

"I'm sorry again about your hand. I really was trying to help."

"I know. It was an accident, and I shan't hold that against you." Her tone was light, untroubled, as if she actually meant what she'd said. But people did not forgive so easily. I wouldn't trust her ready pardon.

The cork opened with a pop, and she put the flask in my hand. "It tastes vile, but it will help balance the humors."

Gulping the tonic, I forced myself not to shiver with disgust before I put the empty flask back in the countess's hand.

"Very good." She sounded impressed and even peeked a glance at my face but quickly looked away when she met my eye. I almost laughed. Where was the bold, demanding woman from the other night?

"I'll need to change out the poultice . . ." She hesitated, and I wasn't sure why until she pointed to my shirt still covering my side.

"Oh, yes, just let me . . ." I fumbled with the blanket, wrapping it tight around my waist to keep myself decent, which earned another blush from the countess. When I wriggled my shirt up to show her the wound's wrappings, she knit her brows with a determined focus. She cut away the old bandage, uncovering a greenish, leafy mud smeared against my skin, then took a clean cloth from Hatzfeld's tray and gently wiped the poultice.

"What is your name?" Her voice was so soft I almost didn't hear her.

"Friedrich."

"And how were you injured, Friedrich?"

"A lancer hurled his weapon at me. He only managed to graze my side before I buried a lead ball in his eye."

Hatzfeld's eyes went wide, and though Countess Margaretha continued cleaning the mud, her silence suggested my topic might be unfit for refined ladies.

After a long pause, the countess spoke. "It's healing, but not as well as I'd like." She dropped the dirty cloth on the tray and picked up a bowl with more leafy mud, spooning the thick substance over my gash. "It'd heal faster if you kept in your bed."

So she'd caught me hurrying to get back under the blankets. "I was searching for my livery."

"The livery was burned."

I froze. "But . . . I had some things, personal items I always keep with me. What happened to them?"

She put the bowl down to pick up long strips of cloth, laying them out at a frustratingly slow pace before answering. "Put aside when we dressed you." She kept the last strip in her grip. "Belinda, would you send for them?"

Her companion bowed and put the silver tray on the bed, leaving the room.

"You . . . dressed me?" My neck warmed at even the thought of Countess Margaretha doing so.

Her eyes widened, and she shook her head. "Not I. The servants."

Oh. "Of course," I muttered.

We sat in embarrassed silence until the countess cleared her throat. "If you please, I must bandage your wound."

I shifted away from the pillows, sucking in a short breath when the countess set a hand on my waist. It was only the shock of her touch that caught me off guard.

She shot me a glance, then ducked her eyes back to her work. With the cloth strip pinned beneath her palm, she unwound the bandage, fingers grazing the tender skin at my stomach.

I focused my thoughts on the draping bed canopy until the countess shifted to wrap the cloth around my back, her face merely a breath away from mine. She kept her gaze down, and my eyes traced the gentle pull of a swallow in her throat, telling me her discomfort was every bit what I felt. My shallow breaths were steeped in the scent of her: lilacs and sunshine and something distinctly feminine.

The rattle of the door had me straightening, leaning away from the countess as if I'd been caught with the count's gold in my pocket. I tugged the cloth from her hand and finished wrapping the wound myself, only letting her assist me in securing the bandage into place.

"The lady's maid will bring your things as soon as the countess is finished." There was a perceptibly amused tone to Mistress Hatzfeld's words.

I raised an eyebrow. "The countess isn't finished?" As if to prove my point, I let my shirt drop to cover my waist.

The countess looked at her companion. "We can be done, yes? He needs his rest now."

She moved to the door, but Hatzfeld returned to my bedside, picking up the tray and clearing her throat. The countess froze, her hand still on the handle before she dropped it to her side and dragged herself back to the foot of the bed.

Wrapping an arm around the post, she hugged it as if it were the only thing keeping her on her feet.

"There is one thing more." She fastened her gaze on the bedcover, tracing the pattern of the fabric with her finger. I found myself watching her hand dance over the curls and circles. "In a few months I leave for Brussels, to the court of Queen Mary. If I can gain her favor, I might have a chance to win my brother's freedom." Her words were stiff, as if they'd been rehearsed. "I've learned the queen is an avid huntress, and I was hoping you would teach me to hunt."

I waited for her to continue speaking, but that seemed to be it. "What about your huntsman?"

"He's too feeble."

"Then why hasn't he been replaced?"

She tugged on a loose thread. "Father is kind to him."

I held back a snort, seriously doubting the count was kind to anyone. "Countess, I'm in no condition to be teaching—"

"Not now." She looked up. "Not until you've recovered. But once you've regained your usual vigor, I want to be trained."

Something struck me as off. "Why do you make this request when your father could simply command me?"

Ducking her head, the countess tugged the thread of the blanket harder.

"I see. He doesn't know, does he?" I adjusted the pillow behind my back and shook my head. "I will not be teaching you to hunt. I've run afoul of your father before and don't care to risk his anger again. When I'm recovered, I plan to get myself out from under his charity and away from this castle as quickly as possible."

Hatzfeld spoke up from the other side of the bed. "If I may, with the war ending, you'll be needing to find work. Perhaps Countess Margaretha could speak to the count on your behalf, get you a position here. That is, if you agree to act as her instructor."

The lady-in-waiting bowed her head again after speaking, assuming the role of a humble servant despite her bold speech.

I did need the money. And with little training or skills, finding a position would be nigh unto impossible. Still, I loathed the idea of working for the count, knowing I would chafe under his orders. Being conscripted to his army was bad enough, but to work here in his castle? I'd only come back at all to fulfill my duty and deliver news of his son. I had no high opinion of the count. And despite my childhood impressions of the countess, much time had passed. She was likely now as spoiled and selfish as every other woman of her rank.

Living here, working with the pair of them . . .

I shook my head at the thought but startled when my eyes landed on Hatzfeld's venomous glare. She lifted a brow as if daring me to refuse.

The countess pulled herself around the bedpost, actually meeting my eye when she sat down by my leg. "Please," she said, her voice breaking as she scrubbed a hand over her nose. Was she about to cry again? "He is my brother. I must do something to help him. If you agree to teach me, I promise to grant you anything you ask."

I let out a skeptical laugh. "What could you possibly grant—" I stopped short, an idea forming. "*Anything* I ask?"

A sudden, fierce blush came over her cheeks, and she lowered her face. "Anything that will not offend God or my conscience."

It took a moment before I understood her meaning, but when I did, heat crept up over my neck and reached all the way to the tips of my ears. "No, I didn't mean . . . I'm not the kind of man who would demand anything . . . untoward." I rubbed the back of my neck to calm my embarrassment. "I'll agree to your bargain, as long as you give me time to decide how you will repay me."

She looked at her companion, and I caught the slightest hint of a nod from Hatzfeld before the countess spoke. "I agree. And I thank you."

I nodded a bow, telling myself the bargain didn't much matter anyway. The count would need a great deal of persuading to grant me a position, and I doubted the shy countess was much good at being persuasive. "Consider me your new hunting instructor."

She gave me a broad smile, reaching out as if she would take my hand. I folded my arms across my chest. Her smile faltered, but she soon recovered, dipping her head in farewell and signaling her lady to follow her as she left the room. Perhaps my snub was too curt. I was in no danger of falling for the countess, and she certainly wouldn't entertain thoughts of a servant, but something inside warned me to keep my distance. Maybe it was fear that our shared childhood memory might cloud my judgment. Or maybe a healthy dose of self-preservation was warning me away from the count, his daughter, and his whole blasted family. The less to do with them all, the better.

The irony of having just agreed to work for *two* of them did not escape me.

The chamber door squeaked opened, and a young woman—the lady's maid—came in with a basket perched on her hip. "Alone at last." She shot me a mischievous smile, closing the door behind her. "It's good to see you finally awake." Setting the basket on my bed, she leaned her face toward mine. "And your eyes are even prettier than I'd imagined they'd be."

I choked out my surprise, and she laughed.

"My name's Ilsa." When I didn't respond, she cocked her head. "Not much for speakin', are you? That's fine. I like the quiet ones."

Gracious, she was forward. And had a pleasant smile. I liked her easy manner but had no interest in encouraging her. My stay in this castle was only temporary. Still, I could be courteous.

She was already walking away, pulling open the door when I finally answered. "I'm Friedrich."

"Ah, he speaks!" She flashed a bright smile. "Well, Friedrich, if there's anythin' else you need, I'm just a summons away." She gave me a final, saucy wink before letting herself out.

Suppressing a grin, I reached for the basket, rummaging through all I owned in the world: the near-empty coin purse, the small rice-filled leather bag for foot games, and the letter. My touch was careful as I lifted the old paper, unfolding it to study the foreign writing again. The language was just as impossible to decipher as it had been the first time I'd seen it, but the thought of being able to read the words and finally comprehend them made my heart pump harder. I knew exactly what I wanted from the countess, and if she could be relied on to keep her word, I could stand to stay under the count's roof a little longer.

CHAPTER 5

Friedrich

THE SUN WAS BARELY UP, and already the town square was bustling with merchants and children, chickens and dogs. Sinking against the church steps, I pulled in a breath of cool morning air, ignoring the dull ache at my side. My wound was healing well, but not nearly quick enough to remove me from the count's charity or the countess's care. Despite her daily ministrations over the past two weeks, her silent manner told me I was an obligation to her. One she would gladly dispose of if we hadn't agreed to our little bargain. Why had I ever consented to teach her to hunt? I knew better than to trust a noble. The minute she had all she wanted from me, she'd go back on her word and toss me out of the castle before ever attempting to fill her side of the agreement. Better to not waste my time with her instructions and focus on saving every thaler I could earn, maybe getting enough to buy my way into a bowyer's apprenticeship and out of Waldeck forever.

A small, spotted dog bumped its wet nose against my hand, and I shooed it back. The dog was undeterred, snuffling around my hose until it found something to lick on the side of my shoe. Flicking my foot scared him a safe distance away, but he sat on his haunches and watched me. I watched him right back. The last thing I needed right now was fleas.

"Mind your head!"

A leather ball flew past my face, slamming into the stone wall beside me. The dog burst into a chorus of furious yapping as I hoisted myself up to retrieve the ball, grasping it just as a little blond boy with bright-green eyes appeared beside me. "Is this yours?" I asked. "That was an impressive throw."

"Hush, Klumpen," he commanded, but the dog paid him no heed. "Apologies, *Herr*. My aim's never so bad."

"Did you mean to hit me in the head, then?" I smiled, and he let out a laugh. Pulling a bit of dried meat from his pocket, he drew the now-quiet dog over and lifted him into his arms, running his hand down the dog's back.

"Your dog is not above taking bribes."

"Oh, he's Ulrich's, not mine. The count lets him stay at the castle with Ulrich because he's a good ratter."

"I see." I held the leather ball out to him.

He took it, setting the dog down and giving me a once-over. "Should ya like to play?"

I hadn't played ball games for too long now, and a flow of nervous excitement rushed to my limbs at his suggestion. But a gentle stretching to feel out my gash told me I'd better not.

The other boys from the game were coming over now, likely wondering what kept their teammate.

"Did you ask him to play?" I recognized Ulrich from the Walpurgisnacht festival. "Because he ain't fit for it. He's injured. And besides"—Ulrich gave me a wry grin—"he's too old."

Too old? How old did he think me? I stole the ball back from out of the little boy's hands. "I might surprise you."

The boys smiled, talking over each other to explain the rules of the game. It was their own version of the games I'd played as a child, but it didn't take much to settle into the flow. I hardly noticed my injury, panting quick puffs of cold air as my muscles burned with the effort. After so long being confined to a bed, the movement was exhilarating. Passing the ball back and forth between my feet, I traveled down the cobbled church street, finally kicking the ball to the little blond boy. It was near to sailing over his head, but he jumped and gripped it tight in both hands, then launched it against the other team's bucket, knocking it over. Our team cheered, the dog jumping and barking as if he'd played a part in the victory.

I set the bucket upright and collected the ball, carrying it to Ulrich with a grin. "Surprised?"

Ulrich didn't answer. He didn't even look at me. His eyes were trained behind me, and I turned in time to see a troop of soldiers filing into the town square, some with pikes held aloft, others with hands wrapped around their arquebuses.

The children began to scatter. A few women let out surprised cries, one looking frantic as she called a girl's name.

"Get the boys behind the church," I ordered Ulrich. Slinking into the shadows of the buildings, I spotted a small girl whimpering and covering her ears as she rocked back and forth beside a rain barrel. I slipped toward her. Gathering her into my arms, I shushed her fearful cries before reuniting her with her desperate mother and sending them into the safety of an alleyway.

A tall, slender soldier stepped forward from the troop, addressing the townspeople in his heavy Spanish accent. "We've been ordered to quarter here. Our job is to ensure you surrender to the kaiser and return to the Catholic faith. If you comply with his generous terms, we shall have no trouble, shall we?" He clapped his hands—the sound puncturing the taut air—then rubbed them together, giving a toothy grin.

Angry murmurs churned through the town square.

"And what if we don't?" someone yelled.

The soldier's smile didn't shift. "We are to use any means necessary to see that you do."

Protests rang out, the people's voices rising with their rage. One man wrapped a beefy fist around the handle of a pitchfork, his face dark with loathing.

No. No, no, no. If this escalated, these people would be slaughtered.

A wary soldier lifted his arquebus, aiming the muzzle directly at the man. To my left, an abandoned mallet lay across a merchant's table. I'd have enough time to grab it and work my way behind the men on the right, maybe taking out two or three soldiers when the shooting started. It might give the women and children opportunity to hide.

Time slowed as I waited for the pop of the gun, waited for the smell of sulfur, for the blood.

And then I saw the boy, the little blond boy with excellent aim, run into the town square and cock back his arm. Without thinking, I pushed through a pair of women, launching myself toward the boy, but it was too late. His arm swung forward, and the *thunk* of a rock ricocheting off a soldier's morion helmet echoed through the square. The boy scurried to disappear into the crowd, but he was too slow to outrun his victim. In a few long strides, the soldier crossed the distance between them, slapping the butt of his gun across the boy's skull. A streak of red stained the boy's white-blond hair.

"Leave him be!" I yelled. The little dog had reappeared beside me, his body shaking with each of his frenzied barks. I had half a mind to kick him but kept my sights trained on the enemy before me.

The soldier who had first spoken, likely their captain, raised an arm to hold back his men as his eyes studied me. I squirmed under his scrutiny but reminded myself that my bandaged gash was safely hidden beneath my shirt and jerkin. He had no way to know I'd fought against the kaiser.

"You're quick to jump into the fray." His arm lowered to his side. "Is the boy *su familia*?"

"He's defenseless. I won't see a grown man beat a child."

The captain smiled and stepped close, his eyes on my face. "Ah. A defender of the weak. You like a good fight, then?"

"No."

"Then how did you get this?" He lifted a finger and tapped above my brow, where a pike had grazed me. The wound was nearly nothing now, likely no more than a pink line across my forehead, but his keen eyes were narrowed in suspicion.

A bead of sweat slipped between my shoulder blades. "It was a scythe."

His eyes brightened like a cat ready to pounce on its prey. "A scythe? You were harvesting crops in May?" He moved closer.

"Friedrich!" The countess's voice rang out over the square, echoing across the stones in the silence. Every Spanish eye lifted to the church steps where the countess stood, the wind whipping her skirts and golden hair. As the soldiers studied her with unmasked appreciation, I used their distraction to slip away from the captain. I picked the boy up by the elbow, and we melted into the crowd to watch the countess and her lady come down the stairs toward the soldiers.

She was brave. I could admit that much.

And her father was a coward, hiding in his castle and sending his daughter to deal with the Spaniards.

"Who might you be?" The captain stepped forward, his gaze wandering down the length of her body.

Her eyes dropped to his boots. "The countess of Waldeck-Wildungen, sir, and—"

"Captain," he interrupted, flashing a crooked smile. "Captain Carrera."

"Captain." She took a shaky breath. "My people mean you no harm."

He lifted an eyebrow. "The dent in my soldier's morion would indicate otherwise."

"Yes. About that. It would seem . . ." The countess's cheeks flushed. "That is, it's . . . it's difficult to explain."

"I'm willing to let you try." His sultry tone made my skin wriggle like maggots. When his forward step caused the countess to retreat, I felt an urge to protect her, to push back through the crowd and shield her from his prying gaze.

Mistress Hatzfeld intervened first. "The count wishes for peace. If you will allow us to take you to him?" Her smile proved her everything opposite of the countess. Confident. Seductive. With only a few more words and a wave of her hand, the Spaniards fell in line to follow her.

"Shall you come too, my lady?" Hatzfeld asked with a peaked brow.

"I will stay and see to the boy. You take the soldiers."

Hatzfeld nodded and led the men away from the square. Before they'd even gone, townspeople surrounded the countess, pummeling her with questions.

"I do not know how long they intend to stay. Please,"—she raised a placating hand—"we must not provoke the kaiser's men. Be peaceable. Comply with all the count wishes you to do."

Hmph. What had the count done to earn their loyalty? He hadn't seemed to care enough to even warn his people the soldiers were coming.

Dismissing her speeches, I squatted in front of the boy, pushing away the dog when it jumped up to lick my face. "Are you all right?"

He nodded, smearing blood across his cheek as he swiped at his glistening eyes. "I was ready to fight them all." The growl in his voice was fierce despite his little frame.

"I believe you."

"Johannes, that was a very foolish thing to do." The countess dropped down beside me, crouching so near that I could again smell her lilac scent. I quickly stood and stepped back.

"Yes." I cleared my throat. "If only poor Johannes were so fortunate as the count and could send a woman to fight in his stead."

The countess's tense posture told me she fully understood the meaning of my flippant remark, bristling at my cutting assessment of her father's leadership. Her attention stayed on Johannes, surveying his wound when she answered me. "Is it always in your nature to make such gross, unjust assumptions?"

She stood, not waiting for my sputtering reply.

"Had I not decided *of my own accord*," she emphasized the last words, "to deliver electuaries this morn, you might be in chains just now. I think gratitude the more appropriate sentiment." Taking Johannes's hand, she swept through the square, leaving me alone with the blasted terrier licking my shoe.

CHAPTER 6

Margaretha

Pastor Hefentreger's final blessing was interminable. I peeked through slitted eyelids to see him dabbing his kerchief across his brow while glancing, not for the first time, at the Spanish captain leaning coolly against the chapel wall. The pastor stuttered through the chant, his tongue twisting over Latin words he hadn't recited in more than twenty years. His German hearers, ignorant of the language, yawned or drooped their heads in the overheated hall.

The realities of losing the war, of losing our freedom to follow Luther's teachings, were most painfully clear in our Sunday worship. So many in this chapel had endured the death of someone they loved: a brother or a son, an uncle or a cousin—men slaughtered to save our precious beliefs. And now the bereaved couldn't even find comfort in the pastor's words, the Latin language being wholly indiscernible to them.

I had never been brave like Samuel, fighting for our faith, but sitting in the chapel witnessing firsthand the death of the Reformation, my regret tasted bitter. I should have done more when there was more to be done. Instead of wrestling for the victory of our religion, my only hope now was to do my small part to help my brother.

Belinda grabbed my bouncing knee, forcing it steady. "Don't fret yourself," she whispered. "You'll do fine."

I prayed she was right. It had been a week since Friedrich was recovered enough to begin his new position at the castle, and he had yet to approach me about commencing our lessons. With Samuel's situation still unconfirmed, I would wait no longer. Today I intended to confront Friedrich. *The arrogant, ill-mannered mule.* I shook my head. Never in my life had I heard a commoner make such a scathing assessment of nobility. Had he no sense? No instinct for self-preservation?

The pastor's prayer was finally at an end, and we came to our feet. Resting my hands on the wood railing, I let my eyes trail the chapel below for Friedrich, but instead I found the captain with a sideways smile upon his lips, his gaze squarely upon the gallery.

"The captain watches us," I whispered.

Belinda glanced down at him, offering an elegant nod in return for his sweeping bow.

I scoffed. "You won't discourage him?"

"Why should I?" She waited for the pastor and his assistants to leave. "Captain Carrera has power over us. I should like to tip the scales in our favor, if I can."

She was right. It was just these calculations that proved she should be the one going to Brussels and not I.

As I turned to descend the stairs, my eyes met with Friedrich's as he stood below. He dropped his gaze and slipped into the aisle to move out the door. He had a head start. It would be difficult to reach him if we weren't quick.

"Hurry, Belinda." I held my skirts, navigating down the narrow steps and into the press, which parted to allow us through. Once we were outside, I caught sight of Friedrich tucking into another street.

"Friedrich," I barked, trotting after him.

"Be pleasant," Belinda panted. "Remember, more flies with honey."

When we reached him, he bent at the waist in greeting. "You wished to speak with me?"

"Yes." My tone was impatient. "I've waited nigh unto three weeks for lessons. When will we begin?"

Belinda placed a discreet hand on my back, and I added, "I'm so eager for your training."

My delivery must have been flat, for he quirked an eyebrow but answered, "I'm ready today, if you desire it."

I looked to Belinda, who nodded minutely.

"Very well," I answered. "Where shall we meet?"

Friedrich's instructions were simple enough that I knew precisely where Belinda and I were to go after changing our clothes and collecting our things from the castle. The May sun sifted through the beech leaves as we followed the spongy forest path. With each step, my hands shook a little more, and I gripped the basket handle tightly to steady them, but the pain of my scabbed burn made me release it with a hiss. I had to settle for deep, calming breaths until we reached the clearing. Friedrich was already there, resting against a tree with a paper in his hands, but on seeing us, he quickly folded it and tucked it into his jerkin. Belinda was too busy scanning the forest behind us to notice him or the questioning glance I shot her.

Upon our approach, Friedrich pushed to stand beside a quiver of arrows and a bow made with all the simplicity of a piece of wood attached to a string. Not with triggers. Not with bolts. Not a crossbow.

"What is this?" I poked the bow with the tip of my shoe.

Friedrich took it in his hands, pushing out his bottom lip as he tilted the weapon this way and that in mock examination. "It's a serviceable bow. What's wrong with it?"

"It's not a crossbow."

"You didn't ask to be taught with a crossbow. You asked me to teach you to hunt. This is how I hunt. I trained with a curved limb bow, and I intend to train you with the same."

"But no one takes a curved bow on a Par Force hunt," I whined. "Guns perhaps, crossbows certainly, but this is primitive."

Belinda cleared her throat. "Mistress, if I may." She led me by the elbow out of earshot of Friedrich before whispering, "Do not forget your purpose. He could be instructing you in dressmaking, for all we care. Cease arguing, find something pleasant to speak of, and for heaven's sake, rid your face of that dour expression."

I couldn't admit as much to Belinda, but I hadn't fully discarded the idea of gaining skill in the hunt to impress the queen. With this turn in plans, I had nothing to do but grind my teeth against the disappointment and force a cheery smile.

She patted my shoulder. "Very good. Now, if you'll give me your basket, I'll wander the forest a bit and see if I can't find herbs enough for both our baskets before your lesson's done."

"But you said you'd be nearby to offer instruction." I clung to her arm in panic. "What am I to do with him?"

Belinda patted my hands. "Talk. Be friendly. I shall be near enough to observe." She pried the basket from my hand and cut her way through the grassy meadow toward the trees on the other side.

Taking a deep breath, I walked back to Friedrich, prepared to be pleasant.

"Where is she going?" His eye was on Belinda.

"Picking. We're hoping to build up the apothecary's store of herbs."

He raised his eyebrow. "But what if someone came upon us? If she's to chaperone, I think it best she stay near—"

"She's near enough," I interrupted. "Unless you think I have need of protection from *you*." I slapped his arm and laughed a high, trilling laugh like I'd heard Belinda do. He raised an eyebrow and rubbed his arm before picking an arrow from the quiver.

Pointing the arrow at the thick trunk of a distant tree, he said, "That will be our target."

I had to squint to see it clearly, it was so far.

"And this"—Friedrich held the bow out toward me—"will be your bow. Clasp it with the joint of your forefinger straight before you."

I gripped the bow, twisting it in my left hand to find the proper position, but the edge of my scabbed burn caught on the wood and peeled back. Wincing, I forced myself not to let go.

He tapped the arrow against my knuckle. "This is where you'll rest the arrow for aiming."

Then he pointed the arrow at me and waited, as if expecting something from me.

"Should I . . ."

"Load your arrow." He spoke with strained patience.

I swallowed my embarrassment and took the arrow. Resting it on my knuckle and the bow string, I glanced to him for confirmation that my form was correct.

"You have to push the nock onto the string. Good. Now shoot it."

Closing an eye, I centered the arrow tip on the tree. I drew the string back, surprised by how much muscle such a simple task required, then let it go. The arrow flew wide right and clattered against a boulder.

"Again," Friedrich ordered, handing me another arrow.

I loaded the bow and repeated the process, this time forgetting to pull the string back to its full draw, for the arrow went a mere rod's length and burrowed into the ground. My face was hot as I put out my hand to receive the next arrow, but no arrow came. I turned to find Friedrich settling down against the trunk of a tree and folding his hands behind his head.

"Just getting comfortable." He smiled. "Since we'll be here awhile."

I wrenched an arrow from the quiver and jammed the bowstring between the nock, drawing the string back until my muscles burned.

"Don't forget the fletching."

"The what?" My suspended draw made my arms shake.

"The feathers on the arrow. If you release that—"

The string slipped from my trembling grip, and the arrow made a quick dive into the dirt only a few paces from my feet. Friedrich snorted, tempting me, begging me to bring him down to my place of humiliation. "How are your new quarters?" I turned to him. "Father gave you the position, am I right?"

His smile slowly faded.

"Huntsman's page should suit you well. I'm told it's quite comfortable, warm even, sleeping in the kennels with the dogs."

He dropped his hands into his lap and lowered his eyes, as if studying the grass between his feet. My smile grew smug until he tilted his head up to ask, "Does your father know where you are now? Did you tell him these herbs you're collecting would make medicinal tonics to help the poor, sickly people of Wildungen?" He glanced toward Belinda, bent plucking a fistful of greenery. "That must be nice for him, having a daughter whose devotion to Christian duty is outweighed only by her truthfulness."

My jaw dropped. He'd struck deeper than he knew, and I refused to satisfy him with a response. Instead, I jerked another arrow from the quiver and set it in the bow, shooting it off with such careless force that the string whipped the inside of my wrist, leaving it hot and stinging. Behind me, Friedrich laughed outright.

I spun on him. "I'm sorry. I must be mistaken. I didn't realize you'd brought me here to make a spectacle of me."

Plucking up a blade of grass, he settled it in his mouth as he propped an arm over his upright knee. "I brought you here so you could learn. You're making the spectacle all on your own."

He sucked on the grass with an infuriating smile.

"How do you expect me to learn?" My voice was loud enough that Belinda looked up from her place across the meadow. "You've done nothing but sit on your rump barking orders like some kind of noble overlord."

Friedrich's eyes flashed, and he stood up suddenly, pacing over to me with such severity that I stumbled back a step. He picked up an arrow, then grabbed my left hand, forcing it to the center of the bow and holding it in place. I sucked in a sharp breath as the scab of my burn split beneath the pressure.

"You put this hand here," he said, then reached his arm around me and threaded the arrow between my fingers. "You rest the arrow shaft on your knuckle, then twist it until the slit in the nock lines up with the string. The fletching must point outward to avoid hitting the bow when you release the string." He covered my fingers with his own, expertly nocking the arrow. "Balance the nock between your first and second fingers. Draw the string back toward your face until your first finger sits at the corner of your mouth." He squeezed my hand beneath his, using his strength to pull the bowstring back to my face, his finger brushing against my lip. I startled at the too-familiar touch, but he seemed utterly unaware of it, so focused on his target that our rather intimate situation was completely lost on him. "When your form is right, aiming comes easily. Sight your target." His face was so close his jaw grazed my cheek. "Now release."

This time the arrow flew in a smooth line, sailing toward the target and landing with a satisfying thunk in the center of the tree. It was a beautiful shot, an expert shot, and I couldn't help bestowing Friedrich a look of awe.

His face was lit by a smile as he studied his work, but when he met my gaze, his countenance fell, and he dropped my hand. Clearing his throat, he took a broad step backward, then turned on his heel.

"Again," he called over his shoulder and settled back against his favorite tree.

CHAPTER 7

Margaretha

THE BATH WATER WAS FINALLY heated, the steam rising from the tub as Belinda helped me out of my gown. I couldn't raise my arms to take off my chemise without groaning, but when I'd finally managed to slip out of my underclothes, I sank into the water and let the warmth pull the ache from my limbs.

"You shouldn't have practiced again today. You wouldn't be so sore," Belinda said.

"And show up at next week's lesson looking every bit the fool I did yesterday? I think not."

"Well, it wasn't all bad." Belinda gathered my pile of discarded garments. "If it weren't for your incompetence, Friedrich would never have had an excuse to put his arms around you."

"He was crushing me, Belinda. He was angry. There was nothing remotely romantic about it."

"Perhaps not just then, but another time, under less vexing circumstances, it could be very romantic." She folded the clothes and rested them across the bed. "From my vantage point, the only real error was when you slapped his arm like the rump of a horse. And that laugh . . . I would have sworn it was a pig squealing if I hadn't seen it come from your mouth."

A blush crept up my neck, and I buried my eyes in my fists. "I have no skill for these games with men!"

"I promised I'd teach you. If you hurry with your bath, we may have time enough for a little instruction before bed."

I wasn't eager to pull myself out of the warm water, and I was even less eager for instructions on flirtation, but after a decent soak, my curiosity got the best of me. Stepping out of the tub, I hurried to dry myself, then let Belinda slide a fresh chemise over my head.

"Now, I want you to watch what I do and imitate," she said, positioning herself in front of me. "When you touch a man, don't hit him as though you were swatting a beetle. Rest your hand on his arm, like so." Belinda laid a delicate hand on my forearm and looked up at me coyly through lowered lashes. "And when you remove your hand, let it trail down his arm ever so softly before you let go. Allow the tips of your fingers to be the last thing to touch him." She gave a demonstration before dropping her arms to her sides. "Now, practice on me."

I laughed and shook my head at the ridiculousness of the request.

"Ah yes, we'll work on your laugh in a bit, but for now . . ." She held her arm out toward me.

Rolling my eyes, I rested my hand on her sleeve, trying to keep my touch delicate.

"Good." She nodded. "Now the release. That's a bit too lingering, dear," she said when I'd run my fingers down the length of her arm. "Just a short sweep at the end is sufficient. Well done. Now on to the next piece. You have a long, elegant neck; let's use it."

Belinda spent the next hour instructing me. She taught me how to tilt my head to best expose and lengthen my neck, how to gently pout my lips when I've concluded speaking, and even how to fold my hands in front of me to accentuate the fullness of my bosom. By the time I'd made my two hundredth attempt at a light, trilling laugh, I was ready to burrow under the bedclothes and sleep till Whitsun.

"Next Sunday we'll take extra care with your appearance, choosing one of your most flattering gowns." Belinda stirred the fire a final time for the night. "If you can manage to keep the conversation civil and practice what I've taught you, I'd be very surprised if you haven't cracked through Friedrich's austerity by the end of the day."

I couldn't prevent a groan from escaping as I crawled into bed. "And if I'm always with him after church, when will I find time to deliver the people's electuaries and herbs?"

"This is more important, Margaretha." Belinda slipped onto her pallet and puffed up her pillow. "I know you still have doubts, but your success here could determine Count Samuel's fate. And more."

And more. Echoes of the healer's screams played through my mind without warning, and I sprang off my pillow, taking to unwrapping the fresh bandage from my hand to dispel the memory. The scab was still split, and the edges looked raw after this morning's shooting practice. I pressed my thumb against it, fingering the rough, thick scab while I dropped my head against the bedframe. My gaze traveled the dark room, reviving darker memories. Only the little chair beside the fireplace managed to draw a smile as I recalled waking from a fitful sleep to find Samuel sitting there, a thick book in hand. He wasn't allowed in my room. The sickness ravaging the house had already claimed Mother and baby Esther—though I knew nothing of it at the time—and Father was adamant that Samuel and Elizabeth stay far from me.

"You shouldn't . . . be here," I'd croaked. "If Father finds you . . ."

Samuel had looked up from his book to give me a mischievous smile. "Then I'll not get caught."

"You will when you fall to . . . your sick bed."

"Hush. I promise to stay over here. I only want to keep watch."

I was so weak, my throat so dry. "Drink," I'd begged.

"Belinda, the ale," Samuel ordered.

She was always quick to obey him, helping me drink while Samuel fidgeted in his seat.

Finishing the ale, I'd settled back in my bed. "You should go, Samuel."

"I shan't leave you to suffer alone, Retie." His voice was determined.

I gave a feeble smile. "Then perhaps you will read to me."

Face softening, he reopened his book, reading aloud the story of Atalanta and her footrace until I'd drifted back to sleep.

He was always so kind. He'd been the one to cry with me when I'd learned of Mother and baby Esther. He'd done his best to console me after the healer's death, though he didn't understand the cause of my anguish. I could never admit my part in it. And why would I? There was nothing he could do. Nothing *I* could do.

Until now.

Samuel was the key. Rescuing him could do more than save the life of my dearly beloved brother. Maybe it could finally bring a cessation to my guilt.

CHAPTER 8

Friedrich

I BOUNCED THE LITTLE LEATHER bag off my knee before catching it with the toe of my shoe, kicking it up to bounce it against my other knee. Back and forth the bag went, keeping my focus on my footwork and away from the gloves resting beside the tree. It was mere courtesy that had me seeking out a pair of ladies shooting gloves for the countess, nothing more. At our first lesson, I'd caught her favoring her burned hand, and seeing as I was the cause of that injury, it was only right to ease any pain she might have. But the idea of offering her a gift made my insides jump, worrying how she might interpret my gesture. So I bounced the leather bag a little higher, testing my skill, applying all my attention so that I actually startled when the countess offered a soft, "*Guten morgen.*"

The leather bag dropped to the ground. "My lady." I lowered into a quick bow, then picked up the bag to stuff it into my pocket before I retrieved the gloves from beside the tree. Were my hands shaking? Of all the ridiculous . . . "I, uh, noticed at our last—That is, I didn't *notice*. It just seemed like you were strugg—" I cleared my throat. "These are for you." Pushing the old shooting gloves into her hands, I took a step back to put more space between us. Why must she always smell of sun-warmed lilacs?

For a time, she simply stared at them, shock evident in her wide eyes, but then a smile graced her lips, growing until it brightened her whole countenance. "My many thanks," she whispered. Her gaze lifted to meet mine, and I was struck by the force of her beauty. Her porcelain skin setting off the sky blue of her eyes, her smiling red lips drawing my attention down to her mouth.

I pulled off my cap, strangling it between my rough laboring hands as I muttered some kind of reply. This was precisely why I had to keep my distance from her. I didn't need her gentle smiles, her nearness confusing what I already knew about her: as a noblewoman, she was not to be trusted.

Tugging my cap onto my head, I circled the tree to pull the bow from the hidden hollow. The countess followed me.

"You keep these here? Won't the armory miss them?"

"Hardly." I handed the bow back to her while I dug out the quiver of arrows. "I made them myself."

She ran her fingers over the smooth wood. "You made this?" Her eyes displayed her awe, but she straightened her features when she caught me watching. "Impressive. Where did you gain the skill?" she asked, returning the bow to me.

"I lived with a bowyer for a time." I carried the bow and quiver to her shooting line before settling myself down against the tree.

She finished tugging on her gloves and picked up the bow, getting into her shooting stance. On her first attempt to draw the string back, she sucked in a sharp breath. Lowering the bow, she shook her arms to loosen them, then got back into position. It was strange that after a week of recovering she was still sore, but the tremble in her shoulders proved that she was. I supposed for a woman who spent her days sitting in chairs reading or weaving, it should not have been too surprising.

With the countess's arms too tired to make the string decently tight, her shot was weak and aimless, diving headlong into a thicket. I folded my hands behind my head, resting back against the tree. It would be a short lesson today. She wouldn't last long with those aches.

I expected it when she drew the second arrow and loaded the bow. She had to at least put on a show of determination. But when she drew a third and a fourth despite her terrible success, I began to wonder how much longer she could keep going.

As Countess Margaretha reached for her fifth arrow, she asked, "Were you the bowyer's apprentice?"

"What?" We were going to chat now?

"You said you lived with a bowyer." She took aim, her arms trembling so much I couldn't help but feel sorry for her. "As his apprentice, no doubt. Yet your speech is more elevated than the other locals. Did you not attend the same school as they?"

I kept my lips tight, frustrated that my education showed so easily.

The string twanged with her next release. "Self-taught then."

I still made no answer.

"Was it your excellent skill with conversation that convinced Samuel to enlist your aid in Mühlberg?" she asked, a playful smile lighting her face as she reached for another arrow.

Pressing back my own smile, I leaned forward and plucked at the grass. "Count Samuel didn't enlist me. Mine was more of a compelled service after foresters caught me poaching on your father's lands. I was given the choice to serve the count's son or hang from a gallows. Bondage seemed the wiser option."

"So that's what you meant about running afoul of Father. But why were you poaching? Didn't you know the consequence if you were caught doing wrong?"

"Of course I knew." I tossed the blade of grass. "But the greater wrong is to let men go hungry when your lands are full of game."

The countess tucked a golden curl that had escaped its plait. "You don't much care for nobility, do you? Perhaps I can improve your estimation of us." She offered a gentle smile.

"My mother was noble."

Her quiet gasp was expected.

"That is how I learned to speak and read and write. She even taught me Latin so that I could one day be a scholar." My lips turned up at the memory. "She was brilliant and kind, but when her love for a blacksmith led to my birth, her family cast her off and refused to see her again, leaving her a beggar."

"She *was* kind? How did she . . . pass?" The countess was almost whispering.

Her gentle concern was an invitation, almost quieting my reluctance to delve into such a painful topic. But I could be brief. "You recall the plague that ravaged our town?"

She nodded. "It took my mother and baby sister too." The countess rubbed a hand across her nose, hinting at emotion that left me unsure of what to do. Should I continue? Averting my gaze to offer some privacy, I looked across the meadow and caught Hatzfeld staring at us. She instantly lowered her head and picked like mad.

I narrowed my eyes. Something was off about that woman. She always seemed to be . . . scheming.

"An-and what of your hunting?" the countess stammered, pulling my attention back to herself despite the nervous glance she shot at her companion. "Who taught you that skill? To be able to shoot an animal with just a curved limb bow, you must be very good at killing things."

I quirked an eyebrow. "Is that meant to be a compliment?"

She flushed, ducking her head as she reached for another arrow, but the quiver was empty. She excused herself and started gathering the scattered arrows, not even asking for my help.

I was tempted to stay by my tree and let her work alone, to give her a useful taste of labor and struggle, but she'd already shot through a whole quiver without complaint, despite her obvious discomfort. It was impossible not to admire that kind of resolve.

When she began jumping to reach an arrow lodged in a high branch, I sighed and pushed myself off the tree, easily reaching over her head to pull it down, then raking the bundle of arrows from her arms into mine.

"Are you ready for another round?" I baited her.

She surprised me, answering without hesitation. "Yes."

"My lady." I puffed a laugh of disbelief. "I wasn't serious. You're obviously tired. You would improve faster if you gave your arms time to recover."

Looking up at the sky, she swallowed, then lowered her eyes to look directly in mine. "If it pleases you. I only hope to please you." She fluttered her eyelashes so quickly that, at first, I wondered if she was working a piece of dirt from her eye.

I shifted away. "It doesn't concern me. Do as you will."

Her shoulders dropped. Did she want me to insist that she rest?

As we walked together toward the shooting line, the countess reached over and tried pulling an arrow out of my grip, but I held it fast.

"What is it?"

I shook my head. "Do you really believe any of this"—I lifted the bundle of arrows—"will make a difference for your brother? Could learning to hunt really gain you any influence with the queen?"

She kept her gaze on her hands, her thumb massaging her injured palm through her glove. "I'm willing to do anything for Samuel." Then she murmured what almost sounded like, "And for my soul."

She glanced up, and the cloud of seriousness lifted. "Even if it means learning to shoot this confounded bow." She started down the path again, determination in her step.

"Countess," I called, and she turned toward me. "When you begin your draw, pull your arm back at an upward angle. It puts the work of the draw into your stronger back muscles and gives you time to steady your aim."

Her cheeks rounded in a smile. "I thank you. I'll try that."

Countess Margaretha bounded to the shooting line with a lightness in her step, and I found myself smiling to think that I might be the cause of it.

Margaretha

Friedrich deposited his bundle of arrows and moved back a safe distance as I took my place at the shooting line. Drawing the string, I did my best to follow his instructions, pulling it at an angle, and just as he'd said, the strength in my back allowed my weary arms a second more for aiming. The arrow flew, coming closer to the target than any before it.

"Much better." Friedrich's voice behind me made me startle. How had he moved so close without me hearing his step?

"Now focus on your anchor," he said. "Pull the string back until your finger sits at your mouth, then press your hand firmly against the side of your face. Before you release the bow, take a deep breath and tighten the muscles in your back."

I was only half listening with him standing so near, triggering the memory of when his jaw grazed my cheek on our first day of practice. I recalled Belinda's suggestion that, with an altered mood, a replay of the scene could be romantic. All my attempts at flirting up to now had only elicited confused looks, but Friedrich was now here beside me, voluntarily helping me. Maybe he was beginning to soften toward me. Maybe this time I would succeed.

Taking a deep breath, I lowered my eyes, then peeked up through my lashes when I turned to face him. "I'm not sure I understand. Could you show me?"

His brows furrowed, but he took a step closer, reaching out his hand. "May I?"

I hesitated, not certain what he wanted.

"The bow," he clarified, pulling the tip of it toward him until I'd released it.

He would only demonstrate. There went any chance of creating a romantic setting. I hoped my shoulders didn't visibly sag.

Friedrich stepped to the shooting line, lifting my bow with fluid familiarity. "You see, when I pull the string back, I set my forefinger against my lip just here." His finger called my attention to his face, to the dusting of freckles across his nose and cheekbones. The features of both boy and man, both soft and stern, made for a beautiful contradiction. I had always known Friedrich to be handsome, but standing this close, I found him positively striking. "Every time I draw, I pull the string back to this same spot. My elbow is tucked behind the arrow, not flailing out to the side. Notice the rotation of my shoulder down and back."

I did notice. With his shirtsleeves rolled to his elbows, I caught myself staring at the sinews of his arms, stretched taut beneath his bronzed skin. Gracious, where was my head today? Was it his proficiency with a bow that had me gaping? His mastery was evident, even to one as inexperienced as I.

"My feet point away from the target, and I've lined them up with the width of my shoulders. Now that I'm bearing the weight of the draw in my back, I can take the time to look down the arrow's shaft, put the point on the target . . ."

His gray eyes narrowed, and his jaw tightened as he took a moment to shore up his aim. He was focused, his entire body tensing, storing up the energy he was about to let free.

"Deep breath." He pulled his shoulders back and pushed out his chest. "And release."

The thunk of the arrow hitting its target awoke me from my schoolgirl swooning, and I turned downfield to see the arrow buried deep in the flesh of the tree. When I glanced back to him, he was watching me with a boyish grin of self-satisfaction. The endearing smile sent a pleasant fluttering through my stomach, but I responded by rolling my eyes and grabbing for the bow to take another turn. My hand landed on his, though I hadn't time to realize it before he was ripping his hand away, sending the bow clattering to the dirt between us.

Friedrich murmured an apology as we both bent to pick it up, but he was careful to keep his hands from mine, pinching the far edge of the bow and dangling the other end toward me as though it was something foul.

"I hope that helps," he muttered, then stalked to his tree, resting his forearms atop his knees and choking the life from his cap without glancing back at me.

I studied him, wondering what had just passed. Was he intentionally avoiding my touch? He certainly hadn't minded Ilsa's nearness the other day. I'd seen them laughing in the courtyard, her hand resting on his arm in a way that made my veins itch.

"Friedrich, have I—" Was I really ready to ask this? His eyes lifted, eliminating the possibility of retreat. I swallowed and plowed forward. "Have I offended you in some way?"

He raised his brows.

"It's just, you seem eager to keep your distance from me. I had thought it a personal trait of yours, being removed and reserved on the whole, but you and Ilsa . . ." I felt as foolish as I ought. How was I to finish such a statement?

Friedrich leaned forward. "Have you been watching us?"

"Not *watching* you, no, but I did see you together as I passed by a window the other day." Heat crawled up my cheeks. Why did his lips curve into a smirk just then?

"You aren't jealous, are you?"

I scoffed and turned my flushed face back to the target. "That's absurd."

"Is it? Then why be angry that I spoke with Ilsa?"

"I'm not angry." The way my voice rose did not support my claims. "I'm merely trying to understand. You are quiet, often cold with me. You shrink back if I ever happen to touch you. Sometimes I sense something like contempt, but why?"

I turned to find him looking at the ground, rubbing his neck with his hand, but he did not answer.

"My family has done so much for you. I should think—"

"Oh yes." His eyes flashed at me. "They've done so much for me."

"You would deny it?" This time I was angry, but I managed to keep my voice even. "My father could have hanged you for your poaching, but he let you live. He had no obligation to take you into his house, to care for you when you were ill, or to provide you with an income."

Friedrich was back to strangling his cap. "Your father doesn't care for anyone but himself," he said, his voice a low threat. "Don't delude yourself into thinking his help to me was out of any kindness in his heart."

I reared back, blood thrumming in my ears. "How dare you. Explain yourself!"

He searched my eyes, his jaw clenched and his breath coming fast, but he said nothing.

"You insult my father, then refuse to justify it? Coward." I threw the bow in the dirt, called for Belinda to follow, then stormed away.

CHAPTER 9

Friedrich

ULRICH'S LITTLE DOG, KLUMPEN, SNORED beside me as I stared at the dark kennel ceiling, irritated to be woken too early by dreams of the countess. After she'd failed to show for last week's lesson, offering no explanation, I should have been furious with her. But these cursed dreams were clouding my justifiable anger.

At the rustling of hay across the kennels, I leaned on my elbow to listen better. Enough moonlight still drifted through the windows for me to recognize the young varlet's figure creeping around the sleeping dogs. He pulled his sleeveless jacket down from the hooks of leashes, sliding the jerkin onto his body.

"Ulrich, where are you going?" I whispered. Klumpen stirred but did not wake.

"It'll be dawn soon." He buttoned the jerkin. "The countess needs extra hands to gather herbs while the healin' Midsummer dew's still on 'em."

The countess. Just the person I wanted to speak to. I pushed up out of the hay, startling Klumpen awake, and had my arm through one hole of my jerkin before Ulrich put his hand on my chest, stopping me.

"You can't go. The dogs need runnin'."

"You can run them."

His mouth tightened into a thin line. "It's Midsummer Day. In a dark forest. With maids." He shook his head, turning both his hands up as if I should understand. "I have plans."

"Ulrich, you're barely fifteen. What would you know of maids?"

"Enough to court a kiss from one." He pulled his cap firmly over his head and moved out the door, but I followed, Klumpen on my heels.

"Wait, wait, wait." I grabbed his shirtsleeve. "Listen, there will be bonfires tonight and dancing. You'll get a chance with your maids then, but I might miss mine if I don't go now."

A sly smile slid over his face. "Who's the girl?"

I put my arm through the other hole of my jerkin. "Not your business."

"Well enough. Since I outrank you, I'll be choosin' who runs the dogs, and I choose you." He turned toward the gates, but I pulled him to a stop again.

"All right, it's the countess, but it's not what you think. I just need to talk with her."

"Is she the one you've been sneakin' out to meet on Sunday afternoons?" He raised an eyebrow.

Perceptive little beetle. "I've been helping her with . . . a project. Will you let me go?"

He stared at me a while, then let out a sigh. "They're meeting in the dell by Wilde River."

"Good man." I clapped his arm and grabbed my cap, shooing Klumpen toward Ulrich with my foot.

"You'll be muckin' kennels for a week as payment," he called after me as I trotted through the courtyard.

I followed the steep road down the hill, all the while planning just what I would say to the countess when I finally saw her. But upon reaching the dell, instead of being the first to arrive, I found the place busy with servants carrying torches and bending over the ground to search for herbs. The countess stood by a large fire directing them, handing out torches and baskets to a line of waiting servants. I stepped in line behind Bernhold, using his frame to hide me from the countess's view.

From across the dell, Ilsa spotted me and waved, leaving her curious friends behind to speak with me. "What luck finding you this Midsummer's morn. I expected you'd be runnin' dogs."

Crouching lower behind Bernhold, I answered quietly, "I got Ulrich to work in my place."

"Why's that, I wonder?" Her smile was coy.

I cleared my throat, using the extra second to invent a reason. "A love of herbs?"

She laughed. "No doubt."

A pair of girls called to Ilsa, and she sighed. "I must go. Find me tonight?" She gave my arm a quick squeeze and left without waiting for an answer.

I watched her join her friends. If my circumstances were different, I might welcome her attentions. She was confident and knew her mind. She certainly beat out the countess for boldness, though the countess had every outward advantage over her. And why was it that a noblewoman would— Blast it! How had this become about the countess? Casting off such thoughts, I focused my attention ahead.

The line moved forward, putting Bernhold at the front, where the countess greeted him. She gave him a torch and a basket for carrying herbs, then pointed to an empty spot by the river, sending him on his way while she bent to pick up another basket. When she straightened to find me standing there, her eyes widened, and the polite little smile on her face disappeared.

"Here's your basket." She stiffly held it out to me.

I moved close to take it and lowered my voice. "If you've decided to be done with lessons, fine, but I still demand my payment."

Even in the dim light of dawn, I could see her cheeks flush, coloring her snowy skin a soft pink. "I've made no such determination."

"Your behavior on Sunday made me think differently, since you sent no note or explanation for why you didn't come. I sat by myself in the rain for an hour waiting for you."

A flicker of pity flashed in her eyes, but she straightened her shoulders and answered in a detached voice. "You'll be searching for violets and vervain with Bernhold over by the Wilde. Belinda, give him a torch." The countess bent to collect another basket, effectively dismissing me.

I snatched the torch and stalked toward the river, glancing back as she greeted the next servant with a broad smile, all beauty and perfection. She was infuriating. More infuriating still was how often she'd visited my dreams in the last two weeks, her warm smiles and easy manner confusing my resolve to dislike her.

Reaching the shores of the Wilde, I hunched over the ground with my torch, knowing very well I'd find few violets or vervain beneath the shade of the river trees. Still, the countess wanted me to search here, and nobles always got what they wanted, didn't they? Her insult from the other day still rang in my ears. Calling me a coward before marching off with her companion? Fie, but she was proud. The fact that she'd had no trouble leaving me to sit in the rain proved it. But at the memory of our argument, my conscience was pricked. I'd spoken strongly enough of her father's guilt that her anger with me was justified—in her eyes, at least. It was no surprise her love made her blind to his faults; such loyalty was only natural, and it did her credit.

My eyes drifted to where she worked, her sleeves pushed back, her hair falling over her cheek as she bent to pluck herbs with muddy fingers.

Not *so* proud, then. And her efforts at shooting showed a quiet strength of will I could appreciate.

I shook my head, turning back to my task. There was nothing about the countess I should be appreciating.

I kicked against a rock to knock the dew off my shoe, then spent another half hour hunched over the muddy ground. When I finally stood, stretching out my back, Bernhold was putting out his torch in the river.

"Task's done here, boy." He moved past me toward the bonfire, and I handed him my torch as he went by.

"I have some work left to do." I wouldn't let the countess's ignorance keep the people from getting their herbs. Waiting till Bernhold was out of sight, I moved into the forest to find the little meadow. The grass there was speckled with purple and blue flowers, and I had a basketful of them by the time I heard a soft step on the ferns behind me.

"You spoke of payment." I recognized Countess Margaretha's smooth voice before I turned to see her, face smudged with dirt and a wreath of mugwort and vervain in her golden hair. "Have you decided what it is you wish of me?"

Of its own accord, my hand settled over my jerkin, over the letter tucked inside. The countess's promise could finally bring understanding, but it would mean relying on her to keep her word. Trusting a noble at all was a grim prospect, considering they were an untrustworthy lot, but I was left without another choice. "I have."

"And?"

I took a deep breath. "I want to learn the French language."

She furrowed her brows. "Why?"

"The *why* is my business. Will you honor your side of the bargain and teach me?"

She tugged a petal from the pile of sunny flowers in her basket, rolling it between her fingers. "I agree to teach you, but our hunting lessons are not terminated. I'll continue to expect them every Sunday."

"Can I expect you to actually be there?" I gave her a stern look, but she ducked her head, refusing to meet my eye.

"If you promise to keep a civil tongue regarding my father. I'll not have him maligned by you or anyone."

"Agreed," I said.

She reached out a hesitant hand, and I knew I should take it to solidify our reconciliation, but I couldn't. I could not touch her or take her hand in mine without fear of losing the fragile control I was struggling to keep over my confusing feelings for her. But I had no reasonable excuse to avoid it. Lifting my hand to meet hers, I stopped when I noticed the crimson stains on her fingers. "You have blood on your hands."

Her eyes flashed up to my face, and she took a step back. "Why . . . why do you say that?" Her voice was breathless.

"See there." I pointed at her hand, and she pulled it toward her, opening it wide for inspection, then laughing with a hint of relief.

"No, it's not blood. It's the St. John's wort. The flowers leave a reddish stain when their petals are pressed." She wiped her fingers on dewy moss, then dried them on her apron. "Shall we combine our herbs with the others?"

I nodded, and we walked together for a bit. The rising sun colored the sky in shades of orange and pink, prompting birds to trill their songs. It was gentle and pleasant. No wonder Midsummer's morn was known for courting. Without conscious direction, I found my gaze drifting to the countess, studying the way the light accentuated the flowers in her hair. "That's a fetching crown you wear."

The moment the words were out, I wished them unsaid.

Her mouth formed a small *O* of surprise, but then she fluttered her eyes, recovering. "Many thanks." She chuckled while pulling the flowers off her head and running a hand over her hair. "The little girls made one for each of the maidens. It is Midsummer, after all. Time for courting."

"So Ulrich reminded me." I smiled.

We walked out of the forest, meeting Mistress Hatzfeld at the edge of the dell and trekking back to the bonfire together. Before we reached the crowd, the countess turned to me.

"I think the best time for French lessons will be after dinner. My tutor always falls asleep while I'm reading, so it shouldn't be difficult to sneak away."

"Very well. Should we plan on Tuesday afternoons?" I'd be mucking stalls for a year to get this favor from Ulrich, but it had to be done.

"Yes. In Father's library. Only, take care not to be discovered in that part of the castle."

"I will, as long as you take care to keep your father from his library."

Mistress Hatzfeld spoke up. "I'll see to it."

I cast her a curious glance, but she did not meet my eye. Bowing, I said, "Then I'll be there."

Countess Margaretha smiled and moved toward the bonfire, turning the wreath over in her hands a few times before throwing it into the flames. As she watched it burn, she repeated the phrase from tradition: "May all my ill luck depart and be burned up with these."

CHAPTER 10

Margaretha

My tutor's head drooped to his chest, and Belinda and I exchanged looks. We waited for his gentle snoring before creeping from the room and toward Father's library. I only hoped Friedrich had found his way there safely.

Tiptoeing down the hall, we rounded a corner and nearly bumped right into Father, followed by a smiling Carrera with two soldiers.

"Margaretha." Father's brow wrinkled, his worn face looking more weary with each day since the fall of the Reformation. "I was just in search of you. But why are you not at your studies?"

"Taking a small bit of exercise," I answered with a nervous laugh, glancing between the soldiers. "Why should you seek me?" Normally I looked forward to Father's visits, to the snippets of information he would share about Samuel's whereabouts. But with the soldiers here, this seemed ominous.

"I came to tell you I'm leaving for Augsburg." He looked down at his hands. "The kaiser has summoned me."

I sucked in a sharp breath.

"Do not worry yourself, *señorita*." Carrera stepped forward. "All will be well."

His words did nothing to soothe me. I wouldn't trust the Spaniard as far as I could spit, which I had half a mind to do if it could discourage that leering smile of his.

Father took my shoulders in his hands, drawing my eye. "The kaiser won't even be there. I'm to meet with his representative, Bishop de Granvelle."

"Why should that bring me any comfort?" My nose tickled, warning me that tears were not far behind. Drat my propensity for crying.

"If he had any intention of making an example of me, he'd want to witness it for himself." He gave a sad smile.

"Oh, Father."

Pulling me into his arms, he quickly whispered into my hair, "Dalwigk brought word. The kaiser and his court will not return to Brussels until winter."

Winter? I bemoaned the setback. What would my brother suffer in the months between now and then? Was there nothing I could do to help him?

Of course there was. And I was on my way to do it now, though I still hated the idea of deception. But how else would I save my brother? Or save myself and Belinda?

"Do what you must to make yourself ready." Father gave me a squeeze, kissing my hair and whispering his goodbye. "I'll be here with you again in three or four weeks' time."

"Promise me." I clung to his overcoat, refusing to let him go.

"I promise."

Watching my father's retreating back, I swallowed down my fear, clinging to his vow to return. And focusing forward. Five months from now I would be in Brussels. It seemed so far away, but that kind of thinking would do me no good. The time to prepare was now, and so I took firm steps down the hall, leading the way toward Friedrich.

Just outside the library doors, Belinda put a hand on my arm and wished me luck.

"Are you not coming with me?" I asked.

"I must remain here to serve as guard. We can't have anyone happening upon you tutoring the huntsman's page."

The idea of being alone with Friedrich made me instantly anxious, but I thought of Samuel, put my hand on the knob, and pushed into the shadowy room.

Friedrich stood at the desk thumbing through the first tract of Luther's *To the Christian Nobility of the German Nation*, but he flopped it closed when I entered. Tossing the pamphlet onto the desk beside the fruit bowl, he faced me.

"I wasn't sure you'd actually come." He frowned, but his tone was teasing.

I rolled my eyes and walked past him to the fireplace. "Well, at least you wouldn't be waiting in the rain this time."

"Where is your companion?" The question was casual, curious. Not accusatory, as it might have been in the past. It seemed Friedrich was putting on his best behavior since our reconciliation Midsummer's morn.

"She is keeping watch at the door," I answered. "Come. Sit down."

Belinda had managed to order a small fire burning, but the room was otherwise already perfectly arranged with Father's two substantial oak chairs angled toward the hearth. I took my seat, leafing through my papers for the alphabet I'd penned, as Friedrich haltingly lowered himself into the other chair. He leaned his elbows on his thighs, clasped his hands together, and bounced his leg furiously. I'd never seen Friedrich nervous before, and I found I rather liked it. His nervousness buoyed my own confidence. Pressing my lips together to accentuate their color, I held out the page to him.

"Here you are." I tugged my lip between my teeth, hoping it wasn't too overt a display.

His leg stopped mid-bounce as his gaze fell to my mouth, and a soft scarlet bloomed over his cheeks. He pulled the paper from my hand to study, rubbing the back of his neck and concealing his blush behind his raised elbow.

But his blush had betrayed the truth; Friedrich found me attractive.

I tucked back my smile. Though exciting a man's admiration was not a novelty, I felt a thrill in my gut to see it from *him*. It was addictive, and I wanted more.

Moving closer, I caught his subtle scent of cloves and straw as I leaned over the arm of my chair and pointed to the first letter on the page. "This is *A*—pronounced 'ah.'"

Friedrich repeated my pronunciation.

"B is 'beh.'"

He echoed me again. We worked our way through the alphabet, and I took special care to pout my lips when pronouncing "o" and "ku," but Friedrich kept his eyes down throughout the exercise, never once risking another glance at me. My former excitement sagged as I riffled through my papers for the next piece to study.

He waved the paper in his hand. "I'll just go over these again."

Friedrich quietly mouthed each letter of the alphabet to himself, leaving me to glance around the room, unsure of how to occupy my time. Remembering the bowl of fruit on Father's desk, I picked out two red-cheeked apples and brought them back to the fire, holding one out to Friedrich as I sank into my chair. "Apple?"

He glanced up from his studies to the offering balanced on my palm, its shiny surface reflecting the flares of the fire. When his eyes met mine, they were narrow and intense with a weight I couldn't comprehend, as though my deed had some deeper significance. Taking the apple, he muttered a quiet, "Thank you."

I hoped I'd answered politely but was too distracted puzzling out the significance of his look to know what I said.

A long silence followed, interrupted only by the occasional pops and hisses of the fire logs. When Friedrich finally spoke, he was still staring down at the uneaten apple in his hand. "You don't recall, do you? When we met as children?"

"We've met before?" From the beginning he'd seemed familiar, but why could I not remember him?

"I'm not surprised. It likely wasn't significant to you. It's just . . . you gave me an apple then too, and this sparked the memory, is all."

"Tell me of it."

He turned in his seat, facing me. "Your father came to visit the mines. You and your sister were there too."

"Elizabeth?" I'd only ever accompanied Father to the mines once, just after I'd recovered from my illness. Just after they'd burned the healer. The hint of a memory stirred in my mind, of air heavy with heat and smoke, of dwarfs and men scurrying from the shafts like ants from their mound.

"I'd tried to talk with your father, but the overseer stopped me," Friedrich said.

Now I recalled kneeling on the coach's seat, knocking over the food basket as I watched the commotion from my window. A beefy man had held a dirt-covered boy by the shirt front, cursing loudly, then cuffing the boy's ear. The boy crushed his eyes closed, hiding his face against his shoulder as he awaited the next blow. The blow never came.

"Your father intervened."

Father had caught the man's hand in the air, his voice carrying to the coach when he'd warned, *"Not in the presence of my daughters."*

The man had glared down at the boy, waiting for Father to walk away before releasing the boy with a shove. He'd yelled at the gawking miners to get back to work, and the ants scurried again.

Left alone, the boy had begun to cry, and I remembered the pity I'd felt to see it. Enough pity that I'd dug a bruised apple from our overturned food basket.

"You climbed down from your coach, defying your sister when she tried keeping you inside. I was so surprised to see you walking toward me in your clean, fine silks." He huffed a short chuckle. "But then . . ." He looked up as we relived the memory together. "You held out the apple for me."

The boy's eyes had met mine, and I was shocked by their color. Stormy gray. The same stormy gray I'd recognized upon our meeting at Walpurgisnacht.

The boy had wiped his nose on his sleeve, reaching out a tentative hand before grasping the apple and tucking it to his chest. He'd cradled it against him as though it was something precious, his thumb caressing its crisp, red skin.

Just as his thumb caressed it now.

We were quiet awhile, each lost in our reflections, until I murmured, "I remember you now."

"Do you?" He pulled his chair so close our knees almost touched. "When I saw you at Walpurgisnacht, I recognized you almost instantly. You were older, of course, and even more—" He swallowed, looking at the apple he rolled between his palms as he rushed through the rest. "Even more beautiful than I remembered."

I froze, unsure I'd understood him rightly. It was such a bold admission.

"But your eyes," he continued. "They haven't changed. As a child they were colored with sadness, almost a private despair. I see it there still."

He looked up at me then, and I darted my gaze to the fire, working to keep my breath steady. "I'm sure I don't know what you mean." My voice was too pleasant, too light.

I felt Friedrich's scrutinizing stare for a time until he sighed and leaned back in his chair. "Of course you don't." He took a bite from his apple and lifted his alphabet for study.

While my breath returned to its steady rhythm, my mind wandered back over our conversation, one point striking me. "You worked in the mine shafts? I thought only grown men and dwarfs worked in the shafts."

Friedrich raised an eyebrow and gave a surprised chortle. "Dwarfs? There are no dwarfs in the mines."

"I remember them quite distinctly. They wore the driving hoods and breech leather aprons of miners. They even carried pit picks."

His smile faded. "Those aren't dwarfs; they're boys. Or men who've worked in the mines since they were boys."

"But it's a man's work. Why would they employ children?"

"Because some of those tunnels are barely higher than my knee." He put a flattened palm out beside him. "Only children are small enough to fit, and that's only if they're lying down. They have to crawl through the shafts to fill a trolley heavy with ore, then shoulder it back up the tunnels on their hands and knees or pull it with a strap across their chests. The weight of the work makes their spines grow curved. And while their legs stay short and weak, their shoulders and chest grow to the size of a man's. Working twelve hours a day in almost total darkness, never seeing the sun, they end up pale and sickly. The shafts are like a living tomb."

"How dreadful! How did you manage to escape it?"

"A lot of things combined that allowed me to escape, but a small part of it was . . ." Friedrich ducked his eyes, ". . . was because of you and your apple, actually." He turned away, his jaw flexing as he watched the fire. "As a noble child, you had no business worrying about me, spoiling your gown for a poor orphan boy. Yet you disobeyed your sister and helped me anyway. You lived outside your class, not bound by expectations."

His prejudice was showing again, exposing his wrongheaded ideas about how nobility behaved, but I let it pass.

"I decided to do the same," he continued, "ignoring all the expectations of an orphan boy's fate and finding my own way. That act, that apple . . . it was a chance to choose something better."

I very much liked the idea of young Friedrich drawing such grand and grown-up conclusions from my simple deed. And the notion that my small kindness had changed the course of his life created a strange sensation in my heart, like the tingling of blood flowing to a limb once numb. I thought of so many things to say, but none seemed quite right.

Friedrich filled the silence. "But those *dwarfs* are good men. They took me in and cared for me when I was sick, then found me work. I do my best to repay their kindness when I can."

"You still see them?" I asked.

"When I'm not away at war," he muttered. "My friend, Ernst, is in a bad way. I try to make time for him."

"He's ill?" I drummed my fingers against the chair's arm, pondering an idea. "I could help him, Friedrich. You should take me with you the next time you go."

His head jerked back. "To Bergfreiheit? I'm not sure how the miners would feel having a countess in their cottage."

"They needn't know I'm a countess. I could go in servants' clothes."

He shook his head. "They work into the evenings, and I haven't a horse to ride anyway."

"I can arrange for a horse."

"What about your father? What excuses would you make to him?"

"Father is gone." I touched the back of my hand to my nose, preempting any spring of emotion. "And will be for the next fortnight, at least. Now is the time to make our visit."

He still seemed uncertain. "I don't think it's wise—"

"Friedrich, let me help your friend."

His eyes studied mine, the scrutiny slowly softening into something else as the moment stretched on. His gentle gaze released another swell of fluttering in my stomach.

"Very well." He sighed. "On Saturday eve I'll wait for you in the clearing. Meet me an hour before sunset, and we may get to the mines before dark."

I blinked. "I'll be there."

CHAPTER 11

Margaretha

I TUGGED AGAIN AT THE neckline of my chemise, trying to pull it higher.

"Quit fussing," Belinda said, clasping shut the line of hook fastenings at my bosom. "This shabby maid's dress flatters you better than most of your gowns. I think it just the thing to elicit Friedrich's admiration."

Shifting my feet, I turned my attention to our saddled horses munching fresh grass. I hadn't yet confessed Friedrich's admission of my beauty, nor his obvious attraction to me during our French lesson. Though I should have informed Belinda of my progress, I couldn't put down the nagging sense that confiding in her was somehow a betrayal to Friedrich.

Yet wasn't this entire entrapment a betrayal to Friedrich?

I wouldn't think on that. Samuel needed me, so it must be done.

"Are you nearly finished?" I asked. "If someone discovers us changing clothes in the forest—"

"Patience," she sang. "And there." She stood back, taking in my appearance with a smile before picking up our discarded gowns and tucking them into her saddlebag.

Our horses' hooves padded over the soft forest floor as they carried us to the clearing where Friedrich stood, one leg crossed in front of the other and a shoulder propped against his favorite tree. He almost smiled at our arrival, but his mouth turned down when he looked back and forth between the horses.

"You're both riding aside."

I was prepared for his reluctance. "We couldn't very well ask the groomsman for a pillion saddle without drawing unwanted attention. You and I can share." I gave him an encouraging nod.

"What do you think of the countess's disguise?" Belinda called to him from her horse, forestalling his protest. "Is it convincing?"

Friedrich looked me over with a critical eye. "Your headdress is too fine. It will arouse suspicion."

"Oh, I forgot." I let myself down from Lange and started plucking out pins and unweaving braids, using my fingers to shake my hair loose before reaching into Belinda's saddlebag to retrieve the last piece of my disguise. Sliding the thin, black headband over my hair, I turned to face Friedrich.

"Better?" I asked.

He studied my appearance again, but this time his eyes lingered on the length of my neck, his Adam's apple dipping in his throat before he set his gaze on the horse.

"Very nice. We should be going." He took Lange's reins, leading him to a fallen tree.

My cheeks warmed with the excitement of Friedrich's attraction as I followed behind, stepping onto the tree and lifting a foot into the shortened stirrup to settle myself in the saddle.

"You can sit behind me." I patted the horse's rump.

He raised his brows. "I have no experience riding bareback."

"I'll be guiding the horse. You just work to keep yourself balanced."

He still eyed the horse skeptically but used the makeshift mounting block to hoist himself up behind me. Lange's ears turned back, and he stamped a few steps rearward, to which Friedrich responded by clinging to the rail of my saddle.

"You'll have a steadier seat if you hold onto me," I suggested.

"I'll be fine. Make sure you keep to the forest trails to avoid being seen."

Maneuvering the horse through the shadows of the trees, I kept him to a slow walk, yet Friedrich still began to slip. And he slipped again only moments later. We could hardly make progress with how often I had to halt the horse and allow Friedrich to adjust his seating.

"What pretext did you offer the hunt master for your absence this eve?" I asked the fourth time we stopped.

"Bernhold hardly needed one. It's Ulrich who's the real taskmaster," he answered. "What excuse did you give to . . . the person you give excuses to when your father is away?"

I leaned forward to smooth an errant hair from Lange's mane into place. "That I've gone to bed early with a headache."

"You sneaked out? What if the groomsman is questioned about a pair of missing horses?"

I clicked the horse forward. "Well, let's just pray he isn't."

Friedrich let out a quiet chuckle.

"How go your French studies?" I asked.

"Well enough. You haven't managed any shooting practice since our little . . . since our last lesson, have you?"

"No, I haven't," I answered. "And I've enjoyed the respite. From *you* more than anything." I shot a mischievous smile across my shoulder in time to catch Friedrich raising his brows in surprise. But his forehead soon smoothed, and a hint of a smile touched his lips.

"Not much respite, I'd say, with barely three days since we studied French."

"You count the days since you've seen me, do you?" My confidence rose with the success of each playful jest. "At least there I'm not expected to take your orders or put up with your brass."

"Not that you've ever taken my orders anyway. If you did, you'd be a decent shot by now." The smile in his voice was obvious.

I answered with a playful jab of my elbow into his gut. He bent forward with a huff, chuckling until he lost his balance again and slipped. He was half off the horse and struggling to pull himself back into place when his haphazard movements frightened Lange, and the horse reared upward. I leaned forward to counter the steep incline, but behind me Friedrich was falling. He groped wildly for some kind of stronghold, his hands catching at my waist to keep aright, but instead his weight pulled the both of us down. Time slowed as we tumbled to the ground, he landing on his back, and I on top of him, knocking the air from his lungs with a wheeze.

"I cry you mercy, Friedrich. Are you hurt?" I pushed myself off him and onto my knees as he sat up, his arm cradling his side.

It took a bit for him to finally catch his breath. "I think you broke my rib," he puffed.

"Truly?" I tried to pry his arm away to see for myself, but he swatted me back.

"Be still. I was not serious."

I sighed my relief as he slowly got to his feet, stretching himself out with a few grimaces. Seeing him well, I tracked down the horse and gathered the reins to find us another makeshift mounting block.

Belinda called up the trail. "My lady, are you hurt?"

"I'm unharmed." I lifted myself into the saddle and reached a hand down to help Friedrich, but he borrowed my stirrup, pulling himself back onto the horse with some effort. He was again taking hold of my saddle's rail when I grasped his shirt, stopping him mid-motion.

"Friedrich, we haven't the time, and you haven't the ribs to spare for this foolishness. Hold onto me, or we'll never make it to the mining village."

His eyes were wide when I let him go, but he complied, scooting forward on the horse until his chest pressed against my back.

"I'm not sure where to put my hands," he admitted.

"Set them round my middle." I clicked the horse forward, pretending not to notice when Friedrich awkwardly settled his arms around my waist. He was warm—his hands around me, his chest pressed against me, his breath on my ear—but the warmth only made me shudder.

"Are you cold?" he asked.

"I was recalling the horrors of the mines." Not entirely true. "At what age did your mother first send you to work there?"

He cleared his throat. "My mother never sent me. I met the miners after I'd been traveling through the forest and caught a chill. When I knocked on their door, they took me in without question, nursing me back to health. Then I stayed on, not having anywhere else to go."

"And when did you find your way to the bowyer?"

"Soon after I left the mines."

His answers were always so brief. "Does it pain you to speak of your past? You seem reluctant to talk about it."

"I'm reluctant to be a bore. I can't imagine how this dull accounting of my life could possibly interest you."

"And yet it does."

His sigh stirred the hairs by my ear. "I traveled to Wildungen to look for work with the tradesmen. They each had apprentices already, but the bowyer was kind enough to take me on as an unofficial apprentice, second to his nephew. After the old man's death, the new bowyer's fists fell too heavy on me, so I took to the vagrant life."

"Only to be caught poaching and sent off to war." I shifted in the saddle, cocking an eyebrow toward him.

"Well, it did take them a few years to catch me." His impish smile brought back the fluttering in my stomach. "And what is your story? Where did you go after we met at the mines?"

Clearing my thoughts of Friedrich's grin, I turned forward. "To Waldeck for a time, to live with my father's cousins, and then I was sent to the Netherlands as a ward of my mother's brother." I nibbled my lip as I pondered. "It's strange being back here. At first, I dreaded it, returning to the place of the plague. Sleeping in the same bed where I slept while my mother and baby sister died—and I fairly with them. I've always seen the place as a scene of death and sadness and regret, but being here now, it's somehow different. There's still sadness, but now it's touched with something . . . sweet." I murmured the last word.

The pulse of Friedrich's heartbeat drummed on my back, and I found myself leaning into it. There was a tautness, a buzzing in the air around us that words would only taint, and I held very still, afraid that if I moved, I'd destroy it.

Friedrich seemed to sense it too. He didn't trouble himself to speak for some time, but when he finally did interrupt the silence, his voice was gruff. "We're nearing the mining village."

CHAPTER 12

Margaretha

WE BROKE OUT OF THE forest, chasing the setting sun into a grassy meadowland dotted with half-timbered cabins of wood and white plaster. Friedrich directed me toward one tucked snuggly against the wood-laden hills, indistinguishable from the other cottages save for the strange smell, which struck us before we'd even dismounted. It grew stronger as we approached the cabin door.

Belinda and I covered our noses against the scent of curdled milk and spoiled meat but quickly dropped our arms to our sides when Friedrich lifted his hand to the door. Before his fist met the wood, we heard shouting, then a crash from inside the cabin. Friedrich didn't bother knocking. Charging through the door, he headed straight for a pair of boys, catching the arm of one boy mid-swing and ducking from the blows of the other. He shouldered himself between the boys and pushed them apart.

"Heinrich, Emil, stop fighting," Friedrich ordered.

Surprise, then recognition registered on the boys' faces, and a momentary peace ensued as they both greeted their old friend. But it passed as the older boy began to justify himself in the fight, and the younger defended his part. Other, older voices joined the argument, and I wondered just how many men lived inside this tiny cottage.

While the boys continued their squabbling, I followed Friedrich into the orangey glow of a small, firelit room, nearly tripping on an overturned chair beside the door. Pushing it upright, I carried it around shoes strewn here and there to nest it beneath the dish-littered table. The feet of the chair squealed over the dusty wood floor, echoing in the sudden, conspicuous silence, and I felt the weight of every eye upon me. Doing my best to ignore the dumbfounded stares of the men and boys standing about the room, I fixed a smile upon my face, but the silence had me shifting between my feet. I gave Friedrich a pointed plea with my eyes.

"Oh, yes." He moved beside me, announcing to the cabin, "Everyone, this is . . ." He paused, and I realized we hadn't made a plan for what name I should take. "Margaretha," he finally finished. I tensed with the initial surprise of hearing him speak my Christian name. It was startling how much I liked the sound of it on his lips.

"*Guten tag.*" I curtsied as a young maid should. Gesturing to Belinda still standing beside the door, I said, "This is my friend, Belinda. We've come to visit you."

The miners continued to gape. My cheeks ached with the pain of a forced smile until Friedrich picked up a loose shoe, throwing it to land with a thud against one boy's chest. The boy startled to awareness.

"*Glückauf,*" the boy said.

I looked at Friedrich for clarity. "I don't know this expression."

He bent his head to mine. "It's a miner's greeting. To offer luck in finding veins of ore."

"Oh. *Glückauf* to you," I addressed the young man. "And what is your name?"

"Forgive me," Friedrich said. "I forgot the introductions. Margaretha,"—I felt a strange invigoration as he said my name again—"our two fighters here are brothers. The ugly one is Heinrich."

Heinrich picked up another shoe and launched it at Friedrich's head, but Friedrich ducked in time for the shoe to bash against the plastered wall. It left behind a hand-sized dent, one of many pockmarking the cottage.

Friedrich straightened, dusting off his green jerkin while nodding toward the other brother. "The uglier one is Emil."

Emil, who couldn't have been more than eleven, had the audacity to wink at me. I did my best to give him a most serious, disapproving look, to which he laughed, wholly unrepentant.

One man too eager to await his turn at an introduction made his way over to me, bending low from the waist before catching hold of my hand to place a lengthy kiss on my knuckles.

"This is Wilhelm." Friedrich cleared his throat, prompting the man to finally end his kiss. I smiled at him when he straightened but couldn't help noticing his bowed back and stunted legs as he waddled over to give Belinda a greeting every bit as gracious. It was easy to see why a child might mistake miners for dwarfs.

"The resident cook is Daniel," Friedrich said, turning my attention to a man at the fire. Daniel flicked his hand in a sort of wave but continued to stir whatever bubbled in his cauldron. I hated to think it was the source of the rancid smell enveloping the cabin.

Daniel turned a keen eye on Friedrich. "Do we get a red hart today, or were ya too busy fer deer catchin'?" His eyes darted to me, and I blushed from his implication.

Friedrich shook his head. "You know I don't hunt anymore."

I caught the surprised look on Daniel's face before Friedrich pointed behind me across the room to introduce me to an older man sprawled out on a short bed.

"Last of all is Ernst, your patient."

With great effort, Ernst leaned onto his elbow and offered a nod before being overtaken by a deep, chesty cough that multiplied into a fit. Friedrich crossed to him, pulling him upright and beating his back until Ernst's coughing subsided.

"Belinda, the herbs," I ordered, and she slipped out of the cabin to retrieve the packets of crushed herbs from the saddlebag.

I knelt beside Ernst's bed, taking his gnarled hand in mine. "Friedrich tells me you've been unwell."

He nodded. "Pains in my chest and a cough I can't be rid of. Sometimes I'm fightin' fer breath."

"He don't eat much either," Daniel offered as Belinda reentered.

I rubbed Ernst's hand. "We'll get you on your feet again." Joining Belinda at the table, I sorted through the herbs for the thyme.

"How can I help?" Friedrich was at my elbow, his breath tickling my ear.

"Perhaps heat a pot of mead?"

He rooted around the wooden shelf, pulling down a jug of mead and a small, three-footed pot, which he nestled into coals beside the fire. While he poured the mead out in glugs, I untied the thyme packet and sprinkled the crushed herbs into the pot for Friedrich to stir with his wooden ladle. I left him to steep the thyme brew, returning to gather the unused packets of herbs and trying to ignore Emil as he leaned against the table beside me.

"So," he said, "have ya any suitors?"

"Stand down, Emil." Friedrich's words sounded like a warning.

Wilhelm knocked Emil on the head as he waddled past. "She's clearly spoke fer." Taking a seat opposite us, he looked back and forth between Friedrich and me, then asked, "How'd ya meet?"

The room grew warm, and I glanced at Belinda for guidance, but she stood with a hand to her lips, poorly concealing her smile.

"We haven't—there's nothing—" Friedrich stammered.

"We serve together at the castle." I tried to sound composed.

"The castle?" Daniel stirred his pot, looking down at Friedrich. "How's that goin'?"

"Enough, Dan." Another warning. Friedrich was testy with his friends this eve.

"I'm only surprised ya'd take work there after—"

"The tonic is warm," Friedrich said to me. "Cups and spoons are there."

I reached for the wooden shelf where Friedrich pointed, collecting a cup and holding it steady as he poured the hot brew. Giving it a final stir, I made my way to Ernst while Friedrich gathered pillows from the other beds to arrange them behind Ernst's back. When Ernst was comfortably upright, I set the warm cup in his hands. He breathed in the steam, stopping short under another string of coughs until he'd recovered enough to take a tentative sip. His face puckered with distaste.

"It's repulsive, isn't it? Most things she brews are." Despite his words, Friedrich gave me a warm smile, and I sensed something like admiration in the soft way his eyes trailed over my face.

I smiled back, but feeling unaccountably shy, I turned my gaze away, letting my sights drift over the untidy little cabin. Miners' caps scattered halos of dirt wherever they lay. Shirts and hose muddy enough to grow a garden were piling up in corners, and every bed was unmade save one.

"Who sleeps there?" I asked. "He deserves praise for being the cleanest among you."

No one answered. No one spoke at all, and the uncomfortable silence grew heavy enough that even Belinda paused when she'd returned from putting away the herbs, looking around the room curiously.

Friedrich finally replied, "That was Jakob's bed."

I lowered my voice to a whisper. "Who's Jakob?"

Heinrich and Emil started straightening the shoes, but Wilhelm pulled out a chair and patted it, inviting me to sit beside him at the table. By the time I'd taken my seat, he was already staring at the twisting hearth flames with a faraway look in his eyes.

"The mines aren't safe fer workin'," he began. "We do what we can—wear hoods and aprons and such—but there's nothin' fer it when the Meister Hämmerling decides to play his tricks."

"Meister Hämmerling?" I raised a brow.

He nodded. "An evil spirit that haunts the mines. At times he's a giant bear. At others, a black horse with one great red eye. But most often he's a monk wearing flowin' robes of blackest night. And he plays tricks, doin' all manner of mischief, then punishing any miners who get angry. Jakob said he saw him befer we climbed into the shafts, a dark monk standin' back in the trees. Jakob was afraid to go down, but we told him all's well, that he'd only imagined it. He was young enough to fit in the narrow veins, and when we heard the rocks and dirt tumblin', we knew there'd been a cave-in. Emil wriggled down the shaft first to try to dig Jakob out. He and the other boys crawled on their bellies, using shunts to haul out the extra dirt, but they wasn't fast enough."

I glanced at Emil now sitting on his bed, his head bowed low, his hands clasped behind his neck. Was he still haunted by Jakob's muffled screams? Could he hear Jakob's panic until it faded into silence?

I sucked in air, my head dizzy from my abated breath. Without meaning to, I'd put myself in poor Jakob's place, feeling his desperation, his terror. Imagining his frenzied struggle to free himself as his life was snuffed out beneath the dirt. I squeezed my eyes closed, shaking my head to rid myself of the thoughts that left a pit in my gut.

Friedrich

Margaretha—that is, the countess—kept her eyes pressed shut, scrubbing a hand over her nose as if she might cry.

"Wilhelm," I called across the room. "This isn't a tale for young maids. Speak of something jolly. Entertain her with your fairy stories."

Ernst coughed again, spilling his tonic, and I put my hands over his to help bring the cup to his lips. When he'd finished drinking, I looked back at the countess. She seemed mostly recovered. Her broken look had turned into a soft smile while Wilhelm spoke of kobolds hiding coins in his shoes.

Ernst cleared his throat, wearing a smirk that made me realize I'd been staring at Margaretha with a soft smile of my own. I ducked my head and picked my thumbnail.

"She's very beautiful, isn't she," Ernst said.

It wasn't a question, and the statement was too obvious to require an answer.

"What d'ya like about her most?"

"Ernst." I blew out a long breath. "Let me put a stop to such thoughts now. Margaretha is only a friend. She has knowledge of healing, and I hoped she could help you, or I never would have brought her here."

"And yet she came. Eager to help yer friends. Eager to help you."

"You assume more than is there," I answered flatly, wanting to end the conversation.

"Do I?" Ernst smoothed a hand over his whiskers. "Then why does she watch ya so?"

I flicked a glance at the table, meeting Margaretha's eye as she smiled one of her breathtaking smiles, the kind I had to daily pretend didn't make my heart pump a few beats quicker. Heaven and earth, of *course* she was beautiful! And frustratingly thoughtful and kind. But what did it matter? She was noble, I was a servant, and she was set to go to Brussels. Even the suggestion of some kind of affection between us was too ridiculous to consider.

Why did my lungs suddenly feel tight? I sucked in a breath, rubbing a fist over my chest. "Ernst, there are . . . obstacles."

He took another sip from his tonic. "Ya mean yer afraid." I started to object, but he held up a hand. "I don't blame ya. I'm certain I'd be scared too, winning the favor of such a beautiful maid."

"I'm not scared. And I've won no such favor," I protested. "The circumstances between us mean I should never even think about her that way. I *don't* think of her that way."

"Tush," Ernst said. "You young men are all so bent on arrangin' yer lives, ya forget to step out and live 'em. Move now while she still looks willing."

Looks willing? Across the room the countess sat listening to another of Wilhelm's tales, but she kept glancing at me. Why?

When her eyes met mine, she didn't look away. The little smile she wore for Wilhelm's story shifted, smoothing into something more serious, something that sped the blood in my veins. Our locked gazes intertwined, each passing second twisting another strand around the invisible cord that pulled me to her. A strange headiness overtook me.

"Friedrich." At Wilhelm's call, the cord snapped, and I startled to attention. "Who do ya think Margaretha would be?"

I bent my head toward my shoes, rubbing a subtle hand over my cheek. It was hot. "You speak in riddles, Wilhelm."

"In the pagan legends. Heinrich says Margaretha'd be Hariasa, but I'm certain she'd be Ilmr. What d'ya think?"

It took no time at all for me to reach an answer, but my ears burned just thinking about it. Making the comparison would be too bold.

"That's enough of this game," I said, but Ernst spoke up beside me.

"She is beautiful." His voice was worn and scratchy, but he answered with the same confidence a man would use if commenting on the color of the sky. "A beautiful maiden with milk-white skin. She'd be Holda."

"Doesn't that goddess have a swan's foot?" Emil asked. "Check her feet!"

I started to protest, but Margaretha stood and slid off her cow-mouth shoes, flattening her skirts against her stockings.

"No swan's feet," she said. "I suppose I can't be Holda."

"But ya clearly cavort with witches," Daniel spoke from his bubbling kettle by the fire.

Margaretha's smile turned stiff, and she pressed a thumb to the scab of her palm. It was a strange response. Did she worry I'd told him about Walpurgisnacht?

"What makes you say that?" Her voice wavered.

"Ya've cast a spell on my housemates to make 'em forget their empty bellies or the supper 'bout to burn if they don't sit and eat."

At his words, the men scrambled for their bowls, tripping over each other to get the food.

Slapping my thighs, I turned to Ernst. "Well, old friend, I suppose we should be off. I see the cou—" I quickly caught myself, "*Margaretha* left a packet of herbs on the table. Do you want another cup before I leave?"

I reached for his empty mug, but Ernst was quiet, his brows furrowed as he watched Margaretha.

"I saw Count von Waldeck's daughter once when she were a child." He spoke slowly. "Do ya ever see her at the castle?"

I paused, my hand still reaching for his cup. "Sometimes. Why do you ask?"

"I've heard she's grown into quite the woman. 'Unparalleled beauty,' they say, 'with skin as white as snow and lips as red as blood.' I'm told she's clever too. Clever as a raven."

"Then she is truly blessed," I snapped, standing up so quickly I almost bumped the mug out of Ernst's hands.

He nodded. "Indeed."

"Get well, Ernst." Turning, I called, "Margaretha, it's time to leave."

Mistress Hatzfeld was quick to be up and out the door, but the countess ducked a curtsy to the men. "Farewell, everyone. *Glückauf.*" She waved, and I followed her out into the cool summer night air.

The countess tilted her face to the full moon, taking a deep breath before she looked at me with a guilty smile. "Daniel's food smelled terrible."

"You're lucky they didn't make you eat it." I smiled back.

Untying the horses, I led them to the mounting block, holding them steady while each lady mounted. Then I climbed up behind Margaretha. Despite the odor of Daniel's cooking, her hair still smelled of lilac petals in the sun, and I didn't lean away from it this time. When she clicked the horse onto the moonlit path, I eased my arms around her waist, letting my body relax against her.

"You're playing a dangerous game, you know," she said.

I went rigid, heat shooting up my neck. "What do you mean?"

"You're still poaching from Father's woods, aren't you?"

I blew out a long breath. "Not often."

"He could have you discharged," she said. We ducked our heads as the horse stepped under a low branch. "Even whipped or hanged."

"Do I detect concern?" Though it was only a jest, I couldn't dampen my curiosity to hear her answer.

"It would take a great deal of work to find myself another hunting tutor."

My shoulders drooped, but I scolded myself for wanting anything more from the countess. Already I'd let Ernst's words sway me until I was imagining things that weren't true. She wasn't leaning into me, letting me wrap my arms tighter around her. Her heartbeat pulsing against my chest didn't beat quicker when I pressed myself closer. No, it was witless to think the countess would ever care for me, a servant. But the real question was, why did I suddenly want her to?

I tried to force the thought from my mind, to distract myself, but only an utter fool could ignore what was becoming frighteningly clear: my feelings for the countess were shifting. My anger and resentment seemed to have crumbled around me until I stood in the rubble of my carefully constructed barriers, bare and exposed and unable to deny that somewhere along the way I'd started to admire the countess. To care for her as more than a friend.

Thrill and fear warred inside my gut, and I balled my hands into fists at the countess's stomach. How had I let this happen? I was disciplined, practical. I knew her to be mountains above me in station and rank. Where had all my reason gone? Had those blasted dreams done me in? The time spent in her company during lessons? Her repeated attentions and kindness?

No. It did no good dwelling on past failures. What was done was done. I knew my weakness now and would simply need to rely upon my strength of will to fight this irrational attraction.

Just then Margaretha's—*the countess's*—head drooped, falling to her chest until she woke with a start. When it happened a second time, I couldn't stop myself from smiling.

"Countess?"

She straightened, sucking in a quick breath. "Yes, what?" Her voice was thick and muddled.

"You're falling asleep."

She puffed a short, embarrassed laugh. "Apologies. I was up late preparing herbs."

"I can lead the horse," I offered, but she shook her head.

"No, I'll manage. Perhaps conversation will keep me alert?"

"What should we talk about?"

She paused. "Why don't you tell me which pagan goddess I remind you of?"

For the second time that night, my ears grew hot. I looked behind me, making sure Mistress Hatzfeld was far enough back to not overhear as I answered, "A *weiße frau*."

"What is a *weiße frau*?" she asked drowsily.

I kept my voice soft as I spoke. "The *weiße frauen* are elvenlike enchanted spirits who live in forests. Sometimes they bathe in streams or sun themselves on rocks as they brush their hair. A halo—" Did I dare admit the rest?

"Yes?"

Her sluggish speech coaxed me to continue. "A halo of light hovers around them, their unearthly beauty luring mortal men to either doom or ecstasy."

The memory of Margaretha in the woods shaking her braids loose was impossible to forget, the sunshine lighting the golden waves spilling over her porcelain throat. It didn't take much imagination to see her as an elvish spirit haunting the forests. Even now I felt her pull and the promise that she would bring me to either rapture or ruin.

The countess was quiet, only answering with a contented hum, and in a few short minutes, her head nodded again. When it dropped back against my shoulder, I froze, sitting stiffly while her head bobbed against me with each clop of the horse's hooves. I shouldn't have, but before I could stop myself, I lifted my hand to her cheek and guided her head against my neck, safely tucking it beneath my chin to hold it steady. She nestled into me, making my heart drum faster.

I rolled my eyes. So much for my strength of mind. When it came to Margaretha, I was all weakness.

Slipping the reins from her hands, I led the horse through the inky woods as the rest of the ride became an exercise in self-control. When I was tempted by the errant desire to breathe in her lilac scent, I focused on how I could improve my shooting stance. When she stirred and I reflexively held her tighter, I made myself count the horse's hoofbeats into the thousands. By the time we'd reached the clearing, I was exhausted from my efforts.

"Countess," I whispered into her hair. She didn't move. "Margaretha, it's time for me to get down."

"Hmm?" She sat forward, blinking her eyes like she was trying to make sense of her surroundings. "What time is it?"

"It must be nearing midnight." I gave her time to wake up before prodding her again. "I need to dismount."

"But we're nowhere near the castle. Will you be all right walking in the dark alone?"

"I'll be fine. It's better if we don't return too close together," I answered. "But are you awake enough to guide the horse?"

"I'm well rested now." She chuckled.

Hatzfeld's horse padded into the clearing behind us, and my smile faded. Gripping the pommel, I slid to the ground.

"The reins, please." Margaretha held out her empty hand.

As I returned the reins, my hand covered hers, and—curse my weakened resolve—I didn't immediately let go. Our eyes met, and the moment stretched out with her hand in mine, the warmth of my skin building until it reached a fevered heat. I finally forced myself to release her.

"Goodnight, Friedrich," she whispered. Was her breath unsteady?

"Goodnight, my lady." I bowed, holding my hand behind my back, squeezing it into a fist, then flexing my fingers out wide and straight; anything to end the burning. I could still feel the heat of her even after she and Hatzfeld turned their horses toward the castle, and I knew I had to stop this foolish fascination. The countess must be a friend, nothing more.

But the longer I paced, the stars surveying my unsettled tread, the more I feared it would be impossible to bury my newly discovered regard for the Countess von Waldeck.

CHAPTER 13

Margaretha

From the moment I entered the clearing, I sensed the shift. Friedrich stood in the shadows of the trees, his eyes holding that same guarded look they'd had when I'd first approached him with my proposal for hunting lessons. Though he wasn't back to the prior, aloof Friedrich, it was still a change from his friendly demeanor of last night.

Belinda inclined her head in response to his bow, her eyes dark from her restless sleep. The nightmares were troubling her again, though she wouldn't admit it. I gave her an encouraging nod as she left to pick herbs, then took a step toward Friedrich.

He folded his arms across his chest. "Did you get any rest after our travels?" He smiled, but it didn't reach his eyes.

"A little." I smiled back. "And you?"

"Ulrich had me up early with the dogs, but I'll be well. Shall we begin?" He waved me toward the shooting line, effectively ending the conversation.

I picked the bow off the ground, catching a bit of dirt beneath my nails that made me shiver with the memory of my dream. The narrow, black tunnels. The red-eyed monk. His laughter as the dirt tumbled around me, covering my face—its taste spreading over my tongue and its scent filling my nostrils.

Another shudder rumbled through me, but I pushed the suffocating panic aside, reminding myself it was only a dream. That I would never be in a dark mine. That I would never be buried alive. I needed my mind sharp now. Every day brought me closer to when I would leave for Brussels. I was nowhere near ready.

Straightening my spine, I forced my voice to sound light. "I'm glad you took me to meet your friends. They were lovely. I admit it felt like an adventure, traveling dark woods and dressing up as a serving girl."

Friedrich's voice held humor when he answered. "No doubt the thrill of playing the peasant would wear off quickly if it were your lot in life."

"Well, I won't pretend to be sorry for my fine clothes and plentiful food, if that's what you mean." I turned to him. "But there are obligations accompanying a noble's life that I'd rather do without."

"Really? Such as?"

Such as the odiousness of my current task.

"I don't wish to marry for advantage," I answered, absently twisting the tip of an arrow into the dirt. "I want to choose a man I admire and respect, not just one who'll provide financial or political gain."

Friedrich unfolded his arms and took a step toward me, his expression momentarily open, curious. Then he blinked it away as he dropped his shoulder back against his tree. "You want to marry for love? That's a rather modern idea for a noblewoman."

"True." Though the freedom of mind brought about by the Reformation had spread through the lower classes, letting men and women decide on their own love matches, women of rank were still obliged to marry for advantage. "And as it is my duty as the daughter of a count to benefit his interests, I'll be expected to make a match helpful to that cause. Under the queen regent's approval, of course."

Friedrich reached up and snapped a twig from the tree, then ripped the leaves into halves over and again. "So what's the trouble? There aren't any men worth loving in your mob of suitors?"

I laughed. "Having no suitors at all, I'm sure I couldn't say."

"Perhaps you've set your expectations too high. A man writes a poor minnelied and you send him on his way."

I tilted my head, watching him to know if he spoke in jest. "Should I ever have the good fortune to attract a man of honor, I certainly won't be put off from him because he fails to write a heartsick poem or dance the galliard."

Friedrich tossed his pile of torn leaves to the ground while the impression of a smile played on his lips.

"Do you laugh at me?" I asked.

"No, I respect your answer. It does you credit." He nodded in the direction of the target. "Should we collect the arrows?" Trekking through the underbrush, he left without awaiting my reply.

His response surprised me, and I warmed from the small praise. Leaning the bow against a tree, I followed Friedrich to the target, picking my way through the foliage.

"What about you?" I bent down to collect an arrow. "Paint me a portrait of the future Frau Huntsman."

"Huntsman's page," he corrected, untangling an arrow from a bush. "I haven't thought on it much. I'm not in a position to make an offer."

"In a position or not, I can't believe you haven't seen a few *fräuleins* who excited your admiration. Come. Tell me what she'll be like. Dark or fair? Thin, or fat from the feasts of her wealthy merchant father?"

"Poor," he answered. "Poor enough that whatever I provide will feel a blessing."

I scoffed. "And she'd best be unlearned too, I suppose, so that the knowledge you impart will feel a blessing?" I very much disliked the image of Friedrich with this imaginary woman. "For your sake, I pray you marry someone more learned, wealthy, and attractive than yourself."

His eyes wrinkled as his lips tilted in a half smile. "Do you think me attractive?"

My face went hot. "Oh! No, I-I didn't mean . . . wait, not *no*. You *are* attractive. It's just—I hadn't meant . . ." I trailed off, hoping he'd readily jump in to dismiss my awkwardness, but he continued staring at me with that little smirk, as if awaiting an explanation. I hoped he was disappointed when I turned my back and searched for another arrow, seeing one well beyond the tree and far past my usual range. Though the distance was impressive, the way to retrieve it was difficult, with grasping holly rising to knee height on either side of a narrow deer path. I started down the trail, more focused on preserving my skirts than minding my footing, and stepped onto an unbalanced rock, which teetered beneath my shoe. As the rock tipped to one side, I dropped my arrows in a scattered jumble and fell backward, bottom first, into a thicket of holly. Each prickly leaf clawed at me, entangling my hair and skirts. The more I twisted to escape, the more the holly grasped at me, piercing my clothes and flesh.

I was stuck, and as humiliating as it was, I needed help.

"Friedrich!"

His laughter reached me before I could twist my head enough to see him, but eventually he stood before me with one hand cradling his elbow, the other covering his mouth. He pulled his hand back, opening his mouth as if he might say something, but closed it again and merely shook his head. Crouching down on the deer path beside me, he drew a short dagger from his boot and pinched a limb with two fingers. He stretched the prickly limb straight, cut cleanly through it, and tossed it aside.

"You know this is your penance for nearly breaking my rib." He couldn't hold back his smile as he sliced through another sprig.

"I think I'd prefer a pilgrimage," I grumbled. "At least then I wouldn't have to endure your exultant smirk."

He chuckled, his breath warm on my neck as he cut a twig from my shoulder. "True. But with you gone, where will I find your equal for such charming blunders?"

Had he just admitted to liking my company? Or was it only a jest? Best to assume he wasn't serious. "You almost sound as though you'd miss me," I teased back, rubbing at my newly freed arms to blur the pinpoint pain.

"Maybe I would." His voice was quiet now, almost earnest, and though I tried to turn my head to meet his eye, the silk cords of my hair netting were still hopelessly ensnared. "Don't struggle."

Friedrich tucked the dagger into his boot and reached toward me but hesitated, taking a deep breath. Avoiding my questioning gaze, he clenched his jaw, again reaching his hands behind my head. I expected his grasp to be as fierce as his looks, but he surprised me with his gentleness as he patiently pulled the netting loose from the holly. Neither of us spoke while he worked with his arms around me, his face so near that, even in the shade of the trees, I could see the freckles dotting his cheekbones and a trace of dark stubble shadowing his chin.

Another sprig flipped upward as Friedrich set it free, moving his fingers to pick at the next set of tangles. His hands on my hair made me shudder, and I closed my eyes, breathing in his now-familiar scent of straw and cloves and listening to his breath beside my ear. It was surprisingly quick and unsteady.

Odd.

I opened my eyes, alert to his every movement as a suspicion formed in my head. Though he avoided my gaze, he could not conceal the swallow tugging his throat while he pulled the last tangle of my hair netting loose. He moved quickly to free my skirts, and I leaned forward to help, keeping a keen watch on his nimble fingers. They were cut and bleeding. And trembling.

I stared at his shaking hands, not needing any experience with men or any explanation from Belinda to understand what they meant.

I had done it. I'd somehow softened Friedrich's heart of steel enough to care for me.

Instead of my spirits rising with victory or elation, the only sensation I had was cold and leaden, and it took up its familiar place as it slunk down to my stomach.

Guilt.

CHAPTER 14

Margaretha

Belinda waited until I'd stepped out of the gown to hold it up to the window. Pinpricks of sunlight shone through tears dotting the sleeves and skirts. She threw it over the bed, then looked at me, shaking her head. "The petticoat too? You've blood drops everywhere."

"The holly was quite sticky." I plucked a sharp leaf from my hair, and Belinda chuckled.

"Margaretha, you're hopeless. If only you'd managed to use your folly for good!"

I hadn't told Belinda the truth of what had passed, of Friedrich avoiding my gaze, his hands shaking with restraint or fear. I wasn't certain of the exact emotion, only the source of it, and to think on it made my stomach ache.

I pressed my arm against it. "True. I've made no gains with Friedrich," I lied.

"How can that be?" Belinda scoffed. "I've seen the two of you together. Your skills are much improved, and you're certainly too beautiful to be ignored. Perhaps your naivete is making you blind to his attraction."

The assertion rankled me. "Is it possible you don't understand men as well as you think?"

Her eyes flashed, and I instantly regretted my remark. "You in your protected castle. I grew up much faster than you could ever imagine. I know men and their desires."

My silence spoke my contrition, and once she'd slipped a fresh chemise over my head, I wrapped her in a hug. "I am sorry, Belinda. You are right. I could never understand."

She sank into my hug, but only for a moment before she straightened her shoulders and turned toward the window. When she spoke, her voice was calm, as if nothing had passed. "I will admit Friedrich puzzles me."

She had shut me out again, refusing to open up about her life from before she'd arrived. Never an explanation for why she used to sneak food from the kitchens, hiding it in our room as if she didn't trust there would be another meal. Or why she'd clung to Samuel, following him around the castle. He'd said he didn't mind it, that it helped her feel safe, but why she should need Samuel to feel safe, she had never confided in me.

"I thought him an easy target with his sullen temperament and low birth." Belinda's words crowded into my thoughts as I sat on the mattress.

"Who?"

"Margaretha, do try to keep up. I was speaking of Friedrich. What peasant man wouldn't want a countess as his conquest?"

"Belinda!"

"Tut." She waved her hand dismissively. "'Tis just an expression."

Flopping onto the coverlet, I rested an arm over my eyes. "It's useless with Friedrich. I'm done."

"Not quite." Belinda pulled at the used clothes beneath me until I lifted my backside off the torn gown. "You owe him at least a few more French lessons, else he'll think himself ill-used."

"No. I'm finished with the scheme altogether. Send me to Brussels to earn the trust of the queen, or you ask too much of me." I pressed a pillow against my aching belly, waiting for Belinda's protest, but she went on silently folding my torn chemise as if she hadn't heard. Laying it over a chair, she sat on the bed beside me, looking toward the fireplace.

"Do you know how I came to be here, acting as your lady-in-waiting?"

I leaned on my elbow, my attention riveted on her.

"Your father and his men stopped to stay with Uncle during their travels. Samuel was among them." She took a long breath, fidgeting with her ring. "The men did the same as all of Uncle's friends, laughing and drinking and hunting their game, none of them paying me any mind. Those were my favorite times, when I was forgotten and alone. Loneliness was best." She stood and paced across the room, her back turned to me as she rested her hands on the writing desk. The shudder coursing her spine betrayed her struggle to speak of it, even after all these years.

I stayed silent. I would not rush her.

"But Samuel didn't forget me." Her voice held emotion. She cleared her throat. "He found me in the library and coaxed me to speak. We said nothing of importance, but he listened to me. Then he showed me a fox den with cubs, got me out in the garden to take walks. He picked a yellow flower for me, making me smile when . . . when I hadn't even wanted to live. And . . ." Another pause. More silence. "He alerted your father . . . when he saw." Her voice was quiet. "Saw the marks on my wrists." Her last words ended in a whisper. She finally turned to face me. "*That* is a man worth saving."

My heart ached for what Belinda had suffered. It ached with longing for my brother. I sniffed back the sting of tears. "I intend to save him, Belinda. I do! Only let me do it as I will, winning the queen's favor instead of scheming for a man's heart. It isn't right."

"Margaretha!" Belinda's voice was sharp, and I reared my head back, surprised by her tone. We watched each other, neither blinking until she spat, "Do what you will, Countess." She bent to pick up my muddied shoes. "If you're willing to risk your brother's life, then so be it, but it's a wonder you're willing to risk our eternal souls. Samuel's suffering could be brief, but ours will be endless." Her shoes clipped over the stone floor, and she left the room.

I buried my face in my pillow. What had I done? I'd upset Belinda the moment she had confided in me. I'd dismissed her pain, her need to save Samuel, and her need to atone for the healer's death. She had suffered so much. *We* had suffered so much together, having no one but each other to confide our shared shame and grief, yet our guilt alone could never make amends. And now I was putting it all at risk.

Flopping onto my back, I looked up at the canopy, the same red velvet filling my view as when I'd first met the healer. I ran a finger over the rough scab on my palm, remembering that night.

I am so cold despite the layers of blankets piled atop me. A woman bends over me, her wiry black ringlets escaping the confines of her wulsthaube *headdress as she dabs my head with a wet rag reeking of urine. I raise my arm, weakly pushing her hand away, but she nods at someone, and Belinda's face appears above me.*

"It will make you well, Countess." Belinda settles my arms down to my sides but wrinkles her nose, turning her face from the rag.

"You must keep the fire burning," the woman instructs Belinda, "and douse the rag in fresh pig urine every two hours. Wipe her brow and wrists with it, then

squeeze three drops onto her tongue. I will return as soon as I'm able." She stands from the bed, and Belinda stands too, releasing my arms as she nods dutifully.

The woman tucks her loose curls back into her wulsthaube, then takes a pinch of powder from a jar and drops it over my left shoulder. "May the shedding of Saint Nikolaus's blood give health to the sick." She takes another pinch and drops it over my right shoulder. "May his cures be upon thee." The last pinch she smears from the top of my forehead to the tip of my nose, then rests her finger in the hollow of my neck. "O, how the cures of diseases reveal the sanctity of that holy leader."

She covers the jar of powder and tucks it into a basket, then pats Belinda's shoulder and leaves the room without another word.

Belinda's smiling face is the last thing I see before closing my eyes.

I sleep, unaware of the danger I face, of how near my soul is to slipping away, but when I awake, it's to Father's shouts. He stands beside my bed yelling at a cowering, crying Belinda, and though I try to calm him, my voice is too weak. He only notices me at all when I try to sit up, and he rushes to my side, lifting me into a tight embrace.

He growls at Belinda over my head. "You'll need a winning explanation if you wish to remain in my employ. Margaretha almost died for your negligence. I've a mind to send you back to your uncle."

Belinda's eyes shoot wide with fear, tears pooling in them. "Please, Your Lordship. I followed all the healer's instructions. I used the rag and the urine and kept the blankets on her."

"Why was the fire not lit? The healer said to keep it lit."

Beads of sweat forming along Belinda's brow make me suspect her deceit. She fell asleep again. Of course she did. After long days and nights keeping watch over me, I don't blame her for it. And I certainly don't want to see her punished, but if she admits the truth, Father might have her dismissed.

"The fire wouldn't stay," she answers. "Every time I'd light it, a sudden wind set upon it, blowing it cold, like it was cursed."

Father's eyes narrow.

"I wanted to warn you but feared leaving the countess alone. Please," she begs again, tears dripping from her chin. "I did all I was asked, though it was none of it natural."

Father freezes beside me. "What do you mean 'not natural'?"

"The healer. She said a chant over the countess. She dropped some herbs." Belinda wipes the tears from her cheeks.

"I don't see anything unnatural about that."

"Herbs crushed with white powder and a strong scent. And when the healer passed over the door's threshold, she spoke to herself, muttering in an unfamiliar tongue before spitting on the ground." Belinda clasps her hands together, as if begging Father to believe her.

Father holds me at arm's length to study my face. "Is it true?"

I don't comprehend his sudden interest in the healer, but Belinda's wide, imploring eyes and the quiver of her lip are too much to ignore. She gives a slight, almost imperceptible nod, and I realize I must lie or Belinda will be returned to the clutches of her uncle.

"'Tis true," I answer.

"The herbs and the foreign tongue? You saw this?"

I resist the urge to look at Belinda again, meeting Father's gaze when I answer. "I saw it all and more."

Father's eyes bore into me. "What more?"

I tax my brain, searching for some rumor I've heard passing among servants, something else I can say to wholly remove the blame from Belinda. "The healer put a waxen image under my bed."

Father sets me free and gets down on the floor.

Oh, please don't search, I think as he pulls the coverlet up, rooting beneath the bed while I shoot Belinda a panicked look.

"It's gone, Your Lordship," she interjects. "I found and destroyed it just before the countess started to mend."

He stays squat on the floor, one hand still pinning the coverlet against the bed as he looks back and forth between the two of us. "And you say a sudden wind took the fire?"

"Yes." Belinda nods.

Father stands up fast enough that Belinda cowers again, but he only gives me a quick kiss on the forehead before striding out of the room.

The weight of our lies doesn't crush us until the day they burn the healer. Word spreads through the servants in the castle, rumors of angry townsmen storming the healer's cottage and dragging her to the town square for burning. With Father gone to the mines, Belinda and I race to the stables and order the coach ready.

Rolling onto the scene, we leap from the coach and force our way through the press, hearing the healer's screams before we see her.

"Stop this! Set her free!" I yell, but my shouts are drowned beneath the roar of the villagers. When we finally push to the front of the crowd, the flames already touch the healer's feet, grasping at her chemise and clawing up the fabric to her hands bound firmly behind her back. The fire shoots up waves of smoke and heat, lifting the healer's hair while she tilts her face toward the sky, letting out an agonizing scream that chills my blood.

Belinda covers my eyes with her hand. "Look away," she whispers in my ear, but it's too late. I will never unsee the woman's pain, never unhear her anguished cries.

"Margaretha!" Belinda's cry brought me back to the present. "What have you done to your hand?"

I furrowed my brow, looking down to see blood oozing from my scabbed burn, my fingers covered in the gore.

"You've picked it open again. And there's blood all over your clean chemise." Belinda pulled me toward the washstand to run cool water over my hands. The basin turned deep red, the blood and water twisting together like my thoughts. Belinda was right. The stain on our souls had been too black for too long. If there was any chance that rescuing Samuel would also free us from the weight of our sin, then I could not be casual. I knew I'd never impress the queen with my attempts at hunting, but I could marry a man of power if I applied myself with careful study and practice. Still, I needn't torture Friedrich in my efforts.

"I concede, Belinda. I'll abandon my schemes for the queen if they jeopardize my chances to save Samuel."

She sighed her relief and gave me a towel. "You show wisdom by listening to reason."

I patted my hands dry. "But it's time to admit defeat and move on from Friedrich."

"Don't give up on Friedrich entirely. You've still got French lessons to win him over, but in the meantime"—she shot me a sly grin—"I'll start the search for our next subject."

I shook my head. "The poor fool."

CHAPTER 15

Margaretha

PRESSING MY FIST AGAINST MY stomach, I twisted the knob to the library. Friedrich was already seated and studying the set of papers from our first French lessons when I lowered myself into the chair beside him. He didn't look up, and I didn't speak, letting him study without interruption. It seemed he was still in his aloof humor, but today I was grateful for it. The less to do with him, the better my stomach fared.

When Friedrich had nearly finished running through the papers I'd composed, I held out a narrow book. "You're making quick gains. What if we move on to this French reader?"

As he grasped the book, his satisfied smile was replaced with shock when he took in my features. "Margaretha, you're pale!"

I self-consciously touched my fingers to my temple, trying to laugh off his worry. "Is it as bad as all that?"

"Not at all," he said, though his brow was still furrowed in concern. "But are you sure you should be out of bed? You seem unwell."

"I'm well enough to tutor you." I folded my shaking hands in my lap. "Tis stomach pains and nothing more."

"But you're shivering. Can I move you closer to the fire?"

He stood, but I caught his sleeve to stay him. "Truly, I am well enough."

"Do you need food? Can I get you anything?"

I pressed my free hand into my belly, feeling all the worse for his transformation from indifference to eager solicitation. "Friedrich, I beg you not to worry over me."

His voice was nearly a whisper when he answered. "I can't help it." His eyes dropped to my fingers still clutching his sleeve, and I realized the familiarity of such a touch. Releasing his shirt from my trembling grip, I felt his gaze studying me.

"Let's put off our lessons until next week." He tapped his thumb against the book. "It will give you time to strengthen your stomach before I expose you to any more of my atrocious French."

I attempted to press back a smile, but it broke free. His cheek tucked with his answering smile.

"Very well," I agreed. "We can be done for the day." I stood and held my hand out for the book, but Friedrich secured it against his chest, raising his eyebrows as he nodded toward my palm.

"That wound has taken a long time to heal."

My cheeks heated, and I hid my burned hand behind me. I reached for the book with my other hand, but Friedrich anticipated me, shifting the book behind his back.

"May I see it?" he asked.

"My burn?" I chuckled to conceal my embarrassment. "Whyever for? Don't you trust me to tend my own wounds?" I snatched for the book behind him, but he deftly pulled it away, leaving me with my arm nearly wrapped around him, our faces close together.

Our eyes met, and I read his open sincerity when he said, "I trust you. But do you trust me?"

I searched his face. Artless. Guileless. I wholly trusted Friedrich.

With a deep breath, I held out my injured hand for his inspection. He took it into his own, angling my palm to better catch the light of the fire. "This looks fresh. Almost like you'd ripped the scab—"

On instinct, I jerked my hand away, then smoothed my skirts as if to smooth over my awkwardness. Friedrich's momentary distraction left the French book sitting loosely in his hand, and I seized it before moving several good steps out of his reach and thumbing through the book to avoid meeting his eyes. "You may be right about my health. Let's forgo our studies until I'm recovered."

"Certainly." He retrieved his hat from his chair but stopped in front of me.

"I want you to know . . ." He paused and swallowed. "If you ever needed help or if there was ever a time you wished to confide in me, I'd do my best to assist you . . . if you needed me."

My eyes stung, and I had to resist the urge to rub my nose. Nodding, I swallowed back the tightness in my throat, but the renewed ache in my stomach could not be quelled. The pain was like a knife puncture with each clip of

Friedrich's shoes on the stone floor as he moved toward the door. Why did he have to be so kind?

"Friedrich." His name spilled out without thought.

He turned and waited, one hand still on the knob.

"There is something I must tell you." My pulse pounded at my temples as he stepped toward me, his brows arched with curiosity.

"I . . . It's just that . . ." I licked my bottom lip. "You know of Samuel's capture, of course." I began pacing. Was I doing this? Was I truly about to admit my deception to him? "Remember, he is my brother. My blood and kin. Think of my duty to him, my affections for him, and perhaps it will render what I am about to say a little less repulsive to you."

Friedrich raised an eyebrow.

Fear and shame threatened to stop my tongue. But no. He deserved to know the truth.

After a deep breath, I continued. "I must confess I've had no real intention of learning to hunt. That is, it was not my primary motive for our lessons. While I have received training of a sort with you, it is not the kind you'd planned. Mistress Hatzfeld," I took the coward's way out, blaming her, "knows my value in the marriage market of Brussels. Knows I'm poised to make an excellent match, a powerful match that could save my brother, if only I could learn the . . . womanly arts . . . of-of flirtation."

I peeked a glance at Friedrich, but his face was stone.

Releasing the French book, I took to wringing my hands. "She conceived a plan in which I would study these arts by repeated trial and error. With . . . you. I confess there was a great deal of error." I laughed nervously.

Ceasing my pacing, I leaned against the sturdy oak chair, my strength sapped by the effort of my confession.

Friedrich stayed silent.

And silent still.

When he finally spoke, his voice was dark. "So, the entire time I've been teaching you to hunt, you've been trying to bait me?"

I pressed my lips inward and nodded.

His jaw went taut, and he whirled around, turning his back on me. The rapid rise and fall of his lungs kept me in agony as I awaited his inevitable anger.

Then I noticed his shoulders shake. He was sniffing. Was he *crying*? That was worse than anger.

"Friedrich, please forgive me. I cannot offer enough apologies." Eliminating the distance between us, I placed a hand on his arm, and he turned toward me, but instead of crying, he was laughing. Laughing!

"What is so amusing?" I furrowed my brows, irritated. I should have been relieved instead of feeling like the subject of a joke I did not understand.

He leaned against the door with another chuckle. "I apologize, Countess. It's just that I pity poor Samuel if his fate rests on your skills as a *temptress*." He laughed out the last word. "Dressing in maids' clothes? Plowing into a thicket? Yes, those are the marks of a seductress in the making."

My embarrassment burned hot, turning to anger. "Any other man wouldn't have required such . . . excessive designing. Amiable conversation and a soft smile really ought to have been enough, but for you—stone cold and prejudiced as you are—I had to resort to the extreme." My mind accused me of going too far, but I wasn't done yet. "Do you know how humiliating it was, working to attract even a spark of your notice? I would never have endured it if it weren't for Samuel. You mock my abilities, but you ought to measure your own. You haven't even the skills to carry on a conversation, let alone entice a woman to love you."

Friedrich's smile disappeared, and he wheeled toward the door, twisting the knob and pulling it half open before he paused. Taking a few deep breaths, he gently clicked the door closed again and turned toward me, his eyes lowered to the ground.

"I apologize. I shouldn't have provoked you, Margaretha." His words were deliberate and slow.

My name on his tongue was water, cool and sweet, dousing the flames of my anger.

"Friends again?" He held out a rigid hand, and I took it, accepting his unexpected offer of reconciliation. His hand relaxed, surprising me further when his thumb traced slow circles over my skin. He gently pulled me toward him until my legs bumped into his.

"I will forgive you your deception if you will forgive my boorish attack on your efforts," he said. "It is noble that you want to save your brother. He's blessed to have a sister so willing to help him."

With one hand still holding mine, he lifted his other to brush back the hair at my temple and tuck it behind my ear. I stilled under his touch. The buzz, the hum during our ride to the mines returned. As his fingers lingered at the hollow of my ear, then cautiously skimmed down my neck to my collarbone, my eyes flashed to his face. His gaze remained lowered, watching his fingers trace the skin of my neck. What was he playing at? This couldn't be real, could it?

He spoke softly. "But you don't need training to win a man's admiration. Your goodness can't be hidden beneath your quiet facade. It is always there, brimming, almost begging men to love you." He lifted his chin, and our gazes locked, my breath becoming ragged as his eyes held me captive. When he slowly leaned his face toward mine, my mind was in tumult. Had Friedrich just admitted to loving me? Wasn't he angry? Did he truly forgive me? Was he really about to kiss me?

Was I about to kiss him?

I didn't move toward him or away, didn't incline or duck my head.

I wouldn't kiss him, but I wouldn't stop him from kissing me.

I closed my eyes and waited.

And waited.

Until I opened my eyes to find Friedrich a few steps away, leaning against the door with his arms folded across his chest. His all-too-satisfied smile made my cheeks, neck, and ears burn with a sudden flood of heat.

"It seems I'm not too inept at enticing a woman, after all," he said. "But I agree with Mistress Hatzfeld. You'll certainly need to improve your skills if you plan to play this game with the court elite. At least keep your guard higher to avoid being taken a fool. After all, I am but a humble servant with—as you say—little skill in the art of wooing."

Huffing with anger and humiliation at being taken in by his pretense, I looked around the room for something to throw at him. Just as I retrieved the French volume from the chair, he skittered out the door. My breath still hadn't calmed when he poked his head back in the room.

"By the by," he said, "we can end the hunting lessons, obviously, but I still expect you to uphold your part of the bargain and tutor me. Farewell."

He closed the door just in time to avoid the flying book.

Friedrich

I somehow found enough self-control to pull the library door closed with only a click instead of the thunderous slam the countess deserved.

Mistress Hatzfeld looked up from her embroidery to give me a forced smile. I gave her one of my own, then took smooth, measured steps down the corridor. I couldn't focus on anything but keeping my facade of calm as I paced into the courtyard, passing Bernhold on my way to the kennels.

"Clouds are gatherin'," he said. "Make sure to fasten up against the rain."

I nodded but kept my sights straight ahead, ducking into the kennels and stepping around the dogs to throw my cap on my makeshift bed of straw and blankets. Klumpen stood and stretched, wagging his tail, and I dropped down beside him. Resting my elbows on my knees, I ran my fingers through my hair before suddenly turning and fisting my pillow. Then I fisted it twice more. Klumpen startled, barking at me, and I took a deep breath, smoothing a hand down his back until he'd calmed.

How dare the countess? How could she use me thus? I thought her different, better than her noble peers, but she was just as self-serving as the rest.

At the very least, I was grateful I'd schooled my anger in her presence. To expose my rage would have exposed my deluded attachment to her. How could I have been such a fool, letting myself care for her? Putting aside my distrust of her kind and our complete inequality of class, I'd already known her plans to leave for Brussels and probably never return. That, by itself, should have been enough to keep me from forming any attachment, but despite my best efforts, I'd lost the battle between logic and inclination.

But she didn't seem capable of that kind of deception. I'd seen her faults. She was too naive, certainly. That she'd need lessons in flirtation showed how totally innocent she was. Too trusting, obviously. She should have suspected my false advances, but she believed me to be sincere.

Maybe because I was *being sincere.*

I rolled my eyes. My mind never failed to dole out uncomfortable truths when I least wanted to hear them.

Certainly, holding her hand and speaking those words hadn't taken much imagination or great feats of pretense. I'd unwillingly spent the last month and more preparing for the part, constantly fighting my admiration for her courage and kindness or battling thoughts of her ivory skin beneath my fingers. It had taken more self-command than I'd mustered in a lifetime to step back from Margaretha while she stood there, eyes closed and lips poised and waiting. I'd had to tack myself against the door for safety, but there was no stopping my hands from shaking. I could only bury them in my folded arms and hope she didn't see through my weakness. That she saw only untroubled, unattached confidence.

Unbuttoning my jerkin, I pulled out the well-worn paper, trying to make out the French scrawls in the dark kennels, but the words were still too advanced for my beginner's knowledge.

How many more lessons would I have to endure before I could understand the letter? How could I face the countess now? If I'd ever toyed with the idea of trusting her to read its contents to me, such an idea was entirely dead. Only nobility knew how to read the French language, and I would never again trust a noble. Had I enough money to leave Wildungen altogether, mayhap I could forget this nonsense with the count and live a better life, but I was still months away from any escape.

Thunder rumbled outside, and the clouds broke, sending rain pattering down onto the kennels and in through the wide-open shutters I'd forgotten to fasten down. Klumpen buried himself under my pillow, and with the way he was shaking, I didn't have the heart to send him off. Pushing myself to my feet with a sigh, I got to work tying the shutters closed while drops of rain pelted my hands and face. As I tied down the last shutter and wiped my forehead on my sleeve, I knew I had no choice but to keep my current plan. Once I had enough knowledge of the French language to read the letter and had saved enough money to become a bowyer's apprentice, I could finally confront the count, then disappear from Wildungen and the countess's life forever.

CHAPTER 16

Friedrich

I TUCKED OUT OF THE bright street and into the harness maker's shop, blinking against the sudden darkness. A worn man sat at a table holding an awl and leather strip as he squinted up at me.

"I'm here for the count's harness and bridles." I unfolded the paper in my hand, carrying it toward him.

The man looked over the list. "You're not the usual boy. Ulrich's got his own set of servants now, eh?" He chuckled and grunted out of his seat, moving to the back of the room to collect the items on Ulrich's paper, then laying them out on the table for inspection. "The count is back, then?"

"Came back two days ago," I muttered, looking over the tack. The harness and bridles went beyond basic usefulness, beautifully tooled with five-petal flowers dotting the leather on either side of the eight-pointed star of the counts of Waldeck. "These'll do."

He smiled and wrapped the items in a cloth sack just as the countess's laugh wafted in through the window, riding the simmering air. Not her sweet, authentic laugh, but a practiced, sycophantic trill.

Giving the harness maker my thanks, I collected the sack and moved to the window, spotting the countess walking up the market street with a dark-haired man wearing a smug smile. Carrera.

The two meandered to a nearby stall, picking up some of the merchant's wares while Mistress Hatzfeld trailed behind at a respectful distance. The countess addressed Carrera, and he laughed. I was grateful not to hear their words, especially when the Spaniard lowered his head and whispered something in the countess's ear that sent a crimson swell up her cheeks. Her responding chuckle wasn't nearly as confident this time, shaking with a bit of nervousness as she discreetly shuffled back from him.

I'd done so well up to now at maintaining my usual demeanor toward the countess. At our past few lessons, I'd been calm and unaffected, at times even charming in my efforts to conceal the anger still smoldering inside. But now, seeing her already baiting her newest prey, the anger roared back to life. And what a prey to have chosen. He was all predator, and I could watch no longer.

Drawing away from the window, I pressed my back against the wall, earning the curious stare of the harness maker. I shot him an uncomfortable smile while I waited and finally peeked another glance to confirm that the countess and captain were nowhere in sight. Touching my cap to bid the harness maker good day, I pulled open the shop door to realize Margar—*the countess* had not left but was tucked in a nearby stall, invisible from the harness maker's window.

"Oh, Friedrich," Hatzfeld called, somehow immediately spotting me. I froze, and the countess cast her lady a worried look, but Hatzfeld carried on. "We've invited the Spaniards to dinner and are struggling to agree on what to serve."

Carrera would be dining at the castle? I tried not to meet his direct stare.

"What think you of the Brussels cabbage?" she continued.

"I've no experience and no opinion of it." I gave my hasty response and was already leaving when the captain addressed me, stopping me short.

"What a shame. You should try one." He tossed the leafy ball toward me as though hurtling a stone, and I reflexively snatched it out of the air.

That insufferable lazy smile tilted his lips as he sauntered toward me. "You have the build and reflexes of a fighter, perhaps even a Landsknecht. Ever thought of being a soldier?"

"If I ever fought, it wouldn't be for anything as mercenary as money." I pushed the cabbage back into his hand. "Good day." Bowing to the ladies, I made a quick exit, abandoning the market for the cool shade of the church before I risked a glance behind me. Carrera was again engrossed with the countess. The two watched a colorful bunting hop across the branch of a nearby tree until it suddenly took flight, startling the countess. She laughed at herself, and the captain joined in, basking in her glorious smiles and taking advantage of the moment by resting his hand far too low on her back. She stiffened beneath his touch but did nothing more to discourage him.

The woman was completely out of her depth.

When the countess strode into the library late, I tried not to grind my teeth, keeping my nose in my book to avoid speaking to her. She stopped behind her chair, as if sensing my mood before she'd even sat down.

"Are you all right?" she asked. "You seem . . . out of sorts."

I flipped the page of my book. "My temperament isn't prone to much change. I am well, as always."

"Good. Good." She tapped her fist on the top of her chair. After an uncomfortable pause, she added, "I'm sorry about today. About Carrera. I'd no notion you would be at the market."

"And if you had?" I lifted my chin, finally meeting her eyes. "Would that have stopped you from your deceitful performance?"

She reared her head back, and I instantly regretted the comment, the more for exposing my bitterness.

"I did not mean that," I muttered, returning to my book.

"Of course. Friedrich." She called my attention back to her before I could read a single word on my page. "Please let me apologize once more. I was dishonest with you before, and for that I am still sorry, but I beg you to believe me when I say my feelings of friendship for you were at all times genuine. I hope we can remain friends."

I had to unclench my jaw before answering, giving her a tight smile. "Of course. No harm done."

She gave a hesitant nod and settled in her chair with a book, leaving me to my studies, though my distracted thoughts had me rereading the same sentence five times before I could even comprehend it. The silence between us was thick enough that I actually jumped when the countess suddenly slammed her book shut. Her face and neck were aflame and her eyes so wide that I found myself near to smiling, watching her shift uncomfortably in her chair. What on earth could cause her such embarrassment?

Reminding myself it was none of my concern, I turned back to my French, but when the countess began fanning herself, I couldn't stop myself from asking, "What is it you're reading today?"

"Nothing." She pretended indifference as she bent to tuck the book beneath her chair, but I snatched it from her hand, flipping it right side up and thumbing through the pages.

"If you want to succeed in Brussels, you'll have to school that blush of yours," I said, my eyes skimming the text. "It gives you away every time." The first set of pages were all in French, giving me no sense of the book's topic, but when I flipped to a well-worn page at the rear, I recognized the courtly love poem. "Minnesang?" I glanced at her. "Does Mistress Hatzfeld still plot to entrap me?"

"I haven't yet told her . . ."

"That I know the truth?"

She started another apology, but I raised a hand, stopping her. "No, no. It's very clever." I nodded. "While I read over poetry to learn the language, my unsuspecting, simple mind is set aflame with ideas of romantic passion."

She puffed out an embarrassed laugh. "Yes, something like that."

I let my eyes trail over words I'd already committed to memory.

> *How vain my deepest plaint of yearning.*
> *No diviner, fairer form hath pleased my heart so well.*
> *But, can my daily torture aid you?*
> *E'en your demeanor hath forced my heart*
> *It ever pierced me to the core.*

"I've never much cared for Wolkenstein's odes." I closed the book. "In truth, I took to calling your brother a heartsick puppy whenever he received women's letters filled with them." Back before I had any understanding of tortured yearning or the "*ill bargain 'twere to desire*" a woman's love.

The countess's head snapped up. "Samuel? Receiving letters of Minnesang?"

"Often. I think he fancied himself in love at one time, but it seemed that love had faded near the end of the war."

"Samuel in love." She twisted a golden curl around her finger, her brows furrowing as if she did not approve. "Did this poem find him any success?"

I pulled my eyes away from her twirling finger. "Unlikely. Love doesn't bloom out of nothing just because one recites a few pretty words."

"Would that it did," she muttered. "It would ease my work in Brussels considerably. My greatest worry is my brother will never be freed when his sister is so miserably suited to the task."

"*That* is your greatest worry?" I leaned toward her. "You're not afraid for your life? If you're discovered doing anything to aid your brother, you could be killed."

"Well, I admit I do fear death." She bowed her head, tracing a finger over her gown's design. "There is too much left undone, too many wrongs to right. What if I don't live long enough to right them?"

The slight woman—looking even smaller pressed into her father's imposing chair—seemed ready to buckle under the weight of needing to do more. I was half tempted to take her hand and assure her she needn't bear such a burden, but I fought the instinct.

"No doubt we are very different in that regard," she said. "I can't imagine you being afraid of anything after working in mines and going to war and wandering forests alone. With such a life, what could you possibly fear?"

Our eyes met, and I held her gaze, a slow swallow tugging my throat. "I assure you, I have fears enough." My mind reeled with them just then, my head and heart a tangle of confusion regarding the countess.

"Such as?" Her voice was a whisper.

After everything she'd done, I had no reason to trust her, yet I felt that unfathomable pull to confide truth to her. It must have been the spell of her eyes on mine.

Dropping my gaze, I toyed with a string on my jerkin, letting a deep breath clear my thoughts. "I've never been too keen on spiders."

"Spiders?" she asked incredulously.

"Hairy. Jumpy. Spindly little legs and an unnerving number of eyes. They're terrifying."

She laughed out loud, and I returned to my book, concealing the small grin that tilted my lips, but even that smile came with a cost. The ache in my chest reminded me how much it hurt to be near her, enjoying her presence. It would be so much easier to hate her. If only I could shut out the good and remember her manipulation and lies, perhaps I could harden myself against the pain.

The reflection made me curious. "Countess, could I ask . . ."

"Yes?"

"It's just, this new understanding of your schemes has me wondering. What exactly is it you've been doing these last few months to bait me?"

With a flush on her face, she studied the flowers of the rug.

"Do you refuse to tell me?"

Her eyes darted to mine before returning to the floor. "You would make me relive the discomfort over again? And to the very person who would find it most ridiculous?"

"You don't have to answer if it causes you grief." She most certainly needed to answer, considering the pain she'd caused me. "No doubt it was intentional having the two of us share a horse on our way to the mines."

"We couldn't very well take three horses without arousing suspicion."

"What about helping Ernst? Or befriending the miners? And what of the tangle in the holly? Did you intend for that?"

Answering from behind the shield of a raised book, her voice was muffled. "You can rest assured that anything I did with intention, I didn't do well."

My eyes dropped back to my reading, and I muttered a quiet, "Well enough."

CHAPTER 17

Friedrich

THE EXCITED CHATTER IN THE cabin made me regret not bringing fresh game sooner. While the miners sat around the table stripping the meat off the bones of the hare, I went to Ernst's bed and sank down beside his feet. I'd been sitting in exactly that spot not one month ago, watching an entirely different scene play out at the table. The memory was colored in orange firelight and warmth as I pictured Margaretha's soft smile and her frequent glances at me. And to think they'd all been lies.

I whisked off my cap and ran my fingers through my hair.

"What troubles ya, Friedrich?" Ernst's eyes sparkled.

"Your grin tells me you already know."

He nodded. "Womenfolk can be downright maddenin'."

"Especially this one. Would that I had never set eyes on her," I grumbled.

"Ya don't mean that. Not with the way you two were smilin' after each other."

I took a deep breath, pushing down the rising anger. "Don't rely on that nonsense. She meant nothing by it."

"Tush, don't go doubtin'—"

"There are things here you don't understand, Ernst," I barked. "Things I can't explain."

Ernst went quiet before he softly asked, "Because she's a countess?"

My eyes met his, and I considered protesting. But I sensed he'd known the truth before Margaretha and I even left the cottage on our last visit. "So you found us out."

"Her beauty. Yer name slip. It weren't hard to figure." Ernst creaked his legs over his bed and scooted himself beside me. "Yer spot might be tougher'n most, but it's not hopeless."

I let out a humorless laugh. "That's exactly the word to describe it, Ernst. Hopeless. If you only knew the things she's done and the lies she's told. And all in the name of aiding Count Samuel, as if that could justify anything."

Ernst tapped a finger against his lips, pondering a moment. "Did I ever tell ya 'bout the accident by Reddighausen? Noblewoman and her children on their way home when the coach broke a wheel?"

I shook my head. This was a large shift in topic.

"I'm not sure if the coach tipped the young boy into the river or he fell in while wandering, but he was drownin'. Course the mother jumped in after him. She got him up on her back, though she could barely keep her own head above water. It weren't a swift river, but it were deep, and the strong current was washin' 'em both downstream. The servants ran along the banks, cryin' out to let the boy go and save herself, but the mother wouldn't give up on her child. Even when the water covered her head, she still clung to him. They both drowned."

I closed my eyes. "Why do you tell me this, Ernst?"

"If that woman didn't fight fer her child, the regret would gnaw 'n wear at her 'til all she's eatin' and breathin' and carryin' 'round with her is guilt. People do foolish things, maybe even mad things, to save the ones they love."

That did sound like the countess, willing to suffer if it meant saving someone she loved. I could easily imagine she'd have no concern for her own happiness when it came to helping her brother, but she didn't seem the kind of person who'd readily hurt others along the way. She was different from her father. Kind. Sympathetic.

Although, the scheme to save her brother hadn't started with her. She'd admitted it was Hatzfeld's doing. Hatzfeld's manipulative designing—I should have suspected it. I'd seen the flash of superiority, the cunning in Hatzfeld's eyes despite her attempts to play the docile maid. I'd seen how the countess looked to Hatzfeld for answers and approval that what she did or said was right. Though it was no surprise a young noblewoman would follow the direction of her older, more experienced companion, Margaretha's faith in Hatzfeld was something different. She'd followed Hatzfeld even when it went against her very nature. Why? What hold did the woman have that caused Margaretha to trust her counsel?

Ernst sighed. "No matter what the countess has done, she loves ya, Friedrich."

I scoffed at his bold statement, picking at my cap and shaking my head.

"It's plain. The way she watches ya, aligns herself to ya where'er ya are in the room. Whene'er ya talk, she's lookin' at ya like a thirsty man to a cup, like she's dyin' to know yer every thought. It's love, a'right."

I stayed silent, wishing his words didn't bring a thrill to my heart. Ernst didn't know of her schemes. Maybe she cared for me, or maybe it was all part of her tricks, contriving perfectly timed smiles to win me over. I'd be a fool to trust any of it.

Except that she never was that skilled when she acted a part. Now recognizing her attempts to entice me—batting her eyes, finding awkward ways to touch me, her laughable compliments—they were all painfully obvious. But the frequent flushes of her cheek or her unsteady breath whenever I grew close . . . were those practiced too? Or did I have the power to affect her as much as she affected me?

"Ya see it now, don't ya?" Ernst studied my face.

I warmed, realizing he'd been watching me. "Whatever her feelings, it doesn't matter. What good could come from a countess loving a serving boy?" I beat the dust from my cap.

Ernst put a hand on my knee, and I was struck by the strange bluish hue of it. "You, of all people, should know rank means nothin' where there's real fondness."

"I, of all people, know the consequence of loving outside your station."

Ernst scoffed. "Their story needn't be yers."

"Ernst, leave it be. She travels to Brussels soon to marry some fool-of-a man just because he's friendly with the kaiser. If she's determined to throw away her happiness to make sure her brother is safe, why should I stop her?"

"Because ya love her."

I ground my jaw. This wasn't love. It couldn't be. Love would never come with such frustration and anger and—

"And ya know she loves you."

"I know no such thing," I protested. "I couldn't even begin—"

"Cares fer ya, then," he interrupted. "Enough that she might one day come to love ya?"

I silently picked my thumbnail, not daring to hope.

"Friedrich, if ya want her, you'll have to get off yer backside and show the girl ya love her. Convince her to stay."

No.

No!

Excitement shot through me, not heeding my rational thought, betraying all my attempts to rein in this impossible affection. And forcing me to face the truth: as frustrated as I was with Margaretha's deception, my feelings for her hadn't changed.

I still cared for her.

I still wanted her to stay.

But Margaretha might not appreciate me trying to talk her out of saving her brother. Of course, I doubted Count Samuel would appreciate his sister risking her life for him, and shouldn't his opinion matter too? He wasn't a child needing protection. The man was a soldier. He could easily calculate that there was no tactical advantage in exchanging places with his sister, consigning Margaretha to prison in his stead. Because that was what a loveless marriage would be. A lifetime of bondage and subservience to a man she did not care for.

Maybe my selfish interests were twisting reality. The more I thought on it, though, the more certain I became that her plan would only bring her misery. Could I convince Margaretha of that? Would it even be right to try? And if she truly wished to marry for love, could I be that man? Still, to pursue a girl so far above my station was too big of a risk. Even Ernst had to see that.

I opened my mouth to argue against his plan, but a new perspective dawned on me. Here I was, already suffering the pain of affection for Margaretha with no hope of a future with her. But if I followed Ernst's counsel and opened my heart to her, what harm could come of it? That she'd reject me? I'd be no worse off than I was now, pining without hope. Maybe it would even be better, knowing her feelings for certain instead of this wondering and fretting. And if she admitted to never caring for me, it would definitely fuel my determination to banish every gentle thought of her . . .

The longer I thought on it, the more the idea captivated me until I was filled with a foolhardy determination to do precisely as Ernst said. I would show Margaretha I cared for her. I would attempt to convince her to stay.

CHAPTER 18

Margaretha

WHAT ON EARTH, BELINDA? THE passionate, illicit embraces of Beltenebros and his lady love, Oriana, fairly set the book on fire.

"Mistress Hatzfeld sends us more reading?" Friedrich's query drew my eyes to him. Rather, to the French primer in his hand, for I couldn't bring myself to meet his gaze with my cheeks aflame.

"No, this assignment is for me alone." *Thank the heavens.* "I'm to study the romances favored in court."

"Ah." He tapped a finger on his lips. "And what sort of tale is it that makes your eyes widen so?" He pulled his chair next to me, his arm bumping against mine, and I had to school my shock that he would even be near me, let alone touch me, after his recent coldness. Casting him a curious sideways glance, I closed the book lest he somehow decipher the words.

"'Tis only the dim light that makes my eyes widen."

"You know, Margaretha, I'm starting to see why Hatzfeld went to such extremes to teach you to flirt." He lifted a brow. "You're quite the innocent."

I dropped a frown. "And you're full of experience?"

"I thought I already proved myself." A smirk twisted his lips, and I threw him a withering glare. "You see, just there," he said. "Though not an expert in courtly romance, I know that glower of yours would have more impact if you had actually met my eye."

Reopening the book, I pretended to read. "I'm meant to be learning ways to attract men, not frighten them off."

"Then you might want to soften your expression into something that isn't wishing me harm."

I answered with silence, but he hooked his finger over my book, pulling it lower until I couldn't avoid his gaze. "Think, Margaretha. Isn't this precisely what you've wanted from me all along? Lessons in flirtation?"

That was the second time today he'd called me by my Christian name. What was this sudden change, this excited energy that was frightfully near to charming?

His finger still hung on my book when he added, "I'm here now, ready to help. You may as well take advantage of it."

He made a fair point. "Very well." Working to force down my embarrassment, I rested my book in my lap and offered him my best attempt at a genuine smile.

"Beautiful," he said, and my cheeks warmed. "It's an innocent, shy smile, and it suits you very nicely. But it's not very encouraging."

The heat spread down my neck, making me check the time on the clock. Only ten minutes more. I could endure this mortification for ten minutes.

Friedrich stood, setting his primer on the mantel. "I can tell you, as a man, your expression is barely enough to convey interest, let alone love."

"You expect me to feign love with half the court?" I scoffed. "Ridiculous."

"Strategic. What could be more attractive than thinking a beautiful, intelligent woman is in love with you?"

My eyes went wide. He'd called me beautiful? Intelligent? What had prompted such a shift in behavior?

"Come. Try it on me," he pressed on without hesitation. "Use your expressions to convince me you love me."

Somewhere in the corner of my mind a distant bell rang a warning, but with my sudden nerves, I could hardly hear it, let alone trouble myself to decipher its meaning. This was Friedrich. With him I was safe from everything except utter humiliation, which I was on the verge of now as I tried to understand the assignment. How was I even to begin to communicate such a look? But Friedrich was offering help with the very thing I most needed to learn, so I would try.

Sighing, I put the book on the chair behind me and drew near to him, narrowing my eyes and puffing out my lips in an effort to be serious and alluring at the same time.

"Is that your attempt?" he asked.

I nodded, and he let out a stifled chortle.

"Try again."

Fighting another flush of heat, I went for a softer approach, forming a half smile with my eyes open wide.

"I'm afraid not," he said.

I stared deeply and solemnly into his eyes.

"I'm uncertain whether you're angry or disinterested."

I tried several more alterations until Friedrich finally stopped me. "Have you really no experience to draw from, Margaretha? No time when you felt yourself falling in love?"

That warning bell sounded again, louder now, but I could only see the challenge in Friedrich's eyes.

"I suppose not," he said. When he turned toward his seat, I instinctively reached out and grasped his hand, pulling him to a stop.

"Let me try once more." I hadn't meant for the words to sound breathy.

His eyes were on mine as he curled his hand over my fingers, making that fluttering spring to life in my gut. Making me realize my boldness. I slipped my fingers from his grasp, slowly, for he seemed reluctant to let me go.

"Very well." He sank into his seat, watching me.

I closed my eyes and took a deep breath to focus my thoughts. For this to work, I had to make myself believe I was in love. Having spent no significant time around any man but Friedrich, I'd have to draw on my experiences with him.

This time the bell clanged in an almighty clamor, warning me it would be dangerous to proceed. Telling me that if I did this, I risked something momentous. But what?

Pushing the question aside, I set to my task, sifting through my history with Friedrich. I let myself relive those moments when I'd felt admiration. Attraction. I remembered the warmth of his arms around me, his breath tickling my ear as we rode to the mines. My surprise when he'd gifted me the shooting gloves, betraying his quiet concern for me. The smell of straw and cloves surrounding me as his trembling fingers grazed my skin to cut me loose from the thickets. His gentle manner in caring for Ernst, and his sense of duty, defying Father's laws to provide for his friends. He'd been a brave child, leaving behind the security of the mines to find his own way. And then again as a youth, living alone in the forest. It had shaped him into the man he was—disciplined, independent, unafraid of society or its judgments, and I admired him for it.

Then I remembered the day I'd confessed to using him. There'd been a fire in his gaze before he'd closed his eyes and leaned toward me, his breath coming faster when he'd moved to kiss me. I let my imagination toy with the memory, Friedrich no longer stepping back to tease me, but actually coming closer, pressing his lips to mine. What if he'd wrapped his arms around me and pulled me against him? What would it feel like to let myself kiss him, to let myself love him?

Something in my chest warmed, spreading heat through my veins, driving back the cold as a glimmer of hope flashed through me. Fear made me tamp it down before I could grasp hold of it, analyze it, face it. Instead, I focused on the numbness, letting it expand, cool and familiar, over my heart until the bells of warning had all but disappeared. In their place was an emptiness that left me rubbing a hand over my nose, fighting back the tears pricking my eyes as I whirled away from Friedrich. Why on earth was I crying? Of all the ridiculous—

"Margaretha?"

I sniffed discreetly but couldn't face him. Not yet. "I'm afraid I'm not up to the challenge." I barked an awkward, forced laugh.

Friedrich's hand slid over my shoulder, his body so close the heat of it warmed my back. Wiping my eyes, I twisted out of his grasp.

"My tutor will be waking soon. I must go." I knelt to collect my things from under the chair.

I felt Friedrich watching me, his posture tense, but then he let out a sigh. "Mistress Hatzfeld will scold me for keeping you from your reading, no doubt." He lifted my book from the chair, sifting through the pages. "Is this story of yours full of the usual intrigues? Unsanctioned loves? Abandoned children? Magics? Future telling?"

"Just so."

When I reached for the book, he pulled it back, catching my hand in his empty one and lifting me to my feet. I kept my gaze on the rug.

"You know, I've a little experience with that." His thumb slid over the back of my hand, stealing my breath.

"With what?" I squeezed out the words.

"Future telling, like in your romance. Shall I tell you your future, Margaretha?" In one swift movement, he discarded my book and flipped my hand over, staring into my wide, surprised eyes. "It is not fated. What I see is only a prediction of what will come if you keep on your current life path."

I nodded without hearing. My thoughts were on the warmth of his calloused hand gently chafing beneath my smooth knuckles. He raised his other hand to my palm, tracing the crease just below my fingers and sending a subtle shiver rolling from my neck all the way down my spine.

"I see a past weighed down by years of sadness. And here, a flash of great pain." His finger settled on a slight circle within the crease. "A crisis born from a moment of decision."

I stiffened. Did he somehow know about the healer? Was this his way of drawing me out?

He continued, not seeming to notice my worry. "Your lifeline makes a sharp curve, showing a sudden shift in behavior as your once open nature became reserved and hesitant to trust others."

"Perhaps because the world is full of charlatans like yourself." My attempt at levity was sabotaged by my raspy voice. "You promised to tell me my future, not make up stories about my past."

"Patience, Margaretha. I'm coming to that." Dropping his eyes back to my hand, his lips turned down. "I see a future of many lovers. And a chance for wealth and glory, though it will mean loneliness."

"Loneliness? Where have all my lovers gone?"

He muttered something that sounded very much like an oath with regards to where exactly my lovers could go, then he added, "A married woman can still be lonely if she makes the wrong choice. And this"—his finger hovered near the scar of my palm—"this is a point of crucial decision. Your fate line is soft and unsettled, but in it I see another path. A future of quiet happiness. It all comes down to this moment." His thumb rested on the burn, covering it from view. "Will you make the right choice?"

My breath hitched in my throat, and I looked up to find him watching me. He stepped so close his shoe tips touched mine, while his thumb began grazing back and forth over my skin, the intensity of his eyes sending my stomach into a volley of flips.

I swallowed. This was all just nonsense anyway. Magics and fortune telling were not to be believed. "You're not even looking at my hand," I said, my voice wavering.

He kept his steady gaze on my face as he turned my hand over and brought my knuckles to his lips, his mouth parting to bestow a gentle kiss.

Though men had kissed my gloved hand in the past, their touch was nothing to the intimacy of Friedrich's lips on my skin. I felt weak and exhilarated, heady and focused, simultaneously thrilled and terrified, and I wasn't sure how to break myself away. Or that I even wanted to.

"Friedrich, I think—" Another swallow caught my words, and Friedrich took advantage of my silence, pulling my arm toward him and resting three soft kisses on the inside of my wrist.

"I-I had b-better go."

"Am I not doing it right?" he asked, an impish grin betraying that he knew very well the effect he was having on my equilibrium. "You wanted me to teach you to woo. I'm only doing my duty."

This was more than I'd bargained for. "I think it best we avoid anything so . . . serious."

He reached up to tuck a stray hair behind my ear. "What if I am serious?" His gaze smoldered, making my head swim.

"Friedrich, I—"

The door sprang open, dumping icy reality down my neck. Friedrich and I quickly pulled apart, but the scrutinizing look on Belinda's face told me she'd seen enough.

"We must go now, my lady." She addressed me, but her eyes were on Friedrich.

I picked up my books from the chair, stepping past Friedrich as I hurried toward Belinda. Just before she ushered me out the door, I cast a backward glance to find Friedrich meeting Belinda's stare with a steely gaze that looked much like a challenge.

CHAPTER 19

Margaretha

Captain Carrera sat on the low platform of the dais, looking quite pleased with his honored place between Father and me. Spending occasional afternoon outings with the Spaniard was bad enough without dining with him too.

Picking up a cut of bread, Father turned to the captain. "Is it true the Elector of Saxony's death sentence was commuted to imprisonment for life?"

"Yes. He had to sign away his electorship to get it." The unmannered Spaniard scooped up his pork with all five fingers and shoveled it into his mouth. "His cousin Maurice is the new elector."

Thank goodness no such sentence had been passed on Samuel yet. He wouldn't have an electorship to trade for his life.

Sucking the juices from his fingers, Carrera added, "You've no doubt heard the Landgrave of Hesse is a captive now."

"What?" Father dropped his bread.

"He traveled to Halle to give himself up."

Father's face turned red, and he balled his hand into a tight fist. "And the kaiser didn't hesitate to take him prisoner?"

"Is the kaiser still in Halle?" I asked. And was Samuel with him there? It was only a day's hard ride away.

Carrera shook his head. "The kaiser's in the Netherlands preparing his territories to receive their future sovereign, Prince Felipe."

"What do you know of the prince, *mein Herr*? What sort of man is he?" Belinda's eyes darted to me, revealing that she still held fanciful hopes of me winning one of the most powerful men in the world, Catholic or not.

"The German accounts of him are always unfavorable." Carrera frowned. "Either he's too carefree or too cold, too learned in Spanish customs or too ignorant to rule." He picked up another slab of meat, and it seemed that was all the answer we were to get.

Belinda tried another tract. "Does he hunt?"

"Not as well as I do." He wiped his coat sleeve across his mouth. "Hasn't the vigor for it."

Belinda kicked me under the table, and I looked at her wide-eyed, unsure what I was meant to do. She gave a pointed nod toward Carrera, evidently expecting me to say something.

I cleared my throat. "I know a little of hunting myself. Shooting, anyway. I haven't yet practiced with game."

"Is that so?" He twisted to face me, leaning his elbow on the table as he looked me over. "I'd be happy to educate you."

I started to decline, but another kick from Belinda had me nodding my begrudging consent.

"The countess would be so grateful to you," she said. "But we must not presume upon the good count's generosity." She peeked at Father through her lashes, and he froze with his spoon halfway to his mouth.

"Oh, certainly." He lowered the spoon to its bowl. "I would take great pleasure in having you hunt my lands. In fact, I'll take you out myself, and we can make a day of it." It seemed Father was employing Belinda's logic, making friends with his enemy to tip the scales a bit in his favor.

"If the countess comes, I am happy to accept." Carrera bowed his head.

Belinda kicked me again, and this time I responded by grinding her toe under my heel. She sucked in a sharp breath while I gave her my most innocent smile. It was small retribution for the way she'd lectured me after French lessons with Friedrich, accusing me of losing my heart to him. I'd assured Belinda that her fears were wholly unfounded.

Entirely.

My eyes flitted to the servants' table, where I spotted Friedrich's dark head bowed over his bowl. Yes, I felt warmer and lighter whenever I was with him. Yes, I looked forward to our lessons, storing up things to tell him, eager for the next time I could talk with him. But that needn't be more than friendship.

Friedrich lifted his chin, and I braced myself to meet his gaze, but he only turned toward the woman beside him, his lips parting in one of his scarce, bright smiles. When she gave him a playful elbow to his arm, my eyes narrowed, focusing on the back of her head to see if it was Ilsa.

"Whom do you study?"

Carrera's voice made me jump, and I quickly laughed to cover my embarrassment. "No one."

"But you do." He lowered his head by mine and murmured, "You bear the look of a jealous woman. A woman grown up since our first meeting."

My cheeks burned, and I floundered for something to say, but Carrera didn't wait for an answer. His hand found mine beneath the table, caressing my fingers as he whispered, "Perhaps I can cure you of your jealousy."

Panic tumbled in my gut, and I fought the urge to push his hand away, settling for a subtle scoot of my chair while leaning out of his reach. It was enough that he didn't pursue, but he turned back to his meal with a grin that proved him not the slightest bit deterred. I'd need help undoing whatever it was I'd done.

I turned to Belinda, but she was looking past me, a shy smile curving her lips as she seemed to be gazing at my father.

"Belinda," I said, and she lowered her eyes, a rare blush coloring her cheeks. "Why do you smile so?"

She shook her head. "Something amusing, that is all. You were too distracted with Carrera to notice."

"Distracted?" I could barely keep my voice at a whisper. "He was seconds away from abandoning all propriety."

Belinda choked on her wine, wiping her lips with the tablecloth and fighting a smile. "Lively, isn't he? Don't fret yourself too much over him; I'll help you keep the dog on his leash."

"Very well." I nodded. "See that you do."

CHAPTER 20

Friedrich

THE HOUNDS STRAINED AGAINST THEIR leashes as we waited for the signal from the hunting horns. The hunters were more relaxed. Count von Waldeck sat on his horse, fiddling with his gloves as he and Mistress Hatzfeld engaged in a quiet conversation. Carrera lounged in the grass, his attention entirely on Margaretha, and mine on every word he spoke to her.

"You said you had some experience hunting. Do you practice falconry?"

"Something closer to Bercletti, but without a dog. Or prey." Her tone was almost apologetic.

"Bercletti? And no prey?" He laughed. "What, have you been shooting hand bows at hay butts?"

Margaretha looked past him, giving me a pointed stare. "Something like that."

"How very primitive. I can see you *do* need me to educate you." He jumped up and turned to Ulrich. "You there, bring me that crossbow."

Waiting with outstretched arms, Carrera's hands flapped impatiently until Ulrich set the bow in them. He looped the cranequin's rope over the back. "Though I still prefer my spear and sword, I know these are gaining favor in Par Force hunting. For men, at least. I won't pretend to know the trends of the ladies."

I doubted him ignorant of anything when it came to ladies.

He wound the cranequin, pulling the bow to its full draw, then loaded the bolt and shot it off at nothing in particular. The wasted bolt disappeared into a thicket.

Carrera tugged Margaretha to her feet, then put the crossbow in her hands. "You see? Easy enough for a woman." He walked behind her, dwarfing her tiny frame beneath him as he reached his arms around to slide the cranequin onto the bow. Her cheeks flushed a lovely scarlet.

"Turn the cranequin like this," he instructed, covering her hand with his and moving their arms in circular unison to wind the crank.

"Now raise the bow. Keep your hands steady." His arms lay under hers, supporting her aim as she looked down the deck of the crossbow.

"What am I aiming for?" Her voice was tense. Nervous.

"Don't worry about aiming yet. Simply feel the weight of the bow in your hands. Take note of the change in the winds. Breathe deeply."

What an obvious bid for more time with Margaretha in his arms. Did I need to step in? Did I have any right to?

I looked around for Hatzfeld, but she was too consumed in her conversation with the count to give any notice to her lady's predicament.

Carrera lowered his mouth to Margaretha's ear, his lips brushing the rim of it as he whispered something that made her shiver. My blood churned.

The sudden thwack of the crossbow sounded, and Margaretha's bolt sank deep in the bark of a tree. "I think I've got the idea of it." She extracted herself from his cage of arms.

"You're a quick study, but there's more I could teach you if we have time."

She returned the crossbow to him. "I know all I want to know. Thank you."

"Then perhaps I might educate you in other subjects."

Though he was subtle, I still noticed him run his fingers along her back. But I was robbed the pleasure of landing a solid punch against his temple when "The Game's Afoot" trumpeted from somewhere through the trees. The hunting party jumped to action. Carrera dropped the crossbow and mounted his horse. Drawing his sword, he urged his horse beside the count's, seeming to forget Margaretha entirely in his excitement.

With Carrera gone, Margaretha's gaze moved to me. Horses and servants and dogs scurried every which way, but the chaos disappeared the moment we locked eyes. She watched me approach, letting out a small gasp when I settled my hands on her waist. I'd intended to lift her onto her horse, but that gasp . . . I couldn't move. I couldn't even blink as we watched each other, my hands burning with the heat of her. She was feeling this too, just as she'd been feeling something in the library before Hatzfeld burst in upon us. But would she confess it?

"Friedrich, the dogs!" Ulrich shouted, reminding me of my task. As if reading my thoughts, Margaretha leapt upward at the very moment I strained to lift her, the two of us moving in fluid synchrony like we'd rehearsed it a thousand times. Seeing her safely settled on her mount, I left to untie the leashes from the tree, pulling the anxious dogs to heel. I hovered over them, ready to unhook their collars.

After a few tense moments, a ten-pointed stag jumped through the camp, and I released the raches, sending the volley of dogs racing after the hart with near-deafening barks. Carrera was quick to join the chase as he reached his long sword out to slash the hind leg of the deer darting past. Blood spilled from the gash, leaving a trail of red scent for the dogs who herded the stag toward the next volley of waiting hounds. Dogs, hunters, and horses—all clamor and frenzy—melted into the green of the forest, leaving the houndmen in sudden silence to collect and tie up the first round of spent and sweaty raches.

Looping the leashes through their collars, we led them along the trail of crushed plants to the inevitable kill site. It was hot, dirty work pulling them over fallen trees, down hills, and through streams, but when "The Mort" sounded, we knew we were close to finding the hunters. Even the tired raches lifted their heads and picked up their pace, drool dripping from their mouths in anticipation.

We arrived at the kill site just as Carrera dug his knife into the deer's throat for the breaking, slicing through the hide down to the tail while blood bubbled out over Carrera's hands. Having had the honor of the first cut, he passed his knife to the count kneeling beside him, and the count continued the grisly work of unmaking the hart. Carrera stood, mopping his brow with his sleeve before settling his fists against his waist. He looked around with a smile, his gaze landing on Margaretha atop her horse. Her eyes were as wide and innocent as a doe's as she witnessed the ritualistic disemboweling of the game her father served at suppers. Shaking his head, Carrera came to stand beside her horse, resting his arm over his jennet's mane.

"I think you've never seen a breaking before." He likely thought his words safely covered by the noise of chatting huntsmen, but I'd moved close enough to hear.

She shook her head, her eyes still focused on the dead hart.

"It's a beautiful game," he said. "Tracking down the hart, the relays of hounds being slipped as they sprint after the prey. The hart's pulse beating faster as the fear of capture intensifies. It may perform its ruse, doubling back on its trail to confuse the dogs, or running through the water to cover its scent. It may even seek out and cross the path of another deer to distract its predators, but I wouldn't be satisfied with anything less."

Margaretha looked down at him with a dark glare as he toyed with the ribbon of her shoe.

"I expect the cleverest and fittest hart and the finest pursuit. I expect the prey to run hard and the chase to last long. I'm confident I'll last longer." His hand slid from her shoe to her ankle, leaving traces of blood as it slipped higher up her hose.

Sucking in a shocked breath, Margaretha kicked out her leg until Carrera released her with a laugh.

The burn in my blood returned in an overwhelming flash, and I dropped the leashes of the dogs to march directly toward the filthy blackguard. I'd taken all of three steps before Ulrich moved in front of me, his hands up to block my way.

"It's not worth it," he whispered.

From behind Ulrich's shoulder, Margaretha noticed me, and her face turned bright crimson.

Ulrich pushed a handful of leashes into my fist. "These dogs've had their reward. Get 'em back to the kennels and clean 'em off. I'll take over your lot."

I stared at Margaretha, my breath coming fast and my blood still burning. I didn't want to listen to reason. I wanted to sic the hounds on Carrera and have them chase him all the way back to Spain.

But I could only turn on my heel, jerking the dogs' leashes to lead them toward the castle.

I had enough time to water the dogs and clean the blood off their muzzles before the hunting party returned. Hoping to escape into the castle without being noticed, I walked in the shadows and was halfway to the door when the count called my name.

"Rowohlt. Water for the horses." He was full of energy after his successful hunt, jumping down beside Carrera to relive the events of the chase with animated hand gestures.

Pulling a bucket from its hook on the stable wall, I plodded back into the courtyard, not acknowledging Margaretha when she tried to catch my eye. Not even stopping when the fresh clatter of hooves brought an unknown rider wearing unfamiliar black-and-red livery. With the hunting party's attention stolen by the stranger, Margaretha softly called out, "Friedrich, wait."

I slowed my pace but continued around the corner of the castle toward the well while Margaretha's light footfalls pattered on the stone behind me. She caught my sleeve, turning me to face her.

"Carrera's behavior was all his own," she said. "Above basic civility, I've done nothing to encourage him."

"I know. It's only—" I looked around us, suddenly feeling exposed. Taking her arm, I led us around the jutting stone and into a recess in the castle wall. "Is there nothing you can do to rebuff him? It's painful seeing him touch you with such familiarity. He paws at you like an animal leaving its mark."

"His mark?"

Using the toe of my shoe, I lifted her gown to uncover her bloodstained ankle. "And he assaults you while I stand right there, helpless to do anything. It's infuriating!" I strained to keep my voice a whisper.

"Friedrich." Margaretha's tone was calm, but I was too agitated to be calmed. She gathered the bucket from my grip, setting it on the ground as I whipped off my cap to rake my fingers through my hair.

"Friedrich," she said again, and this time she lifted her hand, her hesitant fingers touching my cheek and guiding my gaze down to hers. Those steady blue eyes were a clear winter sky, soothing my temper, cooling the flare of jealousy and replacing it with a different heat as Margaretha's fingers lingered on my cheek. Raising my hand to cover hers, I gently pressed her palm against my face. She didn't pull away.

I stepped closer, relishing the way her breath went ragged, matching mine.

Boots striking against the cobblestones broke our solitude, and we pulled apart just as Carrera's face came into view. Margaretha ducked her eyes, but I didn't hesitate to meet his curious gaze.

"This is snug," he said, looking around the recess. "Countess, your father asked me to find you that he might speak with you."

"Very well," she answered, her eyes still on the ground.

Look up, I thought. *Show him you're not afraid.*

Carrera didn't step aside when she tried to leave, forcing her to brush against him as she passed, all the while smiling at me until the sound of Margaretha's shoes faded.

He picked up the forgotten bucket from the ground, fiddling with the handle. "Boy, remind me of your position here."

"I tend the hounds," I answered flatly.

"That's right." He pushed the bucket into my chest, forcing a gust from my lungs as he whispered in my ear. "Remember your place."

When he backed away, his smile was a threat.

CHAPTER 21

Margaretha

BELINDA STOOD INSIDE THE COOL of the castle, taking shelter by the great front doors when I walked in. "Your father is in the library," she said and turned to lead the way.

"Wait," I called out, halting her step. "Should I not go before you? It was me Father summoned." I marched past her, doing my best to keep my stride long and quick enough that she had to trot to keep up.

"Margaretha, you walk too fast," she panted behind me. "Slow your pace."

I reeled on her, and she nearly plunged into me. "Am I to be mindful of your needs now, when you took no consideration for mine?"

She blinked and stepped back. "Whatever do you mean?"

"What happened to 'keeping the dog on his leash'? You didn't give a fig for Carrera's grasping or insinuations."

"I didn't see anything untoward."

I lifted my skirts to show just how high his bloodied hand had traveled. "I hope whatever stole your attention was worth leaving your friend in the mud." I shook my gown to straighten it, then turned toward the library, Belinda following as we coursed the path without another word.

I could hear Father's pacing before we'd even entered.

He waved us inside. "Come in quickly and close the door behind you."

"What is it?" I pulled the door shut with a click.

His eyes gleamed when he answered. "Dalwigk just learned that not only is the kaiser en route to Brussels as we speak, but he is traveling with prisoners in tow. He will arrive in a matter of weeks, at which time I'm hoping you, Margaretha, will be there to greet him." He crossed the room and took my hands in his. "Now is the time for action. Are you ready to do all you can to bring my boy home?"

The chance to finally do something to save my brother ought to have filled me with joy instead of sitting like a boulder on my chest, squeezing the very breath from my lungs.

"Lady Margaretha is more prepared than she gives herself credit for," Belinda answered behind me.

"Is that so?" he asked her, then he looked back at me. "Then you will do it? You will go now?" His eyes bored into mine as he awaited my answer.

It should have come easily. This was precisely what Belinda and I had been preparing for these last few months, but of a sudden, my throat seized, and I couldn't respond. What was holding me back? What was this sinking sense of dread now overcoming me? I tried clearing my throat, but in the end, the only answer I could muster was a halting nod.

Father pulled me into a tight embrace, kissing my forehead. "You're too good," he muttered against my brow. He didn't know the truth.

Releasing me, he sat down at his desk, pulling out a paper and dipping his quill. "I shall write to Queen Mary immediately, telling her you will arrive within a fortnight."

A fortnight? Accounting for the time to travel, that meant I had a little under a week before we left. The familiar, comfortable routine of my life in Wildungen would end.

"You are dismissed." Father's quill danced over his paper, the cloud of melancholy that had hovered over him the last few months now completely evaporated. His excitement to finally be aiding his son was almost palpable.

Belinda and I dipped our bows, and we were moving to the door when Father called out, "Mistress Hatzfeld, I should like you to stay a moment, if you please."

I gave her a look of wonder, but she ducked her eyes, a blush creeping over her cheeks as I opened the door and stepped out of the room. Father followed me to the door and closed it behind me, cloistering himself and Belinda in the library.

As curious as I was about this strange, private meeting, I knew I had very little time before Belinda joined me again, and there was something I needed to do. Hurrying to my tutor's room, I riffled through his papers until I found a blank one, then scratched out a quick message to Friedrich.

Must speak with you. Meet me in the apothecary tomorrow after dinner.
—Margaretha

"You seem nervous," Belinda whispered, casting a careful glance at my tutor's nodding head. In a few moments, his chin would drop to his chest, his breath coming slow and deep, and I'd be running to the apothecary to meet Friedrich.

"My stomach aches," I lied. "Perhaps you could fetch me a glass of wine."

Belinda stood, setting down her needlework.

"More still"—I grabbed her hand—"some buttered bread?"

"We just finished dinner," she whispered, but I put my hand to my belly, and she rolled her eyes, then crept out of the room. I strained to hear her fading footfalls, counting each step and holding my breath until I was sure enough time had passed. Tiptoeing to the door, I slipped through it, then closed it behind me before taking off in a near-sprint toward the south wing. The stairs winding up to the apothecary were steep, and when I arrived, I had to pause just outside, pressing a hand to my burning lungs until my breath steadied. I pushed into the room to find Friedrich wearing a trail into the floor as he paced by the table.

"What's wrong?" he asked, crossing the room to meet me.

I signaled him to be quiet, peeking into the hallway once more before I closed the door behind me. "Father spoke with an informant yesterday. He learned the kaiser is on his way to Brussels. Father's determined to send me there within the fortnight."

Friedrich hissed. "So soon?" He rubbed a hand over his jaw and paced again but abruptly halted, his gaze settling on me. "But why did you call me here to tell me this when a note would have done as well?"

I hadn't even considered that, hadn't let myself think through the reason I so urgently needed to see him, and now with his eyes probing mine, I suddenly felt foolish. "You're right. I suppose that would have sufficed."

I stepped toward the door, and his eyes widened.

"No, that isn't what I . . . I didn't mean . . ." He tossed his cap on the table, scattering the pile of chamomile petals I'd crushed the day before. Taking a deep breath, he tried again. "Was there something else? Something more you wanted to tell me?"

"No." I shook my head. "Nothing more."

"Very well. I have something I'd like to say."

My stomach tightened, but I gave him a hesitant nod.

"I know I've no right to an opinion on this"—he picked up the pestle, absently tapping it inside the mortar—"but you should forget your schemes in Brussels."

"Friedrich . . ." I sighed. "You know that's impossible. I must help Samuel."

"And sacrifice yourself in the process? Is that how wars are fought now, exchanging the lives of maidens for soldiers?" His tone was reproving.

"I know the risk I take," I snapped back but, recalling myself, answered more gently, "My brother would do as much for me."

"But what would he *want* for you? Shouldn't his wishes matter too? All these games, these deceptions . . ." He shook his head and went back to grinding the pestle into the mortar. "They will only bring you misery. If it's discovered you're trying to free your brother, you'll be given his same fate. Imprisonment, maybe even death. If not, you enter a loveless marriage simply for advantage, and you'll have to live a lifetime with that decision." He released the pestle with a clatter. "That's its own kind of prison, Margaretha. And consider that if you do nothing, he might still be freed! Too much is unknown."

We stared at each other in a silent stalemate.

This was nothing like how I'd imagined the conversation going. But despite wanting to stay, to make peace with Friedrich somehow, the seconds were dripping down on me like cold water, their collective weight an uncomfortable reminder of how long I'd been gone.

"I have to be going or I'll be missed." I gathered the chamomile, stirring its sweet scent into the room as I returned it to a neat pile, then offered Friedrich his cap. Instead of taking it, his hand landed on mine, drawing my eyes up to his.

"Margaretha, I know your brother well enough to guess at how angry he'd be that you'd risk your life and happiness on a plan that might not work. He would never ask you to trade your life for his." Friedrich took a gentle step toward me, his eyes still locked on mine. "He'd want you to stay. Here. Where you're safe."

I shook my head. Samuel might not want me taking risks for him, but I couldn't give up. Not on Samuel. And not on my chance for redemption.

Yet, despite my convictions, Friedrich's words brought hope flaring to life inside me, and I couldn't seem to stomp it out. He was giving me reasons to stay. Reasons that forced me to acknowledge how much I wanted to.

Pinching my eyes closed, I shut out such selfish desires, but Friedrich's fingers moved soft and slow across my skin until my eyes fluttered open to meet his.

"What do *you* want, Margaretha? Can you think of any reason to stay?" He stepped so close I had to tip my head back to meet his gaze. His eyes flicked back and forth between mine, begging me, willing me to find that reason.

My head was ringing, the alarm sounding afresh, and this time I heeded it. Ducking my eyes to break free of Friedrich's gaze, I took a step back, forcing down the rising warmth, wrapping myself in the safety of empty numbness before I could explore my feelings further.

Friedrich let out a frustrated sigh. "Margaretha, I have been through war and never found an opponent as challenging as you. You keep an entire army posted around your heart." He stepped toward me, setting his finger on my chin and tipping my head up to meet his eye. "Can you not think of any motive strong enough to stay in Wildungen?"

My stomach turned flips inside me as truth battled against the numbness, clamoring to be heard. Of its own volition, my head nodded.

His finger moved from my chin and traced a trail up my jaw, his voice all gentle persuasion. "Can you tell me what it is?"

No. I refused to face it. What good could come of acknowledging these . . . feelings? *Feelings that have grown from friendship to something more.*

The thought shot bright currents through every vein, each winding its way to my center. Warmth joined with warmth, filling me with a heat that stirred in my chest, sending the ghost of a pulse beating through my long-dormant heart. This was why the bells cried their warning. This was the momentous risk, the shift with Friedrich that could never be undone. Had my heart not been numb, I would have sensed it sooner.

I would have known that I'd somehow fallen for the soldier.

I opened my mouth to speak just as my name echoed down the corridor and footsteps sounded outside the door, robbing me of my courage.

"Friedrich, I must return," I whispered, trying to pull my hand from his, but he held it fast.

"You were about to say something."

I shook my head. "No, we can't be found here together."

His eyes brimmed with frustration, but he loosened his grasp, and I slipped my hand away, throwing him a final, apologetic glance before opening the door to find Belinda pacing the hall.

"There you are." Her words were an accusation. "Seems your stomach is feeling bet—" She knit her brows, looking past me into the room before I could whip the door closed. Her eyes turned icy. "So that's what you've been doing?"

Taking a painful grip of my arm, she half-dragged me down the corridor. "What were you thinking, risking your reputation like that? Anyone who saw you secreting yourself alone with serving boys would think the worst."

I twisted my arm from her grasp, shocked by her audacity. "It was no different than any of our French lessons."

She scoffed. "Except then I stood nearby enough to warn you should someone approach. What would your father have done had he seen you?"

I didn't answer.

"You have exactly one week before your farewell banquet. You're potentially days away from seeing your brother." She paced ahead of me. "Don't let your foolish romantic inclinations get in the way of what we've worked so hard to achieve."

"What if this isn't the right path?" I asked. "What if Samuel wants something more for me?"

She stopped at the top of the stairs, rounding on me. "You think you're in love, is that it?"

"No, it's not—"

"You think someday your father will grant you permission to marry a peasant and be thrilled to let you and Friedrich live here under his charity? Never. And even if there was the slightest chance of your father not throwing Friedrich out as soon as he'd learned of your infatuation, how could Friedrich ever accept you if he knew what you'd done? How could any man love you if he knew the truth?"

I sucked in a sharp breath and fell back a step. A physical blow could not have struck harder.

"How dare you!" I straightened my spine. Belinda's troubled past gave excuse for her shifting moods and dagger tongue, but this was a step too far. "You have no right to speak to me thus. You're every bit as guilty as I."

"Precisely," she snapped. "Which is why I know you could never be happy with Friedrich. Not when your life would be a lie. Not with your brother's corpse rotting in a grave you could have spared him from. Forget this nonsense. Don't hope for a marriage filled with love; seek a marriage to save the brother you love, and that will be enough to give you a lifetime of peace. That's worth far more than any temporary fluttering of affection you think you feel."

I narrowed my eyes at her, refusing to let her see the impact of her words, how she'd shaken my rising hope to quicksand.

It was only when Belinda turned and descended the stairs, leading us back to my sleeping tutor, that I felt an uncomfortable heat emanating from my hand. The scar on my palm had been rubbed an angry red.

CHAPTER 22

Friedrich

I HADN'T MANAGED TO CATCH Margaretha's attention all night, even when she stood with blush-brightened cheeks while her father raised his cup in her honor. And with Mistress Hatzfeld browbeating poor Bernhold into assigning me more work all week, tonight's banquet was the first time I'd seen Margaretha since our apothecary meeting. Going an entire week without so much as a glimpse of her had turned me sullen, particularly because of Hatzfeld's annoying interruption just as Margaretha was on the verge of admitting something vital. I felt almost sure she was about to confess her feelings for me, but with her party leaving tomorrow for Brussels, now I might never know the truth.

"Don't think I don't see right through you." Ilsa's voice intruded into my thoughts, and I turned forward at the table to face her.

"Staring up at the dais with all but drool drippin' from your chin. You've a fire burning for the countess, don't you?"

I gave her a bored stare and picked up my spoon, taking a loud slurp of my soup.

"And I've seen the way you watch her at church, your eyes always flickin' up to the balcony. It's too obvious to ask why you've come to care for her—certainly she's comely—but I thought you were a great deal smarter." She fished through the breadbasket for a roll, then picked off the black seeds. "Ah, poor Friedrich. You're just a servant; did you really believe she cared for you as anythin' more than a bit of fun?"

I clenched my spoon so hard my knuckles turned white. Ilsa had managed to hit on the one fear I couldn't easily dismiss. The difference in our stations put the countess far beyond my reach.

"I've lost my appetite." I gave Ilsa a pointed look and pushed away from the table, pacing toward the great hall doors. Instinctively glancing at Margaretha, I was surprised to find her watching me, her eyes meeting mine for the first time tonight. But I didn't even have a moment to give her a quick smile before Carrera spoke to her, stealing her attention away.

I needed to find a way to meet with her before tomorrow. There was still so much left unsaid between us. How could I let her leave without learning the truth of what she was about to confess in the apothecary? Without making a confession of my own? I didn't need to worry about station and class, thinking so far into the future when all I had left was this one night. One night to convince her to stay. One night to admit my feelings for her.

Margaretha

I could still feel Friedrich's gaze locked on me, his eyes speaking words I didn't want to hear, even after the musicians' melody petered out and Father rose to his feet with a nervous smile.

"Friends"—Father leaned his splayed fingers against the banquet table—"you well bore a father's long and affectionate ramblings for his beloved daughter, but I beg your patience once again, as I have a little more to say now at the close of our meal. Lady Margaretha was but a child when she lost her mother, and though she might have suffered much from such an early separation, she was blessed with the affection and care of so many in this house. Chief among them, she had the good fortune to be guided by one young in years but wise beyond her age. Baroness von Hatzfeld."

As applause echoed in the hall, I shot Belinda a look of surprise, wondering at this unusual distinction, but she did not seem to notice. She stood, offering the room a timid smile.

"Margaretha, you have always loved Mistress Hatzfeld as a friend." Father stepped behind me, moving to Belinda's side and holding out an open hand to her. "Now I hope you will love her as a mother."

Mother? The word was lead in my brain. I couldn't swallow, couldn't blink as Belinda lifted her hand and placed it in Father's. A ringing started in my ears, growing louder when Father pressed a kiss to her knuckles. It drowned out the cheers of the servants, consuming all sound. Even the flames flickering in the candelabras went dim, draining the room of color until it turned a flat gray.

"Nothing will give me greater honor than to call myself your wife," Belinda said to Father, with her head demurely bowed.

What was this? Though she'd never confessed it, I thought her in love with Samuel. And now she was marrying Father? Her shifts for power had been a mild annoyance in a lovable friend, but this was too much. When had she managed to win over Father? How? With the very same tactics she'd been teaching me?

Father raised her chin with his finger and set his arm around her waist, facing her toward the string of servants approaching the table to offer congratulations and deep bows to their master and future mistress. I hardly noticed who passed or whose hand I took as, one by one, the household filed through to offer me congratulations. My gaze remained there on my father's arm wrapped tightly around my lady-in-waiting. My future mother.

I couldn't stay in the room.

As I pushed forward to leave, Carrera suddenly took my hand, holding me fast. "*Felicidades*, Countess. What a blessed event."

"Yes, thank you." I twisted out of his grasp and found my way to Belinda.

"This is quite a surprise," I said. "I offer my congratulations." My words felt as rigid as the hand I held out toward her.

She ignored my hand and pulled me into an embrace, but I kept my arms stiff at my sides.

"Thank you, Margaretha. I wish I could have told you earlier. It was never . . . I didn't want . . ." She sighed and finished with, "I will do my best to be a good and loving mother to you."

Was that all? The only explanation I was to be given?

Wriggling free of her, I moved to Father and wrapped my arms around his neck. "Sincerest wishes for your joy and happiness, Father," I whispered, swallowing back the hitch in my voice. An idle tear slipped from my eye, and I rubbed it out against his velvet doublet, breathing in the sweet scent of his pomander and letting myself lean into his strength one last time before pulling away. "I am fatigued and must rest before my journey. Please excuse me."

"Of course." He placed a kiss on my head, and I mustered a smile before turning and fleeing.

Friedrich intercepted me by the doors, concern painted plainly on his face. Unable to trust myself to speak with my emotions so close, I tried stepping past him, but he moved in front of me, blocking my way.

"Margaretha, how are you faring?"

I turned away, concealing the unshed tears gathering in my eyes as I rubbed the irritating itch of my nose. "Fine." My hand paused when I caught the dark smile on Carrera's face from across the room, his eyes watching Friedrich with frightening diligence.

"I must speak with you, please," Friedrich begged. "Tonight. Alone."

"How would I manage that?" I shifted to face him.

"Meet me in the courtyard when the house is still."

I shook my head. "Friedrich, that's unwise. I doubt I could even get away. It's my last night with Belinda, and I'm certain she'll wish . . ." My voice trailed when I glanced up to the dais to see her standing there, all smiles, beside my father. Anger surged inside me. I owed her nothing.

"Yes." I turned back to Friedrich. "Yes, I'll be there."

CHAPTER 23

Margaretha

BELINDA'S SNORES WERE SOFT BUT rhythmic. She'd slept more soundly the last few weeks, her sleep no longer disturbed by frequent soft whimpers. As I watched her, I wondered what had driven the nightmares away. Love for my father? Or was it his security? I slipped my feet out of bed, pausing when the floor creaked, but Belinda didn't stir. Still holding my breath, I padded over to the clothes press, fetching shoes and a long cloak, then giving Belinda a final glance before softly closing the chamber door behind me. The corridor floors were cold on my bare feet, but I only risked donning my shoes once I was almost out of the castle.

Outside, the wind stirred, sweeping away the crunch of dead leaves beneath my steps as I moved along the edges of the courtyard. I pulled my cloak tighter around me, leaning into the castle's shadows and bracing my back against the cold. When a hand gripped my arm, I nearly shrieked, but it was only Friedrich.

"You're here." He sounded surprised.

"I said I'd come. Why did you wish to speak with me?" I glanced around us nervously before meeting his eye, and when I did, his jaw tightened, and he stepped toward me.

"You've been crying."

I ducked my eyes. "I haven't."

"You have. Even in the dark I can see your eyes are red. It's because of Mistress Hatzfeld, isn't it?"

I didn't answer.

"Did you have no idea of their engagement before the banquet?"

"None." I shook my head. "She never gave a hint of it. Belinda was to be my one comfort in Brussels." I rubbed my nose, fighting the threatening emotion.

"Traitorous snake," he muttered.

I dropped my hand and took a breath, reminding myself of the truth. "Friedrich, that is unfair. You do not know what her life has been before now. How she craves . . . security and safe—"

He stepped into my space. "Why do you do this, Margaretha? Why do you tolerate and forgive and accommodate everyone else's wishes? What of *your* desires?" His eyes burned into mine, and he moved impossibly closer, the heat of him searing me. "What of your heart?"

The threat of tears vanished. "What do you know of my heart?" I challenged.

"That it is stubborn," he growled.

I cast my gaze aside with a huff, but he took a gentle hold of my arm, his voice turning soft. "Why won't you admit what you want?"

My gaze shot to his face, my body tensing.

Because what I wanted was impossible. Selfish. How could I even consider abandoning my brother and abandoning my very soul's redemption to stay here in Wildungen? Belinda needed me. Samuel needed me.

But I wanted Friedrich.

Though I would never confess it.

I stood my ground, matching the fire in Friedrich's eyes as the first drops of rain plinked around us, then fell faster, drumming on our heads and dripping frigid drops down our necks. When I started to shiver, he finally broke his gaze, squinting through the rain as he searched around us.

"Over there." He took my hand and led me to the same nook where we'd hidden earlier, urging me inside it first, then tucking in just as a sudden gale caught the rain and threw it sideways.

Though I watched the storm outside of the small, warm space, all my focus centered on Friedrich's fingers still clutching mine, his thumb brushing the back of my hand. The movements were tentative, skimming soft patterns across my skin. A shiver rolled up my spine. I needed to pull free. Instinct would have me withdraw from his touch, jerk back as if I'd grazed a hot stove, and yet I did not move, foolishly relishing the burn.

"Margaretha." His rough voice brought my eyes up to his, the intensity there making me pull in a quick breath. "I did not ask you here to fight with you. I needed to admit . . ."

Fear and desire swirled together as I anticipated what he would say.

"I must confess that I . . ." He ducked his gaze, the rest of his words coming out in a rush. "I have developed feelings for you. I care for you. And I'm asking you to stay."

Emotions swarmed, my stomach becoming a hive of fluttering and swooping and soaring. Then piercing little stings as reason attacked desire.

I could not give in.

With a sigh, I attempted to slip my hand from his grasp, but he wrapped his fingers tighter around mine. "Don't do this, Margaretha. Don't push me away." His whisper was fierce.

I took a deep breath of rain-stained air. "Friedrich, I don't—"

"Please stay." He released my hand and set his cool fingers on my cheek. "Stay for yourself. Stay for me."

My cloak waved as Friedrich's other hand moved beneath it, landing on my waist and sliding around my back to slowly pull me closer. I was rigid, every nerve taut with the effort to resist his pleas. To resist my selfish longing.

"Stay for me." His voice was gentle, a whisper, and when his eyes dipped to my mouth, I melted into his strength, fear and doubt and resistance all evaporating in the warm way he held me. He lowered his head and I—weak and human—tipped my chin up, lifting my face to his and relishing the way his hand splayed across my back to pull me closer to him. His touch was his soundest argument, convincing me that I should fight for this. That I should find a way to stay.

Warmth flickered in my chest, and this time I did not push it out. Instead, I rolled onto my toes, brushing my nose along Friedrich's rough jawline, then sliding my cheek against his until our lips touched. His gasp of surprise made me smile, but my smile fled the moment he took control of the kiss, his hand traveling up my back to cradle my neck. He tipped my head to the side, the angle bringing him closer as his mouth captured mine again and again. With every caress of his lips, the warmth in me grew, the heat reaching through me and seeping deeper into my core until a gentle rhythm pulsed in my heart. Friedrich wanted me to stay. He wanted me.

But would he want you if he knew the truth?

Ice blasted through me, and I pulled away from Friedrich with a sharp gasp.

"What is it?" His forehead creased with worry. "Did I—Have I offended you?"

"No, it's nothing you've done."

He silently waited for more, fear and vulnerability shaping his features. I couldn't stand to see him that way. Turning aside, I watched the leaves nodding in the rain, wrestling with whether or not to admit the guilt of my past. Was Belinda right? Had my offense made it impossible for any man to love me?

"Margaretha, what's wrong?"

"I'm only worried about . . ." I squeezed my eyes shut, the confession rolling to the front of my tongue just as Friedrich's fingers traced along my cheekbone, robbing me of my breath and my courage.

"You worry how to explain your choice to stay?" he asked.

"Yes," I agreed, gratefully taking hold of anything to delay speaking the sickening words. "How could I justify myself to Father when I'm the only one capable of saving his son?"

Friedrich looked heavenward. "After what he did to you today, do you really think your father cares about anyone but himself?"

"Friedrich, that's not fair." My tone was empty, wearied out by this old argument. "He knows how much I love Belinda. I should be happy to have her as my mother."

Friedrich's features hardened, his lips pressing into a tight line as he dug into his jerkin.

"You have no idea the kind of man he is. It's time your delusions about him end." He handed me a worn, faded paper. "Read this."

Furrowing my brows, I unfolded the paper and leaned it toward the haze of moonlight outside the nook. It was a letter of some kind, written in elegant French script. I read it quietly to myself.

> *Dearest Lord Philip,*
>
> *I find myself at your mercy once more. My neighbors, whose eyes were once merely suspicious, now look upon me with unfettered hatred after the illness of your child. It would seem that you, too, have come to doubt my innocence, if rumors prove true. Let me defend my name, swearing by all that is righteous that I have prayed the Lord's blessings on you and your family. You well know how tirelessly I worked to save your wife and baby, God rest their souls, and I did the same for your sweet little one, using all my skills of healing against her ague. I didn't even leave her bedside until the worst of her fever had passed, and only then with strictest instructions for her care. I have never—*

My pace slowed as I took in the next words.

> *—consorted with the devil. I have never cursed your family. I do not know where the lies began, but I deny them vehemently. I beg you would publicly speak out against these rumors, lest the*

paranoia of the villagers leads them to violence. I serve God, and I loyally serve you, a most honorable count.

Ever your friend and servant,
Lady Gertraud

There was a pounding in my ears as I looked up at Friedrich. "What is this? What does this mean?"

"It's the evidence I suspected, isn't it? It proves your father is not the man you thought he was, that he let the people murder the town healer over naught but rumors. She was innocent, but he did nothing to save her, and I plan to confront him with his treachery."

"But this letter. Where did you get it?" I demanded, shaking the paper at him.

He looked down at his hands. "She gave it to me, telling me to deliver it to the count at the mines. I waded half a day through snow, but by the time the count had read the letter and tossed it to the ground, the townspeople had already burned"—his last words were a whisper—"my mother."

When his eyes met mine, all that he'd said came together in one awful moment of understanding. Despair plunged down into my gut as heavy as a fist to the stomach. "But you said . . . you told me your mother died of the plague."

He cocked his head, confused. "I only meant that she died at the time of the plague, a victim to it, though not in the way you have imagined."

"But . . . what of . . ." It couldn't be true. And yet it had to be. Friedrich's past, his years alone, his hatred of nobles—and of my father in particular. It all fit.

My mind returned to the awful scene, to the woman who'd burned because of my lies. Eyes pricking with pain, I brushed my hand over my nose. "The healer had a child," I whispered, looking down at the paper in my hands. "You're the healer's child. I didn't know. God, forgive me, I didn't know."

I shook my head, pushing the letter into Friedrich's chest. "This was folly to think I could remain here. I must go to Brussels, now more than ever."

Shoving past him, I raced into the storm. Friedrich chased after me, catching me by the elbow and spinning me around to face him.

"What does any of this have to do with Brussels?" he asked, the rain streaming down his face. "Do you think banishing yourself will somehow make up for your father's doing? He bears the shame, not you. The consequence is all his."

"*I* did this, Friedrich." I huffed. "*I* told the lies that got your mother killed. My father is innocent." Warm tears mingled with the cold rain on my cheeks while I watched emotions of confusion and doubt play over Friedrich's face.

"You needn't . . . lie for your father." His voice was slow, uncertain.

"I speak the truth." I flicked a hand over my wet cheek.

"But you'd have no reason to. What could you possibly gai—"

"I lied to protect another. I never could have foreseen such a consequence. I didn't know the town was already against your mother, but it was my words that led to her death, and I will forever burn with the guilt of it." I flattened my palm against my heart. Whatever warmth had been trying to penetrate it had already drained away.

A long, wintry silence passed as I watched Friedrich's doubt shifting, his eyes growing cold and his back straightening. "If this is true," he finally spoke, "then maybe you're right to go to Brussels."

I bit my lip, nodding as I tipped my head back, blinking against the rain.

His voice was bitter when he added, "Since you come by deception naturally, I have no doubt of your success at court."

His words were the last shock of ice, the final freeze of my already chilled heart.

"Goodbye, Countess." He gave a low bow, then paced across the courtyard to the castle gates.

As I watched him leave, three words turned around in my mind like thread on a spinning wheel.

Belinda was right. Belinda was right. Belinda was right.

CHAPTER 24

Friedrich

THE RAIN DRIPPED FROM MY hair, rolling down my forehead before I wiped it away with the back of my hand. The wet cold was a relief, an antidote to the anger burning through me as I relived the countess's words. It had been she all along, and not her father, who was responsible for my mother's death. And all her accusations were lies! She'd admitted as much, knew full well it was her deceit that had killed my mother.

But the count was not blameless.

Kicking a rock down the muddy hill, I remembered the easy way he had discarded my mother's letter, dropping it in a crumpled heap on the ground. He could have saved her if he'd cared enough. Or did he truly believe her to be a witch? She'd had a gift with healing, or so Ernst told me. Most considered it to be from God, but when the plague ravaged the town, people needed something to blame. Accusing the healer of consorting with the devil was too easy, but what if the count believed the rumors? What if he thought my mother's death would save his people from the awful sickness?

Then the blame sat squarely on the countess.

Mud splashed over my hose as I tromped down the hill. A niggling in my mind whispered that she had been but a child, one who'd lost her mother and sister, but there was a pattern with her. She'd admitted to lying to protect another, just as she'd admitted to using me for Samuel's sake. Had she learned nothing from my mother's death?

I pulled to a halt, rain soaking my shirt and jerkin. Margaretha's face filled my mind, her blue eyes pooling with tears, rain streaming down her cheeks. What had I done? What should I do? My heart was bloodied, torn by the sharp fangs of painful, lonely memories, of years without my mother. But was it fair to blame a child?

Squatting down, I rested my head in my hands, taking deep breaths to calm the confusion and turmoil and ache. My soul was not peaceful, not forgiving, but I couldn't think of the countess without remorse. It wasn't right to send her away with such cruel words. Where was I even going, storming from the castle in the dead of the night through the pouring rain?

Cold drops slipped off my nose and eyelashes as I took a few more breaths and forced myself to stand. The walk back to the castle was not long. Hopefully it would give me the time I needed to form the words I should say to the countess. Not words of forgiveness. Not a request that she stay. But something to soften the brutality of my last goodbye. If I could find her. She'd probably gone inside already, but I couldn't let her leave like this.

Tucking into the castle gates, my arm was immediately seized in a strong grip while a hand covered my mouth. I twisted, blinking against the rain at Ulrich as he mouthed, "Soldiers." Behind him a pair of horses stood in the courtyard. When had those arrived? They would have had to pass me up the hill. Was I so lost in my thoughts to have been blind to them?

Ulrich slowly lowered his hand from my mouth. "You must leave," he whispered. "Carrera's in the kennels searchin' through your things. He's out for blood."

"I can't go until I've spoken with the countess."

Ulrich's grip squeezed my arm. "He wants you dead, man. You don't have time for goodbyes."

As if proving Ulrich's point, voices sounded from the kennels, the windows dancing with torchlight as something crashed inside.

"Hurry. Leave."

But where would I go? How could I ever speak with Margaretha? "Ulrich, tell the countess—"

"Go!"

Footsteps grew louder, men's voices moving to the entrance of the kennels, and I turned from the castle and ran, unsure if I would ever see Countess Margaretha again.

CHAPTER 25

Margaretha

COUDENBERG PALACE WAS EVEN MORE imposing from the inner courtyard than it had appeared when we'd first spotted it, perched like a giant vulture atop a massive sloping park. My neck ached just trying to see all the way to the top of the *Aula Magna*—the great hall where Elizabeth had spent her time dining at banquets and dancing with courtiers. There were other places I recognized from Elizabeth's letters: the Senne River snaking through the heart of the walled city; the *Warande,* with its wooded leisure paths and free-roaming deer; the gallery Queen Mary had been building during Elizabeth's service, now complete and filled with statues of regal men I was too ignorant to name.

"How will we find our way to breakfast in that pompous hut?" Ilsa eyed the polygonal towers flanking the Aula Magna, massaging her backside with both hands. Her loose tongue would take some getting used to after years of Belinda's careful composure.

"It will feel like home soon enough," I said, but didn't believe it myself. Home was days away, in the heart of the lush green forests and familiar little shops. It was with Father and Belinda. And Friedrich.

I shut my eyes against the thought, hoping to close out the memory of Friedrich as I closed out the vibrant courtyard. I would not allow myself to think of him again.

Dismounting, I forced my attention on the courtyard, abuzz with the rough voices of men and the clattering of hooves and coach wheels bumping over cobblestone. Above the din, a sharp, staccato jingle sounded as a tall woman with sunken cheeks and sharp ears walked straight toward me. Tied to the girdle belt round her waist was a large silver ring bearing an impressive array of keys.

The woman clipped to a stop in front of me. "*Comtess de Waldeck?*"

"Yes."

"*Très bon.* I am Dame de la Thamise et la Thieuloye, mistress of the *filles d'honneur*. I am to introduce you to the queen. You and your maid follow me; your menservants can follow my husband to deposit your things." She indicated a man standing beside an arch-covered walkway, then glanced at my small retinue of servants and horses and raised an eyebrow. "Is this all?"

I nodded.

"Hmm." Dame Thieuloye turned on her heel and walked away without waiting to see if I followed.

Ilsa and I looked at each other, then quickly fell in line behind her, with me translating for Ilsa everything Thieuloye had said. The woman moved expertly through the bustle, pausing to avoid a pile of collapsing trunks or quickening her pace to cross ahead of an oncoming coach, all while keeping her sights straight ahead. We bungled along behind but managed to keep pace with her all the way to the entrance of the Aula Magna. Two separate staircases faced opposite each other, each leading to the large arched doorway adorned with high spikes in a dated architectural style that reminded me of my home, though on a much grander scale.

Thieuloye led us up the stairs and through the arch before opening a door to let us into the largest room I'd ever seen. The ceilings soared like a cathedral's. Windows slashed the walls, stretching up to reach impossible heights and lighting the checkered tile floor with slices of hot sun. Peppered between the windows were no fewer than ten man-sized fireplaces, the chimneys of which I'd seen peeking out amongst the many spires of the impressive great hall.

"This is the Aula Magna." Thieuloye leaned against the open door. "Here is where you will eat your meals when you are not attending to the queen regent. During festivals and banquets, you will sit with her on the dais." She pointed to the high tables on the platform, then waved us toward her. "We haven't time to dawdle."

We stepped into the bright courtyard again, trailing after Thieuloye's quick steps back to the building bottomed with the open corridor of arches. She ducked into the shade of the arched walkway, her jangling keys echoing against the stony walls as she kept a swift pace down the arcade. "Behind and to your left is the passageway for the chapel. This first floor is where you will bathe and relieve yourself. We use latrines here, *not* chamber pots. Do not mistake the ornamental vases in your room as such."

Ilsa snickered when I explained it all in German.

At the end of the arcade, Thieuloye passed through a narrow doorway at the base of a turret. We followed her up a circular set of stairs to the second floor and down another long corridor lined with doors. I hardly had time to admire the opulent tapestries or the rugs lining the floors before she stepped inside a room to her right, sunlight streaming into the hall as she held the door for us to enter.

The room was beautiful, paneled in deep ebony and draped with alternating crimson and gold curtains, but nothing was so fine as the view from the two large windows on the opposite wall. An empty jade lawn sloped down into the great park of the Warande, which was scattered with ponds and crisscrossed with lush hedge mazes. In the distance, buried between houses and roofs, the Senne was almost invisible, save for one or two glints of sunlight winking from its smooth surface.

"That is where you will sleep." Dame Thieuloye called my attention from the windows and toward one of many modest, velvet-covered beds. "And when your trunks arrive, what clothes you have will be kept in here." She opened a narrow press door. "Most of your clothing will be provided to you by the queen. She will expect your appearance to be above reproach, as when you are part of her retinue, you represent the majesty of the empire."

I nodded. "I am most eager to please the qu—"

"We have strict rules of decorum here, and I expect you to keep them," Thieuloye continued. "You will arise at dawn for breakfast in these quarters. Once you are dressed, you will attend morning mass, after which you will either be at the queen's disposal—accompanying her on matters of state—or using your unoccupied time for education and study. Your tutors and lessons are gifts from the queen. Do not squander them."

"No, mistress," I answered.

"Dinner is served midmorning, and then, weather and obligations permitting, the queen will take the court hunting. You have brought your own horse and page for the hunt?" she asked.

"Yes."

"Good. After seven o'clock supper, you will be allowed a few hours in the evenings for socializing with your fellow noblemen and women. You will not pair off. You will not separate yourselves from the group. You will not leave the room." She gave me a direct and lengthy stare despite my eager nod.

"At nine, you will return here with the other ladies and prepare for bed. During this time, all rooms, alcoves, and hidden corners will be subjected to a thorough search. Anyone found outside this room will be dismissed from the queen's service and sent home. At ten, this door is locked, and I am the only one with the key." She patted the bulk of metal at her side just as my father's servants waddled into the room bearing my trunks.

"Set them here," Thieuloye ordered the men, then turned to me. "You have a few minutes to change your clothing and prepare yourself after your journey before I take you to meet the queen."

We stood in awkward silence while the men finished depositing the trunks. When they left the room, I expected Thieuloye to follow, allowing me privacy to dress, but she stood just as she was, eying me without embarrassment.

I took a deep breath. "Ilsa, my things."

Ilsa went to the trunk and pulled out the dress I'd planned to wear when meeting the queen. Though simply made, the deep blue was a perfect complement to my light features.

Ilsa laid the gown on the bed before unlacing the sleeves and bodice of my mud-splattered travel clothes. She cinched me into the new gown and reset the plaits of my hair with impressive speed, considering the nagging of Thieuloye's impatient foot tapping against the tiled floor.

With the final pin in my hair, I faced the austere mistress. "I am ready."

"You"—she pointed to Ilsa—"remain."

Ilsa looked to me for understanding, and I motioned her to stay.

"Comtess, come with me."

Giving Ilsa a nervous glance, I stepped into the hall, moving only a short distance to the center of the second floor, where we came upon a set of doors large enough that I suspected it was another dining hall. One of the two porters standing guard smiled at me, but I was focused on following Thieuloye into the room when she suddenly rounded on me.

"You will bow when you meet the queen, and keep your head lowered until she invites you to stand," she whispered.

"These are the queen's chambers?" I whispered back, but Thieuloye didn't answer.

My stomach tightened as I crossed the room, anticipating a grandmotherly woman cushioned atop a sumptuous, canopied bed. I imagined her stroking an ugly lap dog while scores of ladies sat about, but I was wrong. Though the room was ornate, it did not seem to be a bedchamber at all. In the center sat a large wooden desk scattered with papers and broken quills and surrounded by several plush chairs. There were ladies in attendance, but only eleven. Nothing near the twenty-six I'd heard the English courts boasted. The older women sat in chairs while the younger ones, my fellow ladies-of-honor, were grouped to the right of the chamber entrance, singing a chanson to the accompaniment of a lute. The only piece that remained true to my imagination was the dog, though instead of one, there were two, and each was so massive that its back stood as tall as the arms of the queen's chair. She petted one's head as she listened to the music, never turning her eyes even a degree or two to see the people who'd just entered her chamber.

Thieuloye waited, unmoving, beside the chamber door until the ladies finished their singing and the older women applauded gently. We stepped forward, finally drawing the eye of Queen Mary, and I mimicked Thieuloye's deep curtsy as the soft murmurs and rustling skirts indicated the ladies-of-honor were resuming their positions beside the queen.

"You may rise," a deep voice spoke.

I straightened, facing the queen for the first time. Though she was older, her face was hard and masculine. She had a protruding jaw and large, heavy-lidded eyes that made her look fierce and tired all at the same time.

"Your Highness, I present to you Comtess Margaretha de Waldeck, daughter of Philip IV, Comte de Waldeck. She is your newest lady-of-honor."

The queen stood and approached, her dogs shadowing her as she walked in a circle around me. "Very good," she murmured. "The rumors of your beauty were not exaggerated."

My cheeks warmed. "*Je vous remercie, Votre Altesse.*"

"Your accent is good. Do you speak only German and French?"

"*Et Latine quoque,*" I answered.

Her stern mouth softened into almost a smile, but she turned before I could see it, returning to her chair and stroking one hound's head again when he plopped down beside her.

"I am aware of the personal cost of the Mühlberg battle for your family. Do not think you will find any sympathy for your brother's plight in my courts. We do not tolerate Luther's teachings here. Even owning his bible is a crime punishable by death. Do you understand?"

I hid my trembling fingers in my palms, reminding myself that her warnings were just as I expected. But I would not be deterred from saving Samuel. From fighting for my redemption. "Yes, Your Grace."

The queen did not speak again. In the uncomfortable silence, only the pop of fabric sounded as the ladies-of-honor stabbed their needles into their sewing. I pretended to study the woodwork around the ceiling just to avoid the penetrating gaze of this forbidding woman. When she finally spoke again, it was with one side of her mouth raised into what I could only assume was a kind of smile.

"I'm grateful you have chosen to accept my invitation. You seem intelligent and well-mannered. Your beauty is quite extraordinary. I think we shall have no trouble finding you a husband. Perhaps one of our Netherlander noblemen will suit."

Beside the queen, several of the younger ladies looked up from their needlework for the first time, scanning my clothes, my hair, and my face. A few narrowed their eyes and lifted their heads higher, studying me over raised noses.

Belinda had prepared me for their assessments. Fighting down my urge for harmony and humility, I straightened my shoulders to a perfect line and raised my chin, unflinchingly meeting each of their gazes. When I turned my attention back to the queen, I had my sweetest smile ready. "I want nothing more than to honor Your Highness with the gifts God has bestowed upon me, praying you may find my service ever valuable."

I finished with a small curtsy, and when I stood, the queen's mouth was curved upward, her eyes approving.

"Then let us proceed with the Oath of Allegiance."

An older, elegant woman rose from her seat beside the queen. "Repeat what I say, inserting your name," she instructed, then began to recite the oath.

"I, Comtess Margaretha de Waldeck," I repeated, "do promise and swear, by God and His Holy Gospels, that to my rightful queen—Mary, by the Grace of God, Queen of Hungary and of Bohemia, governor of the Netherlands for His Imperial and Catholic Majesty, and his lieutenant—I always shall be true and faithful. I shall also with my life and blood agree to live in accordance with the fundamental laws of the realm, which I, in all their parts, shall obey and follow. This I pledge on my honor and conscience to do, so truly help me God to life and spirit."

And so, I was bound.

Part Two: *March 1549*
Brussels, Habsburg Netherlands, Holy Roman Empire

CHAPTER 26

Margaretha

I shifted on the bench, angling myself to peek between the trio of men standing around me. Across the room, Count Egmont was still speaking with that wretch, Lady Jakelina.

"But, Comtess, weren't you frightened of drowning?" Baron Pempflinger asked me. "I'm sure I should be."

I turned my attention from the count to the fluffy-mustached baron, masking my irritation behind a smile. "I doubt that. With many a lady whispering of your valor on the battlefield, I'm certain you're incapable of fear."

He straightened himself taller and puffed out his chest.

Not to be outdone, Sir Lamberg stepped closer, commanding my attention and cutting off my view of Egmont.

"*I* should have enjoyed it," he said. "In fact, I've boated downriver alone many times. At night."

The other two men exchanged skeptical glances, but I answered with an arched smile.

"Ah, Sir Lamberg is of my way of thinking. Boating downriver is far more exciting in the dark." Glancing away from Lamberg's surprised face, I scooted to the right, regaining my slotted view of the count. Though still in conversation with Lady Wretch, his sights strayed from her, moving across the room in my direction. But could he even see me through the assemblage of buffoons standing before me?

"Lord Krell." I reached my hands out to capture the massive paw of the third, quieter man in the trio. "You are forgotten on this side of the party. Come. Stand over here where I can better hear you." I pulled him closer to me, moving him to my left until I had a perfectly clear view of the count. Egmont glanced over then, his eyes meeting mine for the first time that evening, and I smiled and dropped my gaze to affect embarrassment at being caught watching him. If Belinda could see me now, I suspect she would be proud. The subtleties of flirtation had taken a keen eye and a concerted effort to master, but over the last eighteen months I had made that effort, studying the other courtiers and putting into practice all Belinda had taught me.

Squeezing Krell's hand, I asked, "That's much better now, isn't it?"

He reddened and nodded.

"And what do you have to say about my daring boat ride?" I asked him.

"I, uh . . . that is, if your ladyship is . . . I wouldn't presume, uh—"

"I've no doubt you're an excellent oarsman. Should you like to take me on your boat sometime?" I glanced back toward the count but found only Lady Wretch picking up her needlepoint frame to pierce away her solitary evening. Where had Egmont gone? My eyes scanned the room until they landed on the count sitting down at the chess table. He nodded a bow, and I answered with a broad smile before realizing Krell was still stammering through some kind of invitation to join him at boating.

"You are too gracious. I should enjoy that immensely. Would you gentlemen please excuse me?"

The men spoke over one another—granting me leave and thanking me for my time or expressing hopes to have our conversation again repeated—while they stepped back to let me pass with my wide, swishing skirts.

Count Egmont watched me bid the men farewell, but when I moved toward him with singular focus, he dropped his sights and bowed his head over the chess board, resting his fists against his cheekbones.

I set my hands on the back of the chair opposite him, an excited smile hovering on my lips. "Here you are again. You haven't tired of defeat?"

"I'm persistent," he answered without looking up.

Pulling back the chair, I took a seat and moved my black piece. "So am I."

I folded my hands in my lap, watching the top of his bowed head with hopes that he might speak first this time, but he remained silent.

"How is Lady Wr—Jakelina?" I coughed to cover my near blunder.

"She is well." He put his white pawn into play. "And how is your passel of admirers?"

I moved another pawn. "Take care, Egmont, or you'll raise my hopes that you harbor jealousies."

He met my eye, a hint of a smile playing on his lips before he set out his piece. "Where is the queen this evening?"

"Preparing for her brother's arrival on the morrow." I answered his move with another hasty advance of a pawn. "I'd hoped to meet him when he was last in Brussels, but he was too ill with the gout." The ache of remembered disappointment smarted as I recalled the kaiser's last visit. Dalwigk had been wrong about the prisoners; Samuel had not come.

"He is quite regal." Egmont's observation returned me to our conversation.

"So I've heard. His son is said to be regal too." Leaning over the table, I bent my head to be on a level with his own and added in a whisper, "But rumors speak to the queen developing a nervous spasm whenever her councilors talk of Prince Felipe's arrival. As the queen's favorite adviser, I should think you able to confirm such reports."

The count lifted his hand to take up a piece, but withdrew it, tucking his fist with the other under his chin. "I might," he answered, still studying the board. Deciding on a piece, he made his move, capturing my pawn. His smile was self-satisfied.

"Well done." I moved my black rook to capture his pawn before answering his smile with a smug one of my own. We watched each other for a moment, each waiting for the other to concede defeat, but he finally broke into a chuckle, shaking his head.

"Very well, I'll admit that, in private councils, Queen Mary has expressed concern regarding Prince Felipe. I suspect she feels a great deal of pressure, maintaining the dignity of the Habsburg family with a nephew reported to be haughty and distrustful of his foreign councilors." He moved another piece on the board. "The Habsburgs may rule the Netherlands, but they do it with the support and input of our noble families. Should the prince come here and disregard his Netherlander councilmen, he will upset a delicate truce, and the queen is wise enough to know it. I worry her nephew, the prince, is not."

"Have you met Prince Felipe? Is he everything he's rumored to be?"

"Your turn." Egmont nodded to the chess board. "No, I haven't met the prince yet. I suppose we shall each have the chance to form our opinions of him tomorrow."

Tomorrow. The day I'd see Samuel again. He would surely be with the kaiser this time, and I could hardly heel my excitement. "Perhaps once we've formed our opinions, we can meet to discuss them. At another round of che—" A page entering the room behind Egmont caught my attention. His movement was fluid, his build and dark hair strikingly familiar.

"Friedrich?" I whispered.

The count turned to look behind himself. "Who?"

Squinting to study the page more closely, I realized he couldn't be Friedrich. Too short. Nose too pointed.

"It's no one." I smiled at the count but couldn't stop myself from giving the page another studious glance before returning to our match. "Can I count on you for another game of chess on the morrow?"

His cheek tucked with the hint of a smile. "I am at your service, my lady."

CHAPTER 27

Margaretha

THE LADIES-OF-HONOR DASHED ACROSS THE courtyard with hands over heads, shielding themselves from the rain as they made their way to the waiting coaches. I trotted along behind, wrestling down the nerves and excitement that had kept me awake half the night. For the first time in years, I was going to see Samuel.

Pressing into the coach, I smashed down Lady Jakelina's gown to make a seat for myself.

"Margaretha, you're pinching my leg," she complained.

"Then it will pair nicely with your nose," I snapped, earning dark glares from the other ladies.

Mistress Helena pursed her mouth. "You'll not impress the prince with your saucy talk."

"Do you think he'll be handsome?" Lady Anna asked, pinching her rounded cheeks for color.

"Not if he looks anything like his aunt," Mistress Dorthea muttered.

Helena elbowed her in the ribs. "You cannot speak of the queen that way."

The coach lurched forward, and we clattered over cobblestone on a steady decline toward the city's streets before twisting our way through town. With the window sashes pulled, every breath of air became saturated with the stink of damp slippers, yet no one seemed eager to brave the rain when the coach finally rolled to a stop at the city gates. We waited, stone still, listening for any happenings outside. Mostly we heard only rain tapping on the roof or horses' hooves shuffling over cobblestones. Occasionally a man's voice carried on the wind, but the words were diluted in the air until they were only sound.

A sturdy breeze raced by, slapping the window sashes against the coach and affording me a flashing view of men hunched with their backs to the rain. Count Egmont was among them, looking handsome perched atop his steed. He was a good and kind man, blessedly. The sort of man I felt certain would speak for Samuel, once I'd secured his proposal. Thus far I'd only procured his commitment for another game of chess after supper. Or had I? I couldn't remember anything after the shock of seeing that page boy.

The sudden burst of trumpets made us all jump.

"They come!" someone yelled. A groom opened our door, and we poured out of the coach, blinking against the gray daylight. The cool air made my teeth chatter as I followed the other ladies toward the shelter of the queen's canopy. We tucked in behind the ladies-in-waiting, no one seeming to mind the close quarters for the warmth it provided.

A surprising number of spectators had turned out, enduring the wet weather in their eagerness to greet their sovereign. Subjects of all ages stood on the sides of the street with excited smiles while they hid under capes and blankets. In front of them, noblemen astride their horses split into two opposing rows, as though pitted in combat. I scanned their faces until my eyes met with the steady blue gaze of Count Egmont. He looked away but didn't repress the smile that came to his lips. I smiled too, glancing down at my hands before looking back to find him watching me again. This time he didn't turn away, and we held each other's gazes.

A movement at the gate stole my attention as two men on white steeds rode in, each bearing the unmistakable yellow flag emblazoned with a double-headed eagle of pure black, the imperial banner of Kaiser Karl V. And just behind them came the royal father and son. The son, dressed from shoulder to toe in satin and velvet of blood-red scarlet, sat atop an impressive battle charger, staring straight ahead and showing interest in no one. He was everything I expected him to be, save for his looks, which were striking. His wide, dark eyes were framed by even darker lashes that matched his neatly trimmed beard and the black curls peeking out from under his cap. The kaiser shared his son's fine dress and imposing steed, though where one was youthful and handsome, the other was graying and haggard. His body rocked with each clop of his horse's hooves, and his eyes matched his sister's for their heavy lids.

Catching sight of Queen Mary, the kaiser raised his hand, signaling the train behind him to halt. I lifted myself onto my toes, peering around the royals to spot my brother, but there were only courtiers and servants as far back as I could see.

With the men and horses now at a standstill, the young prince looked around himself for the first time, his eyes going straight to the queen's retinue to study the faces of the women in his aunt's service. When his gaze came to me, he leaned forward in his saddle, resting his forearms across his pommel and giving me a rakish grin. I returned his smile but briefly, shifting my eyes back to his father and hoping my neglect would discourage the prince. I didn't need a decidedly Catholic prince ruining my hopes with Egmont.

The kaiser crossed his arms over his left knee, resting while the queen went forward to greet him. She clasped his hand, and though she spoke quietly, her words carried in the breeze. "You are not improved."

The kaiser shook his head, and Queen Mary set her hand on his face, caressing his bearded cheek with her thumb.

"Will you ride with us?" The kaiser's voice was deep and stronger than I expected from one so frail.

"Gladly." Mary ordered her horse.

While we waited, I glanced at Egmont, hoping to cast him a smile, but his stern features were intently pointed in another direction. Following his gaze, I found the prince still staring unabashedly at me. He gave me a quick wink, then shifted his attention to the queen before I had the chance to put him off with my disapproving glare.

I let out a huff of irritation.

Queen Mary mounted her horse and took her place beside her brother. "My ladies will return to their coaches and join in the train behind us."

My irritation bled into disappointment, which left a hollow feeling in my gut. How would I ever see Samuel now?

The ladies moved in one body, catching me up in their flow so that I could only make a last desperate scan of the train of men before I was pushed into the dark depths of the coach.

The damp of the day hovered in the palace like my disappointment, and I couldn't escape either, no matter how I shifted in my place on the bench. Down the row, Anna quietly groaned and pressed her hands over her belly. "If we ate such feasts every day, I might be sick," she whispered over the performance of the queen's musicians.

"Then temper yourself next time," Helena whispered back, smoothing her skirts and painting a pleasant smile over her lips.

Anna straightened. "Prince Felipe is more handsome than I could have hoped."

"You have no reason to hope for anything when it comes to the prince," Dorthea whispered over the lutes closing out their madrigal. "He's a Habsburg. They marry for advantage, and I doubt he'll be wanting your little duchy."

I followed the ladies' gazes to the prince. He sat in a gold chair at the other side of the room, ignoring the conversation of his Dutch attendant and staring directly at me with that same rakish grin.

An awkward shyness came over me that I'd not had since my days in Wildungen.

Anna sniffed. "You're right, Dorthea. He isn't worth troubling myself over. I hear he's nearly betrothed to Queen Mary of England anyway." Anna cast me a sideways glance, no doubt intending to upset me had I set my cap on the prince, but I paid her no heed. My sights were on a different target.

Egmont leaned against the wall with his arms folded across his chest while he watched the prince watching me. The muscle in Egmont's jaw tightened, and I bent my head to conceal a smile, relishing his jealousy. I'd succeeded in winning at least a small bit of his admiration. Now to encourage it . . .

The courtiers applauded at the close of the madrigal, and I excused myself from the ladies, sweeping up my skirts and sitting at the empty chess table with my back to the prince. When Egmont met my eye, I used my foot to push out the chair opposite me. His scowl lifted, and he shrugged away from the wall, making his way over to sit at my table.

"You are right," I said when he took his seat. "You are persistent."

He cast me a small smile that disappeared when he glanced behind me. I turned to find the prince watching us.

"And what of it?" I said, moving my chess piece.

He harrumphed and moved a piece in return. We progressed in silence, with Egmont more reserved than usual as we played.

"Are you fatigued after your long ride in the rain?" I asked.

"So it would seem. I find myself out of sorts this evening." He moved his rook, then placed his fist beside the chessboard.

I gently covered his hand with mine. "Then I hope you'll let me buoy your spirits." I rubbed my thumb over his fingers until he uncurled his fist, opening his hand enough to let me caress his palm. But when footsteps sounded behind me, he wrenched his hand away to conceal it beneath the table.

A smear of bright scarlet moved in my periphery, and Prince Felipe of Spain stepped into view. Beside him, his short attendant gave us a low bow. "Pardon the interruption, but the prince expressed a wish to play against the lady."

"Oh, I don't think—" I began, but the attendant hushed me with wide eyes, as if anticipating my refusal and warning me against it.

I turned to Egmont, my eyes pleading with him to stay, but his countenance was already an apology. He rose from his chair, giving the prince a curt bow before leaving.

The prince took Egmont's place, leaning back in the chair with casual ease as he moved his knight. "What is the name of this woman I am so fortunate to play against?"

My Latin was not as strong as my French. I studied the board, looking for my next move while I interpreted what he'd said. "Comitissa Margaretha de Waldeck."

"Waldeck? That is in the German lands, yes? I had the chance to visit Augsburg when my father defeated the German rebellion. It is beautiful country. The hunting there is excellent."

He captured my rook with his bishop.

"I wouldn't know. I have no interest in hunting." I took a defenseless pawn.

"Really? Yet my aunt tells me you are quite a horsewoman. Seems a waste of skill to not apply it to the hunt."

I held my tongue, conveying my disinterest through silence while we exchanged a volley of predictable moves.

"Perhaps you will let me be your teacher," he said, breaking the quiet. "I am no novice in the art of the chase." His black knight slid across the board toward my key players, and I felt his eyes rest on my face. He was baiting me.

"Yes, I'm certain you've made many conquests of both beast and man," I answered, cutting straight through his allusions as I put my bishop in play.

"And a woman or two." He winked at me before capturing my other rook.

"It's the men I'm more particularly interested in," I persisted. "Most especially those you took in Mühlberg. As they are fellow Germans, I'm concerned for their wellbeing."

He didn't respond, and we moved through another series of plays as his pieces took gradual control of the board.

"You may discover the welfare of your friends next week." He moved his king close to my queen. Far too close. I studied the board, trying to understand the advantage of such a move. "I believe they'll be included in the parade of the Ommegang."

"They'll be in the procession?" The same nervousness from this morning sped through my blood. I wasn't certain why the city would allow the inclusion of known rebels of the kaiser but was glad for it. For the chance to see Samuel.

"Your move," the prince prompted. My thoughts were too muddled for the game now. I pulled the queen back out of instinct.

The prince smiled. "Since you are so interested in seeing the German nobles, I will ensure you a seat beside me on the platform. You'll have a better view of them there."

I didn't know what to say. My gratitude weighed heavy against a sense of foreboding, but I nodded my appreciation.

"Checkmate." The prince stood, his attendant rising in tandem. "Until next week, *mea columba*." He walked away as I studied the board, searching for an exit from the square prison in which he'd bound my king.

CHAPTER 28

Margaretha

THE GRAND PLACE WAS AWASH in color. Jagged buildings with posts and knobs spiraling to heaven were striped with scarlet banners and studded with guild flags wafting in the June breeze. Row upon row of formerly blank and black windows were now filled with vibrant plumed hats and peeking, eager faces.

Our procession took a path around the square, the royals and their retinues leading the way with all the pomp and flair of their station. Sitting taller and nobler than when he'd arrived in Brussels, the kaiser rode atop his steed, accompanied not only by the members of his court, but also by his hounds, his bulldog, and his falcons—the latter poised on the arms of elegant ladies wearing matching livery.

Reaching the *Maison du Roi*, our three sovereigns dismounted amidst the fanfare of trumpets and the cheers of subjects packed around the square. They climbed a short set of steps onto a canopied platform draped entirely in red velvet, taking the few seats appointed for the higher nobility. A flurry of servants approached their retinues, helping the ladies dismount and ushering us up the steps in a dizzying but efficient manner. I stood on my tiptoes to catch the prince's notice, hoping he really intended to provide me with a seat, but a smartly dressed page was already cramming us into the tight spaces on the floor surrounding Queen Mary's chair.

"Mistress Schirstet, you sit here, *s'il vous plaît*. Mistress de Waldeck, over here," he directed.

I started lowering myself to the cushion when the smooth voice of Prince Felipe arrested my movement.

"The *comitissa* will be sitting beside me." He extended a hand down to me, and I took it gratefully, allowing him to pull me up off the cushion.

As we picked our way with careful footing through the crush of bodies surrounding the royal chairs, several of my sisters-of-honor gave me glares capable of freezing the Senne. Some whispered to each other behind their hands, but I forced myself to ignore their prattle and focus on the prince. He did not immediately release me, keeping hold of my hand as he helped me into my seat. Using the excuse of straightening my skirts, I pulled it away. One corner of his mouth quirked upward, but he took his seat beside me, saying nothing.

Despite not forgiving him for driving Egmont away the other night, I did need to acknowledge my gratitude for the softer seat and better view he'd provided. "*Gratias tibi ago.* I did not think you'd remember to save me a place."

"How could I forget a promise to such a beautiful woman?"

I ducked my head and smiled as I knew I ought.

Cheers from the multitude sounded as men wielding massive flags marched into the square, their footsteps pounding in time to the beat of the drummers behind them. They zigzagged between one another, stepping out to form a wide circle, then tapping their flagpoles twice against the ground before spinning them in their hands and tossing them in a flowing arc to the men at their right. The drumbeats came faster, and the twists and soars and pounding of the flagpoles only fueled the nervous turmoil inside me at the prospect of soon seeing Samuel.

Of a sudden, the drumming stopped, and the men and flags became statue-still, save their chests, which heaved from their vigorous efforts. The return of the crowd's applause freed the men to move, and they left the square as the next entertainment took place.

We had to clap for the crossbowmen guild, the sawyers guild, the farriers guild. We clapped for the magistrates, the soldiers, the jesters and fools, the men on stilts. At every new display, I craned my neck, searching the faces for Samuel, but was repeatedly disappointed.

"Are you always so agitated?" The prince nodded toward my bouncing knee, and I reined it steady.

"Do you know when we can expect the German nobles?"

He clapped for the departing guild but shook his head. "If you're in need of a distraction . . ." He glanced at me with a tantalizing half smile, but I was spared the burden of responding when a horrible screeching echoed in the square. Rolling toward us on the newest float was a black bear pounding the keys of a heinous instrument. Twenty ragged, sorry cats were trapped in twenty narrow cages, strings tied from their tails to a set of organ keys. The cats became the music, as every note the bear struck rang out in painful wailing from the unfortunate performers. The only sound to compete with the cats' pitiful wails was the deep belly laugh of Prince Felipe, guffawing and slapping his knee until he settled back against his chair with a sigh.

"I've been to processions and parades until I am sick of them, but that was exceptional."

I glared at him, but he looked past me. "Ah! The food."

At my right, a page held out a silver platter covered with pickled salmon, candied pine nuts, and a grape-and-melon arrangement atop mint sprigs. I waved him away, and he moved to the kaiser and his son, this time kneeling to prevent obscuring their view. The prince pulled off a glove and reached for the salmon, coming away with a small handful, but the kaiser's hand hovered over the tray while a short, bearded man whispered in his ear. A sour expression came over the kaiser's face, and he dropped his empty fist in his lap, sending the page on.

"Who is that man?" I whispered to Prince Felipe. "The one standing behind your father?"

"Vesalius, his physician."

"Andreas Vesalius? Of *De Humani Corporis Fabrica*?"

The prince twisted in his chair to face me, his eyes wide with appreciation. "You've heard of him?"

"Of his works, yes. The unorthodox dissection of human corpses certainly garners notice. And overthrowing Galen's assertion that blood circulates from the liver is rather noteworthy. Though, in truth, I still find it difficult to believe."

"You are well researched," he answered. "I'm happy to find a mind so evenly matched with an enchanting face."

"I'd be surprised to find the same of you." The words were out before I'd realized, and I instantly regretted them. "I most humbly beg your pardon, Your Grace," I said, ducking my head in submission, but my ears were attuned to every shift and creak in his chair as I sat in suspense of what he would do.

His finger touched my chin, turning my face up to his. "I'm flattered you think me handsome." He brushed his thumb over my bottom lip, then released me, and I felt a familiar heat creeping up my neck. I would not allow it. I fought back my blush with a renewed focus on Samuel and the parade.

A two-storied float rolled into the square, the upper story bearing replicas of the kaiser and prince standing proud and resolute, surrounded by billows of white fabric and Grecian columns painted like marble. They rested their fists on their hips, triumphing over a hole that dropped down to the first story, where a miserable figure lay amidst flames of fabric and plaster. In replica, the German monk Martin Luther cowered, his mouth frozen in a scream, his hand covering his eyes as he shied away from the burn of hell.

Despite my anger, I noticed the sudden shift of mood in the crowd. Some onlookers clapped more vigorously, nodding their heads in emphatic agreement with this pronouncement of Luther's fate. Others folded their arms across their chests with tight lips or stared at the ground. A third set of people clapped softly but shook their heads all the while, as if wishing to display disapproval without outright defiance. Their reactions gave me hope. Hope that, regardless of the kaiser's wars and his edicts, Protestantism could not be crushed.

Brussels was not in the kaiser's hand. The firm set of his mouth proved that he understood as much and was not at all pleased by it.

The prince seemed too caught up in his own emotions to take notice. He clapped with great vigor, actually standing as the float rolled in front of us. When he sat down again, he tipped his head toward me. "I think I see your German brethren yonder."

It required a great deal of self-restraint to keep my seat, but I leaned this way and that, hoping to catch a glimpse of the kaiser's captives. The first hint of them was a small wagon with thick metal bars supporting the roof. As it rolled closer, I saw a group of seven men inside—some standing, some sitting in hay strewn over the floor, as if the wagon housed animals instead of people.

The first figure I recognized as the Landgrave of Hesse. He did not have on the cloaks, furs, or jewels he'd worn whenever my family visited him in the past, but he wore the black round hat that I knew well. Searching past him, I scanned a few forlorn, unfamiliar faces until I spotted Samuel, slumped against the bars in the corner of the cage. If I hadn't known he'd be there, I wouldn't have recognized him. His typically neat and trim hair was now long and shaggy. His once-pointed beard clung to his gaunt cheeks and flowed to his chest, looking more like that of a biblical prophet than a German prince. He was thin and pale. And ill.

Indignation burned in my veins. "Is this how you treat your prisoners? Parade them around like animals in cages?"

An amused smile tugged at Prince Felipe's lips. "Should we offer them horses for escape?"

"Of course not, but this . . . Look at that one, there." I pointed at Samuel. "That man is ill. And thin. Are you keeping them from food? From medicine?"

"The men are given sufficient attention. Not all tolerate captivity equally. The weaker ones waste."

"And that is your excuse?"

"That is my answer." His tone was sharp.

I turned away, exasperated, refusing to speak to him for the rest of the procession. Even when he thanked me for joining him, I merely bowed and returned to the other ladies, who mostly feigned disinterest. Only Dorthea peppered me with questions about the prince, about our conversation, and about how I'd come to find a seat beside him. I gave her half my attention, unable to stop thinking of Samuel and how changed and sickly he looked.

That evening, I waited at the chess table, eager to talk to the one person in the best position to speak for Samuel's freedom, but Egmont did not show.

CHAPTER 29

Margaretha

THE HUNTING PARTY WAS ABUSTLE. Huntsmen ordered dog keepers, whose hounds bayed in their eagerness for the chase. Servants collected discarded food and dirtied plates, shaking blankets free of crumbs before repacking them in trunks.

I'd tried, but failed, to catch Egmont's eye during the entirety of the Gathering's repast, but as nobles dispersed to mount their horses, I found my chance to separate from the ladies-of-honor and approach Egmont.

"I missed you at the chess table last night," I said.

He continued adjusting the strap of his stirrup without looking up. "You couldn't find another partner?"

"I didn't seek another partner."

He cast the briefest of glances at me before again tugging the stirrup belt. I let the silence play out, let him feel the discomfort of it until he was compelled to speak.

"Is that because I'm so easily bested?" He sounded testy.

"It's because I enjoy your company." I moved a step toward him, and he froze but did not retreat. "I should like your company now, if you care to ride by me during the hunt."

Egmont barely nodded, but after straightening, he gave a more certain nod, and I smiled to see it. He was mounting his horse when another rider approached. The morning sun lit the newcomer from behind, casting his face in shadow, but I didn't need to see him to know who he was.

"There you are, *mea columba*. I'm glad to have found you. Won't you ride with me for the day's hunt?"

I gritted my teeth, annoyed by the prince's forwardness in calling me "his dove." This precise thing would be my undoing with Egmont. Still, I offered the prince a low bow. "I wish nothing more than to please Your Grace, but I'm afraid I just promised the day to Comitem Egmont."

"Oh, the *comitem* shan't mind. Shall you, Egmont?"

The two men stared at each other astride their battle chargers, with me poised between them, small and insignificant. I drew closer to Egmont, petting his horse's neck as I looked up pleadingly.

"You said you were persistent," I whispered to him.

Egmont continued to glare at the prince, but eventually he dropped his gaze to me, his brows lowering in defeat. He gave me a sad smile, and in his eyes, I could see his goodbye. All my efforts at enticing him, all my hopes of him saving Samuel, withered when he clucked to his horse, twisting the reins to lead the brute away. I stared after him, willing him back, while behind me the prince's saddle creaked, and his feet thumped to the earth.

"Very good," he said. "Let's get you mounted. Where is your page?"

I took a deep breath and turned to face him, painting a smile across my face. And if not a smile, at least not the angry scowl I worked hard to conceal.

"My page was sent home. Family concerns," I answered.

"But surely you have another."

"I expect a replacement whenever my father can spare a man."

"Spare a man?" The prince looked surprised. "Just how impoverished is your county? Gah! Never mind. You may borrow one of my pages. Patricio!" He called behind him to a boy standing at a respectful distance. "The lady's horse, please."

I pointed the boy to my palfrey, a gift from Lord Krell. The dutiful page did not move until his master waved two fingers forward, and then he worked with impressive skill and speed for one so young, retrieving the horse and bringing a mounting stool. I gathered my skirts to climb the first step, but Prince Felipe captured my hand, guiding me up the stool until I was settled atop my palfrey. Mounting his charger, he led us past the other ladies-of-honor with their surprised looks, past Egmont, whose interest was suddenly claimed by his horse's reins, and to the head of the hunting party. Queen Mary glanced twice when she noticed my presence.

"Comtess de Waldeck. What a surprise to have you here." She eyed her nephew, though she spoke to me.

"I invited her," the prince answered without hesitation, either oblivious to his aunt's raised brow or intentionally ignoring it. Steering his horse left and pushing mine along with his, he moved us until we were effectively sequestered from the rest of the group.

"You ride well," the prince said when we were alone.

"I thank you, Your Grace."

"*Comitissa*, please, we cannot be friends if you are always bowing and speaking with formality. Call me Felipe."

"As it pleases you, Felipe." I had to force out the name, which felt strange and foreign on my tongue. The prince must have noticed for he laughed.

"And another thing, Margaretha—I may call you that, may I not?—I cannot enjoy real discourse with you if you insist on speaking with obeisance. Express your true thoughts with openness."

I cocked an eyebrow but kept my face straight ahead. "After our last conversation, I sensed Your Grace would that I keep my opinions private."

"Felipe," he reminded. "And if you refer to our discussion of heretics at the Ommegang, I grant you I have no interest in pursuing it further. This dissension would never be tolerated in Spain. My aunt hasn't managed this place with the strict discipline and watchful eye that's needed to keep such ignorant backsliding in check."

My blood surged. Mining gems of truth from Catholic lies was "ignorant backsliding"?

"But never mind that," he continued, his tone light. "I did not like the way we left things the other week. I could see I'd upset you."

"You have a habit of doing that," I answered.

"Oho!" He twisted in his saddle. "What have I done now to deserve your sharp tongue?"

"Your Grace can hardly be ignorant of your offense. You take great pains to get me alone with you, frightening away any other prospects I have and effectively clearing out my chances for a good match." I glanced to our right, past the pages beating the brush and over to Egmont, who rode alone.

The prince followed my gaze. "Men who are so easily frightened are hardly worth your regret, my lady. Besides, they may scatter like sheep now, but when I am gone, your prospects will return again. You are too beautiful to be left alone for long."

I ignored his compliment. "You mean to use me for your amusement, then? To flirt and make me a mere dalliance until duty calls you to another town? Another woman?"

"You wound me." He pressed a hand to his heart, but his amused smile betrayed the truth. "Wound me when I have done nothing but show an interest in your company. You are clever, Margaretha, and I should like to pass my time in Brussels in the presence of such an intelligent, comely woman."

I shifted in my saddle, looking forward without deigning an answer.

"You're angry!" He gave a surprised laugh. "I have never met a woman who was angered by my attentions. Am I too poor a prospect for you?"

I rolled my eyes and shook the reins to push my horse ahead.

"Did you have your sights set higher than the emperor's son?" he called after me. "Perhaps I'll introduce you to my father. We'll see if he is good enough for you." His laugh carried on the wind, but I ignored it, keeping my horse just ahead of his to discourage further conversation.

With the hunt about to begin, I had to wait through the chase, through "The Mort," the breaking, and the hounds getting their share of the kill, before the party disbanded and the prince finally abandoned me. Once free, I sought out Baron Pempflinger, who received me with an uncertain smile.

"What a relief you are," I said. "I haven't spent more than two hours in the prince's presence, and already I'm exhausted by his self-absorbed talk. I'm glad to have found you. You've always known how to please me with your conversation."

His smile brightened. "I have just the thing to amuse you."

As we trotted together toward the palace, he regaled me with a clever story about a fox and a bear drinking blackberry wine, and my laughter brought over Sir Lamberg, who had a story of his own to tell. By the time we'd pulled into the stables, I'd managed to collect the familiar trio of men around me.

"I think you incapable of such a feat," Baron Pempflinger challenged Sir Lamberg's story, dismounting from his horse. "To carry a wild boar that distance is impossible."

"Not at all," I interceded. "If anything, Sir Lamberg is being too modest."

A page set a mounting stool beside my horse, and I was about to climb down when Sir Lamberg was up the steps and lifting me off my horse. I couldn't stop my eruption of surprised giggles as he carried me down the stool, spun me in a circle, then very gallantly set me on the ground. Holding my hand to my chest to catch my breath, I turned around to thank the page for the stool.

"Did Prince Felipe ask you to tend—" I stopped short, finding myself looking directly into the familiar, stormy gray eyes of my new page.

Friedrich was dressed in the queen's livery, almost unrecognizable for the stubble spread over his jaw and the untrimmed hair curling up to catch on his turned-brim cap.

Neither of us spoke.

"Lady Margaretha?" Krell had come up behind me, silent as silk. "Are you unwell?" He looked back and forth between Friedrich and me, then took a protective step in front of me.

"No, no, I'm all right." I set a gloved hand against his brawny arm and gave him a winning smile but couldn't help glancing at Friedrich again.

"Shall we dress for supper?" Baron Pempflinger offered his arm, and I reluctantly took it, my mind grasping for anything I might say to Friedrich, any kind of parting or greeting I could offer to pay particular attention to him without arousing the suspicion of the men around us.

"Page, will you be sure to polish the saddle? The leather is drying." It was nothing close to what I wished to say.

"*Oui*, Comtess." His voice was so familiar, so much like home, but so distant from me that I ached to hear it.

Pempflinger led me toward the stable doors. "I still think carrying a woman as delicate as yourself no proof of strength."

"You needn't worry, Baron," I whispered. "Sir Lamberg must prove his strength for his pride, but your silence speaks volumes. There is no contest."

He smiled as we wound through the confusion of nobles, pages, and horses in the stables. Before we entered the courtyard, before I joined the other ladies-of-honor, I took a last look back to find Friedrich, but he was gone.

CHAPTER 30

Friedrich

"Hurry up, Rowohlt," the varlet called over his shoulder, raking hay in the stalls. "Food'll be on the tables, and we'll get naught of it if you keep dallyin'."

I polished the saddle faster, putting all my anger and humiliation into making the leather gleam. To have the countess speak to me that way, dismiss me like I was nobody . . .

I had expected to be unsettled by seeing her again. When the count had found me and requested that I come to Brussels, my greatest agitation was knowing I'd encounter Margaretha here. Eighteen months of working and sweating in the mining pits, of hiding away from Carrera, had not been enough to decide my feelings on the countess or her actions. At times my blood still burned with a bitter anger for all she'd taken from me, leaving me alone in a pitiless world and depriving me of my mother's love. At other times, I pushed myself to see reason, telling myself the countess wasn't truly to blame, that she'd been just a child.

But all thoughts of forgiveness fled the moment she'd danced into these stables with a man on each arm. A lifetime of my suffering was not enough to call her to repentance. The woman had learned nothing. She'd lied before, hurting others to meet her ends, and she was doing it still. Those men were dupes to her charms, hanging on her every word and brightening at each of her beautiful smiles. Deceitful smiles.

Finished with the saddle, I set it over the rack and raked out fresh hay for the stall. The day was warm, with only an occasional breeze surprising the stables and blowing over the beads of sweat trickling down my neck. When the breeze carried with it the loud laughter of boys, I put the rake aside and followed the sound, ready to go about my true purpose for coming to Brussels. Still lacking sufficient funds to pay my way into an apprenticeship, I was quick to agree to the count's generous terms for this assignment. If seeing Margar— the countess again had been a second motive, it certainly wasn't any longer. My only focus now would be fulfilling my small, but dangerous task, being the means of allowing the count to communicate with his imprisoned son.

Turning the corner of the stables, I came upon a quartet of page boys playing dice. Precisely what I needed.

The boys were too engrossed in their game to notice me at first, but when they did, they clawed the dice in their fists or scattered them into the dirt, trying to hide their game.

"You there." I pointed to a boy with dice in his hands. "Come with me."

I did my best to sound commanding, but turning on my heel and expecting him to follow was a gamble that paid off. His footsteps clomped on the cobblestones behind me.

When we were inside the dark stables, I faced him. "You seem like a man in need of a friend like me."

He puffed his chest when I called him a man but still squinted a skeptical eye. "How so?"

"As I see it, you could either face three days' imprisonment and the stocks for playing dice, or you could take this taler." I set the silver coin in his hand, then rested a letter on top of it.

He poked his chin at the letter. "Who's it for?"

"A prisoner."

He whistled. "Goin' to need a few more talers than that." He pushed the letter back at me, but I put a hand out to stop him.

"There'll be more when you have a letter to give me in return."

He bit the taler, his eyes narrowing in thought, then spit in his hand and shoved it toward me. "Two talers now, four when the job's done, an' you've got yourself a deal."

I eyed the dribble in his palm. "I'll take your word."

"A'righty." He wiped his hand against his hose just as the varlet called for me to return to raking.

As I finished my work, I hoped the great hall would be cooler, but the heat that greeted us when we stepped through the arched doors was almost worse. The sun baking through the windows showed hot steam wafting up from hundreds of platters piled high with unfamiliar foods. I thought the count ate richly, but his meals were breadcrumbs next to this decadent feast.

The varlet pushed me from behind. "Stop gawkin' and go sit with your people."

I looked around for which people were "mine," then spotted Ilsa, her fingers wriggling in the air to catch my attention.

Meeting her at the table, I swung my legs over the bench, sliding into place on the smooth, polished surface. "You don't seem surprised to see me," I said.

"Oh no. I knew all about your comin' from Mistress Hatzfeld. Lady Belinda now, I suppose."

"You keep in touch with the count's wife?"

"Every so often. She wants reports on how *your lady* is doing." She tossed a nod at the dais, most likely at the countess, but I didn't dare look. Too afraid the countess would notice me. More afraid she wouldn't.

"She's not my lady. She doesn't care for anyone but herself." Picking up my cup of wine, I emptied it in three swallows.

Ilsa raised an eyebrow. "You are changed. Rather more rangy and dangerous than I remember. And quicker to be in your cups."

"It's devilishly hot," I answered. "How do you stand this place?"

"The weather's no different from home. Cooler, if anythin'."

"Not the weather—the sea of bodies. The constant orders."

Ilsa folded her arms and propped them on the table, leaning her smiling face toward me. "The frustration of watchin' your lady flirt her way through court and naught for you to do to stop it, you mean."

I did my best to give her a withering look. "It's too bad you don't apply your wit to a more useful purpose, like being the queen's jester."

"Tell me I'm wrong, and I'll leave you be."

I stopped chewing my bread and stared her straight in the eye. "If you think I harbor any hopes when it comes to the countess, you couldn't be more mistaken."

CHAPTER 31

Margaretha

F*riedrich is here. Here somewhere, living in this palace where I live.* Though weeks had passed since his arrival, my mind still hadn't settled with the notion. Why was he here? Why would Friedrich have ever agreed to come when Ulrich could have served in his stead? Would that I could ascribe his presence to some softening toward me, but I held little hope of that.

"Are you excited for the tournament?" Ilsa secured the hennin to the wire comb around my head. "Joustin' and knights and maidens. It'll be just like the olden days. Likely the biggest court spectacle the queen has ever put on."

I turned to face her, nearly knocking her in the head with my long, cone-shaped hood. "I'd be more excited if I didn't feel so ridiculous."

"Well, you don't look ridiculous."

A compliment. Ilsa had been in a rare mood of late. Arranging the hennin's gauzy veil, she asked, "Shall your prince be joustin' too?" It seemed her understanding of French was enough now that she understood court gossip.

"Ilsa, I have no claim on Felipe—the prince," I corrected when she raised both eyebrows. "In truth, I don't even want him."

"Hmm." Her pinched lips said what she could not.

"Go on." I sighed. "What have you to complain of?"

"Nothin'." She shook out my skirts, straightening them as I waited for the truth to come out. "Except that I'm sure *I* shouldn't turn up my nose at a prince. Even if he weren't so handsome, I'd be grateful for his gifts of jewels and ermine cloaks and anythin' else he wanted to give me."

As Ilsa left to fetch my shoes from the press, her words struck me. *Grateful for his gifts. Anything he wanted to give me.*

"I've been a fool," I whispered to myself, sinking onto the bed. I'd been so focused on the idea of finding a powerful man to marry, of influencing him as his wife to speak up for Samuel, that I hadn't considered the favors a very smitten, very uncommitted prince might grant. His religious conviction was still a massive obstacle to overcome, but perhaps I could charm him enough to release one minor German count. And with Samuel freed and the prince gone to marry his English cousin, I'd be at liberty to marry whomever I wanted.

The memory of Friedrich's kiss came to mind unbidden, but I hurriedly tamped it down. He would not have me now. No matter the stumbling blocks between us—our differences in station, my inescapable purpose here in Brussels—the most insurmountable obstacle now was Friedrich himself.

"Ladies!" Dame Thieuloye clapped her hands, summoning us to line up at the door. Ilsa finished fastening the latchets of my shoes, and I tucked into the train of women following Thieuloye out the door, forgetting the height of the hennin strapped to my head until it knocked against the door frame and went tumbling to the floor. Ilsa rushed to pick it up, sliding it back over the basket weaved into my hair, but delaying me enough that I was last in line to enter the stables. The other ladies were mostly up and on their horses by the time I found the stall where Friedrich was working. Alone. This might be my best chance to ask the question I'd been wondering since his appearance in Brussels.

"Friedrich," I whispered, "what are you doing here?"

He kept his eyes on his work, buckling the bridle's throat latch as he answered. "Preparing your horse, my lady."

"I mean, why are you in Brussels? Why did Father send you and not Ulrich or Hans?"

He gave no answer.

I shouldn't have been surprised. I deserved his silence.

Following him to the mounting block, I put my foot on the first step, but Friedrich amazed me by taking hold of my wrist to stay me. While he looked around him, watching the other pages lead their ladies' horses toward the exit, I could feel only the warmth of his hand bleeding through my gown. It was wrong that his touch still excited a trilling in my nerves, and I fought for the self-command to subdue it. But just when I'd gotten control of myself, Friedrich turned to me, his face abruptly close to mine as I still stood perched on the bottom step of the mounting block.

He seemed as shocked by the sudden closeness as I was, his cheeks flushing as he dropped my wrist and cleared his throat to whisper, "Your father sent me to communicate with Count Samuel. He'd heard the kaiser's prisoners were in

Brussels and dispatched me with a letter to give your brother. I receive letters in return, so I may report back on how the young count fares. I'm to report on how you fare too. It seems you're playing your part well." Even in a whisper, he couldn't conceal his annoyance.

"Yes, thank you for your part in my training," I retaliated, moving up the steps, but my cursed hennin was too tall. It rammed into the stable's ceiling beam, knocking me backward down the mounting block. In a flash, Friedrich's hands were around me, settling on my stomach and back to steady me.

"Are you all right?" The concern in his eyes held me captive, transfixing me with memories of the many times he'd shown me tenderness. But as quickly as it appeared, it vanished, that cold distance slipping over him again as he let me go.

"Mind your footing," he muttered. Turning his back to me, he took hold of the reins and waited until I was secured atop my mount before leading us into the warm afternoon sun.

I told myself to be grateful for Friedrich's anger. It kept me on course, reminding me of what I needed to do today.

Find Prince Felipe.

We approached the lists, joining the train of pages and ladies just as a trumpet sounded and a booming voice announced the name of Lady Jakelina Prues. Applause echoed before another trumpet burst, another name was announced, and the cycle repeated itself, the line before us steadily dwindling. It was nearly my turn, and Friedrich led my horse onto the field, waiting while Helena and her page took the wide arc around the lists to the applause of the spectators. I used the moment to seek out the prince, easily finding him in the center of the gallery beneath the shade of a broad canopy. Despite looking handsome in his red-and-black slashed doublet, he also looked incredibly bored, stifling back a yawn as Helena dismounted to take her seat. I'd do my best to change that.

The trumpet burst, drawing all eyes to me as my name was read, but I kept my steady gaze on the prince. He took notice, leaning forward in his seat and resting a hand across his knee. I smiled, biting my lip and dropping my gaze, making myself the very essence of the beautiful, modest woman of the courtly romances. Until the horse lurched forward as Friedrich gave the reins a sudden tug. By the tight set of his jaw, I sensed he'd witnessed my exchange with the prince, yet what should he care? He didn't want me.

I shifted my attention back to Felipe, finding his bright eyes watching me as I made the wide arc around the lists. He rested his templed fingers over his lips, only half-concealing the mischievous smile that tilted the corners of his mouth, and I couldn't resist smiling back all the way to the gallery.

Ignoring Friedrich's arm as I dismounted, I took my seat. It was a disappointing spot, too far in front of the prince to catch his eye without directly turning my back on the joust.

Friedrich led the horse off to the sides of the gallery, joining the other pages. If he'd intended to shun me, I wouldn't have known it for all my efforts to avoid watching him. I had a hazy impression that I might be acting childish, but the commencement of the joust saved me from exploring the idea further.

Horse hooves pounded down the tilt yard again and again, culminating with the inevitable crash of lances against armor and shields. With each match, the ladies court huddled to debate if either jouster showed exceptional chivalry or horsemanship. One man was becoming the clear favorite. Donning the alias of Knight of the Red Falcon, in nearly every one of his passes he'd narrowed his lance onto the small metal jousting shield bolted to his opponent's left shoulder. Such skill was impossible to ignore.

The sun tipped deeper into the sky as the Knight of the Red Falcon lined up for his final pass in a match he was sure to win. The men began their charge. As they neared the center of the tilt, they let down their lances. The Red Falcon was all smooth movement, lowering his lance in such a graceful arc it startled me when it slammed into the other jouster's shield, shattering the coronel crowning the tip. The nobility were on their feet, applauding his final victory, to which he tore off his helmet, proudly announcing his true name—Georges de Lynden. As he approached the knight marshal seeking his reward, the marshal stood, yelling over the din, "Hold your rejoicing! The tournament is not yet complete!"

Lynden pulled up short.

"We have another jouster. The virtuous knight-errant Beltenebros."

The entire crowd turned to see the self-proclaimed Beltenebros ride onto the lists. His thick, powerful black armor was impacted with ribbons of gold and crafted to fit around him like a protective fortress. His helmet sported the longest train of feathers I'd ever seen, trailing white plumes down the length of his back. This man's false name and covered face couldn't disguise his true identity as the prince of Spain. When had he crept off to dress and ready for this grand entrance?

I offered the prince a smile, not sure he saw me through his narrow visor until he trotted toward the gallery. I stood to greet him.

"Doth a poor knight merit a token from the goodly maid?" he asked.

I pulled out my kerchief, leaning over the gallery wall to tie the fluttering cloth around his upper arm. "May it bring you health and good fortune."

He rested his gauntlet over the kerchief. "Earning your token is fortune enough." Shaking the reins of his horse, he left to find his place on the tilt field.

As I took my seat, I unexpectedly met Friedrich's eye, and my cheeks flushed with a sudden consciousness of being watched. And not by Friedrich alone. The ladies around me gave me cold stares, while behind me I heard the indecipherable whispers of courtiers.

Never mind. I'd secured the prince's notice, as I'd hoped.

The jousters began their charge, stealing the attention of the gallery away from me. As the men approached the center of the tilt, there was a clear difference in the entire bearing of the Red Falcon. His precision was gone; his grace had vanished. The prince struck a decent blow against the Red Falcon, though nothing impressive, yet on the second pass, the Red Falcon made no answer. His lance barely grazed the prince's arm. The Red Falcon was curbing his talent, reining in his skill. Not so much as to embarrass his future sovereign to eliminate the thrill of conquest when the prince's inevitable victorious blow came on the third pass.

The crowd offered what applause was expected as the prince approached the knight marshal, bowing humbly to claim the jewel-hilted sword as his prize. All humility vanishing, he turned to the gallery and threw his sword arm in the air, rallying the nobles to convincing excitement, as if they hadn't known the conclusion of these games the moment the prince came onto the field.

With the tournament completed and the sun disappearing behind the horizon, the ladies left the gallery, following Dame Thieuloye up the circular turret steps toward our chambers. The evening and the palace carried cold winds, and I found myself missing the heat of the day as we passed the men lighting the hallway lanterns. Thieuloye opened our chamber door and was about to step inside when a clamoring din had us all stopping in our tracks, turning to see the prince in full armor making his way down the hall.

The ladies' wide eyes spoke to their shock at the prince's renegade behavior, coming to the very doors of our chambers and without his retinue. Thieuloye was more self-possessed, urging the ladies inside and leaning herself against the door to hold it open as she waited for me.

"Lady Margaretha," the prince called, his voice muffled behind his helmet. "Wait a moment."

I turned from Thieuloye and offered the prince a bow. "Your Grace."

He lifted off his helmet with a smile that was not marred by his sweaty, matted hair, as he looked every bit the dashing knight of the courtly romances.

"Today I am not your prince, but Beltenebros, the knight-errant." He crossed an arm over his waist and bowed low.

I stepped toward him, dropping my voice to keep Thieuloye from hearing. "Then call me Oriana, his lady love and most ardent admirer."

His smile brightened. "Ah, a fellow enthusiast of *Amadís de Gaula*, I see."

"Of many chivalric romances. They are a weakness of mine." It wasn't entirely true, but I felt sure it would please the prince to hear it.

Thieuloye tapped an impatient foot against the floor. "Lady Margaretha, we must dress for supper."

The prince didn't even look at her when he answered in broken French, "Run along, madame. The countess join when she readies."

Thieuloye slammed the chamber door, and I cringed. She might well put needles in my mattress as retribution for such flagrant disrespect.

"I came to thank you for your token," he said. "With your colors on my arm, I feel I could conquer the world."

"Your Grace, with the colors on your family's flag, the world is already yours." I shivered, hoping he'd notice how ready I was for a change of clothes and warm food.

"You are cold." He pulled off his gauntlet, tucking it beneath his arm as he pressed a hot hand against my cheek. "You know"—he moved closer—"I might be able to warm you." Though his tone was playful, he allowed his fingers to slide down my jawline to the hollow between my collarbones, his eyes dropping to my lips.

My stomach leapt, and my pulse danced as his head bent toward mine, but I would not let him see it. Taking a great step backward and schooling my voice, I said, "Tush, Felipe, I thought your feelings deeper than these hollow sentiments. Find me again when you're sincere." I patted his hand and was turning back to my chambers when he caught my wrist and spun me to face him.

"I have been nothing but sincere with you, my lady." His eyes bored into mine as he brought my knuckles to his lips. The kiss he bestowed was warm, the heat of his lips saturating my glove and settling into my skin until a shiver rippled through me that had nothing to do with the cold.

CHAPTER 32

Margaretha

THE LADIES IN THE QUEEN'S chamber laughed in conversation, but I kept to myself, using the light of the windows to reread Belinda's letter. All at home were healthy, she assured me. Though the family's growing debts continued to be a constant source of distress, she would not dwell on that. She and Father longed to visit and would in a heartbeat if Father were not banned from Brussels after his part in the rebellion. She was not yet in a family way but hoped to be soon, and the letter went on much the same. The very idea of Belinda carrying Father's children was every bit as unsettling as their marriage announcement had been. Service to the queen had prevented me from attending the wedding, and Belinda seemed to feel the loss, for her letters to me since then were full of cheerful reports and declarations of how desperately she missed me. Time and her persistent attempts to repair the breach had done their work, however, for I found myself missing her too and eagerly anticipating each of her letters, even if I was not quite prepared for news of a new sibling. I truly wished her happy and my father even happier. He'd been so long without Mother that he deserved to find joy again.

"Do I interrupt your solitude?" Felipe's whisper at my ear made me jump. When had he come in?

"What are you doing here?" I whispered in return. "I hadn't expected to see you until dinner."

"I couldn't wait that long." He glanced behind him, putting his back to the ladies' stares and curious looks as he quickly slipped a paper into my hand. "Please come," he whispered, then disappeared out the door.

Felipe's missive seemed a hot coal in my pocket as I walked the castle corridors toward the Aula Magna just a few hours later. While the other ladies chattered about court gossip, I mentally recited Felipe's instructions to meet him in the north corridor before dinner. Slipping away from the ladies-of-honor would be easy enough, but secretly meeting the prince was gambling with my reputation more than I'd ever dared. Still, it was broad daylight, and we were meeting in an oft-traversed hall. Ignoring the prince's entreaty after boldly seeking his favor seemed the greater risk.

With the entrance to the north hall nearing, I let myself fall to the back of the train, hugging the wall as I walked. I kept my eyes forward, waiting, watching to be sure no one saw, before darting north into the empty corridor. Holding my breath until the soft scuffle of shoes faded, I tiptoed through the hall, wincing at every rustle of my gown and clip of my shoe.

"Margaretha, here." Felipe's whisper echoed, and I put a stern finger to my mouth to silence him.

He answered with a grin, reaching out his hand to pull me into a small room and closing the door behind him. There were no windows, but enough light came from under the door that I could still see his rakish smile.

"I think you like the danger of sneaking about," I whispered.

"I would say I do, only I fear you'd find some new accusation to level at me."

I chuckled. "Perhaps. Though it appears you've forgiven me my abuse of last night."

"Wholeheartedly." He took both my hands, and his smile turned serious. "Though you may still doubt me, I hope to convince you I am earnest in my attachment to you."

"Attachment?" I reared my head. "Felipe, you hardly know me."

He laced his fingers through mine. "I have known many women, but I've never before felt this kind of longing. You're in every thought, in every dream, churning my mind into a fevered haze until I can't think clearly." He ducked his eyes, his voice dropping to a whisper. "My feelings for you are deep and real, and I intend to prove myself sincere."

"And how do you plan to do that?"

I expected his seriousness to fade into levity, for the flirt to win out over the pleading lover, but he proved me wrong. Lifting his head, his eyes surprised me with their openness when he answered, "Any way you ask."

My thoughts leapt to Samuel in an instant, but it was too soon. Too soon to know if the prince's affections were real, and too soon to test them with such a heavy request. Keeping my tone light, I said, "You can start by letting me out of this closet. Though you so enjoy these intrigues, I fear it puts a strain on my reputation."

"Certainly. Though I had hoped to finish what I started yesterday." He wrapped an arm around my waist, pulling me against him. "Just another way to prove myself earnest."

"I'm not sure it doesn't prove the opposit—"

His lips were on mine before I could finish, urgently drinking me in as if my kiss were the only thing keeping him tethered to mortality. I hadn't kissed a man since Friedrich, but Felipe had the power to free my brother. He had almost declared he loved me. Then why did I struggle to return his affection?

Lowering his lips to my jaw and kissing a soft trail to my chin, he whispered, "I've lost sleep imagining this moment."

Bumps raised over my arms at the warmth of his breath on my skin, but my mind was back in Wildungen, surrounded by rain and Friedrich's scent. There was a stirring of guilt in my belly.

Friedrich didn't want you, I reminded myself. *You have every right to kiss other men.*

Felipe released me with a frustrated sigh. "You are stiff. You think me too forward."

"No, it's only . . . I'm uncertain of myself. I've never kissed a man like this before."

He cupped my face in his hands, slowly bringing his mouth toward mine. "Do not think," he whispered above my lips. "Only let yourself feel."

When our lips met again, his kiss was slow and gentle. His thumb traced feather-light circles over my cheekbones, occasionally slipping between our mouths to brush my lip.

Felipe was right. I *was* thinking too much, and it only made me miserable. Shutting out my distracting thoughts, I focused solely on the feel of Felipe's warmth against me, on the excitement shooting through my veins.

And I found myself responding to his kiss.

My hands resting against his chest now slid up over his shoulders and wound their way into his dark, curly hair. He stepped closer, his nearness propelling me back until my shoulders touched the wall, but I only tightened my grip, my lips capturing his. His hands cradled my neck, his heated touch searing my flushed skin. When he stopped for breath, I pulled him back to me, and he smiled, setting his hands on the wall behind me to steady us in our kiss. His passion was intoxicating, deep and raw. Very different from Friedrich's heartfelt, tender kiss.

Thinking of Friedrich brought the thrill of the prince's affections to a sudden end. I broke the kiss, and he moaned in protest.

"We should be going," I prodded. No doubt dinner had commenced, and we would be missed.

He answered by moving his lips down to my throat.

"Really, Felipe. Everyone will have noticed our absence."

"We can be late," he said between each kiss of my neck.

"It isn't right to be alone like this."

His breath puffed against my skin with his chuckle. "Very well, I shall behave. But only for your sake." Releasing me, he opened the door. "I'll return first. You follow in a few moments."

He gave me a final kiss and an encouraging smile before leaving me in the dark.

I waited, counting the minutes until I felt enough time had passed, then I trotted toward the Aula Magna. With the bustle of servants carrying food, it would be easy to slip into my seat without drawing much attention. I thought I'd managed it, even casting Felipe a triumphant little smile, but beside him the queen's shrewd eyes were upon me, and her dark gaze filled me with sudden dread.

CHAPTER 33

Margaretha

DAME THIEULOYE CLAPPED HER HANDS, the bursts echoing against the tiled walls of the privy. "Bathe faster, Lady Margaretha. The other ladies are nearly done dressing."

I scrubbed the soap harder against my skin, ignoring the sudden commotion at the privy doors until Thieuloye rushed past me, nearly tripping over herself in her haste to greet the queen.

Thieuloye dipped a bow. "We are near to departing for the hunt. If Comtess de Waldeck were not so slow—"

Queen Mary raised a hand of silence. "I wish to speak to the comtess alone."

The women shot a few inquisitive glances my way before scurrying to finish dressing, some bearing exultant looks as they followed Thieuloye out of the room.

Queen Mary studied the clothes Ilsa had set out, running a finger over the gown and toying with my ruby necklace as she spoke. "It appears you've proved me right, Comtess. Upon your arrival I predicted your success at court, and here you are, winning the hearts of many a prominent man." She released the necklace from Baron Pempflinger and turned to face me. "It seems you've even won the heart of my nephew. Well, his admiration, at least."

Trying not to break eye contact, I skimmed my arms over the bathwater in search of a cloth for cover.

"I like you, Margaretha. You have a lovely career at court ahead of you, if you manage it well, so with your best interests in mind, I wish to offer some advice. Stay away from Felipe. He will bring you nothing but trouble and ruin."

I lifted my chin, attempting to look dignified. "I thank you for your concern, but the prince's behavior toward me has been above reproach. He's made no untoward advances, and I should never succumb to them if he did."

Mary's lips twitched, and a little huff of laughter escaped her mouth. "Comtess, you're as innocent as a newborn lamb if you believe you can outwit my nephew. I know you've taken great pains with your reputation, winning yourself an abundance of admirers while keeping yourself pure as the driven snow, but if you think you can play that game with Felipe, you really are naive." She moved to the door, then turned back to me. "So long as my brother remains, there's little I can do about his son's behavior, but once the prince is gone and you're left in ruin, don't expect me to intervene when Thieuloye throws you out."

The queen left the room, closing the door with a loud thunk.

Despite the warmth of the tub, I couldn't abate my shaking. I ran the soap over my arms, I splashed water on my face, I focused on scrubbing the roots of my hair, but it did little to assuage the anger lit by the queen's words. She really thought power and a handsome face was all it would take to persuade me into sullying my honor? She'd practically accused me of being a harlot! How could she think so meanly of me?

Stepping out of the bath, I wrapped myself in a towel and looked over my gown's articles: the necklace from Pempflinger, the decorative combs from Cobaron, and the handkerchief from Egmont bearing my initials. The queen was right: I had made conquests and all while keeping myself above reproach. Did she think I was fool enough to risk my reputation now? I'd known precisely what I was doing with those men, precisely where to draw the line when in banter or play. It was what I'd studied and practiced and sacrificed for. And now to be found morally wanting when I'd done nothing to bring my honor into question?

Remembering Felipe's impassioned kisses in a dark closet, heat rushed to my cheeks. It was no compromise of honor to kiss a man, but secret rendezvous were harder to explain away. Why had I taken such a foolish risk?

My skin was almost raw when I finished toweling myself dry. Ilsa poked her head around the door, closing it softly behind her. "We must dress you quickly. The ladies are readying to mount for the hunt."

I stood numb and silent while Ilsa turned me this way and that, cinching and pinching to tuck me into my riding garb. She plaited my hair and coiled it at the back of my head, pinning a hat atop my crown before prodding me out the door. Blending into the line of ladies, I sneaked side glances at Anna and Jakelina, at Helena and Dorthea on our walk to the stables. Did they see me as the queen saw me, a would-be doxy just waiting to be plucked? Could a few short months be enough to bring my carefully guarded reputation crumbling to the ground?

Perhaps the queen was right. Perhaps the naivete of Wildungen clung to me, as impossible to shrug off as my own skin. Maybe it was that naivete that had cost me Egmont. A savvier woman might have found a way to keep his attentions without spurning Felipe's. A savvier woman might have won her brother's freedom in half the time, not be plodding along a year and more later, having yet to broach the subject with anyone.

We entered the stables, where I came upon Friedrich—my biggest blunder of all. A savvier woman would never have let herself fall for someone so impossibly beyond her reach.

Friedrich

I recognized the countess's soft step but kept my eyes down, only acknowledging her presence by walking the horse toward the mounting block. I was required to offer my arm but half-expected her to shun it like she had at the tournament. Instead, she rested her gloved hand on me, even giving my arm a gentle squeeze before settling into her saddle.

"Thank you, Friedrich."

Her words caught me off guard, and I looked into her soaring blue eyes to see genuine gratitude. And a little more sadness than usual. Clearing my throat, I pretended to adjust the stirrup latchet, hoping she couldn't see how much she still had the power to affect me.

"Will you come with me today?" she asked. "I need a foot huntsman."

"I am your servant; I will do as you command." I moved around the horse, adjusting the girth strap.

"I would never command you, Friedrich. I've no right to. After what I did to you, to your mother . . . It is I who should be serving you." She scrubbed a hand over her nose, going silent.

I felt I should say something, but what? That I'd forgiven her? I couldn't lie, no matter how unhappy she looked up there on her horse with her head bowed.

I said the only honest thing I could. "I fear you'd make a poor servant, my lady."

She lifted her chin, quirking a smile. "Then I shall spare you that, at least."

We ambled into the courtyard, joining the slow-moving train on its way to the royal hunting grounds. The weather was hot and uncomfortable, but after arriving at the grounds, it became almost unbearable. The prince took quick notice of the countess. He left his horse with his page, separating himself from the milling nobles and taking the countess by the waist to help her off her horse.

"Where were you, *mea columba*? I couldn't find you at the palace."

"The ladies-of-honor fell behind in the train. I'm afraid I am to blame for our tardiness."

The prince clucked his tongue. "And I thought my kiss would leave you eager to see me."

Kiss? My head snapped to attention. Margaretha's glance told me she'd noticed.

"You would make a flirt of me, Your Grace." Her voice took a scolding tone, but he laughed.

"And you would make a feeble lover of me, my lady, dismissing my kiss so easily." He caught up her hand, leaning close to whisper in her ear. I only caught the words *soft* and *skin*, but it was more than I wanted to hear. I prayed for a stiff breeze to blow the prince's words to oblivion.

"Friedrich, I think the foot huntsmen are assembling." The countess pointed to the men and boys holding beaters and getting instructions.

I bowed my departure and escaped toward the other foot huntsmen, pausing near a grove of trees to grab a sturdy branch for beating. When I joined the group, I couldn't stop a reflexive backward glance at Margaretha. The prince was shamelessly close, running a gloved finger over her jaw as she looked in his eyes.

The hunting horn blew, and I was grateful to leave them both behind, beating my branch against the brush with more energy than I cared to explain. But no matter how hard I thwacked through the grass, the sweaty work wasn't enough to put my thoughts to rest. The countess I'd known back in Wildungen was lost to me forever. Her innocent blush, gone. Her naivete, gone. The change was painful to see, especially with the prick of guilt telling me I was to blame. Would she have stayed with me if I'd forgiven her? Was it because of me that she was forced to demean herself with the prince? Though from the looks of it, she didn't seem too troubled by his attentions . . .

Panicked shouting pulled me from my thoughts, and I turned to find a pair of foot huntsmen waving wildly at me. Their words were buried beneath a snorting sound, a low, hollow growl coming from my left. A dark blur streaked toward me, and I didn't even have time to lift my stick in defense before it bowled me over with its head, its sharp tusk tearing through my hose and into my leg. Scrambling to stand, my feet slipped through slickened grass, and I was back on the ground and beneath the wild boar's hooves before a deafening crack echoed above me. The boar let out a short squeal, then dropped on top of me, its dead weight squeezing the air from my lungs.

With shaking hands, I pushed against the boar, wriggling myself out from under its stinking carcass to find a nobleman with a smoking arquebus still pointed in my direction. A distant round of applause made us both turn.

"Good shot, Egmont!" The prince prodded his horse forward, ducking under a branch to meet us in the clearing. "I'm glad to see your skills as a marksman outrank your success with the ladies."

"Felipe!" Margaretha chided, entering the clearing close behind, but the prince continued unchecked.

"Particularly for the *comitissa*'s sake. Lady Margaretha may well have lost a servant today."

I turned back to Egmont and bowed. "I thank you, Your Lordship."

He nodded and handed his arquebus down to his attendant for reloading. Turning his horse out of the clearing, he called over his shoulder. "Your leg will need attention."

Confused, I dropped my gaze to see warm blood dripping down my hose. My lower leg suddenly pulsed in pain.

"You're cut?" Margaretha slid from her horse and knelt to inspect the gash.

The prince sauntered up beside her. "That a good scratch," he yelled to me in broken French. "A story for telling your *enfants*, yes?" Did he not know the language of those he ruled?

"It's not just a scratch." Margaretha bit off her glove and pried the wound with her fingers. I sucked in a sharp breath through my teeth, and she looked up with a furrowed brow. "This cut is deep. It will need stitching."

The prince bent down to see, then barked in Spanish to one of his pages. The boy ripped the tail of his shirt before coming forward to wrap the linen around my wound.

"Ah, that better now, yes?" The prince smiled and nodded at me. I didn't think I was allowed to disagree.

"Yes." I hobbled over to retrieve my stick.

"Very good." He took hold of Margaretha's hand, guiding her back to her horse, but she pulled away.

"It will not do. He's limping, and in short order, the blood will overwhelm the bandage. He needs stitches and a physician." She was watching me as she spoke, but in the end, she met the prince's gaze with surprising conviction.

His furrowed brow softened, and he snapped his finger at his attendants. "We'll put your servant on your horse, Lady Margaretha, and you can ride back with me." He'd returned to using Latin.

"No, I can't," she protested. "I should stay with the queen and her ladies." But the prince's servants were already giving me a leg up onto Margaretha's horse. The prince mounted his steed and reached his hand down to Margaretha. When she glanced at me, I pretended to fiddle with the reins, avoiding her gaze until she'd settled into the prince's saddle.

The prince guided his horse out, and I followed close behind, seeing only his frame, his body and arms covering all but Margaretha's hat as she sat in front of him. I hated to think how much he was enjoying this. Would he breathe in the lilac scent of her hair and neck? Did she want him to?

I had to stop myself, had to focus on the pain in my leg, which pulsed and ached, yet it wasn't enough to distract me from the prick of jealousy's thorn piercing from inside.

CHAPTER 34

Margaretha

EVEN THROUGH HIS DOUBLET, FELIPE'S chest was warm against my back. What did Friedrich think, seeing the prince with his arms tight around my shoulders the way Friedrich's had once been? The memory of that visit to the miner's cottage summoned an ache of longing, and I questioned yet again if I would rather have lied to Friedrich about his mother or never met him to begin with. But all was done with him now. I had no right to think of Friedrich, save what I stole from him. My duty to Samuel, my need for redemption—that was where my focus must be.

We pulled into the courtyard, and Felipe was quick to throw orders at his attendants, getting them to help Friedrich from his horse and into the palace to find the kaiser's personal physician.

"Not the court physician?" I asked Felipe, following him up a flight of stairs.

"That flesher? It's Vesalius you need." He turned into a deeply recessed doorway, putting his hand on the knob. "You wouldn't want just anyone taking care of one you value so much."

I reared my head. "Whatever do you mean?"

He smiled. "You can't afford to 'spare a man,'" he quoted me, then pushed into the room. "Vesalius, I've got a live patient for you."

Hearing the physician's name, my stomach twirled at the prospect of meeting the great Andreas Vesalius. I followed Felipe, eagerly taking in sights and smells both familiar and foreign. The crushed herbs beside a mortar and pestle and the little pot bubbling over the fire reminded me how much I missed my days of healing sicknesses and brewing electuaries, but the rest of the room was far different from what I'd expected. Sunlight poured across tables covered with a jumble of dissected animals, fluid-filled jars, and scattered papers, illuminating the chaos of scientific progress.

And in the middle of it all stood the great Andreas Vesalius. I had expected him to be taller, but his long, black beard and unruly curls matched in every way the eccentric image I had painted of him. His dark eyes narrowed as Friedrich hobbled into the room, white-faced and leaning against Felipe's attendants. The physician searched around himself, snapping his fingers a few times, then pointed to a table. "Put him here," he said, pushing aside a mess of papers and bent quills and scooting a half-dissected porcupine out of the way. Friedrich sat atop the cleared surface, perching his leg on the edge of the table to be examined.

Vesalius ripped back the blood-soaked hose and grimaced. "What caused this?"

"A wild boar," I answered.

Looking at me for the first time, Vesalius's cheeks colored, but he turned again to Friedrich. "It's deep. It will need stitching."

Felipe smiled at me. "You were right, clever girl. How did you know?"

"It takes almost no medical skill to draw such a conclusion," I answered distractedly, watching Vesalius threading catgut through a needle. "Have you any brandy for my page to drink?"

The physician began rooting through a cabinet of glass bottles when a gentle tap sounded at the door and a footman entered. "Your Grace, His Noble Highness the Emperor wishes to speak with you."

"Very well," Felipe answered, then took my hand, pulling me close to whisper in my ear. "I can think of nothing but having you in my arms. I count each painful second until I hold you again." Lifting my ungloved hand to his mouth, he gave it a slow, soft kiss, pulling back to meet my gaze as he massaged his kiss into my skin with his thumbs. Although my eyes looked at him, my attention was at my periphery, watching Friedrich watch us. I must have nodded, for the prince wore a satisfied smile when he turned to go, taking his attendants and leaving only Friedrich, the physician, and me in the room.

"Drink this." Vesalius gave Friedrich a cup, then took to his nervous snapping as he walked around the different tables gathering a few towels. Handing them to me, he instructed, "You'll need to wipe the blood between stitches."

I raised my eyebrows, surprised he would expect me to help, but he was oblivious to it, already collecting his needle and thread and bending over Friedrich's leg. He pinched together the skin at the top of the gash and forced the needle through the two sides of the split. Friedrich's back stiffened, and he gripped the table.

"I forgot to ask, my lady." Vesalius pushed the needle into the pinched skin again. "You don't sicken at the sight of blood, do you?"

"Never." Friedrich's voice was strained as he answered for me. "She's fearless."

I couldn't stop myself from smiling at his reply, but Vesalius paused mid-stitch, looking between Friedrich and me with questioning eyes. I drew his attention back to his work by wiping the blood spilling down Friedrich's leg, and Vesalius returned to stitching the needle through Friedrich's skin.

Poor Friedrich's knuckles were white and his lips pale by the time Vesalius finished. I tapped the damp cloth against his leg another time to wipe up the last drips of blood while Vesalius cleaned his hands in the washstand.

"We should get him lying down," Vesalius said as he dried his hands on a towel.

Friedrich's eyes looked heavy. I washed my hands, then stepped close to remove his jerkin, feeling his gaze roaming my face as I slipped the first button from its hold. His breath brushing across my neck made my fingers stumble over the simple task.

Rough and warm, his hand covered mine, stopping me. "I'll do it." His sluggish speech matched the lazy way his eyelids lifted and dropped.

"Do not trouble yourself," I whispered. "You must rest." Tugging my fingers out from his grip, I managed to undo the rest of the buttons despite the weight of Friedrich's attention still heavy on me. I slid the jerkin over his shoulders, bundled it into a pillow, and eased Friedrich down to rest on the table. The rise and fall of his chest soon slowed, and his breathing deepened with sleep.

"It's the brandy," Vesalius whispered. "And the pain. Those always rob the injured of their strength."

I nodded. "I've seen it before. It's strange how the body works."

Vesalius turned to face me. "You surprise me, my lady. Your experience with healing goes beyond a noblewoman's customary study of herbs and electuaries. You do well with the macabre and speak as if you've practiced the healing arts."

"A little." I continued watching Friedrich's steady breathing. "My tutor gave me a thorough understanding of potions, but I've done my best to study beyond that, even reading some of the more technical books on doctoring. I've read *your* book. The details of your illustrations are stunning. Was it unsettling posing dead bodies?"

A nervous laugh reverberated in his throat. "I know it's unusual spending so much time in the company of the dead, but studying the bodies of animals will never fully teach us how the human machine works. One must get in there. Cut things up. Look inside."

"It seems you do well with the macabre too. You surround yourself with it." I turned my gaze, taking in every dead thing in the room. Various breeds of fish, birds, and reptiles were splayed out and pinned. Some even hung suspended from the ceiling. The most curious display by far was a neatly organized row of at least seven dead rats.

"Do you have an infestation?" I pointed to the vermin.

"Oh! Oh, no. Those are my experiment. I'm working on a way to dull pain."

"With dead rats?"

"Well, um, no." Vesalius scanned the ceiling, snapping his fingers until he found what he sought. "You see this fish here?" He scrambled up a table and pulled down something that looked more like a ball with thorns than a fish. "This is a species from the New World." He handed me the string from which the fish was suspended, then leaned against the table with the dead rats. "The people there eat these fish for the unusual tingling it causes in the mouth and lips. Sometimes their mouths go numb altogether. Of course, sometimes they die." He furrowed his brows, lifting the tail of a rat and letting it drop. "But if I could make a paste or draft that would cause that kind of numbness over the whole body, why, your servant there wouldn't have felt a thing while I stitched him together."

At the mention of Friedrich, I returned to his side. "Will his leg take long to heal?"

"I recommend at least a few days without walking. After that, no vigorous activity for several weeks."

Friedrich's breath came slow and even, his features calm with the kind of peace only sleep can bring, and in that peace, I was free to study him without reserve. With the shadow of a beard covering his chin, he looked so much older than he had only a year and a half ago, but his long, dark lashes were just the same. The brush of freckles on his cheekbones—almost unnoticeable atop his tanned skin—hadn't changed. His hair, no longer covered by a cap, disheveled and untidy as it was with a lock resting over his forehead, was every bit the Friedrich I'd come to care for. My chest tightened with him so near yet divided from me by a chasm of my own making. Though I reached out, brushed back the hair from his forehead, let myself touch his skin, there was no bridge I could build to reach his heart, and it was there I longed to be.

Vesalius cleared his throat behind me, and I startled, quickly pulling my hand back to my side.

"I wouldn't worry, my lady. He ought to be right enough by the time of the masque."

Pretending to be interested in a greenish powder on his table, I asked, "Which masque?"

"Another of the queen's spectacles meant to entertain her brother and nephew. But it's not for the court alone. The townspeople have been invited too. And the servants . . . I'm sure your page will be well enough for dancing when the night arrives."

"That would be—"

The door hinges creaked, and I turned to see Felipe duck his way into the room.

"Shall we join the hunting party again, my lady?" He extended an arm, and I crossed the room to take it.

"I thank you, Master Vesalius." I nodded a little bow, wishing I could say more as Felipe pulled me out the door.

We walked a ways through the castle corridors, Felipe's attendants keeping enough distance that our conversation felt private when he asked, "How does your servant fare?"

"The doctor says he will be well in short order. In time for the masque, it would seem."

"Ah, so he told you of the masque? I hope to dance with you there." He brushed his fingers over my hand resting in the crook of his arm and pulled it up to his lips. When he turned my hand over to kiss my palm, he came to a halt. "What is this here? This scar you bear?"

I pushed back the creeping heat of a blush and answered dismissively, "An injury from my youth."

"You are still in the bloom of youth." He replaced my hand in the crook of his arm. "Do you mean your childhood?"

I nodded.

"What was your childhood like, Margaretha? Was it a pleasant one?"

"I imagine it was much the same as that of most poor noblewomen. I had a great deal of schooling, though. Father wanted all his children to be well educated, but I enjoyed learning more than the rest."

"So you had siblings?"

We were outside now, walking in the shade of the arcade as a cool breeze tugged my hat, hinting at the approaching autumn.

"Yes, two sisters and a brother. The eldest, Elizabeth, worked for a time as your aunt's lady-of-honor. She met her husband here in Brussels."

"Aha, it is a place of romance." He raised a sultry eyebrow. "No doubt they are very happy."

I looked at the ground. "She's dead. Died in childbirth nine months after she wed. My younger sister died too, when a plague ravaged our town."

Felipe didn't answer. Some time passed in silence before he asked, "And what of your brother?"

"He went away to school, then spent time fighting with the Schmalkaldic League."

"This explains your sympathy for the heretics." He squeezed my hand. "Did he die in the war?"

I hesitated, wondering how the prince would respond knowing my brother was his prisoner. But with my hand cradled inside his arm, feeling his heart beating beneath his doublet, I decided to be honest. "My brother survived the war, but I still fear for his life. In truth, he lives in the *Maison du Roi* as one of your father's particular guests."

Felipe stopped and studied my face. "Your brother is a captive from the Schmalkaldic War? Why have you said nothing of it until now?"

"I half-suspected your aunt had already told you. She's known of it since my arrival. And"—I continued walking to break away from his penetrating stare—"I wasn't sure of your response. I'm still unsure. If you're angry, see that I am punished, not he."

"Why would I be angry?" His tone was curious.

"For my being related to your enemy?"

"I am surprised, not angry. When my attentions to you have been so marked, I'm astonished you'd suspect them so changeable." He took my hand and slid it back into the crook of his arm as we approached his waiting horse. "If your heart is troubled with worry for your brother, let me ease it. I shall make inquiries to see how he fares."

"You would do that for me?" It was a small favor, but a good beginning. Enough that excitement rippled through me. Without thinking, I lifted onto my toes and wrapped my arms around his neck. "Thank you."

He pulled me back with a laugh, holding my elbows in his hands. I found myself laughing too. A genuine laugh that erupted without rehearsal.

"But wait," he said. "I do demand payment."

My smile dimmed. "Of what nature?"

He led me behind his horse and leaned his face by mine, whispering, "I'll have more of your lips." And then he kissed me again.

CHAPTER 35

Friedrich

SHATTERING GLASS AND CURSES WOKE me from my sleep, and I shot up faster than my sore muscles were ready for.

"Sorry to wake you." The physician groaned as he bent, picking up pieces of a broken vial from the floor. "Or perhaps I'm not all that sorry, as I've been waiting to talk with you about your story. How is it that you find yourself in such a dangerous position?"

I froze, not sure of his meaning. Just how much about me had he guessed? I watched him with narrowed eyes, but between his casual posture and my *not* being in a dungeon cell, it was safe to assume he didn't suspect the full truth of my task regarding Count Samuel. After relaxing my tense posture, I noticed the sting of pain in my leg. "What dangerous position is that, sir?"

The physician dumped his pan of broken glass out the open window, then, leaning against the windowsill, he turned to face me with his hands clasped over the pan. "Your mistress is very beautiful. In a court of glittering jewels, she shines brightest."

I didn't move.

"I'm sure you have noticed. You'd have to be blind to not see—"

"I prefer women with dark hair," I blurted.

The physician studied me before an understanding smile lit his face. "Dark hair," he repeated. "Ah, well, 'tis nothing, then. She seems a sweet, intelligent girl, whose affections for you are none too concealed. But as her hair is too pale for your liking, I see you're in no danger from her. I'll let you be on your way, then." He pointed his pan toward the door.

I tilted my head, confused. "That's all you wished to say?"

He nodded, and I haltingly tried to stand, but the moment my foot touched the floor, fire shot up my veins. I smothered a cry and dropped back against the table.

The physician tapped his temple and shook his head. "Thoughtless of me." Putting down the pan, he offered me a walking stick. "For the next few days, walk only when you must. If you heal quickly enough, you may even be ready to dance the masque away with an assortment of dark-haired women." The odd little man made no sense, but I didn't trouble myself to try to understand him as I took one tentative step after another. I was almost to the door when I turned back to him.

"You're wrong about my mistress. She wields her beauty as a weapon, using it to gain her own ends. You don't know the harm she's done me—done her whole village."

"Aha! There it is." Vesalius snapped his fingers and paced in front of a long table. "I knew there was more. So she's hurt you, has she?"

"No, I didn't mean . . . not just me."

He squinted an eye at me, tugging his beard. "But yours seems a particular kind of injury. She won you over with her beauty and sweetness, didn't she? And now you think to blame her for your pain while remaining obstinately oblivious to her suffering?"

I snorted. "Living in luxury while you charm your way into any man's heart you desire doesn't look much like suffering to me."

"Because you'd rather be blind to it."

"I know exactly the—" I stopped myself, suddenly struck with a thought. "Pray, why do you take such interest in whether the countess and I are on good terms?"

The physician released his beard and lowered his eyes. "I have a long history with the Habsburgs. I can pretty well guess the prince's designs for any woman he distinguishes above another, and he has taken a strong interest in your mistress."

I ground my teeth.

"She impressed me with her kindness toward you. It was impossible not to notice her gentle touch while you slept. She cares for you."

Gentle touch? I caught myself leaning toward him to hear more, but straightening, I let the anger return with a roil. "It doesn't change what she did. No apology could ever repair the injury she's done."

The physician watched me with thoughtful eyes. "My young friend, in my work as a physician, I've seen what hatred does to people's minds, to people's bodies. It festers inside like an infection, killing every happy thought and feeling until there is no joy in life, only raw anger. I see that anger growing in you. Only the tonic of forgiveness can stop its spread."

I shook my head. This man couldn't understand how badly the countess had wronged me. He might assume she'd broken my heart, but if he knew what she'd done to my mother—what she was still doing, playing the pretender for all these men—he would never ask me to forgive her.

The physician pushed himself from the table and took my shoulders in his hands. "Some men are born noble. Others must create nobility in themselves. Never does a man exhibit truer nobility than when he forgives the undeserving."

I nodded to appease him, then shrugged out of his grip and hobbled from the room.

Over the next fortnight I followed the physician's orders, keeping off my feet as much as meals and trips to the latrine allowed. The time spent was miserable. My inactive body allowed my mind to race like the waters of a river leading nowhere. I couldn't forget the physician's words about forgiveness. Or his cryptic comment about me being blind to the countess's suffering. What suffering? I'd never seen her smile so much since coming to Brussels.

Though in truth, the smiles never quite reached her eyes.

But this was what she was born for, what all noblewomen were born for. To marry themselves off to the richest, most titled man that would have them so they could bring honor and gain to their families. It was little different than breeding dogs for better speed or strength. No wonder the countess hadn't been eager to come here. She'd said she hoped to find a man to love, and she resented being tasked to marry only for advantage. Maybe she was as much a victim as I, both of us caught in the tangled web of the count and his schemes. Were her smiles nothing more than a mask to conceal her misery?

Seeing things from that light made me more than pity her.

It made me want to protect her.

But she would never stand for it, would she? Hadn't she rejected me as much as I'd rejected her that night in the rain, her wet locks clinging to her face and her eyes pooling as she'd gripped Mother's letter? *"I must go to Brussels, now more than ever."*

She'd as good as said the twisted history between us made her anxious to be away from me.

Yet the odd little physician claimed Margaretha had displayed unconcealed affection toward me. Had I misunderstood everything about her from the beginning?

And why did that thought, the hope of her continued affections, lift my spirits? What kind of morbid man would harbor hopes for the woman who'd killed his mother?

Even if I truly forgave her, it wouldn't solve anything between us. There were too many obstacles to consider, none of which could be overcome by a simple "I forgive you." It was easier to dislike her. It hurt less than admitting I still cared for a woman so impossibly beyond my reach that it was almost ridiculous to imagine.

Almost.

Except for those nights when my thoughts floated to her, wherever she was in the palace, and I let the day's controlled, tightly contained thoughts out of their glass jar to float where they may. And oh, how they soared!

I dreamed of how different life would be if my mother hadn't been cast off. If she'd never met that blacksmith and I'd been born a noble. Would Margaretha and I have been friends on equal terms? Would she have married me if I'd asked?

I remembered our days in Wildungen in the cool, lush forests and her bright smile. Not the simpering, sultry smile she gave to these men in the palace, but her true smile. Warm and open and reserved just for me. And when I recalled that smile, I thought of her lips, deep red and soft under mine . . .

My thoughts, exhausted by their flight, would eventually settle down into their glass jar, where I'd tamp a tight cork over them. In the end I was always left with a pain that ached through my bones like I'd been put to the rack, and I would promise myself not to think of her again, only to repeat the sweet torture the very next night.

On the eve of the masque, I ran the gauntlet of my feelings again. Though I'd learned the servants were invited, I tried my best to stay away from the great hall but found myself wandering into the room just as the play was drawing to a close. Men in masks tripped over each other to reach a trunk of false gold as they performed for the royals on the dais and the servants sitting against the walls. I spotted Ilsa among the servants and slowly made my way to her, while searching the nobility for Margaretha. If I was going to be at the masque, I ought to use the opportunity to thank her for helping after the boar's attack. It was basic civility.

Ilsa caught my hand from her place on the floor and pulled me down beside her, almost toppling me over.

"I was afraid you wouldn't make it," she whispered. "When the masque is done, the actors and court will dance together. Have you recovered enough from your hobblin' that I dare risk my toes for a dance with you?"

"I wouldn't dream of stepping on your slippers," I answered. "Spare your toes and your dance for someone more skilled."

I returned my attention to searching for Margaretha until Ilsa answered, "I'd spare my whole evening for you if you asked, bruised toes and all."

Pity pulled my gaze down to her. I knew the pain of disappointment and would never want to inflict it on anyone, but it was kinder to help Ilsa see the truth of my feelings. "Really, Ilsa, I have no interest in dancing."

Her beguiling little smile turned to a pout. "Why attend at all if you've no intention—"

The crowd burst into applause, drowning her words. With the play now done, costumed men ran around the hall, hovering their hands over their eyes in the exaggerated pose of looking for something. One actor pulled a chambermaid up from the floor, leading her to the open center of the room as music started playing. A second actor collected Queen Mary's dwarf, and a third collected the queen's favored lady-in-waiting. I wondered how the lady would feel about dancing in the same circle as the servants, but no one acted surprised by the mix of classes, as if the spectacle of the masque dissolved all social barriers.

Two more actors wandered the room looking for partners. One climbed onto the dais, stepping over the ladies-of-honor sitting on their cushions until he stretched his hand to the very lady I'd been searching for, pulling Margaretha to her feet. Dressed in crimson and glittering in royal jewels, Margaretha absolutely extinguished all the other women in the room, leaving herself the one bright flame surrounded by guttering, spent candles. The entire hall seemed entranced by her beauty as she followed the actor onto the open floor, but with all eyes on her, her lightning gaze was riveted on me. I was helpless to look away.

"Here." Ilsa pushed a handkerchief into my gut. "You'll need this to mop up the slaver."

I shoved her hand away, irritated that she'd made me lose sight of Margaretha even for a second. Standing and finding her again, I weaved through the crowd of onlookers, matching my place in the room with hers as I watched the hopsteps, lifts, and turns of the dance. Indulging my thoughts of Margaretha all those nights was definitely playing havoc with my willpower. Her partner took his backward step, and without thinking, I pushed my way into his place, putting my hands on Margaretha's waist and lifting her in a turn. When I set her back down in front of me, her wide eyes exposed her shock.

"You are recovered," she panted. "I am glad of it."

"I too." I would have been sorry to miss seeing her in that dress.

Lifting her into another easy spin, I was disturbed by how familiar it was being close to her again. That after all the time apart, it felt natural putting my hands on her waist and breathing in the smell of the red flowers crowning her hair. Natural and alluring. Despite hoping to smother every last spark of desire for her, I felt its burn even now, reminding me how much I cared for her, whether I wanted to or not.

But I hadn't joined the dance to rekindle impossible hopes.

"I wanted to thank you for your help the other day," I said while she leapt before me. "To keep beating in the forest with a gashed and bloodied leg is a pain I'm grateful to have avoided."

"You should be grateful to Felipe for letting you see his physician. The man for the servants is a butcher."

I didn't have any gratitude toward the prince.

"Friedrich, you press my hand too tightly."

I relaxed my grip, but my eyes wandered to the prince, whose steely gaze was locked on me. I nodded with a smile of forced politeness.

Margaretha caught the exchange. "Though you may not care for the prince, he has the power to grant my brother's freedom. That should make you happy."

"It does." My answer was clipped.

The dance was winding down, the moment slipping through my fingers like rain. I wasn't yet ready for it to end. Lifting her in the final leap, I set her down so close in front of me that our faces were a breath apart as we stared into each other's eyes, neither of us moving.

"Friedrich," she whispered.

I swallowed, and my hands gripped her waist tighter.

"I-I don't expect," she stammered. "If you never find it in your heart to . . . to forgive me, I hope that, in my saving Samuel, you can at least see I do not value human life so meanly."

I sighed. "Margar—Countess, the only life I think you value meanly is your own."

The song ended, the crowd's applause dissolving our intimacy, and she took a step back. I couldn't let her leave yet. I seized her hand, bringing her eyes up to mine. The vulnerability on her face stabbed me with a sudden ache for her. "I wish, *I wish* I could find a way to—"

"*Mea columba.*" The prince grabbed Margaretha's hand right out from mine, not even acknowledging my presence. "Are you ready for our dance?"

The smile she offered him did not reach her eyes. "Always."

Throwing me a sorrowful final glance, Margaretha left with the prince.

I made a straight line to the wine table and raced through a cup, reaching for another just as Ilsa appeared at my elbow.

"I thought you had no interest in dancing," she hissed, then whirled around and stormed out of sight.

Margaretha

Friedrich was still at the wine table, alone.

"Felipe, I'm parched. Can I bow out of this dance to fetch a drink?"

"I'll fetch you one myself," he offered.

"Many thanks." I masked my disappointment. His chivalry thwarted any hopes of speaking to Friedrich again, of learning what he was on the verge of saying when Felipe had interrupted. My mind was playing over our conversation, guessing, hoping what he was about to say, when my name stood out in the flow of ladies' conversation behind me.

"Do you think Lady Margaretha stained her dress in blood before the masque?" It was Dorthea's voice.

"I think her dress is divine," Anna pitched in. "The perfect color for a harlot."

The women giggled. "Yes, doesn't the Bible say your sins will be crimson if your name is 'White as Snow'?" Dorthea asked, and they laughed harder at her distorted recitation of the verse.

"I think she's given up playing Lady Snow White now," said Lady Anna. "You see her singled out, arm in arm with the prince, alone with him all the time."

"Hush, ladies," Jakelina whispered. "She'll hear you."

"And what if she does? Yo-ho! Snow White!" Anna called.

Dorthea giggled while Jakelina continued to shush them.

I didn't move. I wouldn't betray that I'd heard them, but I couldn't stop myself from squeezing my fists into balls so tight it strained the seams of my gloves.

Felipe returned with my drink. "For you, my lady." He handed it to me with a gallant, overacted bow.

I took the cup from him, guzzling down the spiced wine, preferring the burn in my throat to the burn of my tears. When I finished draining the cup, Felipe gently took it from me.

"What troubles you?" His eyes were soft.

I shook my head, but he wouldn't heed it, taking my elbow and leading me from the hall into the cool night and the beautiful gardens of Coudenberg Palace. I knew what idle prattle our time alone would cause, but considering what I'd just heard, there wasn't much more I could do to tarnish my reputation.

Felipe stopped us at a fountain gushing perfumed waters. The strong scent, combined with the hastily drunk wine, left me in an odd, dreamy state.

"What happened?" Felipe asked. "Was it that servant man? Did he say something to you?"

"What? No! No, it was only idle court gossipers," I answered, using the moonlight to inspect my gloves.

The prince took my hands in his, leaving me no excuse for a distraction.

"You worry too much what other people think. Do not let them rob us of our evening. I envied the men who danced with you tonight. I wished it to be me. I still wish to dance with you."

Music from the great hall floated over the trees and shrubs into our little perfumed pocket of the gardens, and Felipe swayed to the beat.

I laughed. "Won't we need more couples to dance the galliard?"

He paid me no heed, catching my waist with his hands and pulling me against him.

"This isn't the galliard," he said. "It's a new dance entirely. Forget what you've learned and let the music teach you how to step."

I felt the rhythm of the crumhorns and cornets, allowing Felipe to turn me and lift me and sway with me as he pleased until he wrapped his arms around me, pulling me to settle against his chest.

"I don't think this dance will be taking hold in the courts anytime soon," I said, and Felipe's laugh rumbled through his jerkin.

"Tell me, what was it you heard that upset you so? Do the women tell sordid stories of your love affairs?"

I sighed. "Of one love affair in particular."

"Ah, they speak of us, do they? Say you're my mistress?" He held me tighter, and when I rested into his embrace, the weight of guilt sank in my stomach. Was it right, being here with the prince when part of me wished to be somewhere else? Tonight, for the first time in ages, I'd been back in Friedrich's arms, the feel of them dulling the ache I'd carried since the day he'd cast me off. But he did cast me off. And even though I wanted to believe he was softening toward me, how could I really expect him to forgive me? Yet here was Felipe, a man who cared for me, who could provide exactly what I needed, and whose heart was pounding in his chest at my nearness. He was the one I should focus on now. I took a deep breath, letting the scent of Felipe's pomander chase all thoughts of Friedrich to the quiet recesses of my mind.

"It's not such a bad notion, you know," Felipe murmured.

"What's not such a bad notion?"

"You being my mistress. I can think of very little that would please me more than having you in my arms day and night."

"Felipe!" I pulled away, slapping him across the shoulder, then covered my mouth when I realized what I'd done. "I cry you mercy, Your Grace."

He laughed and caught my wrists, tugging me back to lean against his chest. "Come, Margaretha. Don't tell me you haven't longed for more than this." He lifted my chin with his fingers and bent down to kiss my mouth. "Or this." He tugged the glove off my hand, then his lips trailed down my fingers until he kissed the insides of my wrists.

His kisses made me dizzy. I swallowed, trying to call my muddled thoughts to clarity. "I am human, Your Grace."

His breathy laugh was warm against my skin. "I'll rely upon that."

CHAPTER 36

Friedrich

I PRESSED MY CAP TO my head as cold gusts slashed the caravan winding its way toward Coudenberg Palace. With summer now in retreat, all future court hunts were likely to be as cold and miserable as this one had been. At least the wind cleared out the foul stench of rotting garbage and human waste hovering around the palace like an invisible bog.

Cresting the hill, Margaretha and the prince led the train into the round enclosure of the *Place des Bailles*, passing between the brass statues mounted on top of bright-blue columns. I jogged ahead of them through the tunneled ramp to the inner courtyard, then into the stables to get the horse's stall ready. The building blocked out the winds, making me warm enough that my nose and cheeks tingled while they regained feeling.

Picking up the rake, I laid out fresh hay as a stealthy step sounded behind me. One trying to be silent but failing. I rounded to find the young page who'd taken my taler. "Ah, master of the dice. Have you something for me?"

"'Ave you somethin' for me?" He held out his open palm, but I shook my head, falling into the comfortable pattern of our exchanges over the last few months.

"Letter first."

He pulled two missives out of his jerkin and dangled them from pinched fingers, still offering his open palm. "It'll be six talers now. I used the last two to bribe the guard."

It was the same story he gave me every time he brought one of Samuel's letters, but I studied him with narrowed eyes, trying not to show my surprise at being given a second missive. "Very shrewd." Digging into my pocket, I pulled out six coins and stifled a smile as the page boy bit each one.

"Hope to do business with you again." He touched his cap with his finger, then meandered out of the stables.

I couldn't even wait for him to be gone before I ripped open the first letter, finding nothing more than the standard communications Count Samuel sent his father. But the second missive was different. Short and clearly not meant for the count, it was still written in Count Samuel's shaky scrawl.

Glad you survived Mühlberg. My health is failing. Still worth it to escape the attentions of a certain lady.

The letter was not addressed to anyone, but I knew it was for me. Somehow he had guessed or learned that I was the courier of these messages. Despite my aloofness, or maybe because of it, the young count had always been friendly with me, leading me to form a sort of begrudging tolerance for him and his persistent jokes about going to war to escape the ladies. But the comment on his health made me uneasy. He wasn't one to complain. Speaking about it at all was a clue to how much he was suffering.

Horses' hooves clopped on the stones outside the stables, and I slid the letter into my jerkin just as the prince rode in on his charger. Margaretha wasn't far behind, but I didn't even have the chance to offer her my arm before the prince appeared beside me, taking her by the waist and setting her down in front of him.

"When will I see you again?" he asked.

She laughed. "I'm sure I shall see you at supper."

"Too long from now. We could meet back together and ramble the Warande once we've changed from our riding clothes."

I pretended to inspect the horse's shoe as a reason to stay nearby and hear Margaretha's answer.

"And what excuse would I give the queen?" she asked. "I must stay with the other ladies-of-honor."

"They will assume you are with me." The prince's hands were still on her waist, and he pulled her closer to whisper, "As royal mistress, you have the freedom to move about as you please."

My breath gusted out as if the horse had kicked me in the stomach. Did the prince really just call Margaretha his mistress?

"I am *not* your mistress." Margaretha stepped out of his grasp. Her voice was cool and steely, unfriendly enough that the prince's smile fell.

"Regardless, when everyone suspects you of it, you have the same privileges. Whenever you will it, I give you leave to come to me."

The prince left on much less friendly terms than he'd entered, waiting for Margaretha's parting bow before striding off with his attendants.

I gave Margaretha a few moments to recover before I handed her Count Samuel's letter.

"What is this?" She threw me a curious look as she unfolded the paper. Reading the short note, her eyes met mine with wide excitement. "Is this—? How did you get it?"

"It's what your father sent me to do," I murmured.

She read over the letter again, shaking her head. "I knew he was ill, but to have him say it outright means he's worse than I'd suspected."

Looking to where the prince had just exited, her features settled with determination. When she moved to follow him, I stepped in front of her, stopping her.

"Take some time to think this through," I said. "If you go off so rashly . . . I wouldn't want you doing anything you'll regret."

Her eyes softened, and she gave me a small smile. "Don't fret about Felipe. I know how to handle him."

Then she cut around me and followed him out of the stable.

Margaretha

My sights danced over the courtyard as I frantically searched for Felipe, spotting him leading his retinue across the entrance porch of the palace. I picked up my skirts to dart between servants and up the steps of the porch, skipping every other stair in my haste to reach him. Each minute was precious to me. Each moment I delayed risked putting Samuel beyond my reach.

"Felipe!" I called to him.

He turned, his face brightening with a smile when he recognized me hurrying toward him.

"Already seeking me out?" he asked.

I puffed a laugh, reaching him and catching hold of his hand for support. "You said I need never fear to ask anything of you." I swallowed and took a few deep breaths until my lungs began to steady. "I worry for my brother. He was ill at the Ommegang. He might be further still with so much time in captivity. You said you would inquire after his health. Have you yet?"

He dropped his eyes. "Not yet."

"Will you?" I begged. "Quickly?"

He nodded, bringing my hand to his lips.

Knowing Samuel was suffering, I dared to ask more. "And will you send Vesalius to him?"

Felipe reared back his head. "That is a hefty request."

"Yet I know you can meet it." I stepped closer, my eyes begging him to agree.

His gaze studied my face, and his mouth lifted in a sideways smile. "How easily you persuade me." Shaking his head with a sigh, he said, "I'll send Vesalius."

I beamed at him. This was it. I could feel it. This was the beginning of securing Samuel's freedom.

CHAPTER 37

Margaretha

THE BALL CRACKED AGAINST THE racket, echoing in the tennis court as Felipe grunted to return the volley. Egmont easily shot it back, sending the prince dashing to the back wall to make the return while the spectators offered their "oohs" and "aahs." I was more interested in the little physician entering the viewing gallery, snapping his fingers. Three days had passed since I'd begged Felipe to send Vesalius to Samuel, and each night at supper the prince would promise me, "Soon." Today the physician's snapping was more pronounced than usual, and my suspicion of his news made the rapid pace of the game intolerably slow.

Egmont was gaining in points, showing the prince no clemency as he hit the ball with great force into the tightest corners of the serving court. Where Felipe was dripping sweat and frantic, Egmont's confidence only increased, his hits becoming surer until he launched the ball into the grille and beyond the prince's reach, winning the game.

The spectators applauded, and the two men came together at the net, bowing to each other in a display of respect, though Felipe's flashing eyes betrayed his true feelings. Egmont did not cower. He straightened his shoulders and faced the prince, each man staring the other down until Felipe's rushing attendants collected his racket and offered him a towel.

Egmont took advantage of the diversion by leaving the tennis courts ahead of the spectators ambling toward the doors. The little physician was fighting his way through the departing crowd in an effort to reach Felipe. I did the same, earning the condemnation of more than a few ladies in my hasty efforts to "chase after the prince."

Meeting the two men standing at the net, I tried not to notice the prince's bare chest beneath his gaping white silk shirt or the hard curves of his arm as he toweled the back of his neck. He seemed to know my mind, for he flashed a tantalizing smile that drew me unconsciously closer. He responded by reaching for my hand. The simple gesture calmed my racing nerves.

Once the building was finally empty of spectators, I accosted Vesalius with my questions. "Have you seen to Samuel? What is your opinion?"

"Vesalius hasn't seen your brother yet." Felipe gave me an amused smile. "He goes now. With you."

"With . . . me . . . ? I'm going to see Samuel?" My voice rose an octave in my excitement, and I hugged Felipe.

He laughed. "If we're quick."

We trotted up the steps from the Coperbeek Valley, crossing through the arcade and into the main building, where we navigated deep into a corridor that was wholly unfamiliar to me. When we'd passed through a short, thick set of doors, Vesalius retrieved a waiting lantern and pouch from a table, then led the way to a flight of circular stone stairs.

"Where are we going?" I asked. "This isn't the way to the *Maison du Roi*."

Felipe and Vesalius exchanged glances.

"Your brother isn't with the Landgrave of Hesse or the Elector of Saxony," Felipe answered. "They keep the lower nobility here. In the dungeons."

I stared in disbelief. "The dungeons? Then it is little wonder my brother's health is failing."

Felipe dropped his eyes but didn't answer me directly. "I go no farther," he said. "Vesalius will take you on."

My hands shaking and my breath coming fast, I let the physician lead me down the steps to the palace dungeons. At the top of the stairway the windows had been wide, pulling warmth and light to flood the space, but down here, they were nothing but begrudging slits, jealously holding back all but the barest slivers of sun. The damp was heavy, and the smells of filthy bodies and waste grew stronger. With every step downward came the rising panic of walking into dark, icy waters that would soon cover my head. The physician's lantern light was the only thing of warmth, and I leaned toward it.

Reaching the bottom of the stairs, Vesalius offered a handkerchief. "For the smell."

"I thank you." My voice was muffled behind the kerchief.

I followed him down a row of barred cells, past guards and dim torchlights.

"Why is my brother here, Vesalius?" I asked. "Why is he not with the Landgrave and Elector?"

Vesalius shrugged. "Is there ever sense in the rules of war?"

I pulled down the kerchief. "But he's ill!" My protest echoed off the walls.

"Margaretha?" A weak voice carried from somewhere deep in the dungeon. Though hoarse and rough from misuse, I'd have known that voice anywhere.

"Samuel!" I ran ahead, finding my brother struggling to prop himself up on a filthy tick mattress.

The physician motioned to a guard standing outside the cell, and the man flipped slowly through a ring of keys until he'd finally unlocked the door. I yanked it open and found my way into Samuel's arms, giving him a hug so tight he started coughing.

"Careful, Margaretha," he panted. "I've only one set of lungs."

I prompted him to lie down, helping his head to his pillow before pulling the ratty, moth-eaten blanket up to his chest.

"Best stay back." He scratched his neck, exposing red bumps. "I'm f-food for the fleas. Fleas now, maggots later." He smiled, but a shiver overtook him.

"Samuel, your humor is as ill-timed as ever," I chided, fighting back emotion with a smile of my own. I knelt in the filthy straw beside his cot, pulling off my gloves to hold his hands in mine. They were warm. Too warm. "Do you get enough rest? Do they feed you well?"

The tremor of chills shook his hands. "Food is better than anything Cook served," he teased, and I wondered that, even as sick and in danger as he was, he was still Samuel, making jests at every turn.

"How fare Father and M-Mistress Hatzfeld and . . . everyone?" he asked.

"All well, though Father worries about you. So do I. When I saw you at the Ommegang, you looked so ill. Though the light is dim, I still think you too pale and thin," I prattled as I watched the rapid, straining movements of his chest, tallying all the symptoms of his malady in my mind to form a frightening conclusion: pneumonia.

"*You* accuse me of being pale?" He closed his eyes, his bravado fading with his strength. "I'm tired and cold."

I looked to Vesalius, whose expression showed some of the concern I felt. He settled his lantern in the straw and moved to my brother's mattress, resting two fingers on my brother's neck. He touched the back of his hand to Samuel's brow, then studied the bumps on Samuel's neck.

I quietly waited while Vesalius moved through his examination process, squeezing Samuel's hand whenever the rattling wheeze vibrated through his chest.

"His pulse is quick, and he's febrile," Vesalius whispered. "I'll prepare a tonic." Carrying the lantern to the corner of the cell, he surveyed the contents of his pouch to retrieve his supplies. A desperate helplessness weighted down my limbs. My elder brother, always bigger and stronger, always my protector, lay frail and weak before me. I studied him—his brow beaded in sweat, his eyes swollen, and his lips cracked—and a tear escaped down my cheek. Scrubbing a hand against my tingling nose, I sniffed.

Samuel cracked an eye open. "There you go, rubbing your nose again. I th-thought you would have outgrown such a habit by now."

Kissing his hand, I rested my cheek against it, turning my face to conceal my anguish. "I beg you will forgive me, Samuel," I whispered. "For nearly two years your freedom is all I've striven for, and now . . . I should have had you out sooner. If only I were more capable—"

"Th-there is nothing to forgive," he chattered. "I never meant to put such a burden on you. I'm only grateful I got to see you once more." He slid his hand down to my chin, turning my face to meet his. "You've grown up so much."

I shook my head. "Don't talk this way. You're not beyond saving yet. I will try harder, find some way to free you."

"There's nothing more you need do," Samuel said. "It was never your responsibility to save me. My life is in God's hands."

"I can't lose you." My eyes filled again. "Don't give up yet."

"Never, Retie." He forced a trembling smile. "I'll outlive you and d-dance on your grave."

My laugh made the tears drip down my face. "You're a buffoon."

"Comitem de Waldeck, I have tobacco water for you." Vesalius returned to Samuel's mattress. "Can you lift your head to drink it?"

Samuel nodded, straining to raise himself while the physician set a cup to his lips. When Samuel lay back down, the doctor began snapping and cleared his throat. "I'll need to examine his urine." He avoided my eye as though he were embarrassed, and realization dawned on me.

"Oh, yes. I'll be with Prince Felipe if you need me."

I gave Samuel a parting smile, which quickly faded when I was alone on the walk out of the dungeon. I wouldn't let myself cry again. There was hope to be had, and I was walking toward the very man who could give it.

When I neared the top of the stone steps, Felipe rose to his feet. "How does he fare?"

"Not well. I suspect pneumonia."

The prince took my hand, and his brows lifted. "You're shivering." He pulled me into his arms, letting me lean into his warmth, his security.

"Felipe, what am I to do?" My voice cracked with emotion. But I knew exactly what needed to be done.

We stood in silence for a time, Felipe stroking my back as I gathered my courage. Taking a shaky breath, I asked the question I'd been longing to ask since my arrival in Brussels. "Could you . . . help him? Could you speak to your father on my behalf and see if Samuel could be released?"

He did not even hesitate, as if he'd already anticipated my request. "Of course."

"Of course? Do you really mean that?"

He chuckled. "You should know by now, I cannot deny you anything."

My elation soared. I had finally done it, finding the right man to grant my brother's freedom. I lifted my head, offering him my brightest smile despite the tear trailing down my cheek. "Felipe, my gratitude would know no bounds. I'd be forever in your debt."

His thumb brushed away my tears. "Then could I ask that in return you be forever in my arms?"

My veins pulsed with nervous energy. "Is this . . . a marriage proposal?" I had not expected this. Had never even believed it possible.

"Of a sort." He ducked his eyes. "Not one bound by laws of man, but a marriage in every other respect." He raised his gaze to meet mine, watching me as my brows furrowed in confusion. Then, slowly, understanding began to sink in, and I narrowed my eyes to slits. Anger, thick and hot, pulsed through me, and I pushed against the prince's chest to free myself of his conniving grasp. "So all you've said and done has been a lie? Was it only part of a long scheme to seduce me?"

He caught up my hand, keeping me there, forcing me to face him. "Don't misunderstand me, Margaretha. I do . . ." Felipe averted his eyes, and his cheeks almost pinkened, ". . . love you. I know what I ask offends you, but you must understand my situation. Things are such with England and my father's empire that you know I must make an alliance for the good of my family, my people. I cannot think of myself."

"You think of no one *but* yourself, Your Grace." I tried again to wriggle my wrist free of his grip.

"I know the kind of woman you are, that you would never come to me without persuasion, but you must know the kind of man I am. I won't give you up. I would that you be my wife in spirit. Live with me, love with me in every kingdom and court I travel. I need you with me, Margaretha. In time I hope you will forgive me my coercion. Your brother will be free and well, and I will show you such love that you'll not regret having chosen me."

I stopped struggling against him, knowing I must wait for him to release me if I ever hoped to leave. He took it as a sign of compliance, using the opportunity to pull me closer.

"I know you're human." He gave me a teasing smile. "You admitted it yourself."

He brushed the back of my neck with his fingers until the hairs on my arms rose, then he slowly, carefully moved his lips toward mine. I didn't move, didn't close my eyes. I stayed a statue under his soft kiss. He hugged me against him, nuzzling his face in my neck. "Even after the stink of the dungeons, you still smell of flowers."

His lips traveled over my neck, my jaw, my earlobe, then he whispered, "Be with me, Margaretha. I will make you happy. Let me love you as my heart dictates." His voice was not commanding, nor seductive, but pleading, and it seemed he truly thought he loved me.

He didn't know what love was.

True love meant a willingness to sacrifice anything, even your very life to protect those you hold dear.

And he'd just told me he could save Samuel. He *would* save Samuel.

How much did I love my brother? Was I really willing to sacrifice anything to save him?

Footsteps echoing up the stairs made us separate, but Felipe gave my hand a squeeze before letting it go.

"What do you think, Vesalius?" he asked the physician.

"It's not good. Not good." Vesalius shook his head at the ground. "An advanced case of pneumonia."

"But what can be done?" I asked. "How will he be treated?"

"Given permission"—Vesalius glanced at Felipe—"I could administer more tobacco water, maybe do some bloodletting, but I'm not certain how much it would help. Without a change of location, I fear his time is short. A few weeks. Maybe a month."

My sharp intake of breath drew the eyes of both men. "Weeks?"

"Do not worry," Felipe soothed. "You can get him the help he needs."

Vesalius looked back and forth between us but said nothing.

"I wish to bid him farewell." I started down the steps, but the physician stopped me.

"He is at rest now. Sleep is vital."

I nodded, working to swallow the tight ache in my throat as we moved outside the short doors and back into the palace corridor.

"It will be supper soon, and I must change." Felipe took my hand, pressing something cold and hard into my palm as he whispered in my ear, "It's a copy of Thieuloye's key. Whenever you've a mind for escape, I'll await you in my chambers." He gave my earlobe a quick kiss, then turned to Vesalius. "See her to her rooms."

My hand curled around the key, and I bowed as the prince departed down the corridor.

"Shall we?" Vesalius motioned me forward, allowing me to take the lead out of the corridor and back into the arcade.

We walked in silence, my head roiling with half-thoughts and internal arguments. Beside me the physician snapped once or twice as though he would speak but seemed to think better of it and remained silent. The snapping became a humorous distraction, and I found myself actually smiling when I asked, "How are your rats?"

"Hmm? Oh, the rats. Well, yes, they're mostly very dead. All dead now, though the strangest thing happened with rat number four. When I'd left my room the other night, he lay dead on the table beside the others, but the next morning when I returned, his tiny squeaks caught my attention. He was breathing, and his body trembled. He'd even revived enough to move his limbs. Now I'm wondering if he had been sustained with food or kept warm by a fire or blanket, would he have lived?" He rubbed a hand over his beard.

"You mean he's dead again?"

"Oh yes, quite. I threw him out the window with the others. But it reminded me of the stories I'd heard from the emperor's Spanish sailors to the New World. Stories of people, dead and buried, who came back to life, stumbling into their homes wearing their burial clothes. Maybe they, and my rat, weren't truly dead but in a stupor. A sleep or paralysis that, if I could learn to manage, would allow my surgery patients to undergo painless operations. No more brandy or biting sticks."

"You are quite different from the barber-surgeon of my village. When his patients complain of pain, he blames them for being weak, yelling over their screams and demanding they calm their hysterics."

"Yes, I've seen that before. It's guilty work putting someone through agony, especially if the chance of helping isn't as great as we hope. But we do want the best for our patients. Physicians go into this work because they wish to help."

I smiled at him, and we resumed our silent walk, the weight of my worries again falling heavy on me when another round of his snapping caught my attention.

"I'm very sorry about your brother, *Comitissa*."

I nodded my gratitude for his sympathy.

"I would help you, if you ever needed it."

"Help me?" I raised an eyebrow.

"I've traveled the courts with the Habsburgs for many years. I know the prince. He's used to getting his way no matter the means, and though it must pain you to hear it, your brother's life will soon be beyond saving. Yours is not." He set a hand on my elbow, stopping me in my walk and prompting me to face him. "Truly, I will aid you in any way I can."

Vesalius's words made me wonder how he understood so well my situation with the prince. Squeezing his hand still resting at my elbow, I offered my thanks. "I promise to ask for your help if ever the need arises."

But there was no way he had the power save my brother and no way he could help me out of my situation with the prince. That choice was mine alone to make.

CHAPTER 38

Margaretha

THE QUEEN'S CHAMBERS WERE UNUSUALLY silent. No gentle lute melody floated in the air. No pleasant conversation or even hushed whispers interrupted the quiet. I kept my eyes on my needlework, especially when I felt Queen Mary's gaze resting on me, which it did quite frequently.

A page boy entered the room, earning everyone's watchful eye as the only distraction for the last hour. He seemed to feel it, for his self-conscious gaze darted over the ladies as he handed Dame Thieuloye a letter. She read it and presented it to the queen, who glanced it over, then nodded her chin at me. Instead of bringing me the letter, Thieuloye only motioned for me to follow her.

Setting aside my needlepoint frame, I trailed the dame out the door. We were up the stairs and moving down the third-story hallway of nearly empty chambers before she offered any explanation.

"You have a guest. Your stepmother has come from Waldeck."

"Belinda is here?" Joy made my steps quicker, and I soon outpaced Thieuloye to reach the one open room. Inside, Belinda sat on the bed while Ilsa worked with a servant girl I didn't recognize to unpack a set of trunks into the press. The sheer number of trunks weighed down with new, fine clothes had me gawking. How on earth had Father paid for all of this? Hadn't Belinda been complaining of money troubles in her letters to me?

"Margaretha!" Belinda jumped to her feet, wrapping me in a fierce hug, and I had to hold back the threatening tears, realizing how much I'd missed her. She'd been the one constant in my life. Her voice, her scent—everything about her was so familiar. After nearly two years apart, her embrace was like coming home.

"Stepmother, what are you doing here? I had no word you were coming."

Belinda puckered her face. "Don't consign me to that odious title. It makes me feel twenty years your senior." She took my hands in her jeweled grasp and sat me down on the bed. "I hadn't time to write of my coming. After your last letter regarding Samuel, your father and I agreed I should leave immediately. But tell me, how fares your brother? What is being done for him? The prince is ensuring his good health, is he not?"

"The prince offered to help, even having his father's physician look Samuel over last week. Felipe said he would have Samuel freed by week's end, but only if . . ." I shot an uncomfortable glance at the maids and lowered my voice, "if I consent to be his mistress." I didn't fight the blush creeping over my cheeks as I anticipated Belinda's shocked gasp, but it didn't come. Her face was expressionless, almost bored.

"Well, did the physician think Samuel will last the week?"

"He hopes so . . ." I spoke slowly, confused by her dispassionate response.

"Good. I'll send word to your father that I'm bringing Count Samuel home and that he is to have our physician ready." She moved to the little writing table and dipped a quill in the ink bottle.

Surprise bound my tongue, leaving me mute until I choked out, "What? You encourage me to do this?"

"Hoyday, Margaretha, the whole court already thinks you have. I can't tell you the kind of gossip Hette heard after less than an hour here."

The little maid glanced at me with a guilty look.

"This isn't about your name's honor anymore," Belinda continued. "That honor is gone. It's about saving Samuel, doing whatever it takes to save him, as you promised you would."

"I was willing to risk my life, not sell my soul."

Belinda returned to me beside the bed, kneeling in front of me to whisper, "Our souls were lost long ago. But if we rescue one so noble as your brother, maybe God will forgive us our lies."

Looking down at my hands, my eyes traced the borders of my scar.

"I would do it," she said. "Be the prince's mistress to save Samuel."

I scoffed. "You would do no such thing."

"I would," she insisted, "but it's you he wants. Does that not soothe you some to know he cares for you?"

If I could believe he cared. He'd seemed so sincere. "He said he would marry me if he could, that he wishes to be my husband in spirit."

"There, you see? No doubt he'd even let you perform a ceremony if you wished. Unsanctioned, of course."

Belinda spoke madness.

And yet, seeing my brother free and well was a heavy temptation. "But, no." I pushed myself off the bed and whirled to face her. "Becoming a man's mistress was never part of our plans. I have more respect for myself than to stoop to playing the harlot."

Belinda approached me carefully as if I might startle and take flight. She lifted my hand in hers, her thumb brushing against my scar. "Do not forget what we have done, the life we took. That thing you call self-respect is only pride, and you have no right to it, considering your sins. You should be humbled beyond the lowest beggar, even as I am humbled. Samuel is in prison. *Dying*." Her voice cracked. "There are no other options, no other suitors lined up willing to speak for his freedom. There is only Prince Felipe, a man with greater power than you dared dream of. The man who has offered to save your brother. The time for thinking is done. Now is the moment to act and act selflessly."

I sat with her words, hating that pieces of her logic were beyond argument. Samuel's time was short. There was no one else I could turn to for help. But with no other options, was I really ready to trade myself like a dark-alley purchase for my brother's life? Or maybe Belinda was right there too; the time for thinking was done. We'd spent so long thinking and planning and working and sacrificing that to balk now and see my brother die would be the acutest torture. Could my soul handle the weight of another death, or was this my last chance for redemption?

Belinda's smile made me suddenly conscious that she'd been watching my face and was pleased with whatever she saw. "Ilsa, look through Lady Margaretha's press and fetch me some of her best dresses. I should like a few options for what she might wear when she meets with the prince."

Ilsa pinned me with a heavy stare, lifting her brow in disdain before dropping a quick bow to leave the room.

"Belinda, you are too hasty," I insisted. "I've made no decision."

"But you have. And Samuel thanks you for it."

Friedrich

I slid into the open seat at the servants' tables, scooping up a plateful of mushroom pasties and pork pie.

Ilsa watched me gather food. "I'm surprised to see you. The countess hasn't sent you packin'?"

I paused with my hand over the breadbasket. "Why should she?"

"Well, I doubt she'd approve of you and Lady Margaretha starin' starry-eyed at each other day and night."

It took a few seconds for understanding to click into place. "Mistress Hatzfeld is here? In Brussels? Why?"

She picked up a piece of meat with her fingers. "Somethin' to do with Lady Margaretha's special new relationship with the prince, I'd imagine."

"What do you mean?" I worried I knew too well what she meant and fought to push back the anger.

Rolling her eyes, she said, "You're a smart man, Friedrich. I think you can puzzle it out."

I didn't believe Ilsa's insinuations. I wouldn't. But of its own accord, my gaze jumped to the dais, searching over the faces for Margaretha.

"She's not there." Ilsa smiled from across the table, popping the meat into her mouth with two delicate, dripping fingers. "She has other plans this evenin'." I shot her a warning glare, but she continued. "We spent all afternoon pickin' out just the right gown for the prince—"

I slammed my fist against the table, rattling the dishes. The conversations around us went silent as diners watched with excited eyes to see what would happen next, but I did my best to keep my voice to a low growl. "Your idle gossip does your mistress harm. Steady your wagging tongue."

Ilsa's face was too calm, too confident. "I'm her maidservant, Friedrich. Do you truly think my words only idle gossip?"

A stone dropped in my stomach, burying any appetite, and I pushed my plate away, swinging my legs over the bench and stalking toward the doors. But partway out of the hall, I changed my mind and went back to the table, putting my face right in front of Ilsa's. She stopped chewing and stared at me with her mouth hanging half open.

I spoke low, so only she could hear. "You want to compete with the countess, but if you think your lies will somehow give you an advantage over her, you're wrong. All you do is expose a deep ugliness inside that can never be covered by the beauty of your face."

I left her behind with her eyes wide and her mouth still hanging open.

Pushing out of the Aula Magna, I took a deep breath of the biting morning air. Ilsa was wrong. Margaretha said she could handle the prince, and she'd been doing well enough from what I'd seen. She'd even rebuffed him right in front of me after he'd suggested she was his mistress. Why would that suddenly change?

Clomping through the courtyard, I could think of only one reason. Hatzfeld.

That woman always had an inexplicable influence over Margaretha. If she was here in the palace, I was less sure of Margaretha's resolve. And with Count Samuel being ill, how much convincing would it take before Margaretha justified drastic action? She'd already justified much in the last two years of her work in Brussels, shifting from an innocent, awkward flirt to one easily toying with men to meet her ends.

Black sludge slithered in my marrow, and I worried it might be true.

Margaretha might very well have succumbed to the prince.

CHAPTER 39

Margaretha

Ilsa yanked the brush through a snarl in my hair, muttering an oath under her breath. She seemed particularly ill-humored tonight, and I wondered if it was another display of her waspish mood since the masque or something more.

She set the brush on the washstand with a thump, returning my attention to the key resting beside the pitcher. The dark metal glinted in the light of the flickering candles, looking dangerous and inevitable and making my breath come faster.

"Ilsa, have you finished yet?" The warm room had turned suffocating, the idle chatter of the queen's ladies vexing me like fingers rapping against my skull.

"You would know if I had," she muttered, then added more loudly, "Almost done."

Just a few more moments, a few more twists of the plait, and I would be ready for the evening's gathering. I doubted I would ever be ready to see the prince again, but he was sure to be there, and I could avoid it no longer.

The moment Ilsa's hands left my hair, I bolted out of the chair, my nervousness forcing me to move despite my reluctance to leave the room. I had no notion what I would say to Felipe. I had no desire to even think of it. My brain was sore and bruised from all the mental volleying. Would I degrade myself? Would I abandon Samuel?

"Lady Margaretha." Thieuloye's voice called my attention to the ladies gathering beside the door, and I reluctantly moved to follow them. The corridors were cold against my bare shoulders. Belinda had insisted I wear the scarlet gown gifted to me by the prince, with its dropped neckline and exposed shoulders, and the gown did its work, attracting the eyes of the prince the moment I walked into the nobles' gathering room. He sent me an impish wink, his lips quirking into the grin I once thought charming.

I looked away.

I was not surprised when a short time later his voice whispered beside me, "Shall we talk?"

Still turned from him, I gave a hesitant nod, and he took my hand, pulling me toward the door and away from the nobility. His attendants followed for propriety, but we'd hardly left the room when he ordered them to stay behind. I allowed them to depart without a trace of shock, without a thought chasing through my mind. There was nothing to think, nothing to feel. Even my very limbs tingled with a pervasive numbness as Felipe tugged me to the bottom of a narrow staircase isolated from the main hall. He backed me against a wall, propping an arm over my head and effectively trapping me.

"I'd almost given up on you. You look"—his eyes trailed over my dress, lingering on my neck, my shoulders—"ravishing." Lifting his free hand, he trailed his fingers across my bare shoulder and over my collarbone.

I studied the buttons of his jerkin. How odd that the scrolling patterns there should keep my interest at such a time.

"Will you not look at me?" His voice was as gentle as his finger under my chin, lifting my gaze up.

It was as if I'd been choking, suffocating for want of air, but not feeling the burn in my lungs until my eyes met his. Then frantic panic overtook me, the sheer instinct to breathe, to live, fighting through me, and I pushed against the prince's chest with a force that sent him staggering backward.

His eyes were wide, his chest heaving. I mirrored him, watching him. Waiting.

He straightened, his hands falling limply to his sides. "You despise me, don't you?"

"You manipulated me," I hissed, unable to conceal my disgust.

"Then you are only here for your brother." He took a step back.

"You made it abundantly clear my body was the price of his freedom." I should not be saying these words. Every outburst risked Samuel's life.

"No." Felipe had the audacity to look hurt. "His freedom was only meant to help you see the stupidity of mankind's constraints on love. It would be nothing to overcome such inconsequential laws if you cared for me as I thought you did." Sinking down onto a stone step, he ran a hand through his curly hair, then lifted his sad eyes to mine. "Could you not love me, Margaretha?"

No, I would not pity him. He deserved none of it.

And yet . . .

Was he not, in many ways, a product of his upbringing? A man born to entitlement, with no notion of how to love when life had trained him to command, force, and maneuver to get his way? Though his affections may have been sincere—and I suspected they were—no matter how deeply he felt, he had no idea how to love unselfishly. Maybe we suited each other more than I'd realized, with my own frail, pathetic offering of affection shaded by manipulation, by trying to entice him into saving my brother. With my heart numb and cold, asleep after a lifetime of guilt. With my soul struggling to free itself from the ache for another man. My love was broken too.

I sighed, settling onto the stair beside him. Despite everything, I could not hate him. "I care for you, Felipe."

He took my hand, playing with the ring on my finger. "Every minute apart from you is torture. My heart wrestles to flee from me, pounding against my ribs to escape its cage and settle by you, where it belongs. Can you not see?" He looked at me. "It's not by choice, but necessity that I'm drawn to you, and I beg you to end my torment. You are the only woman I will ever love."

Dropping my eyes, I took a deep breath. "And what of your wife? Where shall I stand when you are joined with England?"

"That union of state?" His voice was laced with disgust. "How could such a cold marriage ever overtake my love for you? In the depths of my soul, Margaretha, you are the only wife I shall ever have."

I stared at the stone beneath us, reflecting on the prince's words, on his claim that I would be his only wife. Pulling the idea apart and piecing it back together in different ways, a notion formed. One that could save Samuel and allow me to keep my honor intact. It would mean closing all other doors, of committing myself to a lifetime with the prince, but my brother would live, and my atonement would be made.

But I would need to convince Felipe.

Curling my fingers around his, I summoned my courage and lifted my eyes to his. "Felipe, if I'm to be your only wife, then I would that you prove yourself to me."

"Gladly." He squeezed my hand.

"Promise to marry me."

His fingers froze on mine, but only for a moment. He almost succeeded in sounding unruffled as he answered, "You know that isn't possible."

"That you marry one so far beneath you?"

"That I abandon an alliance with England."

I cocked my head. "Is not Mary Tudor your cousin? Surely familial bond is alliance enough."

"Hardly. Half the kingdoms are ruled by my cousins. Marriage is the only way to maintain the kind of power we Habsburgs have."

"You already rule half the continent. You can't give up that one little piece of an island for me?" I chewed the inside of my cheek, and the prince eyed my mouth, sliding his thumb across my lower lip.

"It's not just one island. It's my entire kingdom. That alliance with England will give us funds and armies enough to battle the Ottomans, the French, even you rebellious Germans."

I pulled my hand from his and stood, keeping my back to him. "You've managed without England up to now. Surely you can get along without them for the next sixty years."

"Sixty?" He followed me, his fingers caressing the skin of my shoulders. "You plan to live a long life."

I nodded, and he turned me toward him, his eyes dancing over my face before dropping to my mouth.

His head dipped closer. "Will you let me live it with you?" he whispered, then touched his lips to mine.

I should have turned away. Wisdom demanded it, but wisdom was hard to find in the face of Felipe's tender kiss. He wrapped his arm around my waist and tugged me against him, but his lips moving over mine stayed soft and sweet, matching his gentle plea. My defenses were falling, and I was angry with myself that even after his manipulation, some part of me wanted to give in to the heady sensation of his touch. But experience had taught me that Felipe never fought fair, and now he wielded temptation like a weapon.

Twisting from his hold, I left him behind, retreating to the safety of the palace hall. I rested my forehead against the cool stone of a marble pillar, taking a few clarifying breaths before my pulse settled enough to let me face him when he approached. "Felipe, if you truly loved me, it would be nothing to sacrifice alliances and advantages. King Henry of England was so in love with Lady Anne that he broke with the church for her, and I'm certainly not asking you to do anything so extreme."

"You saw how well that turned out for Lady Anne." He folded his arms across his chest. "These are real sacrifices you ask. Not just of me, but of all my people. I am more than one man, more than one kingdom, even. I'm an entire empire, and I must think of what's best for everyone. What's best for you too,

Margaretha. I'm sure you envisioned a life where you'd be at a man's side as his wife, but I cannot offer it. I dare not offer it for what it could mean for you."

I lifted my head to meet his eye. "What do you imply?"

"You take a great risk if you insist on this course. I truly do love you, Margaretha. Maybe even so much, so selfishly, that I could forget about the losses my empire would suffer by our union. But my family would not. Maintaining the empire is all that matters to them, and I fear what they might do to you should you get in their way."

"Are you suggesting violence?"

"Possibly." He stepped closer but avoided my gaze. "Nothing overt, mind you. A convenient accident or unexplained illness. Whatever it might be, I couldn't save you. I wouldn't know how to prevent it." His eyes met mine. "I beg you to accept all that I can give you: gowns and jewels, your brother's freedom . . ." He came closer still, settling his hands around my waist. "And my undying love."

Anticipating his kiss, I turned my face so that his lips met my cheek.

"It's not love," I said.

He pulled back to look at me. "What?"

"What you offer me is not love, else you'd never insist I sacrifice my honor for you. You'd free my brother out of kindness and goodness, not use him as a lure to compel me into servitude."

Clenching his jaw, he caught my wrist in his tight grip. "I use your brother to push you into seeing reason. You have no idea the patience I've shown you. You think it easy to restrain myself?" He dropped my wrist and ran his hand through his hair. "I've waited for you to come willingly. How is that not proof of love?"

I swallowed, forcing myself not to look away or cower. "If you insist on holding my brother's life as forfeit, I can no longer believe your confession of love, but would question your nobility, your decency. Even your humanity."

He flinched, rearing his head back as if I'd slapped him. We watched each other, the silence heavy between us until the prince finally looked away, straightening his jerkin and hair. "It seems we've said all we can on the subject. This must be goodbye." Turning on his heel, he walked away, his boots clipping over the marble floors.

Tears pricked my eyes as I stood, wondering what to do, but I soon found myself scrambling up the stairs toward the only place I could think to go. Belinda's chambers were already dark, but when I quietly tapped on the door, her maid was quick to answer. Belinda sat up so fast I wondered if she'd slept at all. Her gaze was bright with the reflected light of the fresh-lit candle when she asked, "Is all resolved? Is Samuel's freedom secured?"

My eyes welled again. "I may have just destroyed all hope of saving Samuel."

She knit her brows, climbing off her bed to meet me by the door. "But did you not speak with the prince? How did you leave things with him?"

"I'm certain he's angry with me. After I insisted he ask permission for us to marry, he—"

"You did what?" Her face went blank.

"I couldn't make myself . . . I wouldn't be his—"

She turned and stormed back to the bed. "Did you exert any effort at all?"

Tears trickled down my cheeks as I stared after her in disbelief. "I've done nothing else for the last two years."

"And yet you've failed." She whirled on me. "Again."

"Not failed—"

"You pushed too far, Margaretha. If the prince is done with you, who else will you turn to? No other man would dare rob the bed of the kaiser's son, and with Samuel's failing health, you haven't the time to entrap another man anyway. It's the prince or no one, and you just limited your options to no one."

A hollow pit formed in my stomach, swallowing up my anger inside the nagging fear that Belinda was right. I may have lost my brother forever.

"I suppose it's up to me to fix this mess." She threw me one last irritated look before she climbed into bed, lying down with her back to me.

I held in my emotion, waiting until after I'd sneaked back into my chambers, after Ilsa had helped me undress, after I'd climbed into bed and pulled the coverlet up to my chin, before letting my tears trace their warm paths down my face.

CHAPTER 40

Margaretha

Several days passed with no word or looks from the prince, and as I awoke to soft sunlight and the clinking of dishes, I anticipated this day would be no different.

Across the room, Ilsa poured a cup of wine, but the chamber was otherwise empty.

"Where are the other ladies?" I pulled myself to sitting.

Ilsa looked up at the sound of my voice. "All gone to mass."

"No one bothered to wake me?"

She set the wine jug down and crossed the room to put a tray of food on my lap. "I think they all assumed your nights have been busy and you needed the rest."

I choked on my wine and was in a fit of coughs when a knock called Ilsa to open the door. Standing outside the room with disheveled hair and his jerkin half unbuttoned was Felipe, looking much altered since our row.

"Your Grace!" I pulled the coverlet up to my shoulders for modesty, knocking over the tray of food and spilling grapes and oatcakes. It earned me his amused smile.

"I was hoping we might speak," he said.

At my hesitation, he added, "I shall behave, I promise. I only want to talk."

"Very well. Did you . . . right now?"

He glanced down the corridor and stepped out of the doorway, letting the returning ladies-of-honor file past. Their eyes trailed over his untidy state, and with me still in bed in my chemise, I could easily guess the thoughts inspiring their knowing grins and behind-the-hand snickers. He gave them a gracious smile, then turned his attention back to me.

"When you're ready." He bowed and disappeared into the hall.

While Ilsa dressed me, I lamented Belinda's absence. Like the prince, she'd been aloof the last few days, claiming she was working hard for Samuel's freedom and too busy to see me. I suspected she still hadn't forgiven me for botching things with Felipe. But now with him wishing to speak to me, causing me to hope I might still have a chance to help my brother, I wished Belinda was here to advise me.

Taking a fortifying breath, I joined the prince and his attendants in the corridor. He shrugged away from the wall, offering his arm, and I found it strange touching him again with my feelings so conflicted.

"I've missed you, Margaretha," he said, his voice quiet as we turned our way down the turret stairs. "I haven't slept well or thought clearly since we parted."

"If you were so troubled, why stay away? Why send me no word?"

He looked down at my hand on his arm and covered it with his own. "I needed time. To decide what to do. To speak to my father. I toyed with the idea of forgetting you entirely." He gave an embarrassed chuckle. "But it wasn't possible."

"You've spoken with your father? You asked if we might marry?" My stomach twisted into anxious knots. "What did he say?"

He rubbed a hand over his jaw and let out a long breath. "Everything I'd predicted and more."

A wave of relief overtook me, but I chided myself for such self-interest. Samuel fell further into danger every day. "I wonder why the kaiser doesn't release my brother and send us both home if he's so keen to keep you and me apart."

"Father knows me better than that. I won't give you up so easily, and the harder he works to separate us, the more determined I'll be to keep you." Felipe's voice was taut, but then it softened. "Though after your censure the other night, I'm not sure you still want me."

My hesitation lasted a beat too long, but I used a swallow as excuse. "I do."

He tucked my hand deeper in the crook of his arm, pulling me close, and I was grateful for the warmth as we strolled past the frost-covered statues in the gallery.

"Margaretha, I know my father will never agree to our marriage. He'd sooner have one of his bastard sons on the throne than a Lutheran empress at my side. I fear for you. I fear the harm that may come if you persist on this course, and I beg you"—he stopped to face me, taking both my hands in his—"abandon your schemes of marriage. Admit that constancy of affection is the only true union of two souls. It needs no sanction from pope or emperor."

So he was pressing forward on that selfish tract, was he? "And I'm to feel this constancy of affection while I share my bed with another woman's husband?"

"Whip me for a villain, you think me so base! I've no love for Mary Tudor. It's she who steals her way into your husband's chambers. It's she you should abhor, not me. I have no part in it."

"Felipe." I shook my head over our clasped hands. "If it's real love you feel for me, don't ask this of me. Free my brother and . . ." I hesitated, adding with caution, "and let me go." When I lifted my face to meet his gaze, his expression was clouded with confusion.

"Let you go? You censure me for fickleness, then tell me to forget you? You call that fitful, irregular, capricious thing love?" He dropped my hands, chuckling without humor. "Margaretha, to be with me would injure no one. You haven't even your own reputation left to protect. The courtiers all murmur that you are my mistress; your name and honor are sullied and paraded about without any regard for you. What care you for their condemnation? Care for me," he pleaded.

I needed to put him off a little longer, to give the kaiser time to change his mind, or give Samuel the time to miraculously recover, or give space for any other unlikely and utterly impossible occurrence to save me from this fate. "I'll consider it."

Looping my arm with his once again, I directed us back through the gallery.

"Very well," he answered. "I only pray you don't lay blame at my door when your delays cost the young *comitem* his life."

CHAPTER 41

Friedrich

"Hoof." I tapped the horse's foreleg, and he lifted his foot for cleaning. I was thorough with the pick, forcing myself to focus on the dirt packed in the sole of the hoof. It helped keep my mind from wandering to Margaretha, wondering why I hadn't seen anything of her for days.

Finishing with the last hoof, I set the horse's leg down and straightened, startling at finding Mistress Hatzfeld leaning against the stall door, her jeweled necklace glittering in the sunlight.

"Good dawning, Friedrich. It's been a while since our last meeting."

I tossed the pick into the bucket. "Don't pretend you've missed me."

"*Tsk.*" She flicked a strand of straw from her skirt, and her rings clinked together. "You know how keen I was to keep you in County Waldeck."

"To keep me away from Brussels, you mean. Yes, Ulrich said he could hear your fights with the count all the way out in the kennels." Picking up the curry comb, I brushed in circular sweeps over the horse's coat.

"Can we be frank with each other?" she asked.

"I've been nothing but frank with you, my lady."

She flashed a tight-lipped smile. "I've received reports regarding your behavior since you arrived here. At best, you're a distraction, and Lady Margaretha doesn't need distractions." She ducked under the crosstie. "I just want to ensure you won't be a problem for her from now on."

The horse laid back his ears, warning me I was brushing too hard. I softened my strokes but wouldn't let myself answer. There was too good a chance I'd spout the string of accusations uncoiling in my mind.

Hatzfeld seemed to know it, because her smile was exultant. "*'Twere an ill bargain to desire'* the countess's love."

I clenched my jaw and kept brushing until her familiar phrase brought my head up with a snap. Those were Wolkenstein's words, his poem one of many tucked in love letters sent to Count Samuel. But they also touched a memory of sitting with Margaretha in her father's library, reciting those same words from a book. Mistress Hatzfeld's book.

All those jests of Count Samuel's—had he said he was escaping the ladies, or a certain lady? One very devoted lady?

"If I may, as you say, be frank"—I brushed the horse again—"why was it you married the count?"

She cocked her head as if surprised by my question but answered, "The man saved me from my uncle. It was out of gratitude."

"Or was it because Count Samuel ceased to love you?"

Her eyes narrowed, but she quickly recovered, petting the horse's mane with almost-convincing calm. "Did you know the kaiser's Wildungen troops were recalled to Brussels, with Captain Carrera at their head? You and Carrera haven't always been the best of friends, I think." She lowered her voice and leaned toward me. "Imagine what he'd do if he knew about your little letters to Samuel."

I dropped the curry comb in the bucket and faced her. "What do you want from me?"

"Stay away," she spat. "Keep your distance from the countess, or I'll report you to Carrera. He'd be only too happy to see you hanged." She ducked back under the crossties, wriggling her jeweled fingers at me with a cheery smile. "Have a pleasant day."

I watched her leave the stables before grabbing the body brush, whisking dirt from the horse's coat with the stiff bristles. That snake and her threats. She wouldn't dare expose my letter exchanges, or she'd implicate her husband in the plot. A risk I doubted she was willing to take, no matter her talk.

And what did she care about getting Count Samuel freed, anyhow? She was married now. That should be the end of it. Was she still holding on to her affections? Was she expecting the old count to die and leave her free to marry his son? No, none of it made sense, but one thing was very clear: nothing good could come of her being here, back in Margaretha's life. In all Hatzfeld's scheming, she'd kept her hands clean, leaving Margaretha the one holding a hand to the fire while Hatzfeld got the gain. She seemed to make a habit of leading Margaretha down dark paths, convincing Margaretha to entrap me with her flirtations, possibly even convincing Margaretha to abandon any thought of self and throw her lot in with the prince. The woman was poison, and nowhere did her venomous bite sink more deeply than in Margaretha's mind. Why couldn't Margaretha see that? Why was she so ready to believe her life worthless unless she sacrificed it for someone else?

The horse's coat now a glossy shine, I grabbed the lead rope and unhooked the crossties to guide him back to his stall. At that moment, a bird swooped through the stables overhead, startling the horse, and he tossed his head back with a jerk. The lead rope ripped through my hand until the friction burned my skin. When I'd gotten him settled down and stalled, I looked at the red, stinging stripes traveling over my palm and across my fingers and had to shake my hand to let the chilled air ease the pain. As I walked to my chambers, glancing at the burn through puffs of cold breath, it was impossible not to draw a connection to Margaretha and our meeting at Walpurgisnacht. What had been her fixation then, hovering her hand beside the flame? She'd claimed no desire to hurt herself, but I had sensed it. Some kind of desperation rolled off her, drawing her hand closer to the torch. Had the mock burning of the witch filled her with the same painful memories it did me? Was it an unbearable reminder of her lies, filling her with guilt?

The idea pummeled me with the weight of truth, and I had to sink down onto my bed. With my head full of frustration for her self-sacrificing and self-doubt, how had I been so blind to her motives? I should have known it the moment she'd admitted her shame for my mother's death. It was guilt driving her to hurt herself. Not just then, but now too. Why else would she be so quick to follow Hatzfeld's guidance when it went against Margaretha's very character?

But it was wrong to settle all the blame on Mistress Hatzfeld. Though she was guilty of conniving and bending Margaretha to her will, the pang in my heart told me I was to blame too. Margaretha had opened herself up to me, but when she had shared her agony of regret, what did I do? Sent her off to Brussels without even thinking of soothing her ache. I'd treated her like the deplorable person she already thought she was, confirming all her wrongheaded ideas that she was too corrupted to be loved. Too guilty and sin-filled to have worth. And so she'd come here, looking to earn her value through misguided deeds, when I should have shown her just how good and worthy a woman she already was. But it was too late now, wasn't it? She had already chosen her path, submitting herself to the prince. There was nothing I could do.

Or was there?

Why else would Hatzfeld have ordered me away from Margaretha? If her path really was decided, why get rid of me? What power did I have?

And why did I have it?

Nervous excitement brought me to my feet, and I paced in front of my bed. Maybe it was only arrogance or wishful thinking, but I had to hope, to believe that if I wielded some influence with the countess, it was because she still cared for me. My opinion still mattered, and if it did, then it was high time I do the right thing.

CHAPTER 42

Margaretha

THE LADIES-OF-HONOR WERE LINING UP at the chamber door, ready to follow Dame Thieuloye down to dinner, when Belinda appeared in the hall, flanked by a pair of page boys.

"What's going on here?" Thieuloye asked.

Belinda held out a paper to her. "Comtess de Waldeck is moving to my rooms." She directed the boys to my press to fold and pack my things.

Thieuloye broke the seal, perusing the paper with the very conspicuous signature at the bottom: *Moi, l'empereur.* "I, the emperor."

I looked at Belinda, astonished. She'd gotten an audience with the kaiser?

Belinda ignored my gaze, throwing a summoning wave to Ilsa. "Lady Margaretha's maid will need to come with us too."

Ilsa waited for Thieuloye's begrudging nod of permission, then left the room. Belinda took my hand and pulled me into the hall, following closely behind Ilsa as she led our way to the third floor.

"What is this about?" I asked. Her steps were quick, and I had to trot to keep pace. "Belinda, what is happening?"

"The kaiser granted me an audience this morning on account of a conversation he's had with his son," she whispered, releasing my hand. "He was keen to have you out from Thieuloye's watchful eye in hopes that you'll relent and become the prince's paramour."

I slowed. "Is that all?" I'd been hoping my removal to Belinda's rooms meant we'd soon be leaving for Wildungen. "Then Samuel is not free?"

Belinda stopped to face me. "You know exactly how to free him, foolish girl."

Her look was penetrating, but when I refused to answer, she continued walking, leading us down the stairs and into the empty halls of the second floor.

"Should we not be making our way to the Aula Magna for dinner?" My stomach was already rumbling.

"We must stay to direct the page boys where to put your things." She entered her rooms and sank onto the large bed. "You can send Hette or Ilsa down for food, if you wish. I shall be napping." Belinda plopped back into the pillows, closing her eyes and effectively ending the conversation.

"Ilsa." I turned to find her leaning against the washstand, already watching me. "Will you fetch us dinner?"

"Of course, my lady." She didn't move but continued studying me with a raised brow before saying, "So you're not the prince's mistress after all. Seems you deserve the name 'Snow White' in more ways than one." Then she pushed off the washstand and out of the room, leaving me to wonder if her words were intended as praise or insult.

I sat up in bed, holding a hand to my pounding temple and wishing I hadn't succumbed to the temptation to nap. But directing the page boys was tedious work, and after a large dinner, a ray of late-autumn sun penetrating the windows had called me to sleep. Now I was paying for it.

"What troubles you, Margaretha?" Belinda glanced at me in the looking glass as she inserted her earrings.

"Nothing. Just a napping headache."

"Perhaps a cup of wine will ease it. Maybe a bite to eat. Hette brought up a few remains from supper for you."

"Supper?" I dropped my hand, looking out the window to find the sun dipping below the horizon. "I slept through supper?"

Belinda moved to the writing desk, lifting the wine bottle to pour me a cup. "You've been under a great deal of strain. I was glad to see you resting and didn't want to wake you. Ilsa, will you fill a plate for Lady Margaretha?" she asked, then crossed the room to hand me the drink.

"I don't suppose you've heard anything more from the kaiser?" My tone betrayed my optimism. My last hope was that the old mule would consent to the marriage before Samuel was out of time.

"Nothing," Belinda answered, settling on the bed beside me. "Stop irritating your scar and drink your wine."

I uncurled my hand to expose the deep fingernail marks indented in my pinkened palm. Trying to rub them out over my skirts, I gave up, sipping the wine until the cup was empty.

"How's your head now?" Belinda took the cup from me.

I held still, internally measuring the pain. "A little better, I think."

"Good." She smiled, summoning Ilsa to bring over a plate of braised oxtail and tart of apples. Normally my favorites, the food looked less palatable than before.

I picked at my meal, able to get down half a bowl of the oxtail and several bites of the tart before I gave up and pushed them away. The headache still pulsed dull in my brain, and my nerves for Samuel's situation had turned my stomach weak. I needed fresh air and a place to walk that didn't smell of leeks. "I'm going to take a turn in the corridor. I'll just be outside the room," I said to Ilsa, who had risen to join me. She sank back in her chair and picked up her stitching.

"Don't be long." Belinda waved.

With the door closed behind me, I took a deep, reviving breath of the cool corridor air. For now, I would not let myself think of the prince or the kaiser or of my brother's struggle for his life in a dank dungeon cell. I would think of nothing at all. I would walk and breathe and live only in the present.

The halls were almost black, save the ghost-gray strokes of moonlight stealing in from chamber windows and stretching through open doors to light the rug beneath me. I put a hand on the wall and let my fingers trail over tapestries and float the voids of empty doorways as I traveled the hall. The walk was already serving its purpose, lightening the pressure against my brain. One step. Another step. Nothing but now and this moment. Nothing but the soft padding of my bare feet against the rug, until . . . Had I heard a voice? I froze, silencing my swishing skirts and listening harder.

"Margaretha."

My whispered name brought the hairs on my arms upright as a dark figure emerged from an empty room. Shadows only betrayed that the figure belonged to a man, but when he stepped into the moonlight, my shoulders sank with relief. "Friedrich."

"Come over by the window," he whispered. "There's light there."

He waved me to move ahead of him, but as I passed by, his hand caught hold of mine. I sucked in a breath at the shock of his touch but did not pull away, letting it warm me with its rough, familiar feel. His touch was gentle, and now, when I felt so alone, confused and worried, I wanted nothing more than to wrap myself in his embrace and weep. But such things were impossible.

Stopping in front of the moon-flooded window, I turned to face him. "What are you doing here?"

He rubbed his neck, dropping his eyes to the moon-stained rug. "There's something I wanted . . . I'm not sure how to say . . ." Releasing my hand, he pulled off his cap, his hair shining silver in the light as he raked his fingers through the strands. "I'd hoped to speak with you. I thought if you were . . . on your way to . . ." He was still stammering, avoiding my eye as he continued in a rush. "I thought I might catch you on your way to the prince. Maybe stop you from doing this."

He'd heard the rumors. Of course he had. And now he thought me on my way to—

Embarrassment heated my veins, but I kept my tone even. "My many thanks for your concern, but I can manage well enough on my own. I'm no longer the little girl you sent away in Wildungen."

"You're right. You're not the girl from Wildungen anymore. I miss her artless blush." He lifted his fingers to my face, trailing them across the tender skin of my cheek as I stared at him, wide-eyed. "Whenever you smile at the prince or your eyes light up in his presence, it gives me pain. I can't stand by while he's allowed to touch you, to spend time with you—things I've worked so hard to keep myself from doing, though I've felt longer and more deeply than he could ever imagine."

Was this . . . ? Was he being truthful? I remained mute, not trusting myself to answer when I couldn't be sure Friedrich had really spoken those words. It was only a trick of my mind, conjuring what I'd wished to hear.

But then he added, "It pains me most because I know I'm to blame."

"You? Why would you be—" I pressed my mouth shut and shook my head. None of this was relevant. "Samuel is dying."

Friedrich flinched.

"Any change in me is for the better if it means I can save my brother's life."

"Selling yourself is for the better?"

"I'm not the prince's mistress." My voice was flat. Friedrich's jaw dropped slightly, but I continued. "Felipe has asked his father's permission for us to wed."

"Marriage?" Friedrich stepped back. "Do you love the prince?"

His voice held that same open vulnerability as when he'd begged me to stay in Wildungen with him. And I'd almost agreed, thinking it was love that drew us together, until Friedrich dismissed me to Brussels in nearly the same breath. How could I love the prince? I didn't even know what it meant to love in that way.

"I love Samuel," I answered. "And Felipe is proving his love to me by seeking our marriage."

My answer must not have satisfied, for his gaze darted back and forth between my eyes as if he were deliberating what more he might say. I hadn't the time to find out.

"I must get back to Belinda before I am missed. Fare thee well."

Friedrich stepped in front of me, setting a light hand against my stomach to stay me. "If it's true you don't love him—if you're not just trying to spare my feelings—then even if you were to marry him, you'd still be selling yourself. You're worth more than this, Margaretha." His eyes held mine. "Your soul is valuable, and you have a right to live according to your conscience. Don't even consider the prince."

I sighed and softly pressed against his chest to push us apart, to give myself some distance. His arm fell to his side, and he awaited my answer.

"Friedrich, you of all people should understand why I'd consider him. I can't be responsible for another death. I've carried that burden of guilt almost my whole life. So has Belinda."

Friedrich raised an eyebrow.

"We bear our shame in different ways, but her remorse is no less acute than my own." I turned back to the window, staring down at the moon-swept Warande. "And then there's the injury I did you. Though it's impossible to repair, can my penance not in some small way atone?"

Friedrich surprised me with his humorless chuckle. "I can't believe what I've done to you," he muttered, coming to stand behind me at the window. "I came to you tonight to apologize."

I spun to face him. "What would you need to apologize of?"

"Sending you away. My behavior here in Brussels. I've been cold and unfeeling, watching you make the compromises necessary to save your brother. I should have helped you instead of withholding the only aid that's mine to offer: forgiveness."

My brows furrowed, trying to comprehend his meaning.

"But my forgiveness will never be enough if you can't learn to forgive yourself."

Certain I'd misunderstood him, I breathed a skeptical laugh.

His eyes narrowed, scrutinizing me. "You were just a child, Margaretha. You couldn't have foreseen the consequences. You've repented many times over. Forgive yourself."

He was serious, then. I nodded, hoping to convince him I understood, if it meant the uncomfortable conversation could come to a quicker end.

"You don't see." He shook his head. "Of course not. Why should you? After a lifetime of rejecting and condemning yourself, you expect everyone around you to do the same. I was guilty of rejecting you before. Let me fix my error now and help you realize what an admirable person you are. A person worth loving."

My stomach tightened, and I shifted to face the window, running my fingers over the black latticework to shut out the agitation brought on by his words.

"I forgive you, Margaretha."

He forgave me in the sense that it was his Christian duty to do so, and I appreciated his efforts. My lips were tight as I gave a quick nod.

His reflection shifted behind me as he hooked his fingers around mine, gently tugging me to face him. Twisting my palm toward the moonlight, he let his thumb trace the outline of my scar, and a host of opposing emotions threatened to throw themselves into my conscious. I struggled against them, fighting to keep that comfortable, cold numbness.

"I forgive you," he whispered.

The emotions began to take real shape. Pain, anger, fear. Hope and joy.

"I truly, fully forgive you." He lifted my hand up to his lips, setting a gentle kiss over my scar.

I shut my eyes against the prick of tears as Friedrich's words found purchase, cutting loose a weight chained round my soul. The tears came faster. Too many to blink back, they leaked out the corners of my eyes and trickled down my face.

Friedrich's soft lips brushed the traces of my tears—first on one cheek, then the other—before they swept to my mouth, his warm breath hovering over my lips. We'd been here before, on the edge of something momentous, only this time he knew the truth. He knew everything I'd done, yet he erased the distance between us, touching his lips to mine.

His kiss was careful at first, almost timid, but slowly it deepened, his arms curling around me and holding me to him with a hunger born of penitence and longing. He wanted me. Not in the dangerous, passionate way the prince wanted me. He wanted *me*. My spirit, my mind, and my heart.

He moved his arms from my waist, cupping my jaw in his hands as his kiss softened to something achingly tender. It was faithful and honest, and the warmth of it seeped into my veins, spreading slowly but steadily throughout my body until it collected around my quiet, sleeping heart, numb and cold after years of self-loathing.

But Friedrich knew the truth, had seen the blackest parts of me, and cared for me still, forgiving me for every wrong I'd done.

Maybe someday I could forgive myself too.

At that thought, warmth enveloped my heart. A gentle fluttering murmured beneath my ribs, then grew to a rhythmic drumbeat, each stroke bringing the world around me into vivid reality. The dark behind my eyelids now danced with hints of color. A breeze, once whispering through trees outside the glass, now rushed through spinning leaves like a river over rocks. Friedrich's lips now tasted of cloves and honey, mingled with the salt of my tears. And though I was senseless to it before, his heartbeat now pulsed against my chest. My heart sang in rhythm with his, feeling alive, feeling the numbness flee, and feeling totally, wholly loved. Loved by Friedrich. Loved by myself.

I threw my arms around Friedrich's shoulders, crushing my mouth against his while I slid my hand up his neck into his hair. His sudden, shocked breath delighted me enough that I couldn't stop from smiling and ruining the kiss.

He pulled back with a grin, his joy bringing my feelings into overwhelming clarity.

"I love you, Friedrich." The plain, honest words came out without hesitation.

His eyes went wide, but then his features softened, and he rubbed his thumb over my cheek.

"I hid away that truth, too afraid to admit it to myself." I shook my head. "It's still hard to believe you could truly forgive me. I know how undeserving I am of—"

Friedrich put his finger over my lips to stop me, and I smiled.

I pulled his hand away, wrapping it in my grasp. "I want to believe . . . I hope I really am worthy of this kind of happiness."

He didn't speak for a time, swallowing hard as though he were fighting back emotion. Then he whispered, "I love you too."

I tipped onto my toes to meet his lips again, and he was quick to respond, kissing me with an earnestness that left us both breathless. When we broke apart, I had to lean my forehead against his to steady the spinning room.

"I need to go," I whispered.

His fingers traced the outline of my lips, making my pulse dance. "Remember who you are, Margaretha. Remember what you're worth. Don't let Belinda or the prince convince you of anything. You deserve real love."

I nodded, trying to let the words sink in. Trying to absorb them and believe them and make myself understand that all my previous views of myself had been wrong. Such a monumental shift in perspective; it would take time. But it felt beautiful and right and worth the struggle. "I'll endeavor to remember."

Lingering in Friedrich's warmth and gentle kiss for just a moment more, I finally broke away, whispering my reluctant goodbye.

When I walked back to Belinda's chambers, my step was as resolute as my intentions. I was done sacrificing my life to make amends. Though it made my heart ache knowing I would forever lose my chance to save my brother, tomorrow I would meet with Felipe to tell him the truth; that no matter the consequences, I would never submit to the prince.

CHAPTER 43

Margaretha

THE HUM OF CHATTER FROM Belinda and her maid gave the impression that the nervous squirming in my stomach had turned to a swarm of bees. It was bad enough to be refusing Felipe, but I had yet to tell Belinda of my resolve, and I dreaded it. I was not accustomed to defying her, but this time, she was wrong. I took a deep breath, preparing myself to confront her while Ilsa dressed me for my ride with the prince.

"You shake too much," Ilsa complained. "Sit on the bed or I'll never get your foot in the shoe."

My whole body was in a tremor of nerves. "I am fine," I said but swayed enough that I had to use the bedpost to keep from falling.

"Ilsa, get her wine." Belinda took my elbow, helping me settle on the bed. "You shouldn't go out, Margaretha. You are not well enough to walk, let alone ride."

Ilsa doused a hot poker into a cup of wine and offered it to me.

"I must go." I took a few sips of the sizzling liquid, hoping to relieve the headache still pulsing from last night, but the wine landed hard in my nervous stomach. "I must tell the prince that I have made my decision."

Belinda's face lit up. "You will be his mistress, then?"

"I will have nothing to do with him." I raised my chin.

She stared at me, her dark eyes narrowing. "Hettie, Ilsa, leave us."

I watched the maids exchange uncomfortable glances before moving toward the door. When it closed behind them, I faced Belinda again, rearing back at the look of sheer disgust darkening her features.

"So you will let your brother die." Her tone was flat, but I sensed the anger beneath it. If I pushed her too far, she would snap.

"I will respect myself."

"Margaretha, how can you be so blind?" She took the cup from my hands. "The prince could give you everything you ever wanted. Your family's debts would be cleared in an instant, and becoming his confidant would make you the most powerful woman in the empire."

Anger churned inside me. "You would have me debase myself for power?"

"Of course not." Her cheeks pinkened, and she carried the cup to the writing desk. "I would have you save your brother. How can you discard his life and throw away our chance for redemption and call that dignity? Your thinking is backward." She turned to me, leaning against the desk as she awaited my answer.

"Belinda, Friedrich helped me understand."

Her jaw went slack, and I realized my blunder in naming Friedrich. Hoping to distract, I quickly added, "Samuel loves me. He loves you too and would not want us to suffer so on his account. And I would suffer, Belinda. Selling my soul to the prince would leave me miserable all my days."

"And what of the healer? You think our sins nothing, then?"

I joined her by the desk, taking her arms in my trembling grasp as I held her gaze. "I think we've done what we can to atone. The rest is up to God. It's time to forgive ourselves."

Belinda's hard eyes flicked over my face before they shifted to the window, pooling with moisture. She offered a small nod, and I pulled her into a hug, her body shuddering against mine with her quiet sobs. I could not hold back my tears, anticipating Samuel's death, anticipating a newer, freer life for myself. The moment was painful and sweet, and I wanted to both run from it and embrace it.

"I should go, else I'll be late." I gave Belinda a final squeeze, and she turned from me, discreetly wiping a hand over her face as I pulled on my cloak.

As I walked to the stables, I put a hand over my belly to quell the nausea that seemed to go beyond nerves. I felt almost ill. Several times the queasiness compelled me to lean against the wall, but I pushed forward, finally reaching the cold stables to find Friedrich standing ready with my horse. A smile glided over his handsome face when he saw me enter, but it disappeared the moment the prince arrived with his attendants.

"Good dawning, *mea columba*." Felipe bent to greet me with a kiss, but I turned my head, offering my cheek instead.

His brow furrowed. "Are you unwell?"

"Nothing serious," I assured him, but he was pulling off his glove, setting a cool hand to my cheek.

"You're warm. Mayhap we should postpone our ride."

I considered it, tempted by the chance to delay sealing Samuel's fate. But my mind could not be changed. "No, I'm only hot from my brisk walk to meet you."

"Very well." He donned his glove and mounted his horse.

Friedrich helped me up the mounting stool, giving my hand a squeeze. Though he said nothing, the fire he'd ignited last night still coursed through me, sustaining me with the courage I needed. I squeezed his hand back and gave him a quick, nervous smile before following Felipe out of the stables. We couldn't speak as we made our way, single file, down the hill to the Warande, which was just as well, for the bouncing trot atop the horse did little to settle my stomach. The morning's wine made a slow crawl up my throat, but my deep breaths of frosty air pushed it down again. Despite the chill, I found myself patting beads of sweat from my forehead with my sleeve.

On the tree-lined avenue of the Warande, Felipe pulled up beside me. "I'm most curious to know why you've summoned me."

"Yes." I nodded. "I was hoping to explain to you my change of senti—" Suddenly overcome by nausea, I turned away to suck in a hasty breath.

Felipe spoke softly to me. "How about you and I have a little race? You get to display your riding prowess, and we can outstrip any eavesdroppers."

When I faced him, his sights were on his attendants behind us, apparently mistaking my illness as a reticence to speak before them.

"No, Felipe. I'd really rather—"

"Are you more afraid of losing"—his eyes sparkled—"or of having to chase me for a change?"

Before I could answer, he'd spurred his horse forward, leaving me little choice but to follow. Autumn colors blurred, flashing bright yellows, reds, and oranges, until my head swam. My legs and arms felt numb, oddly disconnected from me as black spots punctuated my vision, bouncing up and down on the horizon.

I needed to slow down.

"Felipe."

My voice was too weak for him to hear. I tried calling again just as the spots swelled, painting my vision black. I had the sensation of falling. Then nothing.

CHAPTER 44

Friedrich

MARGARETHA AND THE PRINCE HAD barely left the stables when a soft whistle sounded behind me. Turning, I found that page boy, the master of the dice, motioning me toward him.

I cocked a brow. "Have you another missive for me?" Now that Margaretha had been allowed to see her brother, I thought our letter exchanges at an end.

"I do. And it'll cost you." He held out his palm, wriggling his fingers expectantly. "Four talers, same as last time."

Sighing, I dug into my pockets, pulling out the money and dropping it into his hand. "The letter?"

"In your quarters." He clicked his tongue, then abruptly departed, biting each coin while he walked away.

I made my way to my room, my pace brisk despite the distraction of my thoughts. Margaretha had hinted she was unwell. Though she'd dismissed it as nothing much, her face lacked its usual color, and I'd sensed a tremor in her hand when I'd helped her up the mounting stool. Mayhap it was only nerves at the prospect of facing the prince. If my words last night had persuaded her at all—and I believed they had—she was about to separate herself from the prince for good. No wonder she looked pale. Losing hope for her brother must be a terrifying prospect, and my heart ached for her. I wished I could be with her, hold her hand to lend my support.

A flicker of movement ahead caught my eye, and my steps slowed, my mind catching up with my impulse to seek out the letter.

My quarters were already within view, the little window looking empty and innocuous, but as I stared, I detected the sliver of a yellow uniform shifting ever so slightly from inside. I made a subtle turn, keeping an easy pace until I passed around the corner of a nearby building, then bolted in a dead sprint toward any hiding place I could find. A small gardener's shed met my needs, and I hurtled myself inside only moments before the tromp of boots approached. One man called to another, his Spanish words indecipherable, but I understood his intent. He was searching for me.

The boy had sold me out.

Gripping the door handle, I held it tight as someone shook the other side, struggling to open it. He seemed to think it locked, for he gave up trying, and no one else repeated the effort. My hands were sweating against the handle, but I kept them firm, afraid of what might happen if the soldiers found me. Crouched in the dark shed with the gardening tools, I couldn't tell just how many men there were, but I sensed at least five. They called back and forth to each other, some voices close, some farther, but eventually all their words faded to murmurs.

Was it safe to leave? I couldn't hide here forever. With Spanish soldiers on the lookout, I couldn't stay in Brussels at all. I'd need to flee back to Wildungen. Margaretha would return there, wouldn't she? If she loved me, she'd have no desire to remain here seeking a husband. Then again, I had nothing to offer her. Perhaps it wasn't even right of me to ask that she consider me; her father would most certainly cast her off. But I would let her decide for herself.

These thoughts were nonsense. First I needed to get clear of the shed.

Looking around, I found the nearest source of defense and took a firm grip of the rake's long handle. I quietly lifted it with one hand, still holding the door closed tight and ignoring the pounding in my chest as I strained to listen. A breeze whistled through the cracks in the planking, but there was nothing more to be heard. I took a deep breath and cracked the door, seeing nothing. Resting the rake just inside, I opened the door wider, stepping out of the shed and immediately pulling to a halt. Carrera stood only a few paces away, his brown eyes crinkled at the corners as he smiled at me.

He unsheathed his sword and took a step closer. "I was hoping we'd meet again. You left too soon last time."

"Your German has improved." I took a small step back. "I can almost understand you now."

His smile dropped, but he quickly regained it, moving another step closer as he clicked his tongue. "Spying is not allowed, boy."

"Then it's a good thing I haven't been spying." I retreated into the doorway of the shed, my hand finding the rake just inside.

Carrera came closer. And closer.

I waited until he was near enough, then in a swift movement, pulled out the rake, swinging it toward Carrera's head. He raised his sword to block it but wasn't quick enough to avoid the thick wooden end of the rake crashing against his skull. He dropped to the ground in a heap, and I stared wide-eyed, surprised my plan had worked so well.

He wasn't dead, was he?

His unconscious frame lifted with breath. Alive, then.

I dragged him back into the shed, my chest heaving from the effort, and closed the door behind him. I hoped his disappearance would buy me some time, for I couldn't leave the palace until I'd spoken with Margaretha.

It took some doing, sneaking through the palace unseen, but I managed to make my way to Margaretha's rooms, hesitating with my hand poised to knock on the door. Would Hatzfeld be inside? Would Margaretha already be back from her ride with the prince? Perhaps it was better to await her return in one of the spare rooms, as I'd done the night before.

Yes. I would wait. I only hoped she'd appear before the soldier in the shed was discovered.

I camped in the empty room, glancing at the window with its long, silk curtains. I'd stood there just last night, with Margaretha tucked in my arms as I'd kissed her. She'd kissed me back, whole and unrestrained, not the ghost of the woman who'd been haunting my memories since her departure to Brussels. She was real, and she'd said she loved me.

The door to Margaretha's chambers clicked open, and Ilsa left the room. I caught her arm and pulled her into the empty chamber, putting a quick finger over my mouth to warn her.

She pinched her lips together.

"Where is the countess?" I whispered.

"Not back yet. What troubles you? You're sweatin'."

I dropped her arm. "Carrera. There was a scuffle, and now I must leave. Immediately."

"Is he dead?"

I shook my head. "Will you relay a message to the countess for me?"

She crossed her arms over her chest. "I'm not your errand girl, Friedrich."

"It isn't much, but it's important. The countess must know that I have left. And tell her . . ." I hesitated, aware of the pain my admission would cause

Ilsa. But I needed Margaretha to know. "Tell her to stay strong, and tell her I'll await her in Wildungen, if she'll have me."

Ilsa spun away, turning her back to me, her shoulders rising and falling with her rapid breaths. "You'd better go, or you'll be discovered."

"Promise me, Ilsa."

She did not face me but, after a moment, gave a subtle nod. I took that as my assurance, giving her shoulder a quick squeeze. "Thank you," I whispered, then left the room, seeking my chance to escape Brussels.

CHAPTER 45

Margaretha

VOICES AROUND ME FIRST HOVERED on the brink of consciousness, then grew stronger, more coherent, and far too loud. The prince was speaking, his words rushed and rapid, his Latin slurred with a heavy Spanish accent.

"She was just riding, and then she fell. She'd said her illness was nothing. I believed her. In face and form, she seemed unaltered."

I tried swallowing, but my throat was hot and swollen. My attempt to speak was strangled into an indecipherable groan.

A cool, wet cloth came onto my forehead.

"What happened after she fell?" This voice was softer, somehow comforting, though I couldn't place it.

"She was insensible. I had to lift her back onto her horse, but then she started vomiting."

The second voice jumped in. "Can you describe the vomit?"

"Describe it? I didn't study it." Felipe's voice had an edge of irritation.

"I only meant was there anything unusual or distinctive about it?" The second voice stayed calm, and this time I recognized it as Vesalius's.

Sensation was slowly coming back to my body, and with it, a sharp, piercing pain deep in my belly. I pressed both arms to my stomach, curling my knees up to my chest and rocking to fight back the ache.

"Careful, now. Careful." Vesalius put a restraining hand on my shoulder. "You're on a table. Don't rock too much, or you'll fall."

"Drink," I begged, but Felipe's voice overshadowed mine.

"What do you think it is?"

"Not sure. Not sure." There was a series of snapping. "But until I know what it is, I must ask you to leave the sickroom. Your father would not have me jeopardize your health."

Felipe would leave? But I hadn't had the chance to talk with him.

I willed my eyes open, blinking hard against the bright sunlight streaming into the room. "Felipe, wait."

He took a knee by my side, prying my hand off my stomach to hold it in his gloved fingers.

"She wishes me to stay," he told Vesalius.

"Send for her maid if you fear leaving her comfortless, but I beg you, do not invite the emperor's wrath against me. I protect you *and* my position by insisting you leave."

I spoke Felipe's name again, but through my swollen throat, it came out a hoarse whisper.

"Rest, Margaretha. I'll be back as soon as I sort this out with my father." He lifted my hand to his lips but stopped himself, settling for a soft smile that didn't quite mask his worry. Giving my hand a quick squeeze, he slipped out of the room.

As soon as Felipe left, Vesalius shoveled his arms beneath my back, pushing me upright. The room spun, and a wave of nausea not to be combated took over, but Vesalius was ready with a bowl. I vomited violently, my whole body shaking from the strain.

Vesalius handed me a clean cloth and moved to dump the vomit out the window while I wiped my nose and mouth. When I dropped my hand in my lap, I froze in fear. The cloth was red with blood.

"Vesalius." I held up the bloody rag for inspection.

He nodded. "Blood was in the vomit too. I have a strong suspicion you've been poisoned."

He moved around, babbling, snapping—always that infernal snapping—but it was muted, faraway. Almost underwater for how vague and muffled he sounded. My mind was still twisting around the notion of poison. When could it have happened? I'd been eating in my chambers the last day. It had to be someone close to me. Hette? She'd fetched food from the kitchens. Maybe she'd taken a bribe? Yet, Ilsa had served me. Belinda had been handling my food too. But that was too extreme an idea. She was both sister and mother to me. The very notion of Belinda plotting my murder was too ridiculous to believe.

Vesalius pushed a cup in front of my face. "Drink this."

"What is it?" I gripped the cup between trembling hands, taking a tentative sip of the rank concoction.

"A purgative."

I nearly spat the medicament in the poor physician's face. "I've already emptied my stomach. Twice. Surely whatever poison was there has been expelled."

"We must be certain." He guided the cup back to my mouth. "You must purge everything to minimize the poison's absorption in your vital organs."

Setting the cup to my lips, I tried not to breathe as the sludge tipped toward my mouth. But then I stopped, putting the cup back down. "What good will this do?"

"It's to clean out your—"

"Not the purgative, this effort at clearing the poison. Even if it's successful, I don't think I'll have strength for traveling until a few days hence. In the meantime, I must eat. What use is it to clear my stomach today when the kaiser's determination and resources make an endless list of assassins ready to feed me poison tomorrow?"

Vesalius seemed confused. "Why should the kaiser want to poison you?"

"You don't invest much time in gossip, do you?" I gave him a weak smile. "The prince has asked his father's permission to marry me."

Another wave of nausea hit, and I grabbed the bowl from the table, emptying my already empty stomach and staining the bowl with more blood than bile.

"Lie down," Vesalius urged, putting aside the bowl to lay a cloak over my shivering frame.

My foolish marriage scheme was the cause of all this. A marriage I never intended to enter.

"I d-don't even want it." My teeth chattered.

"It will help the shaking," he answered as if I spoke of the cloak.

"No, the marriage. I must speak with the prince and tell him I will n-not marry him." If he informed his father I'd changed my mind, maybe the kaiser would call his bloodhounds to heel.

The doctor ran both hands down his beard, straightening his whiskers. "I doubt the kaiser will let his son near you now."

"Then I'll write. To Felipe or his father. Y-you could deliver it." I tried to sit in anticipation of penning the letter, but the pain in my stomach stabbed with a sudden intensity, and I couldn't stop myself from crying out.

"Perhaps *you* could write it," I puffed. My hands trembled too much for writing anyway.

"Oh, yes. Certainly. First, I'll just . . ." Vesalius took the bowl to the window for dumping. Rinsing it out and returning it to me, he then rummaged through drawers and lifted up dead creatures in search of paper and quill. His space was every bit as untidy as it had been the last time I was here, with books piled high over tables, bowls scattered beside cups of concoctions, and specimens pulled apart and pinned to expose their innards. There was even another row of rats lying lifeless on the table.

"You're experimenting again," I said.

Vesalius stopped searching and cocked his head, then followed my gaze to the rats. "Yes, I managed to get my hands on more of those fish from the New World. I was careful dosing the toxin, but even still, it was too strong. I don't think any of them survived."

"Perhaps they're too small. You need a human subject to test it on."

"I find myself short on volunteers." He flicked his hand toward the rats. "I doubt this lot would inspire much confidence."

"True. It'd require some d-desperate individuals with nothing to lose." Pain stabbed again at my stomach, and I curled my knees to my chest again, hugging them tight. Even as miserable as I was, it was a greater risk than I'd venture. Only those already slated for death might be brave enough to try.

Slated for death.

Samuel.

"True," I repeated, uncurling my legs as the idea pulsed excitement through my weakened body. "Vesalius, delay for a spell writing my refusal and instead pen a plea to visit my brother in the dungeons."

"But you are too weak—"

"Not I. You. Take him a draft of your fish toxin and see if he has the courage to try it."

Vesalius leaned his hands against the table behind him. "For his pain?"

"For his life. You spoke of the Indians who seemed to come back from the dead. And there was your rat that revived for a time. Couldn't you give Samuel a potion that put his body in a stupor long enough to appear dead, then when he is removed from the dungeons, he'll revive?"

The physician rubbed his hand over his beard, contemplating. When he began to pace and snap, I knew he was considering it with real seriousness, piecing out the specifics of dosing and monitoring and recording.

"What about a funeral?" he asked. "He'll have to be buried."

"We could ask to transport his body back to Wildungen."

He shook his head. "It's not cold enough yet. You'll arouse suspicion."

"But it is cold enough that he won't be buried in the ground. Maybe a crypt?" I sagged back onto the table, the conversation quickly fatiguing me. "I'll suggest it to my stepmother. She is here in Brussels and could see to all funeral arrangements. Then in a day or two, we can sneak back to his burial place and help him when he recovers."

"*If* he recovers," Vesalius said. "This is a very dangerous plan. You understand your brother will almost certainly die."

"If we do nothing, his fate is the same."

We both sat in silence until the physician raised his eyes. "I'll think on it more, but you must tell no one. If my involvement is exposed, it'll be my position or my life."

I opened my mouth to respond when the scrape of a chair beside the door made us both turn to see Belinda, resetting the chair in its place with an embarrassed smile. "My apologies for the disturbance. Prince Felipe's attendants told us Lady Margaretha was sick."

Vesalius nodded toward me, and Belinda came to the table, putting a hand to my forehead. "I knew you weren't well enough for riding. You should have listened." She twisted back to Vesalius. "I thank you for your care."

"Comtess, you should know your stepdaughter is seriously ill." He held his hands behind his back and rolled up onto the balls of his feet. "In truth, I believe she's been poisoned."

"Poisoned!" Belinda's jaw dropped. "Who would do such a thing?"

"I couldn't say with any certainty." Vesalius cleared his throat and leaned toward Belinda to whisper, "Her marriage plans with the prince could well be the root of it."

"Then she'll relinquish them. We'll leave now and get her free of this place."

Vesalius started snapping. "Right now she's too ill to travel. She plans to write the prince of her altered intentions—"

"Certainly," Belinda interrupted. "I'll see that she writes him today and deliver the letter myself."

"Yes, well, in the meanwhile, you must take great caution with her meals. And with your own. It's possible you and your maids could be inadvertently poisoned."

Belinda's eyes widened.

"Your stepdaughter should be in bed. Have you anyone to help take her back to your chambers?"

She nodded, signaling the maids waiting in the hall, and the two of them worked me to sitting. My stomach lurched, and Vesalius barely had time to find the bowl before I vomited again.

"You should take this with you." Vesalius put the bowl in Belinda's hands, and she looked as if she might expel her breakfast too.

The women pulled my arms over their shoulders and managed to get me to the door, but I called over my shoulder to the physician, "I expect to see you again. You must promise to visit me in my chambers."

He looked down at his shoes, then back at me with a solemn face. "I promise."

CHAPTER 46

Margaretha

Belinda's chambers were lit with the mild light of twilight, that soft hue that signifies neither night nor day. I had no notion what time it was, what day it was.

My throat burned with thirst. When I moaned for drink, someone propped me up to set a cup at my cracked lips, but swallowing the wine further pained my bruised, acid-raw throat. I had nothing left to vomit but heaved just the same, my throat swelling with the now-familiar strain of repeated gagging. How much more suffering could I endure before the kaiser relented his persecution? Surely he knew by now that I'd abandoned any designs on his son.

"Margaretha, the physician is here to meet you." Belinda helped me lie back onto my pillows, then sat at the foot of my bed.

Vesalius gave me a quick once-over. "Have you heard anything from the prince?"

"Nothing," I croaked.

He lowered his head and met Belinda at the foot of the bed, leaning against the post as he whispered, "She looks much worse. It's clear she's still being poisoned."

Belinda nodded, swiping a hand over her cheek. She was crying again. She'd done a lot of that since I'd taken to my bed.

"I only wonder why the prince has made no answer to her letter." Vesalius started snapping, and Belinda stood up suddenly.

"Excuse me," she muttered, leaving the room in such a hurry that her concerned maid followed her out.

Vesalius eyed Ilsa stitching in the corner, then pulled a chair close to my bedside.

"I am on my way now to visit your brother," he whispered. "Can you see out the window from where you sit?"

I raised a brow, pushing myself onto my elbow to look outside. A light snow dusted the tops of the trees.

"They'll put him in a crypt, then." I fell back on the bed.

"Yes," he said excitedly. "I'll check on him every two hours, monitor his progress, cover him with blankets. I'm feeling optimistic today." He retrieved a small flask from his jerkin, showing it to me. "My most recent trial with the rats has helped me fine-tune the dosing."

I caught Ilsa watching us, but she dropped her eyes back to her stitching.

"They survived?" I whispered.

"No, not fully, but I was able to predict their revival with a fair amount of accuracy."

The door suddenly banged open as four armed Spanish guards marched in, coming toward the bed.

They were arresting me? Now?

Stopping just short of me, they caught hold of Vesalius's arms and wrenched him upward, sending his flask sliding across the floor. He stammered out protests, thrashing against the soldiers until one jammed the end of an arquebus into Vesalius's gut, and he crumpled to his knees with a groan.

I had to help him. I tried sitting up, but all I could do was roll to my side, kicking limply at the blankets tangled round my legs. Soon my lungs were too heavy to expend even that small effort, and I fell chest-down on the bed.

Another soldier captured Vesalius's hands, pinning them behind his back and pulling the physician upright to drag him from the room.

My thoughts couldn't keep pace with what had just happened. Vesalius gone? To be imprisoned? To be killed? Why?

With my body too weak to go after him, too weak to even right itself, I turned my face into the pillow and cried. After a moment, the bed creaked as someone sat beside me. I turned my head just enough to recognize Belinda. She ran a hand along my back and shushed me while I let out the fear and frustration until I had no tears left.

Sniffing, I twisted my aching head on my wet pillow. "What is happening, Belinda? Why would they take Vesalius?"

"They must have learned of his intent to free Samuel." She ran her fingers along my hairline, pulling away the damp strands clinging to my cheeks.

My body stilled as her words revealed secrets. "How did you know of his plan?"

"Ilsa." Belinda turned to my maid, who stood huddled in a corner watching me with pity in her eyes. "You can leave for supper now. I'll join you in a bit."

The door clicked to signal Ilsa's exit, and Belinda walked to the writing table, lifting a bottle of wine. "Are you thirsty, Margaretha?" She poured the wine without awaiting my answer.

"Belinda," I repeated, "how did you know of Vesalius's plan?"

Setting the bottle down with a soft thunk, she faced me. "I overheard you talking that day in his apothecary." She returned to my side, offering the cup of red wine. When I didn't move, she set it on the stand beside the bed. "I was sorry to imprison him. He seems a good man. But I couldn't have the two of you killing Samuel with your half-witted scheme when the kaiser has promised to release him as soon as you're dead."

Belinda pushed against my shoulder, rolling me onto my back. She adjusted the blankets, smoothing them over my body, then sat beside me on the bed.

"You foolish girl," she muttered. "Why couldn't you have just been the prince's mistress as I asked? Samuel would be free. Our debts would be paid. In the end, all is the same, except now you must die." Her eyes welled, and she ran the back of her hand over them. "Was it really worth it?"

Her words were clear, but my mind couldn't arrange them into any order that made sense. Belinda in league with the kaiser? Then it was she who had been poisoning me? My sister, my mentor, my friend?

"Betrayer," I rasped. Had I the strength, I would have pushed her off my bed. "Don't pretend you care about Samuel. This is all for the money."

Her back straightened, and her eyes went dark. "You cannot say what I feel. I care for Samuel. I love him. His rescue, his kindness is in every thought and is the motive for all I do."

I narrowed my eyes. "Then why—"

"Because he doesn't love me back!" She stood, hugging herself as tears pooled in her eyes. "What else was I to do but marry your father? I needed a home. I needed security."

How, in the face of my death at her very hands, could I still feel any sort of pity for her? And yet, I did. She was selfish and wounded and scared. I could see it in the way she rubbed her hands over her arms, soothing herself because she'd lived a life alone and apart, with no one else to soothe her.

Blinking back the tears, she took a deep breath, letting that cool calm overcome her once more. "Only, your father's position wasn't as secure as I'd expected."

"So you sold your soul to the kaiser for thirty pieces of silver."

A sad smile came over her face. "It's a bit more than thirty, dear. And there are lands too, but you could have had so much more if you had just listened to me. The prince would have given you everything." She shook her head, her features turning hard. "But now it's up to me to secure your brother's freedom, and I *will* see him free."

The door opened, and Hette peeked inside the room. "Supper, my lady."

"I must go now." Belinda reached for my hand, but I pulled it away. Undeterred, she placed a quick kiss on my forehead. "Rest. It will ease your pain."

She swished out of the room behind her maid, leaving me alone in the darkness.

So this was the end, then? I was to die for Father's coffers and Belinda's gowns? I was to die so that Samuel might live? That might have served as consolation before, but now it wasn't enough. Not nearly enough. I'd spent so long living as a ghost, sacrificing myself to everyone else's causes and whims. I was pushed about as a pawn in Belinda's games, slid across the board as a rook in the prince's, and now, finally ready to step forward as the queen of my fate, I'd been cut down.

A hot tear leaked from my eye as exhaustion turned my bones heavy, and I sank deeper into the mattress. My sights followed a slow circle around the room: over the writing desk crowded with breads and fruits, over the looking glass, the clothes press. These would continue without me, cold and dispassionate to my extinction. There'd be no change to mark my time here, no memory of me, no sad little sigh years from now when the cut of my death had dulled to a quiet bruise, only pained when memory touched upon it.

It was such an odd thing, resigning oneself to dying, but I found it happening. Found myself bidding life adieu with surprising forbearance until my eyes landed on the apple poised conspicuously on the writing desk. Had it been there all along? In the dark, its red skin was almost purple, but it drew my attention, the fruit pulling at the memory of French lessons in Father's study. Of a warm fire and my warm cheeks as Friedrich had recounted our first meeting, admitting that I was the reason he'd left the mines. What had he said? That my act with the apple had offered him the chance to choose something better?

Closing my eyes, I rested on my pillow, but the image of the apple persisted in my thoughts. *Choose. Choose something better.* Friedrich's words stirred my pulse to something more than the dull thud of the last few days, the thick beats resounding like a battle cry. *Choose to live. I need to live. I deserve to live.*

I opened my eyes, surveying the room with intention. What resources did I have? What means of escape?

And then like a miracle, I saw it: Vesalius's flask. He'd dropped it when the soldiers took him, and now it lay tucked beneath an empty chair. But it was almost across the room, and I barely had strength to lean up onto my elbow.

Even if I drank it, how would I revive with Vesalius imprisoned? At least the snow guaranteed a crypt burial, but I shivered at the thought of waking to a room of half-rotting corpses. If I awoke at all.

I closed my eyes tight, then pushed myself out of bed, landing with a thump on the floor and retching all over the rug.

The door cracked open, spilling light over me.

"Lady Margaretha?" It was Ilsa's voice. "My lady! What happened?" She rushed in the room, hooking her arms under mine to lift me.

"No." I weakly fought back. "I need it."

She stopped straining. "Need what?"

I pointed across the room at the flask. "Give it me to drink."

"Are you mad? I heard enough from that physician to know you won't survive it."

"My body is stupid, but my mind and reason are healthy. You must trust me."

Ilsa gently lowered me to the floor and retrieved the flask, popping it open and setting it in my hand.

I studied it as I instructed her. "This will make me as though dead. Once I am buried, send Friedrich to check every few hours to see if I've revived. Say nothing of this to Countess von Waldeck."

Ilsa's eyes dropped to her hands. "Friedrich is gone, my lady. He left days ago."

"What?" How had I not heard of this before?

"I meant to tell you. I just . . ." She peeked up at me, her cheeks coloring in the dim light.

Ah. The maid was jealous of me, just as I'd been jealous of her.

I considered who else I might call on, who else I could trust to aid me, but my list of supporters was small and dwindling by the minute. Eyeing Ilsa, I realized this jealous woman was my last hope of survival. She had withheld the truth about Friedrich's departure before, but if she'd truly wished me harm, she could have remained silent still. It seemed I would have to trust her. Giving her hand a squeeze, I said, "Then you come find me."

I was lifting the flask to my lips when she put a hand over the opening. "But we're leavin'. As soon as you're . . . gone. Lady Belinda said the kaiser just agreed to free Count Samuel, and she's eager to get him back home." Her hand pushed the flask toward my lap. "She sent me to her chambers to pack our things, thinkin' you won't last the night."

"She would know very well, since she's the one who is poisoning me," I panted.

Ilsa furrowed her brows. "She warned me not to trust you. She said your thoughts had turned deranged."

Of course she did. "She murdered me to gain favor with the kaiser. He promised her money and lands."

Another spasm in my gut had me doubling over. "Try to find a way to stay, Ilsa. More likely than not I'll die, but I fear being trapped alive in a crypt." My long-ago nightmare of being buried alive in the mines revived, as did the panic, returning with a vengeance.

"I'll find a way. I promise." Her looks were resolute, and I tried to match them, despite my inner terror.

Tipping the flask back, I let the toxin pour down my throat until I'd swallowed almost all of it. I had to fight to keep it from coming back up, but slowly, a tingling warmth spread through my body. One by one, my legs and arms disappeared inside the numbness creeping toward my chest. My lungs became heavy. Every breath was effort, and every effort gave me less and less air, turning my thoughts murky. My mind spun and floated in a way I couldn't get hold of to pull it down to reality. Was this sleep or dying? Would I dream? If I did, I wanted to dream of Friedrich.

I sucked in a strained breath and held it safe in my lungs, not knowing if I'd be able to draw another. I kept the swirling thoughts of Friedrich safe too, harboring my memories of him for as long as I could before I slipped into nothingness.

CHAPTER 47

Friedrich

The hares hidden inside my cloak were so cold they were almost stiff as I knocked on the rough wood door of the miners' cottage. An eerie quiet hovered around the place. There was no laughter, no friendly argument, no sound at all coming from the other side of the door.

I knocked again until the door squealed on its hinges, and Emil stood there, looking solemn.

"Friedrich." His sad face brightened a little. I was surprised by how much he'd aged in the few short months since I'd left.

I stepped into the cottage. The creak of the boards beneath my shoes was as out of place as laughter in a chapel. Everyone was somber, sitting on their beds and picking at their fingers or standing listless by the hearth. Only Wilhelm stood to greet me with a firm handshake.

"We're all glad to see ya, Friedrich," he spoke softly. "It lifts our spirits in these troubled times."

I cocked an eyebrow. "Troubled?"

"Bad news here and abroad. Mostly here." He nodded toward Ernst's bed, and I turned to see the old man, blue-skinned and straining for every breath. I held back my groan. How had I not known it before? He had the miner's consumption, and no amount of thyme brew would ever help.

I pulled a wooden stool up beside his bed, resting my hand on his heaving shoulder.

"Shouldn't . . . be here," he puffed.

"I want to be. Can I get you anything?"

He shook his head and took another wheezing breath. "Waldeck. Dying."

I tilted my head. "What do you mean?"

He was panting, trying to get the breath to speak, but I couldn't wait. I turned back to the room. "Ernst says something of Waldeck and dying? Do any of you know what he means?"

"That's the bad news abroad," Wilhelm answered.

"Ya haven't been to the castle yet?" asked Heinrich. "I thought ya'd have more to tell us."

"I stopped here first. Tell you about what?" My tone was clipped.

"Countess von Waldeck," Emil piped up from his bed.

"The daughter, not the count's bride." Daniel stepped in front of Emil. "The one people call a 'rare beauty.'"

My blood went cold. I was afraid I already knew the answer, but I had to ask. "What about her?"

"She's dyin'." Daniel said the words without emotion. "We heard the count is pacin' the castle, wishin' he could be off to sayin' his goodbyes, but the kaiser's banned him from comin'."

"Say his goodbyes?" My voice grew louder with each word. "She was perfectly fine when I left not five days ago!"

"Did ya know her well?" Wilhelm lifted a sympathetic hand to my shoulder, but I stepped back out of his reach. It couldn't be true. Margaretha was coming home to Wildungen. There had to be a mistake.

A cold hand gripped my wrist, and I turned to see Ernst with bloodshot, entreating eyes. "Go to her," he wheezed.

I was already aching to do just that, but I had to be reasonable. I couldn't just rush off to Brussels, could I? I was no healer, and getting caught by Carrera was a not a risk I took lightly.

But staying in Wildungen waiting to hear news wouldn't do any good either. The only reason I'd come back was for Margaretha. If she died, all my future hopes would be buried with her. I couldn't stay. It would be more torture than I could stand to live through. My home was with Margaretha or nowhere.

I squeezed Ernst's hand. "You're right, Ernst. You've always been right. God be with you, and farewell."

After saying a hasty goodbye to the rest of the miners, I gave Ernst a final smile, moving out the door before I remembered the two hares still under my cloak. I rushed back inside, my hands a hurried tangle as I untied the hares from their cords. Leaving them on the table, I bid the miners goodbye again and almost ran out of the cabin.

It was a five-day walk back to Brussels or a two-hour run up to Wildungen, where the count's stables were ripe with fresh horses.

The sky was already getting dark, only heightening the pressure to make a quick decision.

To Wildungen then, to do a bit of thieving.

I said a quick prayer, asking God to spare Ernst any pain in his passing, asking Him to give me speed in my travels, and begging Him to please, please let Margaretha live.

CHAPTER 48

Margaretha

BLACKNESS.

Even after opening my heavy-lidded eyes, there was only blackness everywhere. I sucked a slow breath, grasping at the air that refused to find my lungs. Putrid air, thick with stink and damp. Thick with death.

It meant I'd survived.

My numbed hands were folded over my chest, still too dead to move, but beneath them I could feel the slow rise of my ribs.

One breath, one pulsing heartbeat, then nothing. Another breath, another heartbeat. Silence. Time had slowed to just this here and now, measured by nothing more than the dense pulse of blood coursing through every heartbeat.

And with each pulse I became more alive, more awake to my surroundings.

The air around me was warm, close to my face as if something hovered over me, but until my hands had the strength to reach up and investigate, I refused to consider what it might be.

Heartbeat upon heartbeat passed as the fog of my mind cleared and feeling slowly returned to my extremities. My toe twitched. My fingers wiggled. My limbs awakened.

My hand quivered as I tentatively raised it up to touch a domed surface, smooth as glass and wet with moisture, which I traced down on either side of me to meet with whatever table or platform I'd been laid upon. I was closed inside some kind of glass coffin. Trapped. A sudden panic threw me into action, and I kicked against the lid, my feeble legs landing dull on the thick glass. I had to calm myself, to slow my frantic breathing and think clearly. The glass was wet and the space warm. If it was tight enough to store my body's heat, it might be tight enough to seal out any fresh air too. I'd need to move quickly, to use my breath and strength efficiently if I hoped to escape.

With my body still trembling, I thrust my arms against the lid, but they were too weak to earn any movement. Keeping my hands on the glass, I pulled my knees to my chest, wedging them between myself and the coffin and hoisting the lid enough to let in a rush of reeking air. When my wobbling limbs could no longer bear the weight, the lid dropped around me with a heavy thud.

I let myself rest, took in a few more breaths, then tried again. This time the lid moved a small distance, pinning my gown beneath it when it fell back down. No air seeped inside. I had no notion how wide the platform was but knew if I could scoot the lid little by little until I came to the side of the table, I could create a gap under the lid to let in more breathable air.

Fabric ripped the next time I lifted my legs and arms to push the lid. More musty air rushed in, more fabric tore with each lid lift, and slowly I made incremental gains. My breath was coming faster with the exertion, eating up the outside air before my muscles were ready to hoist the lid again, but my lungs demanded it. When I dropped the lid for the seventh or eighth or twentieth time, a steady stream of cool air raced in at one side.

I'd reached the edge of the table.

I greedily sucked in the vile air, my whole body sagging against the hard stone as I took in breath after breath until my heartbeat settled. Though my muscles shook with fatigue, the fire had eased out of them, letting me focus on something more than pain.

Ilsa had not come. No lanterns sat by, lit and waiting for me to wake. There were no blankets or food and drink at the ready. Either I'd revived too soon or too late, or no one was coming for me.

I chuckled a dry, humorless laugh. Against impossibility, I'd managed to survive the toxin, only to die of starvation, trapped under glass inside a crypt.

A sudden scurry made me freeze. I listened intently as tiny claws scratched over stone, then faded, leaving me to the iron silence of the dead. How many cold, hardened bodies were in this crypt? What did they look like now that time and vermin had eaten their flesh?

The hairs on my neck raised, but I reproached myself. They were only empty bodies now, with spirits gone. I needn't fear what couldn't harm me. I shouldn't think on them at all when I had to plan for escape.

The coffin lid was the first obstacle. I'd have to push my way out from underneath it. Once free, I'd feel my way toward the wall and follow it to find a door or opening of some kind.

My stomach grumbled and wriggled. No point waiting to start.

Pulling my knees back up to my chest, I set my tired muscles to work, grinding my sore shoulder, hip, and backbone against the stone as I returned to moving the lid portion by portion. The gap of air at my side grew wider, though still not wide enough for me to fit through. I pushed more, widening the gap until I'd scooted far enough that the right side of my body hung mid-air off the table. There was no leverage on that side for me to push off, leaving me unbalanced when I tried to lift the lid again. With the lid teetering at the edge of the table, I dared only the slightest of movements, but it was enough that the lid tilted dangerously. And when it finally tipped, it pulled me down with it. Glass shattered over the stone floor, and I landed in the piercing remains, my head slapping against the ground hard enough that bright circles erupted in my vision.

My mind repeated the sound of cracking glass as my thoughts turned hazy. Pricks of pain morphed into burning wounds all over my arms and legs, stabbing up my stomach and face. And I could smell blood.

As I shifted to kneel, shards tinkled around me, cutting into my bare palms and gown to stab my knees. I pushed searching hands out into the blackness until they hit something hard, like stone, then used the stone slab to gingerly pull myself upward. My brain pounded, and if there'd been enough light to see, I was certain the blow to my head would have turned my vision double. As it was, I had to brace myself against the stony support until the hammering turned to a steady ache.

My shoes crunched through glass as I slid my hands over the slab's edge to walk around the platform. A sticky, webbed thing brushed my face, and I frantically batted it away, but when I reached for the platform again, my hands hit stone much sooner than expected. Only this stone was different. Marbled and with little hills and valleys of intricate carvings. A sarcophagus.

My muted shriek bounced over the walls, and I skittered away, blindly stumbling out into dark nothingness. I swept my hands back and forth in front of me, willing myself to be calm, to not panic. I focused on the clip of my shoes and the whisper of my gown across the paved floor, but something else whispered too. I froze.

A faint, steady hissing came from behind me, exactly in the direction of the sarcophagus.

Terror chased out reason, and I ran, flailing my outstretched arms back and forth to keep from plowing headlong into anything, but I hadn't accounted for the low platforms. I slammed stomach-first against another stone slab, my hands barely saving me from knocking my head against another sarcophagus. Still, I'd touched it, and it started hissing too, joining its raspy voice with the other. I backed away carefully, and when my shoulders bumped into a tall stone column, I pressed my back hard against it to follow its wide arc.

The hissing was behind me, on the other side of the column, and fear tempted me to sink to the floor in a heap, but I had to find a way out. Braving the dark once more, I set my hands in front of me and walked out into the emptiness, forcing my steps to be slow. I moved in the direction I prayed was a wall, keeping one hand high and the other low enough to discover a platform before I collided with it.

My pulsing head was turning dizzy. The panting, frantic breaths of stale air likely made the dizziness worse, but every time I calmed my breathing, the hissing behind me grew louder.

I kept each foot moving in front of the other. Only a few more steps. The wall had to be close.

My fingers finally landed on damp brick, but as I wondered if I should follow the wall left or right, something cold brushed my neck. I pushed my back to the wall and clasped my hands over my neck for protection. A few thick heartbeats went by before I found the courage to run, keeping one hand to the rough brick wall as my shoes clattered across the floor. I kept running until my foot kicked against something, and I went sprawling forward, landing hard on a set of stairs.

The way out!

Laughing from sheer relief, I scrambled up the steps to the first slits of light I'd seen. At the top of the stairs was a rough wooden door, and I passed my hands wildly over its edges in search of a latch. The cold touch of metal on my fingers announced the handle, and I gave it a hard twist, but it didn't budge. I shook it back and forth, rattling the door in the frame, pounding the door with my fist until the side of my hand was riddled with sharp slivers. I screamed, my voice raspy against the scratch of thirst in my throat, but no one came.

Sinking to the ground, I sat for what must have been hours, watching the light under the door fade from white to gray to inky black. The cold air turned icy. I hugged my knees to my chest and leaned against the door, trying to swallow the burning thirst in my throat. My stomach had quieted its gnawing complaints to mere grumbling, but it was only a matter of time before starvation stabbed again. If help didn't arrive soon, I'd truly belong with the corpses. Death might come from cold or hunger or thirst; it didn't much matter. Every prospect was as slow and hellish as the next.

Tears leaked out of my eyes, and I rubbed them against my knees, but they were instantly wet again. I missed Father. I wished I could rest my head on his lap once more and have him pet my hair while he hummed to me. I wished I could see Samuel healthy again and laughing his infectious laugh. Mostly I wished for Friedrich. I wanted one more of his rare smiles, bright as sunshine after a rainstorm, but one more would never be enough. Even a lifetime of his jests, his quiet contemplation, his faithfulness wouldn't satisfy. And his kisses, tender and caring . . . I thought on his kisses until my head drooped to my knees, and I fell into a fitful sleep.

Hours or days or minutes could have passed before I awoke with a jolt, forcing my sore body into rigid surveillance. In the silence between breaths, mice scampered over the floor, but their staccato scurries blended with a new sound. A slow scraping, like long fingernails running down the underside of a coffin lid.

I'm still dreaming, I told myself, but when the hissing started again, I jumped up and searched for the door handle. No matter the terror that fueled my frantic wrenching, the handle refused to move. As the scratching behind me intensified, I beat my sore and lacerated fist against the door, focusing on the pain in my hand—the one thing I knew to be real.

A stream of ice-cold air slipped past me, and I flipped around, looking into the pervading blackness, but there was nothing. I turned and beat the door with renewed vigor, then another gust shot past.

It's just wind. I swallowed hard despite the drought in my throat, but the fingernails scraping below multiplied.

I couldn't stop myself from glancing over my shoulder down the dark steps but kept pounding against the door, trying to call for help just as a sudden iciness touched upon my cheek and brushed over my neck. A cold breeze tickled my ear, and a raspy voice whispered, "Margaretha."

Slamming my back against the wall, I crossed myself, whimpering a prayer that was drowned out as fists started beating inside coffins like drums. The scratching and hissing continued, competing for notice, the sounds lashing over each other in haphazard repetition like a tumult of waves. Then, from below, the coffin lids ground open, and I knew the dead were coming to claim me.

I threw my hands over my ears, pushing my back into a corner and squeezing my eyes shut as I slowly sank to the floor.

"It's not real. It's not real," I whimpered, shaking my head.

Another gust of air passed over me, and suddenly my wrists were seized in a tight grip, trying to pull me down into the belly of the crypt. I flailed against it, refusing to open my eyes and see the specter before me, but it had strength enough to rip my hands away from my ears, flooding my mind with the grating screeches of the dead.

"No, no!" I shook my head again, but over the cacophony of voices came a gentle uttering of my name. A warm hand settled against my cheek, and my eyes fluttered open to find Friedrich's storm-gray, familiar gaze. He crouched before me, his fingers caressing my face. He had found me. He had saved me.

Throwing my arms around his neck, I knocked him onto his backside as I burst into tears. "The-the voices, the bodies. They've escaped. They seek my death," I rambled, tears still streaming down my cheeks.

Friedrich lifted a lantern up to the crypt, then studied me with worried eyes. "There's nothing, Margaretha. You're safe now."

"But the hissing. The scratching. It won't stop!"

"This wound." Gently pulling back the hair at my temple, he hovered the lantern beside it. "This was a heavy blow. No wonder you're hearing things. Are you hurt anywhere else?"

I watched him fuss over me, checking the cuts on my fingers, my face, my neck. His eyes and touch were all tenderness, and my heart rate slowed to a tranquil rhythm under his tender care.

Setting down the lantern, he lightly rested his hands on my face as he met my gaze. "What you're hearing isn't real. I'm real. I'm here with you now."

I focused on his warmth, on the concern in his eyes, and the scraping and scratching seemed to dim. Friedrich really was here beside me, and just when I'd believed I had only memories of him left to cherish.

He took hold of my arms, pulling me to my feet and out of the tomb, away from nearly all the clamor, save the quiet hissing that had followed me almost since my escape from the glass coffin.

We walked across the small landing to the base of the church's steep stone stairs, where Friedrich retrieved his satchel. As he riffled through it, his hands shook, betraying the strain he, too, had been under. My heart warmed, and I had to rub a hand across my nose or risk another round of tears. He gave me a flask filled with water, which I guzzled down, coughing out spurts and trying to swallow more.

"Margaretha, you must sit." Shrugging out of his jerkin, he spread it over the ground.

Nodding, I let him wrap me snugly in his cloak. He helped me down onto his jerkin, then settled against the wall beside me, studying me as he rested his arms across his upright knees.

He was still worried for me.

I sent him a quick, reassuring smile, then took another swig of water, and as I did, I noticed the door to the crypt hanging ajar, with the handle and lock chopped out. A dull hatchet rested on the ground beside it.

The drumming of fists. The hammering. It was Friedrich I'd heard.

I pushed the stopper back into the flask and returned it to Friedrich, meeting his anxious gaze.

"I keep worrying I'll wake up, and this will have all been a dream." He lifted my hand and brushed a gentle thumb against my skin. "You can't imagine what agonies I've felt. When I arrived and saw the crowds in the streets and then the black horses go by, drawing behind it that glass coffin—"

"There was a procession?"

He ground his jaw. "The prince's idea, no doubt. All the pomp and display, and you at the center of it, lying still and perfect. My heart stopped beating, Margaretha. I swear it did. I've never known such"—he took a slow breath—"torture. Hours of waiting for deep night, pacing dark alleys and hiding from soldiers, all while driving myself to distraction wondering if you were alive or dead."

I squeezed his hand. "I'm so sorry for it all. I never meant to worry you."

"You're taking the blame for that now too?" He quirked a smile, making me chuckle.

Nuzzling my head against his neck, I let my fingers caress his hand. "Though it's not my fault, I'm sorry just the same. But let us think on it no more." I lifted my chin to rest against his shoulder, waiting for him to look down at me before I reassured him, "I'm here now, with you."

He leaned over and touched a soft kiss to my forehead. "When I learned about your dangerous plan, I prepared myself for the worst. I was ready to walk into the crypt and find you dead and ruining inside that glass coffin. But I imagined saving you too, reviving you and holding you in my arms."

The pleasant trilling in my stomach was a stark change from hours of hunger and gut-wrenching panic. I scooted closer, pressing my side against his, and he took my hand, cradling it. The quiet, continual hissing from the tomb faded further until it was almost nothing.

"But how did you know to come find me?" I asked. "Where is Ilsa?"

"Gone. It seems your whole household left as soon as Count Samuel was released."

Hearing those words aloud was surreal. My brother was truly free. But I would need some time adjusting to the reality of it. "If they were gone, how did you—"

"Ilsa," he answered, taking the flask from my hand and tucking it back in his satchel. "She sent an urgent missive to Ulrich, knowing I would return to the castle. She spoke of your stepmother's treachery and of your plan to take the physician's toxin." His eyes watched me, his expression soft as he muttered, "Margaretha, you're either brave or mad."

"Maybe a bit of both." I chuckled, shaking off the chilling thoughts of what could have been had Friedrich not come for me.

He smiled and shifted to his feet, lifting the satchel strap over his head and settling it across his chest. "I know you must be tired, but we only have a few hours before sunrise. We should be going."

"To Wildungen?"

"If you wish it." He took both my hands and pulled me to stand. While Friedrich collected his jerkin, I picked up the lantern, my thoughts a distraction.

"Friedrich, Father will never allow us to be together."

He slipped an arm through the hole of his jerkin, his movements slowing. "He won't. But I shall take you to Wildungen if that is where you want to go."

"And if I don't?"

His eyes danced over my face, inviting me closer. "I don't have much to offer, Margaretha." He watched me move toward him. "It is selfish of me to even ask, when it means separating you from your family, but . . ."

"But you love me."

He took hold of my hand, his thumb caressing soft circles over my skin. "But I love you."

"And you wish to marry me."

He shook his head with a chuckle. "And I wish to marry you." Then he rested his forehead against mine, his voice turning serious as he whispered, "I wish it desperately."

My heart swelled, and I blinked back the prick of tears, bringing my hand to his face to trace every line, every curve, every freckle. Did I really deserve such happiness? "Then, Friedrich, I will be your wife."

His face lit with a stunning smile before he wrapped his arms around me, squeezing me tight enough to make my cuts and bruises ache. I almost didn't notice. He dipped his head, and I twisted out of his grasp.

"There shall be no kisses until I've had a chance to at least change my clothes and clean my teeth," I announced.

He looked properly annoyed, prompting me to laugh.

"And then you may kiss me all you like."

"Is that so?" His lips turned up in a wicked smile. "Then what is keeping us here?"

My legs hardly felt the fatigue of the long climb up the stairway and out of the chapel into the cold, starlit night. I took a deep breath of the crisp air, cleansing my lungs of decay and clearing my head enough that the hissing faded into oblivion, leaving only the buzz of a sound blow to the skull.

We slipped through streets to retrieve a horse that looked very much like one from Father's stables in Wildungen. Friedrich helped me up, settling me on his lap and wrapping his arms around my waist as I took the reins. I leaned into his warmth.

"Are you ready?" His breath tickled my ear.

"I'm ready," I answered. "Let us find our new home."

EPILOGUE

Margaretha

Five Months Later

FEATHERS ALREADY CLUNG TO MY damp, exposed arms as I lifted the downy chicken from the boiling pot. I hung it by its feet, waiting for the plumage to cool enough for handling, and was plucking my first fistful when a rattle at the door announced Friedrich. He was struggling with the infernal handle, as usual.

I shook my head with a smile. "Push down hard before you turn it."

After more finagling, he got it, ducking his head as he walked into our little cottage. I dropped the feathers into the bucket and rested the half-plucked chicken across my lap, watching him stomp snow off his boots.

When he looked up, his eyes crinkled with his smile. "You're plucking a chicken?"

I pulled another handful of feathers. "Don't act surprised. You've seen me do it before."

"Yes, only never in the house." He scooted a few feathers with his boot. "It isn't really an indoor activity."

"Yes, well, it was cold outside." I ignored the flush of embarrassment. "And anyhow, you're late."

"I was delayed by news." He came to warm his hands at the fire.

I admired my husband's handsome profile before tugging at the chicken once more. "What news?"

"It's about Vesalius."

My hand froze with a fistful of wet feathers, and I looked at Friedrich with worried eyes.

"Not dead." He shook his head, and I breathed a sigh of relief. I owed the man more than my life. Considering his counsel to Friedrich, I owed him my very happiness.

"Apparently enough time has passed for the kaiser's anger to cool, and Vesalius's sentence was commuted. He's on pilgrimage to Jerusalem as we speak."

"Saints be praised." I dropped more feathers into the bucket and took up another handful, but from the corner of my eye, I could see Friedrich still watching me.

"Was there more?" I asked.

"There is something . . ." He lifted his coat to reach into his jerkin. "Wilhelm gave me this." Friedrich held out a letter with my familial seal. "It's from Samuel."

My stomach wriggled with nerves. I wasn't ready.

"I can't read it now. I'm filthy." My plucking turned aggressive.

Friedrich twisted out of his coat, throwing it and his cap over the back of a chair. "Then I'll read it for you."

"This isn't the best ti—"

He snapped the seal and unfolded the letter, his voice drowning out my protests.

> "Dearest Retie,
>
> Your letter arrived just in time. Father had ordered your maid packing for her accusations against our wicked stepmother, but at your word, there was nothing he could do but believe. Despite her pleas, Belinda is now a prisoner in Castle Höhnscheid, where she can don red iron shoes and dance with the devil all she likes.
>
> I'm overjoyed you still live. Since my release, I was led to believe I'd been freed as pity for the death of my sister. How could I have taken pleasure in my freedom, knowing it came at the cost of your life? I'm particularly grateful you pulled through, since I was too ill when I left Brussels to keep my word and dance on your grave."

I rolled my eyes.

> "To be serious now, your letter relieved a heavy burden from me, though it came as a great shock to our father. Not only as it gave him profound joy over your survival, but also as it gave him great distress concerning your recent marriage."

Friedrich stopped reading to nibble his lip, and I sensed his discomfort. "Continue," I prompted.

> *"Father and I have had many quarrels as I've urged him to accept your union, but I cannot prevail. I fear his heart too hardened on this subject.*
>
> *Take courage. When I am Count, I'll welcome you and Rowohlt back into my house, giving you your deserved place.*
>
> *Until we meet again, address all future letters to me.*
>
> Samuel"

Friedrich finished, leaving me to my thoughts while the fire crackled. After a few furtive swipes of my hand across my eyes, I took a deep breath and put on a cheery smile. "I'm so relieved."

He lifted a skeptical brow.

"Really, I am. Vesalius is alive. Belinda can do no more harm. Samuel is well."

His brow stayed raised, and I sighed, tugging at the chicken again. The feathers were now cold and tough for plucking.

"Of course I miss my family. And it does . . . hurt to know Father cannot accept us." I returned to the fire and dunked the chicken in the boiling pot. "But if you think I lament my choice, you're mistaken. I don't regret it."

"Well why would you, when you're so comfortably set up in this tiny hut with your hands blistered from work?"

"Friedrich Rowohlt!" I glared at him. "I love the work I do, caring for our home and for the sick people of our village. And I love you, so if enduring a bit of physical labor is the only price I pay to be with you day and night, then I pay it gladly."

He hung his head and studied his boots, but then a mischievous smile tilted his lips. When he lifted his face, his gaze slowly trailed down my figure.

I rolled my eyes and turned back to the chicken, pretending to ignore the sound of his long strides coming toward me, even as my heart hammered beneath my ribs.

He came up behind me, his chest warm on my back, his hand trailing the length of my arm until he wrapped his fingers around my wrist. Lifting my hand to his mouth, he blew away the clinging pieces of down, then touched his lips to my faded scar. The heat of his kiss left my palm tingling.

"You are so beautiful," he whispered against my neck.

I laughed and turned to face him. "Yes, in my tattered gown and up to my elbows in feathers, I'm sure I dazzle."

He picked a feather off my face. "Up to your eyebrows in feathers." He smiled, tightening his arms around my waist and pulling me closer. "Margaretha, when will you understand? Whether wearing fine gowns and jewels or standing here in our little shack with your stained dress covered in feathers, you are equally beautiful. Though I would make one adjustment." He reached behind my head, pulling out the pins in my headdress and lifting off the covering so my hair tumbled long and free down my back.

I tried to hide my smile. "And why, may I ask, are these rags equal to my beautiful silver damask gown with the pearl latticework partlet?" I set my arms around his shoulders, careful to rest only my clean sleeves against his jerkin.

He responded with a gentle kiss. "Because it's not the clothes that make you beautiful. It's not even your looks, though I've never met a comelier woman." His gaze moved over my face. "Your beauty is in the goodness of your soul. In who you are. It's *you* who's beautiful. It's *you* I love."

This time when his lips touched mine, I threw myself into his kiss, pressing my mouth against his and curling my arms tight around his neck, chicken feathers and all.

AUTHOR'S NOTES

While this story is inspired by historical events and figures, the majority of it is fictional. I used the theories of German historian Eckhard Sander to draw parallels between the original Snow White fairy tale and the life of Margaretha von Waldeck.

Margaretha really was a German countess who lived in the sixteenth century. To my knowledge, she was not directly or inadvertently responsible for the death of any person. She was renowned for her blonde-haired, blue-eyed beauty. At the age of sixteen, she was sent to Brussels to be a maid-of-honor to Queen Mary, possibly with the hopes that she would be an advocate for the Protestant Reformation in the queen's court. She had many suitors, including Count Egmont and Prince Felipe. I altered her birthdate, as well as changed the fact that she did actually die in Brussels. The suspected cause of death was poison.

Count Samuel really did fight in the Schmalkaldic War and was shot in the leg and captured by the kaiser's forces. It was he, and not his father, who owned the mines at Bergfeiheit, and it was Samuel's wife who suffered the fate of being imprisoned in Höhnscheid Castle due to infidelity. He named his youngest daughter Margaretha.

Margaretha's stepmother's name was actually Katharina von Hatzfeldt. Katharina would have spent little time around her stepdaughter, since Margaretha lived away from home starting at the age of twelve. Having died eight years before Margaretha's suspected poisoning, Katharina is in no way connected with Margaretha's death.

Andreas Vesalius is renowned for his work in the field of biology and was the personal physician to the Habsburgs. Though he did make a pilgrimage to Jerusalem, it was fifteen years after the events of this novel and wholly unconnected to Margaretha von Waldeck.

Felipe, or Prince Philip, was not well liked by the people in Brussels. His Spanish customs seemed cold and distant, and he spoke only Spanish or very hesitant Latin. (For the sake of allowing him to converse with Margaretha without a translator, I gave him a boost in his knowledge of the ancient language.) His staunch Catholic beliefs not only led to a Spanish Inquisition when he became ruler of Brussels, but to an entire national revolt that lasted eighty years and eventually resulted in the independence of the Dutch Republic.

Friedrich is entirely a work of fiction. You're welcome.

ABOUT THE AUTHOR

Rachel Grow Law's interest in romance began at the age of four, when she first kissed a boy. (He was not as excited about the kiss as she was.) She has been chasing that feeling ever since, consuming novels, movies, and Korean dramas filled with sweet and swoony love stories. After finding her own happily-ever-after with her best friend, Rachel turned her matchmaking schemes to the fictional characters in her mind. When she and her husband aren't busy raising their noisy children in the quiet suburbs, they dream of the days when they can travel the world.

Find Rachel online!
www.RachelGrowLaw.com
Instagram: @rachelgrowlaw_author
Facebook: Rachel Grow Law